THE SHAPE-CHANGER

Raudbjorn's reason departed. With a terrible bellow, he drew his sword and thrust it through Sorkvir to the very hilt. Planting his foot on the wizard's chest, he yanked the sword out and lashed off Sorkvir's head. Then he began to chop the rest of the wizard to pieces.

"Now you've done it, you berserk fool!" the eldest of the Dokkalfar counselors shouted. "He's going to change form!"

Raudbjorn staggered back in astonishment, coughing and snorting. Instead of fresh blood, Sorkvir's body oozed only dust. Then a ghostly image began rising and swelling until it was as large as Raudbjorn. It began to solidify into a massive, shaggy bear. The small eyes in its enormous, broad head glowed redly. The bear's teeth parted in a menacing growl.

The wooden dais creaked as it padded forward toward Raudbjorn.

Also by Elizabeth H. Boyer

THE SWORD AND THE SATCHEL
THE ELVES AND THE OTTERSKIN
THE THRALL AND THE DRAGON'S HEART
THE WIZARD AND THE WARLORD

and published by Corgi Books

THE TROLL'S GRINDSTONE

Elizabeth H. Boyer

CORGI BOOKS

THE TROLL'S GRINDSTONE
A CORGI BOOK   0 552 13201 2

First publication in Great Britain
This edition published by arrangement with Ballantine
Books, a division of Random House Inc.

PRINTING HISTORY
Corgi edition published 1987

This book is set in 10/11 Times.

Corgi Books are published by Transworld Publishers
Ltd., 61–63 Uxbridge Road, Ealing, London W5 5SA,
in Australia by Transworld Publishers (Australia) Pty.
Ltd., 15–23 Helles Avenue, Moorebank, NSW 2170, and
in New Zealand by Transworld Publishers (N.Z.) Ltd.,
Cnr. Moselle and Waipareira Avenues, Henderson,
Auckland.

Printed and bound in Great Britain by
Cox & Wyman Ltd, Reading

SOME HINTS ON PRONUNCIATION

Scipling and Alfar words sometimes look forbidding, but most are easy to pronounce, once a few simple rules are observed.

The consonants are mostly like those in English. G is always hard, as in Get or Go. The biggest difference is that J is always pronounced like English Y as in Yes or midYear. Final -R (as in Fridmundr or Jolfr) is the equivalent of English final -ER in under or offer. HR is a sound not found in English. Try sounding an H while you say R; if that's difficult for you, simply skip the H – Sciplings would understand.

Vowels are like those in Italian or Latin generally. A as in bAth or fAther; E as in wEt or wEigh; I as in sIt or machIne; O as in Obey or dOte; U like OO in bOOk or dOOm. AI as in aisle; EI as in nEIghbour or wEIght; and AU like OU in OUt or hOUse. Y is always a vowel and should be pronounced like I above. (The sound in Old Norse was actually slightly different, but I think the sound is close enough.)

Longer words are usually combinations of two shorter words or names. Thus "Thorljotsson" is simply "Thorljot's son" without the apostrophe and joined together.

And, of course, none of this is mandatory in reading the story; any pronunciation that works for the reader is the right one!

CHAPTER 1

LEIFR had not expected any company when he made his furtive encampment among the old barrows of Morken. Someone, however, was out there moving stealthily among the stones, watching him. Quickly he stamped out his small fire and listened again, straining to hear over the hissing of the icy wind that was parting the sere grasses of the barrows and moaning among the lintels of the barrow mounds.

Thinking of the restless draugar, he burrowed into a pouch to find a small gold hammer, which was his last possession of any value worth considering. Hanging the amulet at his throat, he next thought about the three thief-takers pursuing him for the reward on his head. The best defense against those human predators was already gripped in his hand – a precious steel sword he had taken from a dead enemy while he sailed with the viking Hrafn Blood-Axe.

After a long, taut wait, he heard the stealthy crunch of dry grass under a foot, coming from the direction of a small round barrow to the north. Using the lowering gray twilight to conceal his movements, Leifr slipped around the edge of the barrow, approaching the small tumulus. Crouching behind an upright stone blackened with ancient lichens, he waited until another soft sound belied the intruder's hiding place. Leifr crept forward soundlessly.

A cloaked figure crouched behind the largest stone of a ship ring, peering intently around the edge toward Leifr's extinguished fire. Silently Leifr crept forward, still undetected, drawn sword in hand. Then with a rush and a pounce, he seized the spy by the collar, flung him back against the stone, and held him frozen there with the gleaming point of the sword inches from his throat. The stranger gasped for breath, his eyes held in fascination on the poised sword. After a brief appraisal, Leifr had to admit to himself that his captive did not resemble a thief-taker. Skinny, ragged, possessed of no weapons or armor, the stranger more resembled one of the emaciated corpses in a barrow.

'Who are you, and why are you spying on me?' Leifr put as much menace as possible into the questions – an unnecessary precaution, considering the fellow's condition.

The stranger transferred his shadowy gaze to Leifr's face. 'All I was hoping for was to beg a share of your fire, and perhaps your food if you have any to spare.'

'You're a wanderer?' Leifr asked suspiciously.

The man nodded briefly. 'Landless, lordless, and frequently foodless. I get most of my living from scavenging bits of metal, bones, and hides. I also render tallow from time to time, when I can find an unclaimed carcass.'

Leifr's eyes narrowed incredulously, and he darted an uneasy look around the barrows to see if any of them were recently opened.

'No, no, animal carcasses,' the scavenger hastened to explain. 'The tallow is for making candles.'

Slowly Leifr lowered the sword, considering the scavenger. Although he certainly looked like a destitute scavenger and he spoke with a certain degree of forced servility, there was a disturbing note of self-mocking deprecation in his speech, as if he found a source of grim amusement in his desperate situation.

'You don't speak like an outcast,' Leifr said.

The stranger returned Leifr's scrutiny with an unabashed stare. 'I wasn't born to this lot, which is sometimes a great disadvantage. People think I'm an impostor.'

'Impostor!' Leifr chuckled ironically. 'Who would want to be mistaken for a scavenger, if he weren't one?'

'A good question indeed,' the scavenger replied with a faint, quirking smile.

'Show me there's no weapon under your cloak, and I expect I can let you share my protection tonight,' Leifr said. 'There are some outlaws and thief-takers prowling around this barrow field tonight, and there's not one of them you'd like to run into unawares.'

The scavenger opened his cloak to the bitter wind, revealing no weapons – merely an assortment of castoff shirts and tunics hanging to his knees in tatters blackened by grease and soot, some disreputable old trousers, and a pair of ancient, reindeer boots with most of the hair rubbed off and with holes where the grass stuffing was coming out. Only a very ingenious lacing job prevented the boots from falling completely apart. Leifr also observed that the stranger's right arm dangled uselessly in its sleeve – perhaps damaged in a long-ago defense of his former lord. In spite of his wasted and battered appearance, he seemed unbeset by advanced age; what his true age might be, Leifr was unable to guess. Disfiguring scars, obviously of early vintage, had drastically marred the fellow's countenance with swollen white seams. Leifr surmised that most of the bones in his body must have been broken and allowed to heal with painful crookedness to lend the stranger such a raddled and unwholesome appearance.

'Not a splendid sight to behold, am I? Except for a curiosity, perhaps,' the scavenger observed wryly. 'Once I looked like a fine specimen of a warrior, much like yourself – instead of a crushed beetle scrabbling around, half-alive.'

Leifr squinted at him dubiously. 'If that's true, then I suppose I could believe almost anything.'

'I'm glad to hear it. Are you satisfied yet that I'm nothing but a wretched old beggar, of no possible threat to one such as yourself?'

Leifr did not doubt the creature's wretchedness, but it seemed that he was making too much of the oldness, so

9

Leifr's well-conditioned suspicions lingered. The wizened scavenger's beard was still black and wiry, although Leifr had no way of telling how much of its color might have been attributable to soot and grease.

'You'll do,' Leifr said. 'You look almost as destitute as I am right now. I'm afraid that my hospitality is little better than a fire and some stale bread.'

'It's better than nothing, on a night like this.' With a sigh of relief, the scavenger stooped to pick up a sack with some lumpy bulges in its sides and followed Leifr back to the camp by the lintel.

Leifr relit the fire, tore in half a round black loaf of bread, and used his knife to divide a shard of hard, rank-smelling white cheese.

'You're generous to a fault.' The scavenger accepted the cheese extended on Leifr's knife-point. 'Only a poor man shares so willingly.'

'Having so little to share makes it easier. Half of almost nothing is no sacrifice at all.'

They sat chewing the meagre provender in companionable silence, each studying the other with covert glances.

'A barrow field is an unhealthy place to stop for the night,' the stranger observed, brushing the crumbs out of his beard and catching the ones that he could. 'There are friendly houses hereabouts that let a stranger in from the cold and dark.'

'So why didn't you find one?' Leifr retorted suspiciously, shying away from the subtle questioning. 'I have my reasons for choosing this place, and if yours are similar to mine then the less said about it, the better.'

'Quite so.' The stranger nodded. 'I had you pegged from the first moment I saw you and your fire. No horse, no companions, a small huggermugger fire in an unfrequented place — you're an outlaw, running from thieftakers, perhaps.'

'It's not wise to be so curious, my friend,' Leifr warned.

10

'No, it's not. If I were wise, I'd be sitting in my own hall surrounded by the warmth and brightness and friendship that power can bring. Loyal friends to protect me, the fearful respect of my enemies, the gratitude of my neighbors. Instead, I'm here with you.'

Leifr smiled a dark smile, nodding his head in commiseration. 'I've been as rich as an earl many times since I sailed with the viking Hrafn Blood-Axe, but money gained by force goes through your fingers like warm blood. I gambled it, gave it away, had it stolen, lost it—' He shrugged his shoulders and shook his head ruefully. 'It's all gone. Like my luck.'

'For now, perhaps. But no matter how badly beaten you might be, you'd join with the next viking you meet and gladly do it all again. Not so much for the gold as for the getting of it. For you, the hunger is more exciting than the feast.'

Leifr grunted, considering his last morsel of coarse black bread. 'This feast certainly isn't worth remembering. You speak like a soothsayer. What else do you know about me, friend?'

The stranger clasped his useless wrist. 'You're young, for all your viking mannerisms – very young to have fallen so low. I daresay, with all the boldness born of indifference to punishment, that your father would be glad to have you back home again.'

'Not for another five years, he wouldn't. I was banished for ten years. I shouldn't have come back to Skarpsey if I valued my life. My last ship was sunk, and a trader picked up the survivors and left us off on Skarpsey. It was better than drowning or feeding the sharks. I need to get off the island while I'm still alive, though.'

The scavenger shifted his position, leaning against his sack with a grinding of metal on metal. 'Perhaps I can help you out of your difficulties.'

Leifr darted him an incredulous stare. 'You? I have doubts that an old barrow robber like you could do me much good. I think you've sniffed too much poisonous barrow vapor and you've lost your mind. I've seen a great lot of wanderers and beggars, and they all have a marvelous scheme for instant and fabulous wealth. The only trouble is, they need someone else to do the work. No thanks, don't tell me your plan. I'm not interested, and it probably won't work anyway. Real wealth and success are hard-fought and dearly bought.'

'How wise you are for your limited years. Do you see these scars and poorly mended broken bones? Doesn't it appear to you that I have done some hard fighting already and paid a few dear prices with my own hide and blood?' The scavenger's eye flashed hotly in its dark depths, and his withered frame was wracked by a shiver of indignation.

'Yes, you appear to be raddled by something or other.' Morosely Leifr poked at the fire for a few moments before returning his gaze to his companion. 'What's your name? If I'm to listen to your scheme, I ought to know what to call you.'

'I'm called Gotiskolker. A presumptuous name for a scavenger.'

Leifr extended his hand to shake. 'I'm Leifr Thorljotsson. Since we have nothing better to do except shake and shiver, you might as well tell me your scheme. Surely one great scheme has to work sometime, doesn't it? What do you want me to do?'

'Since you are so blunt, I'll be the same. I want you to pretend to be the son of an old man who is dying – and the brother of a famous warrior.'

'Is that all? Suppose I'm recognized and hanged?'

'That's unlikely. Old Fridmundr is almost blind, and the brother is dead. Fridmarr has been away a number of years, and people's memories are not that good when it comes to faces. You look very like him anyway – tall, fair-haired, and inclined to bad temper.'

Leifr scowled. 'There must be more to it than passing for Fridmarr. Isn't there any money is this plot of yours? If there's not, I'm not interested at all.'

'Certainly there's money in it. Let me finish. It's a matter of overthrowing an unpopular warlord, Sorkvir by name. Fridmarr's brother Bodmarr was the first choice, but Sorkvir killed him. Fridmarr, as his brother, will be the next best choice.'

'Why isn't Fridmarr doing it himself, if he's the next in line for it? Is he going to come back unexpectedly?'

'No, he's not coming back. You don't need to worry about him. The people will expect something of this nature from Fridmarr.'

'It sounds like a good way to get myself killed. Supposing I could pass for Fridmarr, all I have to do is kill the warlord and help myself to his coffers?'

Gotiskolker demurred, 'I am compelled to confess that it won't be quite that simple. Sorkvir is clever. In fact, he has led most people to believe that he's a wizard.'

'Wizard!' Leifr repeated. 'Gotiskolker, it would save us a lot of time and trouble if we simply drew our knives and cut each other's throats now and died in relative peace. You expect me to kill a wizard? With no more help than a one-armed barrow robber? I know what wizards are. Most of them are the shiftiest, meanest, most evil men walking the earth. No thanks, Gotiskolker! You can keep Sorkvir for yourself. I'll take my chances with the thief-takers. At least they have the decency to die when you kill them. Wizards are not so obliging sometimes.'

Gotiskolker nodded. 'You've seen a few wizards in your travels through the world?'

'Enough to know better than to tamper with them.' Leifr pulled up his cloak around his ears and turned his freezing back to the fire, while his warmed knees instantly took on the clammy chill of the prying wind.

'They aren't all like Sorkvir,' Gotiskolker said. 'I've known some fire wizards, who are at war with the evil ones. Fire wizards use Rhbu magic when they can get it, which is death to ice wizards, trolls, jotuns, dark elves, and whatnot. I know one fire wizard who would be willing to help us.'

'Not interested. I don't like any kind of wizard.'

Gotiskolker tried another tack, shrugging his thin shoulders. 'Fridmarr wasn't really as bad as everyone believes. To be sure, he had a quick temper and he leaped into things headlong before he thought about them properly, but I doubt if he did half the things everyone said he did. It would let his father rest easy in his barrow if Fridmarr's name were cleared and his honor restored.'

Leifr looked around at Gotiskolker for a moment, knowing what it felt like to be falsely accused. 'What do they say he did?' he asked, interested in spite of himself.

'Fridmarr stole a few things and he kept bad company.'

'Is that all?' Leifr eyed Gotiskolker skeptically.

'Well, perhaps he was too friendly with Sorkvir. Together they profaned some landmarks held precious by the local people. He robbed some barrows and stole a sword, which caused Sorkvir to lay an alog against all sharp metal within a hundred miles of Solvorfirth – except for the weapons held by Sorkvir's followers, of course.'

Leifr passed Gotiskolker the last of the strong dark ale he had cherished so frugally. A few long pulls from the bottle soon loosened the scavenger's tongue.

'I've heard of no such affliction,' Leifr said, watching more of the ale disappear. 'Of course, I've been gone from Skarpsey for several years.'

Gotiskolker smiled slyly. 'You wouldn't have heard of this alog, any more than you'd have heard about Solvorfirth.'

Leifr frowned. 'A small, out-of-the-way settlement, I don't doubt. But tell me more about this alog that made all the sharp metal dull. How could such a thing happen? Couldn't the metals be sharpened again?'

'Nay, not without some powerful magic. All the

swords became pitted and dull after Sorkvir's curse. Nothing could sharpen them. Except—' He paused for another greedy swallow and wiped his mouth on the back of his hand. 'Except for a certain grindstone at Hjaldrsholl. Legend has it that an odd little troll guards this grindstone; and when a battle is coming, he turns that grindstone at dark hours of the night as a warning. A few of the luckiest warriors have had their swords sharpened by the troll of Hjaldrsholl, which guarantees them success in their enterprises, whatever they might be.'

'I wish I could find a grindstone like that.' Leifr took a small sip of the ale and passed it back.

Gotiskolker darted him a shrewd glance. 'So you may, my friend, but you will have to look for it. Fridmarr could not convince the people of Hjaldrsholl to let him sharpen his sword at the troll's grindstone, so he stole the grindstone. But his plan came to pieces when Sorkvir heard of it. He lost the sword and the grindstone, as well as the life of his brother Bodmarr. He tried to kill Sorkvir and was outlawed for life. Sorkvir now has the sword hanging among his trophies, the grindstone is hidden, nobody knows where, and Fridmarr has not been seen for more than forty years. But he swore he would return and avenge the death of Bodmarr someday.'

Leifr smiled. 'A good story. For a moment I almost believed it was real.'

'It is real, you dolt!' The scavenger's eyes burned with a flare of rage. 'I'm offering you the opportunity for fame and wealth and honor! As surely as the stars travel their courses in the heavens, our paths have crossed this night to change the fate of many people, as well as our own. Are you unable to recognize fate when it comes knocking at your door?'

Leifr shivered in sudden unease, peering around at the dark barrows. 'This is no place to speak lightly of fate,' he growled. 'If dying is what I'm after, I'll turn myself over to those thief-takers now and be done with it quickly and relatively cleanly.'

'Fridmarr's father is dying. What could be more natural than asking for a truce until Fridmundr is dead?'

Leifr snorted. 'No, I'm sorry. I don't take such impossible risks with my life. It's the only one I've got, you know, and I want to save it as long as possible.'

Gotiskolker nodded his head. 'Well, I hadn't pegged you for the overcautious sort. I must have made a mistake. By all means, avoid taking chances and your life will be a long and a dull one – not to say impoverished. When Sorkvir took over Solvorfirth and killed our chieftain Hroald, he took all the gold he could squeeze from all the landholders. It amounts to quite a lot, I'd say, but getting it is a chancy thing. You don't like to take risks, as you said, so I suppose there's nothing more to be said about all that gold. Chests of it, so I've heard.'

Leifr turned around and bent an evil glare upon Gotiskolker. 'It's lucky for you that I've learned to tolerate the meaningless jibes of individuals whose worth is negligible. I'm tired of talking. I'm going to try to sleep. But I warn you, scavenger, I sleep with both ears and one eye open and my hand on my sword. If you have any thoughts about scavenging my head for a reward, you're far more likely to get scavenged yourself by the foxes and ravens that pick your bones.'

Gotiskolker wrapped his ragged cloak more closely around himself and huddled nearer the fire. 'Go ahead and sleep. You've nothing to fear from a one-armed barrow robber. I'll watch for thief-takers and keep the fire going. If anyone approaches, I'll warn you.'

Leifr arranged his sword, shield, and axe beside him where he could grab them at an instant's notice. He grunted. 'Now all I have to worry about is watching you. I don't see what I've gained by this bargain.'

As was his habit, he dozed lightly, like a cat, awakening frequently to check his surroundings. Each time he awoke, Gotiskolker was sitting vigilantly nearby, his

16

hood drawn down, with the firelight occasionally catching the sparkle of an eye or the harsh angle of his cheekbones and broken nose.

Near dawn, Gotiskolker uttered a sudden warning hiss. Leifr awakened, crouching over his weapons, all vestiges of sleep instantly dissolved.

Gotiskolker muttered, 'Three men are coming down the ravine from the settlement above. Thief-takers, I wouldn't wonder.'

Leifr took one swift look at the three riders proceeding cautiously toward the barrow field. 'I know those three. They've been following me since Saltaness. I recognize that piebald horse.'

He had his scanty possessions gathered in a moment and slung over one shoulder in a battered pouch. Seizing his lance and shield, he started away to lose his enemies among the barrows – or maybe turn the tables on them, if he found a good place for an ambush. A few well-placed arrows could end him of the thief-takers forever.

His mind was so busy with his calculations that he did not notice Gotiskolker limping along at his heels until he had covered a considerable distance. Halting suddenly, he demanded, 'Where do you think you're going? You'd better get away from me as fast as you can. There's going to be a pretty good fight, in case you hadn't noticed.'

Gotiskolker paused in the lee of a tilted lintel stone. 'I'm going to help you escape, in return for a small favor from you.'

'Oh no, not me. I'm not going to fight your wizard. These thief-takers are almost more than I can manage. They're going to kill me, unless I can ambush them first.'

Gotiskolker seized a handful of his cloak. 'Your means of deliverance is closer than you know. Head for that flat-topped barrow and you'll see what I mean.'

'Let go, you wretched vermin! How do I know this all isn't a trap you've connived with those thief-takers? I'm not easily fooled.' He made a menacing gesture with his sword, but Gotiskolker did not flinch.

'If I don't rescue you from your pursuers, you may cut my throat. I have more to gain by keeping you alive than any tight-fisted prize a thief-taker would give. Besides, that barrow offers more cover than anything else nearby.'

A swift survey of the barren landscape corroborated Gotiskolker's assessment. Leifr started a determined dash toward the flat barrow. The thief-takers spied their quarry crossing an open space and spurred their horses forward with challenging shouts. Leifr stopped to face them in a last defiant stand, motioning Gotiskolker to get out of the way.

'No one will ever say that Leifr Thorljotsson ran from a fight,' he replied in response to Gotiskolker's outraged protests. 'Now get behind that rock and keep your mouth shut. I have my honor to uphold!'

'You sound like Fridmarr exactly!' Gotiskolker gritted his teeth in exasperation. 'Not running from a fight is the same as running to find one. There's three of them and only one of you, fool!'

'I'll take at least one of them down with me,' Leifr replied grimly, peering over the rim of his shield at the thief-takers flogging toward him, with their hairy faces wreathed in triumphant grins. Holding their weapons aloft, they charged forward confidently. They were formidable fighters; Leifr had tangled with them several times already and he did not relish the thought of another engagement.

Gotiskolker tugged frantically at his cloak, measuring the advance of the assassins with a wild eye. With an oath, Leifr shoved him aside, raising his lance for a thrust which he hoped would skewer his vengeful enemy. The swarthy leader wore a particularly gleeful leer on his face. Leifr had wounded him in their first encounter, and he was anxious to repay blood for blood.

As Leifr took his stance, something struck him between the shoulders from behind. Whirling around, he saw Gotiskolker standing on the flat barrow, throwing

18

rocks at him and making insulting gestures. 'One more rock and you're dead,' he warned.

'Here I am, you great dolt!' Gotiskolker called down to Leifr. 'Come up here and make me stop.' As he spoke, he heaved a large stone over the edge, which rolled toward Leifr at a dangerous, lurching gait.

Casting a quick look over his shoulder at the thief-takers, Leifr started up the barrow as fast as he could climb, muttering balefully under his breath. An arrow shattered against a rock beside him, and another pierced his billowing cloak. Gotiskolker laughed hoarsely, dropping more rocks down at him. The thief-takers closed the distance rapidly. Leifr plunged over the lip of the flat barrow, looking murderously for Gotiskolker, who had taken cover inside a ring of sagging black stones. Leifr went after him, since he was the closest.

The thief-takers surged over the edge of the barrow, whirling their axes above their heads, mouths agape in savage bellows of derisive fury. The stone circle offered better protection than where he stood, so Leifr dashed for its limited safety. Dodging behind the largest stone in the center of the ring, Leifr gripped his favorite weapon, his steel sword, and waited for his enemies to come within reach. He did not have time to pay Gotiskolker any further attention, but he had the impression that the scavenger was hurrying around the circle, muttering, and touching each stone as he passed.

The thief-takers came to a plunging halt at the edge of the ring, looking around with expressions of dumb-foundment, and sudden apprehension. Leifr tried to make a rush at them while they appeared to be at a disadvantage, but a wall of mist rose suddenly between the hunters and their prey, and Leifr felt the ground sinking beneath his feet, as if he were unexpectedly walking downhill on a dark night. Missing his footing, he tripped and rolled down a grassy slope, entangled with his sword and shield and a swearing, sputtering Gotiskolker.

By some miracle, they reached the bottom of the hill without being cut or stabbed and disengaged themselves from a tangle of cloaks and weapons and Gotiskolker's barrow loot, which had administered some breathtaking buffets to both of them in its career down the hill.

Leifr gripped his sword in both hands, his eyes upon the hilltop, where he expected to see the thief-takers plunging down at any second.

Gotiskolker chuckled drily as he got to his feet. 'You can relax. They're not coming. They're standing on a windy barrow in the Scipling realm, wondering where we've gone. As far as they can tell, we vanished right before their eyes.'

Leifr slowly lowered his sword, his awareness of his surroundings gradually expanding to include a warm green hillside and a few speckled sheep, who stared at the intruders in wild surmise a moment before scampering away among mossy boulders. The barrows were gone, with their wind-swept rocks and browned mounds of autumnal grasses. The sun shone warmly, and the earth exuded the fragrant, sweet gases of spring growth.

Gotiskolker apparently found nothing noteworthy in the extraordinary changes as he stooped and wearily slung his pouch with its cargo of barrow findings over his shoulders.

'Where are we?' Leifr demanded. 'What happened to the barrows?'

Gotiskolker did not waste any time stopping to talk. 'There are barrows here aplenty, and you'll see some of them shortly. This is the Alfar realm. We'll talk more later.'

CHAPTER 2

LEIFR could scarcely take his eyes off the unfamiliar landscape long enough to follow Gotiskolker, but he had no desire to be left behind.

'We'll talk now, you scavenging thief,' he declared. 'I said I wouldn't help you with your mad scheme. I don't like what seems to be happening here. You've taken me someplace I didn't want to go.'

'I saved your life for you, didn't I? Would you rather go back to the thief-takers?' Gotiskolker found a faint path leading along the side of the fell and started away on it at such a hasty rate that Leifr had to lengthen his stride to stay close enough to hear the words Gotiskolker flung over one crooked shoulder. 'It's not safe to linger in this area. My house isn't far from here. Once we're safe behind a closed door, I'll tell you all you need to know. Hasten along, or something a lot worse than thief-takers might find us.'

The scavenger had lost his furtive, humble attitude. Now his entire lean frame almost quivered with purpose, and his sunken eyes glowed with the combatant's fiery glow upon his return to the battlefield. Feeling the last shreds of his amused condescension falling away from him, Leifr followed Gotiskolker with no more questions. On the other side of the fell, the faint path dipped toward a rocky cluster of old barrows. Against one of the barrows stood a crude hut built of rocks and turves, with bones and old hides to plug the gaps. The roof was covered with more bones and the skulls of animals. A piece of a wrecked ship served as the door, polished to a greasy sheen by years of use. A large, blackened pot stood over a bed of dead coals, half-full of foul-smelling tallow. True to his occupation as a scavenger, Gotiskolker had collected heaps of things which someone might want someday; white drifts of whale bones, odd-colored rocks, dung for fuel, driftwood, sticks, rags, broken pots, dishes, and flagons. Over it all hung a terrible smell, coming from a pile of motley gray hides that had been taken from the carcasses of some animal Leifr could not identify. Whatever beast it was, it had rough hair, a long ropy tail like a rat's, and sharp, hairy ears.

'This is home,' Gotiskolker said, shouldering open the door and casting his bag of findings into a corner. 'It's not much, but kind folk nearby keep me from starving.'

Leifr sank down in a sagging chair with a dreamlike sense of unreality, while Gotiskolker dragged a small feast from his larder – a mutton haunch not quite picked clean, cold, rubbery slabs of cereal mush, a pot of cold rhubarb soup, some hard cheese curds, and cups of dark ale.

'Here's to Fridmundr, benefactor of the feast.' Gotiskolker saluted with his horn cup. 'He'll be glad to see his errant son again before he dies.'

Leifr glowered, heartened by the encouragement of a good meal. 'You think you've tricked me, don't you? You sneaking, thieving barrow rat, I ought to put an end to your scavenging here and now.'

'And remain trapped in the Alfar realm for the rest of your life?' Gotiskolker slung himself into a decrepit chair with a grunt. 'If you want to return to the Scipling side of Skarpsey, you'll take an earnest interest in my continued health – such as it is.'

'What do you mean with this talk of realms and the Scipling side of Skarpsey?' Leifr growled suspiciously. 'Are you a wizard? Have you brought me here by magic?'

Gotiskolker sighed impatiently. 'I've used only the magic that is available to anyone who knows the secrets of the standing stones. I am not a wizard, and surely you are aware that the unseen realm exists. You Sciplings know about Ljosalfar and Dokkalfar – the Huldurfolk, you call us. This realm is the unseen side of your own realm – the opposite side of the coin. You can see only one side at a time, but both are there, nonetheless. You have nothing to fear; mortals visit us frequently and we visit your realm.'

Leifr's eye cautiously measured the distance to the door and next traveled to the remnants of the food he was eating. 'If what you say is true, this might be enchanted food,' he said. 'I might be in your power already.'

'It might be, but it's not,' Gotiskolker replied testily. 'I am a Ljosalfar. But through an accident, I lost all my Alfar powers. Sorkvir holds most of the power in Solvorfirth, and his bands of armed Dokkalfar terrorize and dominate. Wherever they pass, blight and death soon follow. They leave Sorkvir's mark of doom behind, and whatever is marked is destroyed.' He gripped his useless left wrist, hiding his hand beneath the table. 'You're not afraid of a fight, are you, Leifr?'

Leifr drew his sword and laid it across the table. 'As long as I have my weapons, I fear nothing. Why don't these Ljosalfar fight for their freedom? Sciplings would not be so meek and helpless.'

Gotiskolker reached for a long, ragged bundle, which he opened on the table, revealing two swords, several knives, and an axe, all fine workmanship but dreadfully pitted and blunt. 'All our weapons look like this,' he said, running one thumb along the ruined edge of the sword. 'It's an alog Sorkvir has sworn against us in a mighty curse. All our weapons and tools will be dull and blunted until a particular circumstance occurs, which I know you will be interested in, because that is the entire reason for which I have brought you here.'

Leifr folded his arms and leaned back in his chair until it creaked protestingly. 'This is the bad part, isn't it? I knew it couldn't be anything as simple as killing a warlord who happens to be a powerful wizard. I wonder

what I have ever done to deserve being chosen for this.'
He tore his good-luck amulet off his neck and threw it
into the fire in disgust.

Gotiskolker shrugged. 'You were chosen because you
happened to cross my path at the right time, and you also
happen to look a lot like Fridmarr. I knew it for the work
of the dexterous Rhbus, who see all the earth's events and
struggle to preserve peace and virtue. For the first time in
my life, the Rhbus have condescended to notice me.'

'I don't feel as honored as I should. How did Sorkvir
make an alog like this?' Leifr touched the blunted weapons
in silent wonderment.

'By corrupting the beneficial earth magic of the Solvorfirth Pentacle into his own harmful magic.'

'Pentacle?' Leifr sketched a five pointed star on the
table's finish of ingrained grease.

Gotiskolker nodded. 'But this Pentacle is twenty miles
on a side, with a significant site at each point, where
something important was altered by Sorkvir. When all is as
it was before, Bodmarr's sword must be sharpened by a
Rhbu grindstone, and this is the weapon that will end
Sorkvir's journeys back from Hel's kingdom.'

Leifr glanced at his own sharp Scipling sword. 'An
ordinary sword won't kill him?'

Gotiskolker shook his head. 'The Rhbu sword was taken
from Bjartur, one of the points on the Pentacle, but
Sorkvir's alog has dulled it, as well as every other Ljosalfar
weapon.'

'And an ordinary grindstone won't sharpen the Rhbu
sword?' Leifr asked.

'Nor any other blade within a hundred miles of
Solvorfirth. The Rhbu grindstone has been hidden by
Sorkvir, and he took possession of the Rhbu sword when
he killed Bodmarr.'

'It would appear that Sorkvir holds all the vital tokens
in this game,' Leifr mused. 'What is it you expect me to
do to help you? I'm just a common Scipling, with no
magical powers for restoring your Pentacle, and my

sword is an ordinary steel sword which won't kill Sorkvir. I don't see how I could help you, even if I wanted to.'

'When you go to Dallir, you will meet a wizard, Thurid by name. Although he is currently in reduced circumstances and earns his keep at Dallir by directing the thralls and watching over Fridmundr in his last illness, at one time he was schoolmaster for young Bodmarr, Fridmarr, and Ljosa, the chieftain's daughter. Foretelling the future was his claim to renown; but unfortunately, he wasn't much good at it, despite some rather spectacular methods. For the past years, he has been studying Rhbu magic from old rune sticks. He is one whose aid we've got to enlist.'

'Why don't you ask him?' Leifr asked.

'He despises me. In fact, you'd better not mention that you've had any dealing with me at all. My name is somewhat tainted in Solvorfirth.' He smiled his ironic smile, scarcely more than a twitch of his thin lips, and brought his crippled hand onto the surface of the table, turning the grimy palm upward to reveal Sorkvir's spiral mark burned into the flesh.

Leifr stared at the scar. 'What have you done to earn Sorkvir's mark of destruction? You're nothing but a scavenger, no threat to anyone.'

Gotiskolker put his hand out of sight again. 'It was not always so,' he said shortly. 'There's not time to talk about it now. Suffice it to say that my name is better left unmentioned.' He stood up and reached for a walking staff. 'We've wasted enough time here. It will be dark soon, and that's no time to be wandering around these fells. You'd better get yourself to Dallir and make your presence known. You look completely suitable for the part of the returning wanderer – ragged, wasted, and forlorn.'

Leifr got to his feet. 'I never consented to pose as Fridmarr. I'll do it as my own self or not at all.'

Gotiskolker sighed impatiently. 'A stranger will not be

25

trusted. Particularly a Scipling. You would be viewed with utmost suspicion by Sorkvir.'

'And he'll be delighted to see Fridmarr, who once tried to kill him?'

'Just believe me when I say Sorkvir has no advantage in killing you on sight. You'll have to ask for his pardon – a truce until Fridmundr dies.'

Leifr snorted. 'Beg for pardon? I've never done that before and I won't do it now. I came here to fight, not to beg. And what if someone finds out I'm not Fridmarr? What's going to happen to me then?'

'No one will know you're not. I've told you, the two of you look very similar.'

'But Fridmundr will know his own son. I dislike deceiving a dying man more than anything else about your plan. It will grieve him more when he knows I'm not Fridmarr.'

Gotiskolker paused, leaning on his greasy walking staff. 'He will never betray your secret,' he said quietly. 'He's not long for this life. I've seen his fetch myself with my own eyes – an old gray sheep standing outside his door, gasping for breath. When it dies, Fridmundr will die also.'

Leifr shook his head slowly. 'It still won't work. Somebody will know I'm not Fridmarr. I can't fool anyone who has magical powers.'

'I'm not finished with you quite yet,' Gotiskolker replied grimly. 'Do you think my plan will be confounded by something so ridiculously simple as that?'

He limped to the hearthstone in the center of the hut and knelt beside the small peat fire, scratching among the ashes. Trying not too appear too curious, Leifr watched suspiciously as Gotiskolker prised up a section of stone and extracted a small leather pouch from its earthy concealment. With a hand that trembled, Gotiskolker placed the bag on the table, and his ruined face was twisted by an emotion which Leifr could not fathom, but there was a glitter of muzzled anger in his secretive eyes.

'Open the bag,' Gotiskolker directed harshly, moving away as if fearing irresistible temptation. 'Go on, it's yours to take. I've got no use for it. I can't even touch the thing again, or it may cost me my life.'

Doubtfully Leifr hefted the bag. It weighed nothing at all in his hand, for all its dread significance to Gotiskolker. He upended the bag. A brilliant red gem, almost the size of a wren's egg, rolled onto the table, glittering from a thousand inner facets, although its surface was perfectly smooth. Leifr's acquisitive viking instincts awakened instantly. He cradled the gem reverently in his palm as he calculated its immense worth.

'What is this stone? You say it's mine?' he demanded.

Gotiskolker smiled his thin, dark smile. 'You can have it, but I fear it will never be truly yours. This is not a mere bauble to be sold somewhere for gold. It is an Alfar carbuncle – anciently known as anthrax – something which you Sciplings have never known before.'

Leifr's breath frosted the stone's glossy surface as he peered at it, and it felt warm in his hand. For a moment the room blurred around him, and he had a peculiar sensation, similar to being lifted off his feet by a powerful, swelling wave. A series of images flashed through his mind, like memories fluttering in the shadows of his consciousness, half-remembered. They were all unfamiliar to him – strange faces, unknown places, but all somehow infused with an insistent familiarity.

The carbuncle felt almost hot in his hand. With an elaborate air of negligence, Leifr put the stone on the table. 'I don't believe I want this,' he said as casually as he could.

Gotiskolker snorted. 'Don't be afraid of it. In fact, everything depends upon your wearing this jewel next to your skin for the next several days. Without it, you may as well stand up and shout that you're not an Alfar, with no powers and no family memories to guide you. Sorkvir in particular would be impossible to deceive without this carbuncle. It was Fridmarr's, and if you wear it, other

Alfar will perceive you as Fridmarr. Mere physical appearance is easily altered among Alfar, but the signals from this little stone will be forever Fridmarr.'

Leifr touched the stone tentatively with one finger, and was rewarded instantly with a glimpse of a girl's face and tendrils of mist-colored hair. He drew back and scowled at Gotiskolker. 'I've heard of things like this and I want nothing to do with it. I don't want to be taken over by Fridmarr's memories and ideas. This would be like giving myself up to be possessed by a fylgjadraug.'

Gotiskolker sighed impatiently. 'Leifr, I promise that you'll be able to get rid of this stone whenever you want – but you'd be wiser to think of it as merely an identifying badge among Alfar. If you wear it, the others will have the sense that you belong, instead of regarding you as a stray goose among swans.'

Leifr grunted, considering the comparison and not liking it much. 'What is a rotten slinker like you doing with a stone like this? If what you say is true, then this stone is the most precious thing in the world to Fridmarr.'

Gotiskolker returned his suspicious glower. 'Calm yourself, and I'll tell you exactly how I came by it. Before this bodily destruction of mine occurred, Fridmarr and I were friends – practically brothers. He didn't get away from Sorkvir and his guards unscathed. He was ill for a long time, too ill to return if he had dared, not for a good long while, at least. He also left behind a very sorry state of affairs in Solvorfirth, which tormented him unmercifully. I told him I would go back and do what good I could – or harm, in regard to Sorkvir. Since he could not be there to advise me, he gave me his carbuncle, much as I'm giving it to you now.'

Leifr folded his arms obdurately, his eyes resting upon the carbuncle. 'I'm not taking it,' he said.

'It's harmless, I tell you,' Gotiskolker insisted. 'Every Alfar is born with a tiny grain of this substance. It has to do with powers and recall of past ancestors' words –

nothing more than basic instincts for survival. What's so frightening about that?'

'The more I hear, the less I like it. I think Fridmarr is dead, and you scavenged this gem from his corpse.'

'Not quite. He still lives, as far as I can tell. The carbuncle shows life yet, does it not?'

Leifr eyed the sparkling ruby interior and was forced to admit it appeared almost alive. 'It will die when he dies?'

'Unless it finds a place with another host. Haven't you noticed the wartiness of old wizards and witches? Those warts are carbuncles, their own and others they have bought – or stolen. The larger the stone, the more valuable it is.' He rubbed his scarred left eyebrow absently as he talked, his gaze fastened upon the glittering stone. 'This stone is actually rather a small one, or you might well fear being taken over by it. Should you one day choose to become more an Alfar and less a Scipling, all you would need to do is carve a small slit in your skin and sew this stone inside with gut; in a very short while, you would never wish to be a benighted Scipling any longer.'

'You must be mad!' Leifr stood up, his hand on the hilt of his sword. 'I would never do such a thing!'

Gotiskolker favored him with a bitter sneer. 'Not even when you consider how short-lived you Sciplings are? Fifty years is considered a lifetime for you, but to an Alfar, fifty years is a reasonable length of time to spend visiting relatives you're not particularly well acquainted with. With this stone, you could seek knowledge beyond the ken of the most enlightened Scipling sorcerer and attain power beyond your wildest imaginings.'

Leifr unfolded his arms and again leaned forward to contemplate the carbuncle. It seemed to wink at him invitingly. Cunningly, he inquired of Gotiskolker, 'If all this is true, why have you ended up so miserably? Surely you possess a carbuncle of your own, if you are an Alfar, and if these stones can bring you power.'

Gotiskolker lifted one sharp shoulder in a shrug. 'As I said before, carbuncles are sometimes bought, sold, or stolen. Mine was sold a long time ago, but I won't bore you with the story. Fridmarr's is the only one of interest to you.' His tone was almost venomous in its harsh self-loathing. 'Parting with my jewel is partly to blame for the wreck I am now. Alfar do not live well without their carbuncles – or wisely, I fear.'

At last Leifr heaved a reluctant sigh and picked up the stone again. 'I'll carry this stone for the sake of your venture, but I'll never be host to it. As soon as I'm finished with it, I'll give it back to you. I can still scarcely believe that all I have to do is carry it and everyone will see me as Fridmarr.'

'There are curiouser marvels,' Gotiskolker said drily, watching sharply as Leifr fashioned a hanger for the stone and strung it around his neck inside his shirt.

Leifr returned his watchful stare with a belligerent scowl to hide uneasiness and distaste for wearing the carbuncle. 'Well then, do I look like Fridmarr?' he demanded challengingly.

Gotiskolker looked away, reaching for his walking staff again. 'The resemblance is there,' he grunted unhelpfully. 'And it will increase the longer you wear his jewel – whether you like it or not.'

Leifr felt as if a cold wave of air had touched him, awakening him to the utter strangeness of the Alfar realm. All the normal laws of Scipling behavior and expectations had been suddenly revoked, leaving him bereft of guidance.

Gruffly he said, 'Well, I'm not going to like it, so let's get it over with. We'll meet again soon, I trust?'

Gotiskolker shook his head. 'You'll be completely on your own, except for the carbuncle. I'm not particularly welcome at Dallir, except to haul away rubbish that no one wants or to bring tallow for candles. I'll watch out for you when I can, and you know where to find me, if you care to. I'm your dear old friend, remember; but also remember that it isn't wise to be seen with your old conspirator, as far as Sorkvir is concerned.'

'Sorkvir be blasted,' Leifr muttered in consternation. 'You've got to help me at least some of the time.'

'I hope it won't be necessary,' Gotiskolker responded.

The sun was low in the west, casting long shadows behind the rocks, barrows, and thickets. Gotiskolker hurried along with many uneasy glances over his shoulder. Once he motioned to Leifr urgently, and they crouched in a ditch while six riders in long black cloaks went by with an officious jingling of harness and weapons. Leifr stared at their battle banners, hung on long pikes ornamented with fluttering trophies of hair and rattling bones. The devices on the banners were skulls and bats, which matched the symbols on the warriors' shields and helmets. When they had passed, Leifr looked to Gotiskolker for an explanation.

'Dokkalfar,' Gotiskolker whispered grimly and hurried onward, darting from shadow to shadow until they came into view of a turf house and its many sprawling annexes and barns and stables.

As they advanced along a crumbling stone wall, Leifr could see that Dallir was more nearly a ruin than it was a working homestead. Portions, if not all, of each building had fallen into unclaimable ruin, although use of the building continued with stolid determination to endure until the structure finally collapsed entirely. A sullen red light burned in one end of a sagging turf barn, and a few sick sheep stood listlessly in a muddy pen.

As Leifr and Gotiskolker crouched beside the wall among the nettles and thistles, a ragged figure carried a milk pail and a guttering horn lamp toward the main hall. An annex door opened briefly, casting a slim wedge of light into the gloom, then vanishing quickly.

Gotiskolker nudged Leifr sharply. 'That's the kitchen. Fridmarr would never use the front doors. Go on, and good luck to you.'

31

'I'm sure I'll need it. Who will be there that I should know by sight?'

'Just Fridmundr, Snagi the house thrall, and Thurid – you'll know him by his thin hair and his arrogant clothing. His head-gear is typical of Djarfur district, but you'd know nothing of the dress customs. Pretty vain and foppish, but some good wizards have come out of Djarfur.'

Leifr shook his head, which was suddenly filled with images of blue and yellow Djarfur hats, with red tassels and crowns shaped like horses' nosebags.

'Red tassels!' he exclaimed in amazement. 'If this is an example of how that precious carbuncle works—' He made as if to tear the string off his neck.

Gotiskolker fastened his claw in Leifr's arm. 'It will tell you other things. You're not losing your nerve, are you? I hope the Rhbus weren't malicious enough to send me a coward.'

Leifr jerked his arm away. 'If this doesn't work, you old barrow robber, I'm going to come after you and break your other arm and maybe your neck.'

Gripping his sword hilt, he stalked toward the annex door, his heart thudding. He nearly leaped out of his skin when a pair of small, scruffy-looking dogs suddenly erupted from under a broken cart with a vociferous uproar of barking. Sniffing suspiciously at his heels and growling and whining worriedly, they scuttled away in craven terror when Leifr stamped his boots at them. Unfortunately, they took a defensive position on the stoop, growling, bristling, and showing their teeth. Leifr hesitated, eyeing the porch window, where it was considered more polite to knock, and watching the dogs, whose belligerence increased with his hesitation.

Suddenly the door opened, and the dogs scrambled inside, still growling, with their tails curled between their legs. A ragged individual leaned out to peer into the darkness at Leifr, calling out in a nervous, cracked voice, 'Who's there? Answer up quick, unless you're a draug or a Dokkalfar. Once the sun goes down, I don't open this door for anybody.'

Leifr came forward a few more steps, unable to think of any appropriate words for a returning prodigal. The bright eyes of the doorkeeper peered sharply at him around the edge of the door.

'Well, speak up, or I'm going to shut the door and let the Dokkalfar and trolls have you.' He started to suit his words with the appropriate action.

'Wait,' Leifr said, pulling off his hood in a gesture of peace. 'I've come a long way to get here. I heard that Fridmundr – my father – is dying. I don't know if I'm welcome or not, but I've come to see him for the last time.'

The door was snatched open wider, and a tall, glowering individual thrust the first speaker aside and surveyed Leifr from head to foot with mounting suspicion and scorn evident in the harsh glitter of his eyes. With his nose thrust forward like the prow of a ship penetrating enemy waters, he swiftly peered around the farmyard to see if Leifr had any cohorts lurking avariciously in the shadows, then turned on the ragged fellow who had opened the door.

'Snagi, you old fool, how dare you open the door to a stranger this way, with no regard for the safety of the house? How do we know what sort of creature he is?' He turned toward Leifr abruptly, without losing a stride in his rapid fire of questions and accusations. 'How do we know you're not plotting to murder us all in the middle of the night? How do we know you're not one of them?'

Leifr's heart condensed into a cold, hard knot and sweat trickled down his spine. If this hard-eyed, suspicious character was Thurid, Gotiskolker's scheme would be detected immediately, and all due retribution heaped upon him.

'Thurid! Won't you listen a moment!' Snagi at last made his presence known, after a series of unheard protests and exclamations quivering with excitement. 'Look at him, Thurid! Listen to his voice!'

'What nonsense is this!' Thurid flung open the door to let the light fall upon Leifr. 'Stop where you are,' he commanded, striding out onto the porch, his eyes riveted on Leifr with a sudden acute sharpening of his gaze.

Certain he had betrayed himself somehow, Leifr edged a step backwards. 'I think I've made a mistake,' he muttered. 'This must be the wrong house. Sorry I've disturbed you.' He had almost turned away when Thurid spoke.

'Fridmarr!'

Leifr froze, then swung around warily.

Thurid scowled blackly. 'Don't pretend you don't know me. I almost didn't recognize you in that wretched attire. As long as you're here, you'd better come in, before Sorkvir gets wind of your return.'

Leifr's eyes narrowed with dislike. He felt his hackles rising dangerously. Men of this authoritarian, autocratic ilk had always irritated him almost beyond endurance.

'Thank you for your kind invitation,' he said coldly. 'I regret to intrude myself where I'm not wanted, but I wish to see my father.'

'Intrude? It's your hall now, since Bodmarr is dead. You know I'm here only on Fridmundr's sufferance.' He led the way into the shadowy kitchen, fragrant with ancient wood and peat fires, whose pungency had permeated every beam and turf for generations. 'Let me go ahead and prepare him for the shock of your unexpected return.' Thurid arched his left eyebrow, as if to say Fridmarr's return was unwelcome as well as unexpected.

Resenting his officious tone, Leifr's gaze traveled over Thurid's apparel, the long cloak and gown affected by scholars and men of wisdom who often were paid to remain at the halls of wealthy men to enhance the atmosphere. His clothing was of exceptional quality, if somewhat threadbare and shabby, and his fine boots had been assiduously mended and patched to extend their lifespan beyond the normal years for a pair of boots.

'Still down on your luck, I see,' Leifr observed. 'Your study of magic hasn't gotten you far, has it?'

Thurid darted him an evil glare. 'Thanks to your late disgrace and Bodmarr's ill luck, I've lost a lot more credence in Solvorfirth. I can't even get children to tutor. Rhbu magic never prospers those who practise it. Wait here while I see if Fridmundr is in any condition for visitors. I shall summon you in a moment.'

'I'll come with you,' Leifr said, not trusting Thurid out of his sight. 'I'm not a visitor here. I wish to see my father at once.'

Thurid conceded with ill grace. 'Come on, then,' he said, stalking into a cold, dark corridor that led toward the back of the house. 'I can see there's still no reasoning with you. By the way, did you ride a horse, or are you afoot?' He glanced down at Leifr's worn, dusty footwear with a supercilious smile.

'I had to sell my horse long ago for ship's passage. It was either sell it or eat it.' He ignored Thurid's visible shudder of disgust and strode down the corridor at Thurid's heels toward a dim doorway, where a massive carved door stood ajar. In the dim light, Leifr saw intertwining serpent designs that seemed to move in the dancing firelight, writhing up and down the doorposts and across the panels of the door. Leifr gazed at them, hesitating a moment, while Thurid coughed with impatience, eyeing him with a knowing simper.

'You needn't be so nervous,' he said. 'Fridmundr is beyond all anger and disappointment now. I believe he has quite forgiven you for the blot upon the family's name.'

Leifr spared him a cursory scowl and stepped into the room beyond, mustering all his wits for the ordeal that awaited him; the effort resulted in a very stiff and appropriately anxious demeanor.

A large, carved chair stood near the fire, and a tall, raddled figure drooped listlessly between the two heavy dragons' heads ornamenting the foreposts. Completely white, his hair and beard covered his shoulders and chest

35

in a straggling mane, and he raised his head with the fierce weariness of an aged lion at the sound of footsteps. His eyes, white with cataracts, glowed like the eerie phosphorescence of foxfire as they probed blindly at the two dim shapes that stood before him.

'You're lucky,' whispered Thurid. 'Usually he's not much aware of his surroundings.'

'Thurid? Who's that with you? A messenger?' Fridmundr's voice, still deep and mellow, reminded Leifr of his real father, and his throat constricted, rebelling against the lies.

'I have news. It's Fridmarr, your banished son,' Thurid said sombrely, relishing his role as the bearer of news, whether good or bad.

Fridmundr stiffened. 'Not dead, I hope,' he said with a tremor in his voice.

'No, no. Fridmarr is here, as poor and ragged as a traveling beggar. He has come to beg your forgiveness for his past crimes and bring joy to your household once more.' The last words bore a spiteful sting, and Thurid bestowed a sharp glance upon Leifr and a nudge to urge him forward.

'Fridmarr!' The foxfire glow intensified to an amazing, pure radiance. 'The Rhbus are kind to me in my last days. Is it true? Speak, if it is so!'

'It's true,' Leifr croaked reluctantly. 'I am here.'

Fridmundr reached out with his long leathery hands. 'Come closer and let me touch your face, my dear boy, so I can know you're really here. I think it is another dream.' His voice quivered, and a tear started its tortuous course down his eroded cheek, disappearing swiftly into a hundred channels.

'It's not a dream. I have returned.' Leifr knelt beside the old Alfar's footstool and let trembling fingers touch his face lightly, never having experienced a more uncomfortable moment in his recent history.

Fridmundr's gaze faltered upward and seemed to fasten on a point somewhere among the dark rafters overhead.

He slowly sank back in his chair, his strength ebbing.

'You are changed,' he said softly. 'You have endured much, but your travels have left you wiser. Your influence no longer leaps out like a flame to disorder your life. It has gone inward to some far, deep place of darkness and doubt—' His voice trailed away and his brow knotted in consternation. 'Thurid, you must do something to help Fridmarr. His powers are all beyond his reach. Promise me you'll stay by him to protect him. He has a great endeavor before him. He is going to reclaim the honour of his name.'

Thurid flashed Leifr a skeptical glance. 'My lord, I shall be most happy to help Fridmarr in any way I can. In spite, I might add, of some of his past performances.'

'He has changed,' Fridmundr whispered.

'Changed, yes, I daresay that's so,' Thurid replied in an agitated tone. 'But Sorkvir hasn't changed. He won't be glad to see Fridmarr back again. I don't see how Fridmarr can extricate himself from his old troubles, especially if he's let his powers slip away from him – and after all the lessons I gave him as a boy. It must have been your dealings with Sorkvir that robbed you of your powers, Fridmarr. Didn't I warn you a thousand times what would happen to you? Of course you never listened.'

'I'd rather not talk about it,' Leifr said, thinking he had never spoken truer words. 'The past is better left buried. Let new deeds cover old wrongs.'

Fridmundr uttered a ghost of a chuckle. 'Thurid, he's going to keep you in your place when I'm gone. You might come to regret all those thrashings you gave him as a boy.'

Leifr eyed Thurid with cold dislike, and Thurid tried unsuccessfully to stare him down.

'You won't hold that against me, I hope,' he muttered. 'I was only doing my duty. I can see that all these years of fighting, looting, and high living seem to have added a great deal of bulk and girth to your frame, while I have

37

grown thinner, if anything. You can see that I no longer pose a threat to your peace of mind. Maybe I was rather hard on you when you were a child, but never in my life have I seen such an obstinate, ill-tempered, bull-headed, deceitful young fool, who—' Seeing Leifr's expression hardening into wrathful lines, he hastily added, 'I think I'll wait in the kitchen. Surely no one in there will object to my presence. I know when I'm not wanted.'

He sailed out of the room in high dudgeon, leaving Leifr gazing at Fridmundr in considerable alarm at being left alone with that glowing, unearthly prescience. With his head inclined forward, Fridmundr sat clutching the arms of his chair, as if listening to Leifr's deepest thoughts.

'Do not be afraid,' Fridmundr said softly. 'I am the one who is dying, not you. This is the last, bright sputter of a dying flame. For a short while, this old wick will burn brighter than it ever did in life. A small but worthwhile compensation for going out completely.'

'I wish that it weren't so,' Leifr said. 'It seems cruel to lose your sight so near the end.'

'My sight is all inward – and forward. I see the task that lies before you, my lad, and it is immense and filled with danger. At any step you could fail, and Sorkvir's curse would remain unabated. My heart aches for you in your desperate courage, but I am also filled with pride that you have come to put an end to the battle with Sorkvir. For many years it has gnawed at my heart that my son's name is an anathema to all of Solvorfirth, when I knew that it could not be true.' His head drooped forward wearily onto his chest, and his gaze wavered over Leifr sightlessly as he extended one frail hand. 'It grows late, and I must rest. I hope to open my eyes again and know you are here. It strengthens me to know you will take the burden off my shoulders. I feel much lighter now.'

He clasped Leifr's hand in a silent benediction that sent a shiver of invisible strength up Leifr's arm. For an instant Leifr felt as if he were swirling in a vortex of powers and memories, and the mysteries of the Alfar realm were suddenly revealed to him in a blinding glimpse, as if every atom in the carbuncle were thrilling in response to Fridmundr's handclasp. Then the frail hand was withdrawn, leaving Leifr once again in his void of Scipling darkness, relieved only by faint impulse from the carbuncle. No wonder Fridmundr's eyes burned with light, if such powers were consuming the fragile old flesh with their flaming energy.

Leifr silently withdrew. Fridmundr's consciousness had drifted away into a remote area that excluded his immediate surroundings. Pausing to look back, Leifr saw the old Alfar sitting in an expectant attitude, facing the outside doorway. Leifr peered into the shadows, thinking he had glimpsed something there – an old dog, perhaps – but now he could discern nothing. Uneasily he went in search of the kitchen, following a dim glow down the long corridor.

Leifr found Thurid sulking before the fire, clutching a cup of tea and staring stonily into the glowing coals, with his back still stiff and straight from the recent outrage to his pride. Leifr sat down on a stool, wondering where he was expected to stow his scanty belongings and his person for the night.

'I suppose you'll be wanting me to leave,' Thurid said suddenly in an accusing tone, fixing his disapproving eyes upon Leifr and hitching up his cloak around his shoulders.

'I never said anything of the kind,' Leifr replied, mystified.

'You'll be wanting to go to bed, I presume, in your favorite lair.' Thurid nodded curtly toward the shadowy end of the room, where a couple of ancient sleeping platforms built against the walls were now used mostly for storage. Leifr arose to investigate, discerning that this part of the house was by far the oldest. With the additions of the larger annexes, it had been reduced from the main hall to the kitchen. Its mellow ancientness seemed to radiate a homely welcome to Leifr, reminding him of his own ancestral roots at Landslag.

'I don't know why you'd want the kitchen, where the thralls and dogs sleep, when you could have any of the choice rooms in the household,' Thurid grumbled, scrutinizing Leifr mercilessly from under a skeptically arched black brow while pretending to find something of great significance in the pattern of his tea leaves. Quickly he sloshed the tea into the fire and stood up.

'Bah, I don't believe evil tidings in a teacup are as bad as the Rhbus would have us believe. I, for one, am willing to forgive old enemies and let the past perish. One can certainly give someone else a second chance to prove himself, wouldn't you say, Fridmarr?' He spoke with a pompous sneer, barely concealed by his patronizing manner.

'Certainly, Thurid.' Leifr suddenly knew exactly how Fridmarr would have thought and spoken to him. 'I'll never give up the hope that you'll change into a decent, likable fellow, even when hope seems so futile. Goodnight, Thurid.'

The speech produced a pleasant tingle of imminent danger, and its effect on Thurid was most gratifying. Thurid glowered, drawing deep breaths to swell himself up like an indignant cat. Shaking his finger in self-righteous wrath, he cried, 'You wouldn't be so arrogant if you had a true appreciation for what I've gone through on your account. One of these days you'll know me for what I truly am and you'll regret your impudence. You haven't forgotten that old satchel and rune sticks you gave me, have you?' He dropped his voice to a significant whisper, his eyes darting around as if the shadows were alive and listening. 'All I can say now is – beware!' He strode away with a final insulted sniff, letting his cloak billow majestically.

CHAPTER 3

LEIFR spent a few days cautiously acquainting himself
with Dallir and its inhabitants. In addition to Snagi, the
aged house thrall, there were two ruffians who looked
after the few sheep and cows, a couple of girls, and a
great buzzard of an old woman who ran the dairy and did
the cooking. Thurid was supposed to oversee them all
and give them their directions, but mostly they went
their own ways and the work was done haphazardly, if at
all.

'You'd think they were running this farm,' Thurid
grumbled at breakfast, after reciting a long list of the
servants' short-comings to Leifr. He stared blackly at the
bread. To Leifr's surprise, it moved across the table with
a jerk to rest beside Leifr's plate. Gingerly Leifr prodded
it back to its rightful place in the middle. It stayed there a
moment, until Thurid reached for it; then it slithered
toward Leifr again before he could touch it.

'Still up to your old tricks to torment me, I see,'
Thurid snarled. 'I'd hoped you'd grown out of that.'

'I didn't do anything,' Leifr protested.

Thurid stood up and reached for the bread. As he did
so, his chair levitated several inches off the floor, to
come down with a crash when he sat on it. Thurid bent a
slow, angry glare upon Leifr.

'I don't know what's happening.' Leifr gaped at the
milk jug quietly overflowing itself and running onto the
floor, while a shelf full of kettles rattled and danced
merrily over Thurid's head. Thurid glimpsed a heavy
mug just as it slipped over the edge; he dodged its fall
barely in the nick of time.

With his thin nostrils quivering, Thurid stood up to his

full height and composed his clothing, keeping his eyes upon Leifr. 'Do you recall the thrashings you got during the snake episode? You conjured snakes in people's food, in their beds, in their pockets—'

'I did no such thing,' Leifr interrupted indignantly. 'And as for all this—' He motioned to the room, where other objects were jiggling and rattling, 'I don't have the powers. Fridmundr himself said my powers were locked away someplace where I couldn't use them. How could I be doing this?'

'Very easily, for a malicious young troublemaker,' Thurid retorted. 'I know you, Fridmarr, and this is exactly the sort of thing you used to do years ago. If you don't stop it immediately, I shall have to take counteraction.'

His blustering tone began to annoy Leifr. 'If you think you're going to frighten me, you're mistaken,' he said, looking straight into Thurid's eyes and picturing what he could do to him if his temper got the best of him.

Thurid's eyes flew open in consternation, as if he had received the picture perfectly. With a thoughtful grunt, he summoned up a deep interest in finishing his breakfast, which he kept well-seasoned with a barrage of orders flung at Snagi in an irritable voice. Between times, he glared at Leifr, who sat helplessly watching a series of petty annoyances plaguing Thurid. His tea spilled for no reason, any metal objects near him behaved bizarrely, and the bread shifted positions on the table whenever he reached for it. Then he discovered a suspicious, dark fragment floating in his cup.

'What's this?' he demanded, trembling with fury.

Peering uninvited over his shoulder, Snagi volunteered cheerfully, 'Looks like a bit of midden to me.'

Thurid stood up suddenly, fixing a hostile glare upon Leifr. 'If there's muck in the milk, I know who's responsible,' he snapped. 'We've had a peaceful time of it while you've been gone, but the moment you return, all manner of fiendish tricks start happening. It doesn't take a wizard to figure out where the trouble comes from.' He whirled around and strode out the door, half-tripping over a piece of firewood which had crept out of the box to trip him. Another kettle fell off the shelf with a heavy crash.

Snagi kept one hand over his mouth to hide a toothless grin. 'You shouldn't gall him like that, young master, be it ever so funny. You're not changed one bit, are you, lad? I remember how you used to set fire to him.'

Leifr uncoiled somewhat from his wincing and cringing. The ungoverned magical effects seemed to have halted with Thurid's departure. He couldn't help glancing around nervously, and the evidence of magical powers tripping around the room had destroyed his appetite for breakfast.

'He's the wizard, not me,' he protested feebly. 'He must be doing all this himself.'

Snagi laughed aloud and discreetly turned it into a lengthy cough. 'Wizard! And my grandfather was a haddock,' he wheezed. 'You'll never admit it, will you? Still got it in for him after all these years – I declare!' Snickering under a muzzling hand, he turned his back to hide his glee. 'What will you be doing today, young master?'

'I'll have to go see Sorkvir sometime,' Leifr said grimly. 'I'd best not put it off too long, although I never was a great one for obligations.' He knew enough by now about Fridmarr to feel quite safe in that statement.

Snagi's mirth faded. 'If you go to Gliru-hals, you might never come back again,' he said worriedly. 'I remember how it was before. Sorkvir was the grandest thing you ever saw. You were lucky to have escaped from him once. Are you sure he'll let you go a second time?'

'I have a good sword, Snagi, made of Scipling steel,' Leifr assured him, sensing his fond concern. 'Sorkvir's alog hasn't touched it. As long as I have it in my hand, I'll have a fighting chance of getting away from Sorkvir again.'

Snagi wagged his head in solemn agreement. 'I'll have the mare saddled for you. This isn't like before, when you didn't want to be one of us.'

Leifr stared after his patient brown backside, stumping across the overgrown courtyard toward the stable, and wondered if he would ever understand Fridmarr completely. An uneasy sense that he was treading blithely over cavernous depths began to plague him, especially when he considered what he was about to do. Over the past three days he had at least learned in which direction Gliru-hals lay, but everyone seemed to expect Fridmarr to know what awaited him within.

Snagi accompanied him as far as the first gate, which he ceremoniously opened for Leifr. At that moment, a flock of sheep pattered across their path and Leifr stopped to let them pass. As the shepherd went by, Leifr caught a glimpse of a woman's face beneath the closely drawn, ragged hood. Twice she looked over her shoulder with a frown and would have hurried on with her blattering sheep if Snagi had not called out to her.

'Halloa! Ljosa! Stop a moment!' He hobbled after her, anxious to impart his news of Fridmarr's return.

'I've heard it already,' she said, with an unfriendly toss of her head in Leifr's direction. 'Everyone is anxious for me to know that Fridmarr is back, although I fail to see where the honor lies in returning forty-odd years after he's caused his brother to be killed.'

'No! Ljosa!' Leifr gasped, caught completely off balance by an overwhelmingly poignant surge of recognition sparked by the carbuncle. With a wave of revulsion, he wished he were posing as almost anyone else but Fridmarr. The hatred in Ljosa's eyes struck deep. Her anger lent a soft blush to her pale and delicate cheek and added brilliance to her large and alluring eyes. Tendrils of fair hair escaped from her hood like wisps of mist, agitated by her deep, quick breathing as she looked at him. The ragged cloak enveloping her form failed to conceal her regal bearing, made even more haughty by her indignation.

Ljosa gripped her shepherd's staff resolutely. 'I don't know what you're thinking of to come back here,' she said in a low, forceful tone. 'You can't possibly do more harm than you've already done. Or are you dissatisfied with your handiwork? Is there someone else besides Bodmarr you'd like to sacrifice? At least my father is out of your reach now. He died last spring in Sorkvir's dungeon.' Angrily she dabbed at a tear with a tatter from her cloak, turning away to hide her emotion.

'I'm sorry to hear that,' Leifr said unsteadily, flogging his wits for something appropriate to say. 'I know I'm guilty of many things, but I want to make amends.'

'Amends! Do you think that's the way to find peace of mind, Fridmarr?' she retorted. 'Can you ever ease your conscience after what happened to Bodmarr? A lifetime of good deeds will not bring him back. Amends are futile and vain when lives have been blasted and shattered.' She whistled to her dogs to gather the scattered sheep and strode away.

Leifr gazed at her haughty back, but she did not favor him with a second glance. He expelled a weary sigh, totally baffled by Ljosa's hatred of Fridmarr.

'You almost wouldn't know her now in those ordinary clothes,' Snagi observed. 'A far cry from what she once was, when Hroald was chieftain. Still as haughty as ever she was when Hroald was seeking a grand match for her. In a few years of sheep-tending, her fine looks will be all gone, and she'll be glad for some of the offers she's turned down already. If she'd taken Bodmarr—' Seeing Leifr's quick, interested glance and misreading it, he hastily finished, 'Well, I should be ashamed for gossiping. I'll shut my mouth and go back to the house. Good luck, young master. I hope the Rhbus smile upon your endeavor.'

'So do I, Snagi,' Leifr agreed earnestly, turning his horse toward Gliru-hals with extreme reluctance. His only source of comfort was his sword; but that would

45

have no lasting effect upon Sorkvir, according to Gotiskolker. Perhaps these unknown Rhbus were as good a defense as any.

When he came within view of Gliru-hals, he stopped and studied the massive turf-and-timber hall and its outlying buildings, all in good repair and evidently prosperous, as befitted a chieftain's hall. Except for a peculiar lack of the usual clutter of noisy geese, thrall children, dogs, and orphan lambs, Gliru-hals seemed ordinary enough at first glance. Then his practised eye discerned the large number of shields hanging on the side of the hall and the lances standing in clusters by the doorways, ready to hand at the first hint of opposition. In addition to the traditional beaks of enemy ships captured in battle, the doorways of the hall were ornamented with more grisly trophies; the cloven skulls of enemies were nailed up as a silent warning to anyone who thought to cross Sorkvir's might.

Two guards posted along the road leading to the hall returned Leifr's scrutiny in sinister silence, their faces masked in black to protect them from the sunlight. Long black cloaks trimmed with embroidery, weasel tails, and dangling bits of tinkling metal covered them almost to their feet, and they carried shields embossed with the insignia of their rank – spiders, in the case of these two. Leifr urged his horse toward them at a cautious pace. Suddenly they spurred their horses forward, rushing at him with shrill yells and a clashing of weapons and shields.

Leifr stood his ground, recognizing scare tactics when he saw them. The two Dokkalfar charged past on either side of him, making his placid mare dance around nervously. Slowing to a halt, the Dokkalfar circled, making menacing gestures with their lances, and came alongside Leifr to look him over carefully.

'What do you want?' The ranking Dokkalfar was marked by a red spiral painted on his helmet. He peered through his eye slits suspiciously, with nothing of his face to be seen behind the black mask stitched to resemble a spider in a web.

'I'm Fridmarr Fridmundrsson, and I've come home,' Leifr said curtly. 'I've come to beg Sorkvir's pardon so I can remain with my father until he dies.'

'Fridmarr, of course.' The guards exchanged a glance. 'We've been expecting to hear from you again. If you hadn't come back to your old friends on your own, we were prepared to come and find you. Lucky for you that you came willingly.'

Leifr scowled. 'I came here to talk to Sorkvir, not his underlings. Either lead me to him or get out of my way so I can find him.'

The Dokkalfar made a show of reaching for their weapons, glaring balefully, then motioned Leifr to follow them. One Dokkalfar dropped behind, as if to make certain no one mistook the procession for a friendly association.

Once within the walls of the court, Leifr left his horse reluctantly to the care of a thrall and let himself be escorted through the tall, creaking doors into the hall. Leifr glanced sideways at his guards, strengthening his original supposition that the Dokkalfar felt no yearning to express themselves in any other medium than blood and oppression.

The doors were closed against the yellow sunlight and green fells, and Leifr found himself enveloped in the amber gloom of the ancient hall. It was long and high enough to store a full-size longship, and Leifr mentally counted off the paces as he walked the length of the hall toward the dais at the far end. A half-smothered fire smoked on the great hearth and several lamps burned dully, as if something in the atmosphere prevented proper combustion. A knot of dark-clad Dokkalfar stood around a man seated in a heavy, carven chair, talking and darting suspicious glances at Leifr. He tried to determine some essential difference between Dokkalfar and Ljosalfar – Dark Elves and Light Elves – noting among this group an almost deathly pallor and a sharpening of the features. A few of them were hideously marred by vile-looking blotches on their hands or faces, which Leifr attributed to accidental exposure to daylight. These were high-ranking Dokkalfar, ornamented with costly gold chains and emblems of owls, wolves, and foxes. When they turned their narrow backs and moved away like a remnant of a storm cloud, Leifr breathed much easier.

He gave his attention to the man seated in the chair, and Sorkvir looked back at him with the same still, deadly stare that the carbuncle indicated had transfixed him before, filling him with the proper awe for a wizard who held the powers of death and life at his command. Sorkvir's clothing was of the excessively plain and expensive quality usually reserved for burial garments, and his only ornaments were the two brooches that held his black cloak, gleaming gold embossed with his spiral mark. His beard was fine and silken, carefully combed and trimmed around his narrow face.

Returning Leifr's scrutiny with displeasure, Sorkvir spoke in a dry, grim voice. 'Well, Fridmarr, you're much changed. Outlawry has done you good. I can scarcely believe more than forty years have passed since I saw you last. Yet I seem to recall banishing you for life, at the threat of death if you ever returned.'

'Death is a hollow threat,' Leifr replied, in true stoic viking fashion.

Sorkvir tapped one long finger on the chair arm, his eyes darkening. 'So you choose to remind me of that. I have often wondered what you did with the knowledge you gained from me. You have me to thank for teaching you not to fear death, and I have myself to thank for being such a fool as to trust you. Let me warn you that I can devise torments far worse than death. I have died and returned many times, and I find far more torments on this end of Hel's journey than I have seen on the other.' He gazed at Leifr with narrowed eyes through

48

the winding miasma of smoke rising from the lamps.

'I consider myself sufficiently warned,' Leifr replied warily, wondering desperately what it all meant.

Sorkvir leaned forward, his eyes glittering. 'Don't think I haven't heard all this talk about the Pentacle. You can't restore the earth magic to it, Fridmarr. You may know what I did to change the Pentacle, but you don't have enough power to destroy my influence. If you try, I shall teach you the meaning of true wretched misery. I'll make you wish that I had killed you. You'll regret that you ever begged to learn my secrets of immunity from death. Death will be a haven which forever escapes you. Ask your friend Gotiskolker what it is like.' His lips twisted ironically. 'I was disappointed in you, Fridmarr, when you sent your ally here to fight your battle with me, like a great coward.'

Warily Leifr replied, 'I did not send him to fight my battle. What he did was his own choice.'

'And a poor one. I knew at once that the two of you had hatched a scheme to trick me out of Bodmarr's sword. He confessed, after some encouragement, that he had removed his own carbuncle to disguise himself. Then there was a reverse glamour spell to disguise him further that he clung to until I turned him over to my guards to do with as they wished. They tramped on him and broke him down into the crippled and bent old beggar that he came disguised as. The first I knew of his survival was when he hobbled into Gliru-hals, after crawling off the dung heap where they had thrown him to die, to ask for eitur to ease the aches and pains of the bones my men had broken, as if I could be held responsible. So now he's addicted to the poison, and I fear it's consuming his flesh at an alarming rate. He comes to beg for it as often as every fortnight. It continues to amuse me to keep him alive – a living relic to remind me of my triumph over you and the Pentacle.' His yellowed skin creased in an unpleasant smile, reminding Leifr of a snake parting its jaws.

'You're poisoning him by slow degrees,' Leifr said with a shudder of sudden hatred. 'Surely that's too beastly even for you.'

'Not in the least. It's better than he deserves, after trying to kill me and steal Bodmarr's sword. The eitur is all that keeps him alive. Without it, he would die a painful and lingering death. Thus it is he remains here, docile and obedient, lest I withhold the drug that relieves his pain. Is it a pleasant prospect, Fridmarr? The eitur is in your veins, also. Its gnawing agony will eventually destroy you. The only remedy for the pain is more eitur – but there is no remedy for the destruction it has done to your Ljosalfar powers. Gotiskolker is nothing but a hollow carrion shell, and so you shall become, one day.'

Leifr stared into Sorkvir's sunken eyes, fighting a wave of fear, reminding himself it was Fridmarr that Sorkvir was speaking to. Then the carbuncle yielded another memory of Fridmarr's. 'It was only a small taste of eitur that I took,' he said. 'Scarcely enough to make me a slave to it.'

'So you may have thought at the time, but we both know by now that there's no such thing as too little eitur. Surely you've felt some of its ravaging in the years since we parted?'

Warily Leifr considered the gem's spiraling messages. Almost instantly he struck the memory of a paralyzing, bitter agony so acute that even the mere thought of it made him wince despite himself. But Fridmarr would not have revealed the extent of his sufferings to Sorkvir, so Leifr replied, 'Only somewhat.'

'I confess I am disappointed,' Sorkvir answered ironically, with a knowing sneer. Reaching inside his cloak, he produced a small flask with a gold stopper and held it up for Leifr's inspection. 'Come now, Fridmarr, admit that you came back for this. You have endured the random attacks of the eitur long enough – a good, long time, but it will only get worse as the body degenerates. Your friend Gotiskolker would have died long ago, if not for the eitur. He comes and begs for it when he feels the effects coming on. All you must do is ask for it. With the eitur, you can live a long and frequently painless life – as long as you preserve my equanimity by causing me no trouble.'

Leifr shook his head slowly, unable to find Gotiskolker anywhere in the mass of Fridmarr's memories teasing at the edge of his mind. Most likely Fridmarr had done his best to forget Gotiskolker, after sending him off on such a fool's errand. 'I have no need of your poison,' he said coldly. 'I came here to strike a bargain.'

'Go ahead, I'm listening – although I have just offered you the only bargain you will get from me.' Sorkvir opened the flask and inhaled the smell of the contents, keeping his eyes upon Leifr.

Leifr caught a whiff of a cloying scent. With a wrench of fear, the carbuncle reminded him that such stuff was death to it, and for that reason Fridmarr had removed it from his flesh. Once removed, it could garner no memories. Uneasily wondering at what point in his relationship with Sorkvir Fridmarr had parted company with his carbuncle, Leifr drew a deep breath to gather his resolution.

'My father Fridmundr is dying. I wish to stay here in peace until he's gone.'

'And after he is dead? What then, Fridmarr?' Sorkvir inquired mockingly. 'I feel almost certain that you don't intend simply to disappear again, as you did last time.'

'No,' Leifr answered, his eyes shifting to the wall behind Sorkvir's chair, where weapons from vanquished enemies hung as adornments to Sorkvir's fame. 'I'm going to visit the Pentacle and do what I can to restore its original powers, which you destroyed.'

Sorkvir took another sniff of the eitur. 'You must know that you'll have to destroy me in order to restore the Pentacle. You know you can't touch Ljosalfar magic without great harm and pain to yourself because of the eitur you once drank. You will fail, Fridmarr, as you have always failed at everything you have undertaken in the past. I don't believe you have the fortitude to purify the Pentacle. Even if you should manage to steal that sword—'

He leaned back in his chair to gaze upward at a much-pitted, dull-hued sword hanging in a central position among the trophies. Its elaborate hilt formed a guard for the haft, which was made from a walrus tusk, finely engraved. Sorkvir considered the sword a moment, then shifted his gaze back to Leifr. 'You won't be able to find the troll's grindstone to sharpen it. Did you think I would be so incautious as to leave it lying around for some fool to find?'

'It's the Rhbus' grindstone, not the troll's,' Leifr countered, 'and the Rhbus are sympathetic to the Ljosalfar cause. They will help us find the grindstone.'

'You Ljosalfar are superstitious fools if you think there are any Rhbus left, and doubly foolish if you think they guide your miserable fates in any way,' Sorkvir retorted with a quick flare of temper. 'The Rhbus did not exist, as you know them. They were giants who degenerated into trolls through their own folly, as the Ljosalfar are degenerating into weak and powerless beings who will soon be extinct. Don't talk to me about the help of the Rhbus, Fridmarr. Do what you may to the Pentacle, but know that I shall never allow its powers to be disturbed. You must believe you have someone with the power to help you, since a nithling like you could not touch my spells, I sense that all your powers are buried and almost extinct. I have the eitur to thank for that.' He smiled again, or rather snarled, showing teeth that reminded Leifr of a corpse's teeth after the body had been exhumed from a peat bog.

Shuddering, Leifr looked away, not knowing whether it was the hypnotic glitter of Sorkvir's eyes that filled him with such a strong feeling of incipient failure or his own common sense trying to tell him the Pentacle was a hopeless cause.

'I will do nothing about the Pentacle as long as my father lives,' he said steadily, with the sensation of having his back to the wall and facing impossible odds. 'Let's give our conflict that much of a respite.'

'Yes. That will allow you time to realize how futile a task lies before you, should you choose it.' Sorkvir turned his head away contemptuously, treating Leifr to a view of a hideous, black scar that ran from the top of his head and down the side of his neck, like a rather crudely mended split in old and rotten leather. Leifr stared in horror, certain that a small gap revealed the bare bone underneath. For the first time Leifr began to ponder what it meant to die and return repeatedly from the dead.

Belatedly, Leifr realized he was being dismissed and started to edge away cautiously, not wanting to turn his back upon Sorkvir.

'About your friend Gotiskolker,' Sorkvir said suddenly, returning his attention to Leifr. 'Stay away from him. He's my meat now. I can easily imagine the two of you using this truce period to try dreaming up schemes against me. I shall have you watched.' He beckoned to the Dokkalfar still lingering in the hall. 'Fetch Raudbjorn.'

Leifr heard the tramping of heavy footsteps advancing slowly down the passage, accompanied by the unmistakable music made by armor and weapons. A towering hulk entered the hall, stooping his head slightly to clear the door frame. He shambled the length of the hall and presented himself to Sorkvir with a slight, creaking bow. Beneath his much-battered helmet, the face of Raudbjorn was rotund and placid, and his almond-shaped eyes held no more expression than a pair of black, shiny buttons. His leather body armor gleamed with old bloodstains and grease. Around his massive neck, he wore various souvenirs taken from his enemies and hung on chains or filthy strings – hilts of swords and knives, gold amulets, locks of hair or beards, teeth, and more than a few dried ears. At his belt hung several small pouches, a sword as high as Leifr's shoulder, two knives, a grimy bag, and a coil of rope. Over his shoulder, he carried a huge, double-bitted halberd with a long, vicious blade at the top, capable of skewering through a man of ordinary size. Like the weapons of the Dokkalfar, it was untouched by Sorkvir's alog.

'This is Raudbjorn,' Sorkvir announced. 'Raudbjorn was the best thief-taker in the realm before I hired him as my bodyguard. His presence helps encourage the more hotheaded Ljosalfar to keep the peace in Solvorfirth. Raudbjorn, this is Fridmarr Frimundrsson. I want you to watch him carefully. He has a treasonous disposition, and I don't want him conniving with that rubbish scavenger Gotiskolker.'

A ponderous scowl spread itself over Raudbjorn's brow. He grunted. 'This outlaw Fridmarr? Outlaw heads go in sack.' He slapped the grisly bag hanging from his belt, and his eyes lit up with pleasure at the recognition of Leifr as an opponent.

'No, I don't want you to kill him just yet,' Sorkvir snapped.

Raudbjorn's anticipatory look faded, and he lowered his halberd to the ground with a thud. He darted a resentful glance from Leifr to Sorkvir.

'Raudbjorn follow and watch,' he growled.

'You'd better not forget this time,' Sorkvir snarled, pointing a clawlike finger at Raudbjorn. 'Your mind is too much on killing to suit me, Raudbjorn. If you want a warm fire for your backside this winter and food and ale for your gullet, you'd better start following my directions.' He waved his hand in curt dismissal, and Leifr turned away to leave the hall, with Raudbjorn clumping heavily almost at his heels.

The Dokkalfar elders glanced up suspiciously from their whispered conferences, and Leifr heard one of them mutter, 'Day-farers! Sorkvir gets into trouble whenever he trusts one of them.'

'Bah! He has them where he wants them,' another growled. 'Do all in the Owl Society suffer from such old womanish qualms? If the Fox Society were in charge, this war would have been ended centuries ago.'

'I thought the firebrands were confined to the Bat and Spider Societies,' the member of the Owl Society said with an audible sneer.

'Perhaps there's more wisdom in the lower ranks than the societies for aged Dokkalfar would like to think,' the second speaker snapped.

When the great doors were opened, Leifr squinted a moment in the welcome sunlight, still feeling as if a clammy dew had settled on him and dampened his clothing as well as his spirits. Warily he looked back at Raudbjorn, also blinking at the brightness.

'Why would a day-farer want to work for the Dokkalfar?' he demanded scornfully. 'You had much more honor as a thief-taker, Raudbjorn.'

'Not as much gold,' Raudbjorn grunted, cradling his halberd in the crook of his arm. 'Thief-taking is hard life. Thieves very smart. Fight like rats. Cold nights, no food. Sorkvir not so bad.'

'It would be better to starve than be under Sorkvir's control,' Leifr replied.

Raudbjorn's forehead crinkled worriedly, and his breathing became deeper as he put to work the little-used mechanisms for serious thinking. With an expression of pain, he shook his head resignedly.

'Raudbjorn likes warm bed and good food. Raudbjorn tired of thief-taking. Still like to fight, though.' His little eyes dwelt upon Leifr's sword. 'You warrior, Fridmarr. Maybe we fight sometime. Sorkvir won't know.'

'He'll know,' Leifr answered. 'I'll kill you.'

Raudbjorn flung up his head, scenting a challenge, and a slow smile illuminated his battle-scarred features, revealing several missing teeth. With his thumb, he strummed the edge of his halberd as if it were some fine musical instrument whose tone he was testing.

'Then I keep this sharp for you, Fridmarr,' he rumbled pleasantly, looking as if Fridmarr had made him very happy.

'Sorkvir doesn't want us to fight,' Leifr reminded him. 'You're supposed to follow me and watch out for any treasonous actions or dangerous acquaintances.'

Raudbjorn shrugged his thick shoulders. 'Raudbjorn might forget,' he said in a reassuring tone, grinning in amiable delight.

Thus encouraged, Leifr rode homeward, with Raudbjorn following at a casual distance on a huge, hairy-footed horse. Making no pretense of discretion, Raudbjorn posted himself on a hillock outside the gates of Dallir, where he had a good view of all that happened between the house and barns.

Leifr unsaddled his horse quickly and hurried toward the back door of the house, where he encountered Thurid peering around the edge of the door in Raudbjorn's direction.

'Fridmarr!' Thurid cried. 'Didn't you see what followed you home? Look at that creature! It must be an apparition of Sorkvir's vilest art!'

'It's Raudbjorn, the thief-taker,' Leifr replied with gloom. 'Sorkvir sent him to spy on me. He's agreed to a truce as long as Fridmundr lives, but Raudbjorn is part of the agreement.'

Thurid's eyes bulged wrathfully. 'A fine bargain you made! I could have done better, if you hadn't crept away deliberately so I couldn't assist you. It takes a wizard to deal with a wizard. One of these days Sorkvir will learn of the threat that has been growing here while he lords it over us in his ignorance.'

Scarcely hearing him, Leifr strode into the kitchen and glowered around as if it were the worst sort of prison.

'Trapped here! I've got to speak to Gotiskolker,' Leifr exclaimed, swinging around to face Thurid. 'Send Snagi after him. Make it look as if he's fetching tallow. Get him here without Raudbjorn seeing him.'

Thurid shook his head earnestly. 'Something of that nature is exactly what the gross creature is watching for. Let him sit there for a couple of days. He'll soon tire of waiting for you to make a move and he'll fall asleep or go away; then you'll have your chance. Why on earth do you want to talk to Gotiskolker?' He inserted a delicate shudder into the name, as if revolted by the mere mention of it. 'And that reminds me – I've been finding an abnormal number of spiders today, Fridmarr. I hope you're not going to infest the house with them. I can't abide spiders.'

He pointed his finger at a long-legged spider bumbling across the table, and a small jet of flame suddenly sizzled the creature into a knot of threadlike legs. Thurid turned to Leifr with a pleased quirk of one eyebrow, in spite of his temper. 'A clever little spell, eh? That was one from the old satchel you gave me.'

Leifr was only momentarily distracted. He was becoming accustomed to small magics and to seeing inanimate objects misbehaving. A certain amount of unexplained phenomena seemed normal for the Alfar realm. 'Thurid, I must talk to Gotiskolker. Are you going to help me or not? If I have to kill Raudbjorn to do it, that's what I'm going to do.' He looked around for his battered shield and helmet.

'Fridmarr, I thought you'd learned not to be so impulsive,' Thurid said. 'Wait awhile. You're not – ah, seriously considering a real challenge to Sorkvir, are you? You're the last of your line, you know.'

Leifr nodded regretfully. 'It can't be avoided, Thurid, and you promised my father you'd help me.'

Thurid thrust his nose outside again for a look at Raudbjorn. 'I don't intend to help you to your doom – particularly if Gotiskolker is involved. I was afraid you'd want to see him. I have an evil feeling that terrors will descend upon this house if you start collaborating with Gotiskolker. I can see nothing but terrors coming from it.' He sizzled another spider crawling up the wall and resolutely strode outside with his staff in hand, as if to ward off the terrors as they approached.

The terrors were not long in appearing. Gunhildr, the old woman who ran the dairy and the kitchen, was found lying on the flagstones in the still house with a broken ankle, clutching a huge crock of fresh curd to her bosom. Amid much remonstrating and considerable resistance, she was put to bed to mend, and a lesser maid instructed on the management of kitchen and dairy.

That night, a fairly serviceable pigsty collapsed for no apparent reason, and the sole pig vanished into the darkness. The next morning, when Leifr opened the door of the cow stable to help with the milking, the old brindle boss cow Mjoll shouldered open the door roughly and flung it aside as she came bursting out with a wild bellow. The other four cows thundered after her, ignoring Leifr's shouts, and headed for the high pasture as fast as they could gallop. Leifr picked himself out of the gooseberry bushes, as one of the thralls set out in pursuit of the cows. Scratched and prickled, he was in no mood to be set upon by Thurid, who came swooping out of the kitchen with a fierce gleam in his eye.

'Fridmarr, you'd better stop this foolishness,' he began furiously. 'At once, do you hear? The house is crawling with spiders and toads. I even dreamed about spiders and toads last night. These tricks are your doing; and I hate to believe it, but I think it was your influence behind Gunhildr falling down the steps. Now the pig's gone, and who knows if we'll get our cows back?'

'It's not me,' Leifr snapped. 'I don't have any power. It must be you and that old satchel. I'm not sabotaging the farm.'

Thurid gripped his staff. 'Somebody is. We've had nothing but bad luck since you've returned.'

'What sort of luck did you have before? I wouldn't call it exactly rosy.'

Thurid's eyes narrowed to unpleasant little slits, and he jabbed a finger at Leifr, which caused a row of buckets to swing and clatter on their hooks. 'Fridmarr, this is not a warning, it's a threat. Either stop the nasty tricks, or I shall leave.'

'You said you dreamed about spiders and toads, and today the house is crawling with them,' Leifr pointed out. 'You're doing the tricks.'

'Most certainly not!' Thurid huffed indignantly. 'Nonsense! I had nothing to do with the livestock going berserk, nor all the jittering of everything for no reason at all. I'm sick to death of things falling off the walls and these confounded sparks everywhere.' He dropped his satchel and suddenly began pounding at his clothes and flapping frantically until a large coal dropped out of his long gown. 'You see!' he shouted, his eyes fixed on Leifr accusingly. 'Can you say with good conscience that you weren't responsible for that?'

'Yes,' Leifr answered, with a challenging stare. 'I'm not the one with the power, Thurid. Stop denying it, and it will stop pestering you – as well as the rest of us.'

Thurid's lip curled contemptuously. 'Power? Me? Surely you jest. I'm no real wizard. All that boasting and blather is nothing but lies. Do you want to know the truth, Fridmarr? Shall I tell you the real history of the great Thurid of Dallir?'

'No, I'd rather you didn't,' Leifr said hastily.

Thurid was not to be deflated by so small a barb.

'I've got no power,' he almost spat. 'I'm a failure. I failed the tests to get into the Wizards' Guild Academy for my final apprenticeship. I made a total fool of myself before the instructors and masters who examined my skill. The masters very kindly said I was not likely to develop any further powers, despite a promising beginning. Extraordinary skills and potential are required for Guild wizards, so they sent me back to the mundane life of an ordinary Ljosalfar. As if I could so easily forget my yearnings for wizardry!'

Thurid thumped his staff upon the ground, causing a sudden gust of wind to billow his fine cloak around him.

'In only one regard was I praised,' he continued, with a bitter smile. He extended one hand and summoned a small, brilliantly glowing orb to the tip of one long finger. 'My alf-light alone was worthy of the masters' notice. Very pure, they said, very consistent, but simply inadequate for the needs of a full-fledged wizard. Inadequate!' He swung around to glare at Leifr.

Leifr returned his challenging glare. 'Well, from what I've seen, I'd say you have a lot of powers if you'd learn to control them.'

'I can't! I don't dare use those powers! They frighten me half to death! I wish I'd never seen that wretched old satchel you brought me! Those aren't Guild powers, Fridmarr – nor are they Dokkalfar powers. I don't know for sure what they are, but sometimes I think they might be – '. His voice fell to a tortured whisper as he darted a frantic glance all around before continuing. ' – Rhbu powers.'

'You've gone this far,' Leifr said. 'You can't go back, once you've got the knowledge. You'll have to use it, or your life will be miserable.'

'Use it! The knowledge could destroy me if I try to. Do you remember how I burned up those spiders? The same thing could happen to me. Oh, I don't know why I'm wasting my breath talking to you. I can see you don't believe a single word I'm saying!' He turned away with a haughty twitch of his shoulders.

'Wait, Thurid, you great dolt!'

Thurid whirled around, his thin nostrils quivering with indignation, his eyes narrowed to blazing, incredulous pinpoints. Slowly he raised his forefinger, trembling slightly.

'Do you know what these powers could do to you, or any other large, obnoxious creature?' he began momentously. The alf-light gleamed through his forefinger until the flesh appeared transparent, almost too bright to look at.

Leifr drew a deep breath. 'I expect I can imagine, judging from what happened to the spiders.' Thurid started to nod wisely, but Leifr went on, 'However, if what you say is true, then it wouldn't be hard for you to divert Raudbjorn long enough for me to escape.'

Involuntarily, both their heads turned toward Raudbjorn, who was watching patiently from his knoll outside the gate, his gaze trained earnestly upon the cow stable.

'Come on now, Thurid, it would take just one small spell. You can do it. You've had better than forty years to work on those spells. Or are you all threats and bluster and no real magic?' Leifr eyed him challengingly and plunged onward recklessly, seeing the fire in Thurid's eye flickering toward doubt. 'Maybe forty years aren't enough for a blathering old blowhard. Did it take you forty years to learn to kill spiders?'

Thurid gripped his staff, his eyes still fixed upon Raudbjorn, while small curls of black smoke feathered off its glowing knob. Inside the barn, buckets rattled on pegs, unnoticed. 'Saddle your horse,' he commanded. 'Be ready to ride away when I give you the signal.'

He opened the satchel, releasing an ancient, musty smell, and drew out a handful of rune wands, all carved with indecipherable scratchings and stained with some dark substance that Leifr suspected was blood. Selecting one, Thurid read it from end to end several times and replaced it in his satchel. Seeing Leifr watching him dubiously, he pointed peremptorily toward the horse stable.

'Ready yourself for escape,' he intoned. 'Stay in the barn, out of sight.'

Leifr saddled his horse quickly and hastened to apply his eye to a crack so he could watch Thurid.

Thrusting back his sleeves, Thurid strode up and down a few times, muttering to himself. Then he stopped and faced the house. After a long moment, a dark image appeared in the doorway, stepped down off the porch, and walked across the courtyard toward the road that led up to the high pastures in the fells.

Leifr scuttled to another crack, ramming his eye against it and scarcely feeling the pain, overwhelmed as he was by total amazement. A perfect likeness of himself was walking casually out the upper gate, as if intending to help search for the strayed cows. The cloak and hood were the same design and color, even down to the tassel on the tail of the hood and the embroidery around the hem of the cloak.

Raudbjorn watched with great interest a moment, then climbed onto his horse and rode slowly after the image, following along the outside of the wall until he gained the same road, letting his horse take leisurely mouthfuls of grass along the way. When his bulky form vanished into a ravine, Leifr slipped out of the barn to find Thurid.

Thurid stood facing the road, his arms extended rigidly and quivering slightly. His face was contorted into a painful grimace, his eyes screwed shut, and he muttered something under his breath repeatedly. As Leifr watched, Thurid began to sway on his feet and would have toppled over on his face if Leifr hadn't stepped forward hastily and caught him. Spluttering indignantly, Thurid disengaged himself immediately and composed his clothing, still trembling and a little dazed.

'What are you doing here?' he snapped. 'Get going! I kept the image as long as I could sustain it. The old high gate this side of the ford was the last thing I saw. Raudbjorn will be back here when he realizes I've tricked him. Stop staring, Fridmarr, and be off to your reunion with Gotiskolker. You can tell him, by the way, that we're out of tallow, and he'd better not try to cheat us as he cheats everyone else.'

Leifr still lingered, not liking the gray color of Thurid's face, nor the glassy look of his eyes. 'You look like a dead fish,' he observed. 'Are you sure you're all right?'

'I'm fine. Now leave!' Thurid steadied himself against the turf wall and glared at Leifr fiercely.

Inspired with a sudden new respect for Thurid and his powers, Leifr turned and hurried into the barn after his horse. In a few moments, he was galloping over the fell toward the barrows, still marveling at what he had seen.

CHAPTER 4

Leifr found Gotiskolker rendering a pot of unsavoury grease. He scarcely glanced up from his stirring.

'You've kept yourself away a long time,' he greeted Leifr. 'I hope the time has passed agreeably for you.'

Leifr tethered his horse and tried to get upwind of the kettle. 'Agreeably! Nothing has gone right since I got here. There's a great deal you failed to warn me about, you slinking thief. I had to learn almost everything from Sorkvir.'

Gotiskolker raised his head warily. 'You've been to see him already?'

'Yes. I went to bargain for a truce until Fridmundr dies. In the meantime, he's set Raudbjorn to watch me and make sure I don't come anywhere near this place. You never once mentioned that Fridmarr had taken Sorkvir's eitur at one time. I met Ljosa, too. It seems that Fridmarr is universally hated by everyone. And Sorkvir told me about your addiction to eitur, which puts you practically in his power, so what sort of an ally are you going to be? As if that weren't enough, he says that the Rhbus do not exist and that the grindstone and the sword were stolen from the trolls, so they aren't going to break the alog, anyway. Maybe you'd better just send me back to the Scipling realm while I'm still alive. The longer I'm here, the less likely it seems that anything can be done about Sorkvir.'

Gotiskolker listened, his black brows knitted closer and closer until his entire face was twisted up in an incredulous scowl.

'I should have know better than to trust a Scipling!' he

finally burst out. 'Why did you take matters into your own hands so hastily? Now Sorkvir's suspicions arc aroused, and no amount of discretion will allay them. We're doomed before we've even started!'

'You've been doomed for years, since you took that eitur,' Leifr retorted. 'You'd better send me back before you die. You've led me into a trap.'

Gotiskolker wiped his hands on his thighs and spat into the tallow. 'You're not going anywhere until I've finished with you, Scipling. I'm not going to be thwarted by anyone's stupidity, unless it's my own. Now be quiet and let me think. We'll have to move quickly, before Fridmundr dies. This truce of Sorkvir's is no guarantee that he won't suddenly decide to chain you to a wall in his dungeon or let five or six Dokkalfar dance on your face with hobnail boots.'

'I don't know what we could do alone,' Leifr growled. 'Even if I decide to stay. Why don't we get some of these Ljosalfar together to stand up against Sorkvir? Ljosalfar have magical powers they can fight back with, don't they?'

Gotiskolker snorted emphatically. 'That shows what little you know about Ljosalfar. For one thing, their magical powers have deteriorated since loss of contact with Snowfell, where King Elbegast is. Secondly, Ljosalfar are too independent-minded to cooperate much. Thirdly, they're all too frightened of Sorkvir and the Dokkalfar anyway. And fourthly, they don't trust either you or me because of past associations with Sorkvir. That's four excellent reasons for not attempting to raise a rebellion; are you satisfied?'

'No, I'm certainly not satisfied. I'd feel much safer with twenty or thirty men waiting in the fells, whether they had sharp swords and axes or not.'

Gotiskolker was shaking his head adamantly before Leifr had finished speaking. 'No, no, no. There's no one that we can trust. You don't know them as I do. Your way won't work.'

Leifr glowered, resenting his high-handed arrogance. 'Either we get some allies, or I'll leave you to your own devices and do this job the way we would do it in the Scipling realm. If there's one thing I know how to do, it's fight. A scrawny imp like you isn't going to be much use anyway.'

'And your stupidity isn't going to be much use either. I say no allies and no fighting, and that's my final word.'

Leifr and Gotiskolker glowered at one another across the foul-smelling kettle.

'Do you have a better plan?' Leifr demanded.

'There is only one plan which will work. The Pentacle will help us. In the old days, seekers after special powers and hidden knowledge visited the five points of the Pentacle to gain favor with the Rhbus. When the supplicants had passed each site, the Rhbus granted their wishes – if they survived the natural hazards of the journey. If you destroy Sorkvir's evil influence that perverts each site, the Rhbus will show you where the grindstone is hidden.'

'Sorkvir says the Rhbus are nothing but superstition. You could be following a foolish delusion. For all I know, you could be lying. Sorkvir's eitur is in your veins and his mark is in your hand. How do I know you won't betray me for some purposes of your own?'

Gotiskolker spat into the kettle with a sputtering hiss. 'Then go your own way and start a rebellion. A lot of Ljosalfar will be killed – if you can persuade them to trust an old ally of Sorkvir's. You won't find the grindstone. Sorkvir will eventually run you to earth, and you'll spend the rest of your life in torment – like me. How very like the real Fridmarr you've become already.'

Leifr scowled. 'Don't insult me. I see nothing in Fridmarr that anyone could admire.'

'Good. Then you won't be surprised if Fridmarr decides to break Sorkvir's truce by stealing Bodmarr's sword from Gliru-hals. It's exactly the sort of thing everyone expects from Fridmarr.'

'You must be mad. Outside of breaking an honorable truce, there's a trifling matter of thirty or forty Dokkalfar lurking around Gliru-hals, from the number of shields on the walls, and all of them as mean as wild sows.'

'True, of course. We need someone who can slip into the hall and steal the sword right from under their filthy snouts. The only one who can do that is Thurid.'

'Thurid! He sets fires in his own pockets!'

'But he has that old satchel and staff Fridmarr gave him. They were stolen from a wizard's barrow in Bjartur, the old Rhbu hill fort on the Pentacle. There are special powers in that bag, and we need him to exercise them for us.'

Leifr thought of the image of himself Thurid had conjured and he shrugged with an uneasy smile. 'The powers in the satchel may be good enough, and Thurid might master them one day, but right now I wonder if Thurid is ready for a challenge of this magnitude. Thurid's been causing all sorts of accidents and spiteful little tricks wherever he goes. He blames me for it, but I couldn't conjure these things – hundreds of spiders and toads creeping all over the house, buckets jumping off their pegs, strange breezes, strange sounds. Old Gunhildr fell down and broke her ankle, this morning the cows went mad and nearly trampled me, and last night the pigsty fell down. I'd fixed it myself just yesterday. I think I'd rather live in this stinking place than at Dallir. Thurid's bad enough by himself, without these mysterious powers.'

Gotiskolker nodded, his brow puckering in thought. 'Be patient. He's still learning. When he masters the magic in that satchel, he'll be a fit opponent for Sorkvir. Surely you've seen some promising signs, haven't you?'

'Well – a few. I'm no judge of wizards, though.' Leifr heaved a discouraged sigh. 'I suppose Thurid's the only wizard to be found. What am I to tell him? He already suspects that I've come back to make another attempt upon Sorkvir and he doesn't much like the idea. If I tell him that the three of us are going to attack Sorkvir, he's going to think I've lost my wits.'

'Wits? He's never thought you had any. As if he were one to judge. Just tell him that you want to talk to him at his cave in the upper pasture. Fridmarr used to like going there. I'll be watching for you after dusk, when your chores are done and he's finished his nightly spiel to Fridmundr. He may resist the idea, but when he stops shouting long enough, he'll come around. Don't mention to him anything about me. If he knew I was behind this, wild horses couldn't drag him into it.'

He stirred the tallow desultorily, his gaze drifting northward toward Stormurbjarg, where a steep dark fell towered over the headland.

'So you saw Ljosa,' he said in a cautiously neutral tone. 'She used to be the beauty of all Solvorfirth. How does she look now?'

Leifr pictured her as he had seen her. In spite of her opinion of Fridmarr and her angry demeanor, he could not keep the admiration out of his voice. 'She's beautiful still, in spite of the cold wind and the ragged clothes. In all my travels, I've seen few to rival her, even dressed in a shepherd's rags. She would be worthy of a king's ransom in jewels. She has no great opinion of Fridmarr, I might add. If words were poison adders, I'd been so bitten that I'd be green with venom. She accused me – Fridmarr, I mean – of causing Bodmarr's death out of sheer jealousy. He didn't really do that, did he?'

Gotiskolker ignored the question, waving it away with a contemptuous spitting sound and turning his back.

'You can't blame her for being bitter,' he said. 'A chieftain's daughter, accustomed to comforts and the best of all things, and now her father and brothers are all dead by Sorkvir's hand. Her mother died long ago and was spared all this.'

'Did Fridmarr and Bodmarr quarrel over her?' Leifr asked.

'It was always Fridmarr she cared most about, although Hroald had cradle-promised her to Bodmarr. Hroald always hated Fridmarr, even in the early days when Hroald and Sorkvir were cheek by jowl and Fridmarr was Sorkvir's pupil in magic. Then Bodmarr fell out of favor, things went sour between Hroald and Sorkvir, and the real trouble began. Hroald lost his land, his sons, his chieftaincy, and finally he died in a dungeon. Sorkvir waited until then to turn Ljosa out to make her way as a shepherd.'

Gotiskolker seemed almost to forget about Leifr as he recited the tale of woe, and his brusque manner softened perceptibly. 'She has suffered many disappointments – but I think perhaps none was greater than the loss of Fridmarr.'

'You'd never guess it,' Leifr said, shaking his head. 'Wouldn't you think she'd be glad to see him, in spite of the past?'

'She's proud, you dolt. Don't you know the meaning of pride? It means choosing to suffer rather than admit you might have been wrong – even if your happiness is at stake.' Gotiskolker's lips twisted in a bitter grimace.

'There's nothing to prevent her having her choice now,' Leifr said, his hopes suddenly brightening.

'Except for the fact that she could not forgive Fridmarr for going over to Sorkvir, considering what befell her brothers. Besides that, you're not Fridmarr, in case you'd forgotten. I can see that you're captivated by her quite on your own initiative. It makes our charade all the more convincing.'

'I'm not captivated,' Leifr retorted fierily. 'She hates the sight of me. I can see I haven't a chance, so I won't waste my time by trying.'

Gotiskolker pursed his lips sardonically. 'You're going to be proud too, eh? I didn't know you were one to give up so easily. When you restore the Pentacle and destroy Sorkvir, I think Ljosa will forgive Fridmarr for his past mistakes. Don't judge her harshly. It's the way she protects herself from pain.'

Leifr sighed and nodded. 'Just out of idle curiosity – do you think an Alfar chieftain's daughter would consider a marriage offer from a landless mortal?'

Gotiskolker smiled bitterly. 'Perhaps you'd have a better chance than Fridmarr.'

'But with Sorkvir gone, Ljosa will be restored to ownership of Gliru-hals and a position much loftier than mine. If she is as proud as you say, she may look for a duke or an earl.'

'Her pride isn't that sort. She's no more humbled by herding sheep than I am by rendering tallow. It's the forgiving and relenting that she can't abide. My advice to you is to apologize to her for Fridmarr. He was too proud himself to ask her forgiveness – even knowing that he didn't cause Bodmarr's death out of jealousy.' Gotiskolker sighed and shook his crooked shoulders as if he were shaking off something. 'Enough of this useless chatter. There are more important matters, whether you think so or not. Just get Thurid to his cave at dusk tomorrow, and I'll put this matter before him. Now get out of here while I'm still in a good mood.'

'Don't forget the tallow. And don't try to cheat us.'

'Trolls take you and be welcome!'

Of evenings it was Thurid's custom to sit near Fridmundr and guzzle ale and smoke his pipe while rattling off a great list of the day's activities on the farm. Most of the time, Fridmundr's gaze was fixed upon infinity, or he sat dozing with his head bowed down to his chest. It mattered not to Thurid; he talked on as if he had a roomful of appreciative listeners.

It was Leifr's duty to listen also, although he was fast becoming dissatisfied with the procedure, particularly when his thoughts roved from Gotiskolker to Ljosa to Sorkvir and back around again, like an endlessly grinding treadmill.

'Can't you see he doesn't hear you?' Leifr snapped suddenly, unable to bear the mundane dronings any longer. 'He's got far more important things on his mind than sheep ticks and botflies, and so have I.'

Thurid gazed haughtily down the length of his long, aristocratic nose. 'This is important business,' he said with withering reproach. 'It might be of benefit for you to listen. One day soon, this farm will be yours, and you'll be in charge of the running of it. Then perhaps you'll appreciate the long, weary hours of faithful service poor old Thurid has contributed. When you're the master here, I expect I'll be turned out like an old cat to starve on the bitter mountainside, in the middle of winter, if it's at all convenient.'

As he talked, the laces of his boots untied themselves, waving and wriggling in the air like curious little snakes. Thurid slapped at them angrily until they subsided.

'You may think it's humorous to humiliate me with your infantile magic,' he grunted as he knotted his laces. 'Great wizards are seldom appreciated by their old friends. Only my tolerance and self control keep me here where I am so grossly underappreciated.'

'Thurid, for the last time—' Leifr began, exasperated.

'Spare me your fulsome denials,' Thurid interrupted. 'It's time to put the old master to bed. I fear he's even weaker tonight. His days of sitting in that chair are almost done. Since your return, he has no reason to linger.'

They each supported Fridmundr from the side, and Leifr noted again the old Alfar's lightness, as if his bones were hollow and his flesh mere shadow. As Fridmundr rose from his chair, his luminous eyes fastened upon the front doors of the hall.

'Look,' he whispered in a vibrant manner. 'Do you see it? There by the doors.'

Awash with gooseflesh, Leifr turned to look at the shadowy form he knew lurked there. He glimpsed a grizzled old ram with massive, curling horns, down on his knees, panting wearily and holding up his heavy, nodding head with difficulty. So swift was the vision that it vanished almost immediately, but Thurid had seen it also. His eyes were wide and almost transparent, and his breathing was suspended.

'He's down on both knees now, Thurid,' Fridmundr said faintly, his eyes closed. 'Help Fridmarr, Thurid. The time is growing short. Events are coming together. I can see Sorkvir's doom. Promise me you'll help Fridmarr, Thurid. Cleanse the Pentacle of evil.'

His voice trailed away, and they gently put him into his own bed. The light in the dying Alfar's eyes seemed to permeate his withered flesh, like lamplight through a threadbare curtain.

'He won't rise from that bed tomorrow,' Thurid said gruffly, keeping his face averted from Leifr. 'The end comes.'

'Thurid, we need to talk,' Leifr said in a low tone. 'There's no sense postponing it further. Our fates and Sorkvir's are inextricably mixed, whether we like it or not. But we can't talk here. Let's go to your cave.'

Thurid flung up his head indignantly. 'My cave? Never! I allow no profane foot to cross its threshold, for fear of disturbing my concentration with useless distractions.'

'If you ever want to become a real wizard,' Leifr said, 'you'd better listen to me. Do you want to go on forever as you are? This might be your only opportunity to make something of yourself.'

Thurid tugged on his nether lip dubiously. Finally he heaved a ponderous sigh, gripped his staff, and picked up his satchel. With the noble mien of a martyr, he led Leifr through the maze of fallen buildings and crumbling walls, following a detailed ritual. A certain path must be followed, certain stones touched, and Thurid directed Leifr to step over objects that had been there at one time but now were removed. He even went through the motions of opening and shutting a nonexistent gate.

'Why do we have to do this?' Leifr grumbled, as Thurid patiently crawled underneath a toppled beam that he could have easily walked around.

'Ritual magic,' Thurid replied. 'I always do it this way for luck. You must be certain to do everything exactly as I do it.'

Leifr did as he was told, no matter how foolish he thought it was to bow to the circle of standing stones in the upper pasture. As they followed a narrow sheep track through the lava flows, Thurid suddenly plunged between two thickets and vanished into a dark fissure. Supposing it was the cave, Leifr followed Thurid's lead exactly, plunging into the fissure and slithering down a steep, smooth incline, to land at the bottom in the middle of Thurid's back. They both sprawled in a tangle of dead twigs and branches fallen in from above.

'You buffoon!' Thurid spluttered, struggling to his feet. 'I stumbled! This isn't part of the ritual! Now there's no telling what will happen. I should have known better than to trust a disruptive influence like yours!'

Leifr raised one hand warningly and motioned Thurid to be silent. Above, a horse's shod hooves grated against a stone, accompanied by the soft jingle and creak of harness and weapons. In a moment the sounds diminished; then Leifr heard the snort of a horse distantly and the splash of hooves crossing the beck.

'Raudbjorn!' Thurid said. 'He suspects you're up to something.'

'He didn't find us.' Leifr smiled. 'Thanks to your clumsiness in falling down this chute.'

Thurid swelled importantly. 'Keep that in mind next time you feel inclined to deride my rituals. My every action is fraught with significance.'

He snortled gloatingly for the rest of the way to the cave.

Enough light remained for Leifr to discern a door barricading the mouth of the cave. The runic symbols carved into the wood glowed with a faint phosphorescence. The ground in front of the cave seethed with a peculiar mist that hovered over each rock and mossy stick in an eerie aura.

Thurid positively beamed as he watched Leifr's face suffuse with awe. 'Another little spell from that satchel you brought me,' he said, giving the satchel a friendly slap with his hand. 'Follow me; it's damp, but harmless.' He made a few motions with his hands and the door fell inward with a welcoming creak of hinges.

At that moment, a dark shape rose up at Thurid's elbow and a bony hand reached out to give the door a push.

'Well done, Fridmarr, you've brought him here just as we'd planned,' a hoarse voice said. 'Let's go inside, shall we, Thurid?'

Thurid gasped indignantly and planted his feet, but Leifr gave him a small shove forward for encouragement, and Gotiskolker vanished into the dark interior of the cave ahead of them.

'What's the meaning of this invasion?' Thurid demanded, rapping his staff on the floor and summoning a burst of brilliant light to its knob. 'This is my cave. What are you doing here, you purveyor of dead carcasses?' He thrust the light toward Gotiskolker, who was seating himself in a chair unbidden.

'Lock the door, Fridmarr,' Gotiskolker said. 'The trolls will be out before long. Thurid, how have you been progressing with that satchel and staff Fridmarr stole from the Rhbu ruins of Bjartur?'

Thurid rounded on Leifr, his eyes bulging as he watched him shut and bar the door. 'Stolen from Bjartur? My staff and satchel? I never dreamed you got them from Bjartur.'

'Yes, Bjartur,' Leifr replied rather faintly, then added with a flash of inspiration from the carbuncle. 'The staff is hawthorn, cut from the sacred grove of Wotan.'

Thurid ran his hand along the staff reverently. 'Only the Rhbus were allowed to cut wood from those groves,' he murmured, darting Leifr a troubled glance. 'I can scarcely believe that even you would have the nerve to desecrate the old Rhbu ruins. That's worse than barrow robbing.'

Leifr winced. He had not yet stooped to barrow robbing but obviously Fridmarr had shared no such compunctions.

74

'I did what I had to do,' he growled resentfully.

Thurid hoisted one eyebrow skeptically. 'It seems you had to do more than your share of treacherous deeds, such as stealing Hjaldr's grindstone. And that sword you gave to Bodmarr was from Bjartur also, I presume?'

Leifr felt himself nodding. The recollections from the carbuncle were becoming painful and cloudy. 'I never meant for Bodmarr to be killed,' he said, dragging up the words from a great depth of Fridmarr's inmost misery.

'I *hope* that wasn't part of your plan,' Thurid answered. 'Ljosa believes it was, but I could never believe it. Now do you see what comes from using a sword stolen from a barrow?'

Leifr avoided Thurid's piercing, questioning stare. 'I don't wish to discuss my past crimes,' he snapped. 'It's the present that matters the most now.'

'Well, sit down and tell me what you want, then,' Thurid retorted. 'I hope it won't hurt to listen.'

Leifr glanced around the cave for something to sit on and found a chair half-full of a dismaying assortment of objects. He shoved them aside. Bones, sticks, egg shells, bits of hair, rocks, ropes, sea shells, dried flowers, feathers, teeth, and a host of objects Leifr could not readily identify rained down onto the floor.

'Now you've done it!' Thurid exclaimed suddenly, his brow puckering in horrified recognition. 'You've disarranged my absolute proof of a great drought in forty-two years. I had it all in that chair, assembled in true natural form. Totally random objects thrown together frequently surpass all other methods of divination, and now you've destroyed the whole business!'

Leifr shifted uncomfortably, causing several more objects to fall. 'I'm sorry, Thurid.'

Thurid snorted and sat down, wedging his staff in a crack between two rocks to shed its light over the room. 'It doesn't matter,' he growled, darting a malignant glower at Gotiskolker. 'The entire cave is profaned. The only question in my mind is what outrage you are plotting against me now by bringing this unsavoury creature into our midst.'

'You know from Fridmundr that things are about to start happening in Solvorfirth,' Leifr said. 'The reason Gotiskolker and I are here is to make an earnest request for your services as a wizard.'

Thurid's eyebrows hoisted themselves upward, and he swung around to stare at Gotiskolker incredulously. 'You're involved in this too?' he asked.

Dryly Gotiskolker replied, 'You may recall my past unsuccessful attempt to steal the sword. My failure did not cure me of my ambition to see Sorkvir destroyed. Fridmarr and I long ago swore an oath that we would see the Pentacle restored to its former powers. Why do you think Fridmarr gave you that old satchel from Bjartur, unless he intended to return one day when you had mastered its powers? Did you think he returned because he missed your company? You're not a third-rate prophet anymore, Thurid.' He thrust at the clutter on the floor contemptuously with one ragged boot. 'You've got far better powers at your command than this. What's more, they will use you whether you want to use them or not.'

Thurid darted Leifr an accusing glare. 'I thought you were doing me a kindness,' he muttered. 'I've never done anything of this sort before. My skills are untested and my powers are untried. I've practised, but with Sorkvir so near, I've had to use the utmost caution. If he knew that I possessed the knowledge that I do, my life would be worthless.'

Gotiskolker cut off his protest. 'What we want you to do is to steal Bodmarr's sword from Gliru-hals. It won't be your duty to challenge Sorkvir; that's up to Fridmarr, when he gets the sword sharpened.'

'Steal Bodmarr's sword from Gliru-hals?' Thurid gasped. 'You must be mad! How can I do that? Need I remind you that Sorkvir is also a wizard, and much more experienced than I am? How easy do you think it will be to fool him?'

'You're the wizard; you answer the questions,' Leifr retorted. 'Can you do it, Thurid?'

Thurid tossed his head back and pretended to contemplate the ceiling, as if the answer were written there in the dust and bat guano. 'It may take a little time.'

'Take as long as you wish, but once Fridmundr dies, the truce is off,' Leifr said impatiently. 'We'll be too overrun with Dokkalfar to think about stealing the sword. It will have to be done now or not at all.'

Gotiskolker nodded broodingly, his eyes upon Thurid's staff. 'When the ram goes down on his side, you'll know it's the proper time to steal the sword,' he said.

Thurid frowned and tugged at his lower lip. 'That doesn't leave me much time. I fear Fridmundr's fetch will die within a few days. It's down on both knees now.'

'Have your plan ready, Thurid,' Gotiskolker said, rising to his feet and pulling his hood over his head. 'This will be your chance for greatness. Don't make an ass of yourself.'

Thurid lunged from his chair, his nostrils flaring indignantly, but the door closed behind Gotiskolker softly. Snorting, Thurid strode up and down the cave a few times to work off his temper, glancing challengingly at Leifr. 'I don't know what ever induced you to pick him as a friend. There's something about him that gets under my skin like an inflamed sliver. He irritates me as much as you do, if that's at all possible.' Jabbing his finger at Leifr, he sizzled a spider that was creeping along the arm of his chair, and peered around vigilantly for more evidences of mischief. 'I'm not safe even in my own cave,' he muttered.

Leifr stood up and more stuff shuffled off the chair. 'It must be nearly dark by now,' he said. 'The trolls might be coming back for another chance at the livestock – us included.'

Thurid took up his staff, seized the nearest random object, and threw it against the wall, the opening shot in a furius volley that lasted until Thurid mysteriously reached a point of satisfaction with his efforts. With the inquisitive attitude of a hen pecking over some grain, Thurid looked over the mess he had made. 'Yes, it rather looks as if there might be trouble,' he said at last.

'Wouldn't it be easier just to guess?' Leifr asked.

'That would be neither scientific nor accurate,' Thurid replied. 'Look at these juxtapositions and tell me you see nothing significant there.'

'I see nothing significant,' Leifr said agreeably.

'Fridmarr, where most Ljosalfar minds are clear and liquid, yours is a lump of black granite,' Thurid declared. 'I hope there aren't many more like you, or it bodes ill for the future of all Ljosalfar. My own clarity of thought causes my sensibilities much suffering when they are subjected to the obtusities of common minds.'

He flung the epithet at Leifr as if it were a brickbat and strode toward the door with his nose in the air.

As they approached the ruined walls and paddocks of Dallir, Thurid began to glance around warily. 'This is where trolls like to lie in wait sometimes,' he whispered. 'Plenty of rocks to throw.'

They crossed several walls. Then a rock thudded to the ground beside Leifr, followed by several others that missed by an even wider margin.

'Head for the cow stable,' Thurid said. 'I'll be right behind you.'

Looking over his shoulder, Leifr saw several dark shapes skulking along the tops of the walls. As he approached the barn, he noticed that the door stood open a foot or so, but he had no time to think about such an irregularity. A barrage of rocks pelted them from the direction of the sheep paddock, dealing Leifr several breath-taking blows before he dived into the warm darkness of the stable.

Outside, Thurid lit his staff with a spout of brilliant light and raked the surrounding shadows. A sharp explosion suddenly shattered the evening quiet, and Thurid chortled, 'I got you, scumbag! Try throwing rocks at me again, will you!'

Liefr rolled to his feet on the straw-littered floor and went to soothe the cows, who were bawling and kicking at their stalls in a panic. As he passed one of the empty stalls, half a dozen dark forms catapulted out at him, claws and long, sharp teeth reaching for him. Leifr's sword cleared its sheath to meet their savage charge. His first stroke felled their leader in mid-air as the troll leaped for Leifr's throat like a wolf. The others hastily backed off, blinking and squinting in the indirect light, their wizened faces a curious combination of animal and human, with short, snouty noses and tufts of matted fur around their faces like scraggly beards. Their eyes gleamed with a cunning knowing expression that Leifr found repulsive and evil.

Brandishing his sword and wishing Thurid would stop his useless flaring outside, Leifr took a step forward. The trolls shrank back with a ferocious hissing, spitting and growling.

'You'd better run, you filthy little cowards,' Leifr snarled, 'or I'll make you into rat bait for our traps.'

The trolls laid back their ears and growled louder, cringing together in a knot of utter defiance.

'Thurid!' Leifr called hopefully. His only reply was another blast from outside and a triumphant chuckle.

The trolls crouched, their ratty tails twitching.

'Thurid!' Leifr called insistently, taking a step backward, which seemed to encourage the trolls greatly.

Grinning, they sidled closer with a scuttling of long claws which turned into a rush. Eyes glaring with malevolence, they sprang at him with roars and gibbers.

Leifr shouted, 'Thurid!' and flung himself backward.

Suddenly a white wash of light swept into the barn, showing him the wave of trolls rising around him, almost frozen in mid-air by the glare. Their expressions changed from wicked glee to wild terror. Then the stable shook with thunderous explosions. An unseen force knocked Leifr off his feet and propelled him into the midst of a tangle of kicking, threshing trolls, who seemed to be pelting him with a hail of rocks.

'It's all right now, they're done for,' Thurid said, playing his light around the barn. The light blazed from the end of his staff in a radiant beam almost too brilliant to look at. With his toe, he disdainfully nudged a heap of rocks aside into the barn gutter. Barely able to keep his expression neutral, he returned to glance at Leifr.

Too stunned to be properly appreciative of Thurid's technique, Leifr goggled at the heaps of rocks that had been trolls only moments before.

Thurid's voice trembled with excitement or rapture. 'Did you ever see such a burst of alf-light? I don't quite believe it myself. It was nothing like anything I'd ever imagined doing before. Confound it, Fridmarr, perhaps you're right. I could learn to enjoy using powers like this.'

Leifr took some deep breaths to steady himself. 'Thurid, you amaze me. You saved my life with your magic. I'll always be grateful to you.' He extended his hand, and, after an astonished moment, Thurid clasped it warmly.

'Fridmarr, there are moments when *you* amaze *me*,' he said solemnly. 'I never thought you'd learn the meaning of gratitude. I feel as if you're almost a stranger.'

Leifr replied uncomfortably, 'How right you are, Thurid. Let's not get maudlin about it, though.'

Thurid's gaze suddenly sharpened. 'That sword,' he breathed. 'It's sharp. Where did you get it?'

Leifr sheathed it quickly. 'It's one I acquired in my travels – under circumstances I don't care to divulge.'

'That sounds typical. It can't be from the Alfar realm or the alog would have blunted it. I hope you can keep it a secret from Sorkvir.' Shuddering suddenly, he damped his brilliant light to a soft red glow and his expression became brooding. 'Fridmarr, Fridmarr,' he sighed wearily. 'Your past is no less troubled than your future will be. Sometimes I fear you. Sometimes I fear for you.'

Leifr shivered also, feeling that Thurid had spoken prophecy.

CHAPTER 5

RAUDBJORN watched Dallir patiently, seeming oblivious to rain, cold, fog, the odd snow flurry, and the malicious peltings of rocks by the trolls at night. His aspect brightened whenever Leifr appeared on some mundane occasion; but on the whole, his job was a boring one. He prowled about, enlivening his existence only once a day when a closely masked Dokkalfar brought him his food and drink from Gliru-hals.

On the surface, Dallir was the dullest of all the downtrodden Ljosalfar settlements. A keener mind, however, might have wondered at the increased need for tallow at Dallir and the sudden spate of housecleaning, which entailed taking something nearly every day to the scavenger's hut in the barrows. Snagi and Thurid, or one of the servants, did the traveling back and forth, while Leifr remained where Raudbjorn could keep his eyes on him. Gotiskolker received an almost-daily account of Fridmundr's declining condition.

Stubbornly, the old Alfar's fetch labored to release its hold upon life and upon the life of Fridmundr. Leifr was not able to see it every night, somewhat to his relief, since he still felt uneasy in the presence of the mysteries of Ljosalfar magic. Thurid reported to him what he saw, whether the ailing ram managed to rise to one knee or whether he was down on both again. Fridmundr kept to his bed now, his luminous eyes fixed upon the rafters in rapture. His entire body glowed with alf-light, as if the threadbare curtain were thinner with each passing day.

Leifr saw Ljosa twice, herding her sheep past Dallir to water at the beck. With Raudbjorn watching, Leifr had no intention of speaking to Ljosa, thereby casting

81

suspicion upon her. Ljosa glanced toward Dallir and let her sheep take their time drinking their fill, then she went on her way. Later, Leifr heard that she had taken her sheep north to Stormurbjarg, where Hroald's farthest shieling was. Remembering her lingering near Dallir, Leifr wondered if she had wanted to speak to him. At least she was out of Sorkvir's way now, he told himself gloomily.

As a creature of habit, Thurid continued his evening practice of telling Fridmundr all the happenings on the farm for the day, although now he had to sit by the bedside for his recitation. Leifr sat beside Fridmundr also, out of respect for a noble Alfar. In his youth, Fridmundr had been a redoubtable warrior, unbroken in spirit until the death of Bodmarr and the treachery of Fridmarr. After his fondest hopes had been shattered and Sorkvir seemed entrenched in Gliru-hals, Fridmundr turned the running of the farm over to Thurid and retreated into himself in search of the voices of his ancestors. He had found them, and slowly his body wasted away, until at last the nearness of the end was signaled by the alf-light and the burning revelations of the meanings of all things.

'All Ljosalfar don't die this way,' Leifr observed, hoping to pump Thurid for more information.

'No,' Thurid replied rather proudly. 'Only philosophers, sages, wizards, and others who are clever enough to die safely in bed, rather than in a fight.'

Leifr murmured, 'A straw death is held in contempt by the Sciplings. Death in battle is the most honorable death to be bought with one's life.'

Thurid snorted. 'I'm not at all surprised to hear it. Those Sciplings won't last as a species, with that kind of ideas.'

Leifr would have liked to argue that point further, but the dusk was deepening to night; at the boundary of nightfall, Fridmundr's fetch was most apt to be seen. Unwillingly, yet helplessly fascinated, Leifr watched the shadows beside the door. Thurid arose to blow out the lamp, and Leifr head him gasp. Leifr turned around slowly, his hair prickling as a cold wave swept over him.

The fetch lay beside Fridmundr's bed, between Thurid and the lamp. It raised its heavy head to look at them with glazed eyes in mute appeal, gasping for each breath, its lips drawn away from its teeth. With a sigh, it laid its head down on the floor and wearily stretched out its legs – too weary to struggle any longer. Still struggling to breathe, the fetch faded and vanished.

Gingerly reaching over where it had lain, and taking care not to step there, Thurid picked up the lamp and carried it out of the room, with Leifr close at his heels.

'The fetch is down,' Thurid said when they had reached the kitchen where Snagi was polishing boots with bear grease. 'Somebody must tell Gotiskolker.'

'Tonight?' Snagi quavered. 'The Dokkalfar are out hunting with their troll-hounds. If they found my trail, I'd be torn to ribbons.'

Leifr went to the door and listened. The savage howling of the hounds drifted down the fells, a sound that would turn the bravest heart cold and send most trolls scuttling underground as far as they could get.

'I'll go,' Leifr said, reaching for his cloak. 'Snagi wouldn't have a chance with that shaky knee of his. The hounds are hunting in the high fells, so I've little to worry about.'

'Except Raudbjorn,' Thurid added.

'Even Raudbjorn has enough sense to take shelter somewhere when the hounds are hunting,' Leifr replied. 'He should know that better than we do.'

'I forbid you to go,' Thurid declared. 'It's too dangerour. If the hounds don't find you, the trolls might. Snagi wouldn't be that much of a loss. We'll send him.'

'We'll send me,' Leifr said grimly, unsheathing his sword a short way. 'This will discourage the troll-hounds.'

Ignoring Thurid's spluttering and threatening, Leifr

83

let himself out into the windy night, creeping along the walls and hurrying from thicket to thicket, in case Raudbjorn was lurking nearby. By the time he was halfway up the side of the fell, he had detected nobody following, although the baying of the hounds was considerably closer.

Keeping near the running water, Leifr took a rather circuitous path to get to Gotiskolker's barrow field. Twice he was followed by trolls along the opposite side of the water, which they were prohibited by earth powers from crossing. Aside from snarling and throwing a few stones, they did not bother him, uneasy as they were about the hounds hunting.

When he neared the barrow field where Gotiskolker's hut stood, Leifr advanced cautiously until he had reached the large pile of bones and skulls near the door. A faint flicker of light gleamed through the cracks in the makeshift door, but the fire had died beneath the huge, blackened kettle and its foul-smelling brew. Hearing no sounds of human occupation, Leifr crept toward the door and found it unlocked.

Inside, he found Gotiskolker sprawled across the table, still wearing his traveling cloak, with his stick propped against him. It seemed unlike Gotiskolker not to awaken at the slightest noise. Leifr announced himself with a loud *'Hem!'* but the scavenger slept on, his face drawn up in a weary, anxious scowl.

Leifr gave his shoulder a shake, and the motion dislodged a small vial from Gotiskolker's hand. A single red drop oozed from the empty vial onto the table. Leifr touched his finger to it and smelled it. Eitur – Sorkvir's addictive poison! Hastily, he wiped it off his finger and looked hopelessly at Gotiskolker, who was lolling in his chair like a limp doll. His breathing rattled stertorously, and his meagre muscles were completely relaxed.

'Gotiskolker! You wretched rat!' Leifr propped him upright and shook his wasted form none too gently. 'What have you done? We've got to talk tonight! Fridmundr's fetch is down on its side, dying. Can you talk? Wake up, you fool!'

Gotiskolker's eyes opened reluctantly, looking flatly at Leifr with scant recognition.

'Who is it?' he muttered thickly. 'Go away and leave me alone. Haven't I furnished you all sport enough?'

'It's Leifr, you sot – the Scipling you brought here to be Fridmarr. Now pay attention. The time has come to get the sword from Sorkvir. Tell me what to do, Gotiskolker.'

Gotiskolker's head sagged. 'Sorry. Can't tell you anything. We'll talk later. Too sleepy now. The pain – I had to have the eitur. Didn't know the fetch was sinking so fast.'

'Gotiskolker! You fool! If you'd endured it for one more day – don't you know that stuff is killing you?'

Gotiskolker tried to nod. 'No more eitur. This is the last time. Time to let go and die.'

'There'll be no talk of dying until you get me safely back to my own realm, my friend. Why did you have to make everything so difficult?' How long is this going to last? I'd better take you to Dallir, in case you wake up and decide to make yourself useful.'

Leifr bent to free Gotiskolker and the stick, then lifted the limp form to his shoulders and closed the door behind him. Fortunately his burden was not as heavy as a well-fleshed man, but, by the time Leifr reached Dallir, he was staggering with weariness and too exhausted to care if Raudbjorn saw him or not.

Snagi opened the door in response to Leifr's imperious kick, scuttling out of the way as Leifr reeled across the kitchen and deposited Gotiskolker on the old sleeping platform.

'What's this? You've brought contagion into our midst!' Thurid sputtered indignantly. 'Fridmarr! Do you know what sort of bugs he must have from those troll hides?'

'I don't care,' Leifr panted, collapsing in a chair and

85

accepting the horn of ale Snagi put into his hands. 'The fool has taken eitur. Maybe it will wear off tomorrow. If it doesn't, we'll have to plan the theft without him.'

Thurid's brow puckered in consternation. 'Without him? This scruffy rat knows a great deal about Sorkvir and Gliru-hals. We can't do it without him. We'll have to wait until he wakes up.' He rubbed his hands nervously and avoided looking at Leifr.

'The time is now,' Leifr replied. 'Fridmundr's fetch is dying. If we wait until Fridmundr is dead, Sorkvir is going to strike the first blow the moment the truce is off. From what I've seen of his Dokkalfar, I don't think we could survive. Thurid, you must have a plan in mind. We'll put it into action tomorrow, whether or not Gotiskolker is awake. We must have that sword in our possession when Fridmundr breathes his last. You've done amazing things already. There must be a spell on one of those rune sticks that will help you.'

Thurid paced across the room several times, plucking at his sparse beard. 'I suppose this is what it means to be a wizard. One must do the most difficult things alone.'

'I'll be with you,' Leifr said. 'I can put my old clothes back on and slink around like a scavenger and no one at Gliru-hals will look twice at me. You could do the same, Thurid.'

Thurid paid scant heed. He opened his satchel and selected a rune stick. By the firelight, he studied it carefully, his lips moving silently as he read.

'This one is the spell I shall use tomorrow night,' he finally announced with an air of finality. 'Now I must go to my cave and ready myself by seeking the intervention of the dextrous Rhbus. I fear the clarity of my mind isn't what it used to be, before certain disturbances entered into my carefully ordered life.' With a swirl of his cloak, he turned and went out the door, letting in a gust of cold wind as he departed.

Leifr slept fitfully. Snagi insisted upon staying awake to sit beside Fridmundr. 'I'll sleep later,' he assured

Leifr. 'Between chores, or during chores, or instead of chores. You know how lazy this old thrall is. I'm the last of your father's thralls.' He spoke in a tone of mild surprise, as if he had only just thought of it.

'You're a thrall no longer,' Leifr said. 'My father would want you to be a freeman now, and so do I.'

Snagi flapped one hand in disdain. 'Oh, the master tried to set me free many times, but I wouldn't go. This is my place and my father's before me and my grand-father's before him, and on back I don't know how long. I'll stay at Dallir for as long as I live.'

In the morning, Fridmundr was still breathing at slow, shallow intervals, and the alf-light had faded to a soft glow. His eyes were open, but he made no sign of seeing anyone who came into the room. Snagi sat beside him, dozing lightly from time to time. Around midday he sent word to the outside servants to start collecting the wood for Fridmundr's funeral pyre. Word was also taken to Fridmundr's old friends, Einarr the Elder and Young Einarr, Latvi, Birki, and the other old Alfar who had known Fridmundr.

Gotiskolker slept on, as limp and unconscious as he had been the night before. Thurid glared at him resent-fully, still hopeful, until at last the sun was low in the west, and the time had come to depart.

Leifr wore his old clothes, feeling quite at home in them. He looked disreputable enough that Raudbjorn scarcely glanced at him slinking out of the gate like some wandering beggar. Leifr headed down the ravine toward Gliru-hals.

He met Thurid behind the horse stable as they had agreed. Gliru-hals was stirring around them, with the scavengers creeping out of their hovels to beg, the troll-hounds setting up an eager yammer from their kennels in anticipation of another night's hunt, and the Dokkalfar slipping furtively from shadow to shadow, their voices raised in quick, heated argument.

Thurid and Leifr climbed onto the roof and lay in the

shadow, waiting until it was fully dark. Of his plan, Thurid would say nothing, keeping it rather smugly secret.

'You shall see,' was all he would say. 'Stay here and watch. You'll have a splendid view.'

'If anything should go wrong, just shout for me,' Leifr said uneasily. 'I can hear you in the hall from here. Are you sure I shouldn't get closer?'

Thurid glanced over his shoulder. 'That way lies our escape route. Stay close to it and hope that the moon gives us plenty of light.'

With misgivings, Leifr watched him climb down off the roof and disappear into the shadows, which were increasingly populated with skulking Dokkalfar and scavengers. As the smells of cooking food drifted from the main hall, followed by the sounds of the Dokkalfar feasting, the beggars crowded around the doors, waiting for the leavings. Leifr watched them closely, suspecting that Thurid had insinuated himself into their midst and was plotting a secretive entry into the hall by one of the doors.

The Dokkalfar finished their meal and threw out the scraps to the scavengers, then laughed coarsely to see them fighting over their meagre fare. Ten Dokkalfar saddled their horses and rode away purposefully, while the others sat round gaming, sharpening weapons, or whispering in tight knots of four or five, eyeing other knots of conspirators with suspicion and loathing. Six Dokkalfar saddled their horses and went hunting with the troll-hounds. Leifr saw nothing of Sorkvir. Only the highest ranking Dokkalfar did not gamble, quarrel, conspire, or hunt; they stood upon the porch, talking seldom, their grim presence alone enough to quell the most avaricious of scavengers and discomfit the most determined of the conspirators.

Leifr still saw no sign of Thurid and was beginning to hope that Thurid had gotten inside the hall somehow. Then one of the nondescript watchdogs sounded the alarm, leaping off the porch with several others following, all barking furiously, and the lot of them tore away up the lane past the stable. The Dokkalfar glanced up suspiciously from their grooming, polishing, and sharpening.

A lone rider paced slowly down the lane, guiding his horse fastidiously away from the squelching mud holes. At a single word, he silenced the barking mongrels and sent them cringing way to hide in a barn. The Dokkalfar forgot their work and stared blatantly as the strange Dokkalfar rode into the yard at a dignified pace, scarcely glancing right or left. His black cloak, turned back to display its red lining, sparkled with embroidery and bright bits of metal and glass, and his ceremonial headdress incorporated the wings of an owl. He wore a scarlet mask trimmed with owl feathers and stitched with an owl motif. The ceremonial shield he carried bore the owl symbol and more feathers and talons. His horse ornaments glittered with gold nails and owl motifs, leaving no doubt that the stranger was a Dokkalfar of importance.

The stranger halted his horse to gaze around at the Dokkalfar in silent contempt a moment. Then he barked in a harsh voice. 'When you've got your fill of staring, scraelings, you can send word to Sorkvir that I wish to see him. I've come all the way from Djofullholl to see about this alog of his.'

Laden with scorn, his tone lashed at the other Dokkalfar, startling them into action. Three hurried away at once toward the hall with the message, two edged forward cautiously and offered to attend to the stranger's horse, and one held his stirrup for him to dismount. The others cast knowing glances at one another and whispered covertly until the stranger rounded upon them suddenly.

Shaking his beaded whip in one hand, he snarled, 'You slime are the worst of the Dokkalfar worst. Djofull knows about your defection, and he's not pleased. He is your warlord, and none other. The Dokkur Lavardur has spoken to him.'

'The Dokkur Lavardur!' someone whispered. 'He knows! Sorkvir is doomed!'

The stranger raked the assemblage with another disdainful glower. 'Little do you suspect the harm you have done in Solvorfirth, and I don't refer to your infantile wrecking of farms and killings of innocent Ljosalfar. Your plunderings have awakened the wrath of a great wizard, whose powers have been sleeping since the last of the Rhbus. Now he is stalking you with all the might of the Rhbus and the wrath of the Fire Wizards' Guild. His name is Thurid, and he has marked you for destruction.'

With a billow of his red-lined cloak, the stranger strode away and mounted the steps to the porch.

With a weak feeling in his knees, Leifr slipped off the roof and found a hiding place nearer the hall by the kitchen door. A group of scavengers waiting there for a few last tidbits eyed him unwelcomingly, but he sat down in their midst anyway, his eyes upon the door. He knew with a deadly certainty that Thurid was going to need him. Thurid's natural vanity had carried him too far already.

As he pondered his means of getting into the hall, a disturbance commenced in the yard behind him. Looking around cautiously, he beheld Raudbjorn picking his way through a blockade of jeering Dokkalfar, his gaze fixed upon the main hall, as if the Dokkalfar were nothing but a shoal of malicious puppies chewing at his bootlaces. When he reached the doors, however, two of the Dokkalfar put their backs to it and presented their swords defiantly.

'You can't go in there, you blundering ox,' one said derisively. 'Sorkvir has an important visitor.'

'Raudbjorn has important news,' the thief-taker rumbled with a lowering scowl. 'Move Dokkalfar carcass, or Raudbjorn spill your guts.'

'Get out of here,' the guard retorted. 'If you bother Sorkvir now, he'll spill your guts. What is this great news you have to tell him, anyway? I could take it to him later, perhaps.'

Raudbjorn's eye gleamed cunningly, and he shook his head. 'My news, not yours.'

Turning his back, he returned to the yard to wait, squatting down on his hams and leaning against the side of a barn to rest himself. The Dokkalfar took amusement in throwing small bits of sticks, dung, or pebbles at him, grinning wolfishly behind their hands when he opened his eyes to glare around at his tormentors. From his position by the back steps, Leifr could see Raudbjorn's ire rising. The roach of hair atop his head bristled like the back of a mean-tempered old boar. One long lock of his hair dangled down in an ornamental topknot, with a few favorite teeth or bones fastened to it, and one of the Dokkalfar had the misfortune to reach over and give it a tweak.

With a roar, Raudbjorn was on his feet, with one huge hand gripping the Dokkalfar around the throat, lifting him off his feet completely. Instead of breaking his neck, Raudbjorn gave him a toss over the wall into the rear yard, where the scavengers scuttled to get out of the way. When another Dokkalfar rushed at Raudbjorn, he threw him over the wall to land upon his friend. Raudbjorn glared over the wall and growled. 'Learn to fight, Dokkalfar. Sneaking little rats. Trolls in black cloaks.'

Raudbjorn uttered a loud snort of disgust and was turning away when his eye lighted upon Leifr crouching next to the steps, trying not to attract any attention.

'Fridmarr!' Raudbjorn started to climb over the wall, his eyes gleaming. 'Fool Raudbjorn a little while with old clothes. Raudbjorn not so dumb. No beggar went in Dallir, so how a beggar come out? Something evil in your mind, Fridmarr. Better come away from Gliru-hals.'

Leifr leaped onto the porch, shoved open the kitchen door, and slipped inside, pressing the door shut with his back. Some house thralls and women were cleaning up after the meal and they turned and looked at him suspiciously.

'I'm a new house thrall,' Leifr improvised. 'They sent me around here to make myself useful.'

The housekeeper put her fists on her hips and eyed Leifr from head to foot. 'You look better than some I've seen,' she said reluctantly. 'We don't need you in the kitchen. You can go stand watch by the hall. Sorkvir doesn't trust these Dokkalfar not to kill him. You keep them away from him and follow my orders and you'll be a good thrall. Otherwise, you'll be out there with them.' She jerked her grizzled head toward the scavengers and went back to her goose-plucking.

Leifr did not wait around for more of her acrid speech; he dived into the nearest doorway and found himself in a long, dark corridor. No sooner had he disappeared than he heard a heavy knock at the back door and the slow bumbling buzz of Raudbjorn's voice being overridden by the shrill clatter of the housekeeper's irate tongue; then the door slammed shut with a decisive bang.

Leifr grinned in the darkness, hoping Raudbjorn's rout by a shrewish housekeeper had been witnessed by the Dokkalfar, particularly by the ones the thief-taker had thrown over the wall. Creeping down the long passageway, Leifr passed doorways into stables and dark, damp places that smelled of rats. Presently, he reached a closed door with light showing beneath it. He was fumbling discreetly for the latch when a couple of Dokkalfar strode importantly into the corridor, almost colliding with him in their haste.

'What are you doing here, thrall?' one demanded. 'You're not allowed in Sorkvir's private rooms!'

Leifr backed out of the way, chilled by the atmosphere that surrounded them. The nails studding their armor glowed with a dim phosphorescence, and their eyes shone with a feral, red gleam. Remembering belatedly to cower, Leifr got out of their path, keeping his head covered.

'They wanted the doors open because it's too hot,' he muttered.

The Dokkalfar flung open the doors and stalked into the room beyond, leaving Leifr a perfect view. It was a small hall, used by a chieftain and his elect companions to provide a refuge from the restlessness of a larger room crowded with warriors. He saw Sorkvir seated upon the dais with Thurid in his outlandish disguise. A cup of ale sat on the table near Thurid, untouched, and Thurid still wore his mask. The two Dokkalfar bowed respectfully to him and seated themselves below, looking grim and stiff.

The atmosphere in the hall was also grim and stiff. Thurid turned his masked gaze upon the new arrivals, taking in their owl insignia in silence.

'More traitors to the Owl Society,' he said, after the scrutiny had become insulting. 'The Dokkur Lavardur is not pleased. You are causing a division in his power.'

'I am merely increasing his power,' Sorkvir said, without much deference in his tone, but his manner was tense. 'Our lord has nothing to fear from my efforts in Solvorfirth. My loyalty is not to be doubted by any of these Dokkalfar surrounding me. I make certain that any new recruits understand we are all loyal to Djofull and the Dokkur Lavardur first and foremost.'

'That truly sounds well,' Thurid replied dubiously. 'But we've heard alarming reports about your alog. We've heard that Fridmarr Fridmundrsson has returned and has enlisted the assistance of a powerful Rhbu wizard, who is going to make dogs' meat out of the Dokkalfar in Solvorfirth. We've heard that they are going to reverse your spell upon the Rhbu Pentacle for the express purpose of destroying you and all your lives.'

Sorkvir combed his fine-haired beard with his fingers. 'Gossip certainly travels fast to have reached Djofullholl so soon. But like most gossip, it is completely false, and greatly exaggerated. You may assure our lord that the Pentacle is in no more danger of destruction than I am

93

myself. As for this Rhbu wizard, that is the greatest joke of all. He's merely a local antiquarian who dabbles a bit in foretelling and prophecy. He has a habit of boasting to thralls and other simple minds about his supposedly great powers. I have no fear of him; if he has any powers at all, they are maladroit and stunted. Most certainly he is not a Rhbu, since he was born in Solvorfirth, and there is a record of it in the book. The Rhbus are extinct, if they are not a myth concocted by the Ljosalfar to comfort them in their final decline into extinction.'

Thurid nodded slowly, unfolding his arms which were clasped in an unfriendly posture, and reached out to take up his cup of ale, sipping at it warily. 'Your words are a convincing explanation,' he said, managing to convey the opposite impression. 'Yet the matter of Fridmarr is still of concern to the Owl Society. You betrayed highly select knowledge to Fridmarr. Only the Owls are permitted the information that leads us back and forth from Hel's cold embrace, yet you entrusted it to a Ljosalfar. It raises questions, Sorkvir – questions about your competence and integrity as an Owl Society member.'

Sorkvir's eyes flicked restlessly around the small chamber, as if he felt confined by its walls. 'Fridmarr has taken eitur, and it is slowly killing him. I taught him no secrets – merely useless lies. When he dies, I will capture his fylgjadraug and burn his body to ash.'

The two Dokkalfar nodded in silent agreement at this prescription, and Thurid pressed his fingertips together and pretended to consider it. Finally he shook his head regretfully. 'This won't do, I'm afraid. My brother Owls would never agree to it. The only way to destroy someone possessing the death secrets of the Owl Society is to deal him death with that Rhbu sword you stole from Fridmarr. I fear the situation warrants the intervention of the Owl Society, so I am going to remove this matter from your hands, and we shall take it up ourselves. I daresay there will be an inquiry into the whole situation from the beginning, and I shall have to request the surrender of Hjaldr's sword, which I saw hanging on your wall in the main hall.'

Sorkvir stared at Thurid coldly. At last he said, 'This requires some thought. Perhaps tomorrow I could give you my answer.'

'Tomorrow is not soon enough,' Thurid replied. 'And if you refuse to surrender the sword, the Owl Society will interpret your action as blatant rebellion and will take steps against you. Loyalty to the Society is absolute. You must remember the oaths you swore, and the penalties you agreed to. All these others here with you will suffer the same reprisal if you choose to be wrongheaded and turn your back upon your Society.'

One of the attendant Dokkalfar stood up to address Sorkvir, his wrinkled features drawn up in consternation. 'Turn over the sword, Sorkvir,' he said. 'None of the rest of us want to get involved in a quarrel with the Owl Society. We don't want to find our throats cut in our beds one night. Rebellion against the Society is suicide.'

'What use is a dull sword?' the other Dokkalfar added. 'I'd turn it over and be glad to be rid of it.'

Sorkvir leaned back in his chair a little less stiffly and crossed one ankle over his knee. 'I'd turn over the sword without question,' he said smoothly, 'but there's a serious defect about it that I fear will render it useless to the Owl Society. The grindstone meant to sharpen it is a Rhbu grindstone. I had one which Fridmarr stole from the Hjaldrsholl Dvergar – he was a clever thief, I'm compelled to admit – but that grindstone was lost again, I fear, in the commotion of Fridmarr's treachery. The Society may not be interested in a sword which it cannot sharpen.'

'More evidence of your incompetence, Sorkvir.' Thurid stared at Sorkvir rigidly. 'We must take the sword before it is also lost. However, I might put in a gracious word on your behalf to Djofull, if I am assured of your compliance.'

Sorkvir rose to his feet, and Thurid cautiously

followed suit. 'I'll give you the sword, but you can spare your gracious words on my behalf. I shall speak for myself, should this matter ever come before the council. Follow me.'

He led the way to the doors to the main hall and threw them open. Thurid followed, with the two Dokkalfar behind him. They went directly to the dais and stood before the wall where the sword hung. Leifr shadowed them, finding plenty of places to conceal himself. He saw Sorkvir remove the sword and place it in Thurid's hands. Sorkvir stood with his back to Leifr, with one hand behind his back in a casual stance, and Leifr could see his fingers closing around the black hilt of a dagger. Leifr quietly drew his sword and poised himself for a swift and noisy charge.

At that moment, a tremendous thundering shook the door, accompanied by a violent, roaring bawl and the shouts and shrieks of Dokkalfar under attack. In a moment, the door burst open, and Raudbjorn strode inside, swinging his halberd menacingly and peering watchfully from side to side.

CHAPTER 6

'RAUDBJORN!' The two elder Dokkalfar sprang forward to repulse this outrage, but scuttled back again when Raudbjorn brandished his halberd at them.

'I hope you have a good explanation for this intrusion,' Sorkvir said in a deadly tone as Raudbjorn trod heavily up to the dais, his hackles still bristling.

'Huh! Fridmarr!' Raudbjorn waved his weapon around to encompass the hall.

Sorkvir's eyes glittered. 'What of Fridmarr, you nithling? Why aren't you watching him, as I ordered you? Can't I give you the simplest charge and expect it to be fulfilled?'

Raudbjorn ceased his restless prowling about the hall and peering into shadows – just before he reached the doorway where Leifr crouched with his drawn sword.

'Fridmarr in Gliru-hals,' Raudbjorn growled, his eyes still darting. 'Dressed like ragged thrall. Went in back door. Raudbjorn find him.'

The two elderly Dokkalfar exchanged a startled glance, then Sorkvir snorted, 'I don't believe it. Bolviss, go to the kitchen and ask Faedi if she saw anyone come in that didn't belong.'

'He looks dangerous,' Thurid remarked, edging toward the door. 'Should I summon your men to subdue him?'

'No, no, he's quite harmless, except for his stupidity,' Sorkvir explained. 'Come and sit down. As soon as I've disposed of him, I'll show you some Gliru-hals hospitality, now that we've settled our differences so amicably.'

Leifr backed further into the small chamber as Bolviss approached. It would be a nithling's deed to kill such a

withered little Dokkalfar, so Leifr knocked him unconscious with the butt of his sword and dragged his body
into the shadow of a sleeping platform where he
wouldn't readily attract notice. Then he crept back to the
doorway to make sure Thurid escaped with the sword.

Raudbjorn tramped up and down, looking into the
shadows like a restless bear, with the other Dokkalfar
watching warily from the main door. Thurid had reached
the door and was pressing his way through the curious
Dokkalfar. Sorkvir divided his attention between Thurid
and Raudbjorn with increasing impatience. Then he
roared out a command to his men.

'Stop that stranger! He's not going to leave with my
sword!'

Thurid froze. The Dokkalfar shifted their weapons to
menacing angles. Leifr stepped out of his hiding place;
but as luck would have it, no one saw him but Raudbjorn, who uttered a great roar of triumph. 'Fridmarr!
You see!'

Leifr dodged into the shelter of the doorway, peering
out cautiously. Everyone in the hall was gazing at him.

Then the elder Dokkalfar snorted and said, 'That's
just a house thrall. We saw him on our way in.'

The watching Dokkalfar laughed in derision at Raudbjorn, whose head and neck began to turn an ugly red.

'You great dolt,' Sorkvir spat. 'Get out of my way!
Don't let that Owl escape with my sword!'

Thurid halted in his dignified escape and turned to
face Sorkvir. With a twitch at his sleeve he produced his
staff, inquiring mildly, 'Are you calling me a thief?'

The Dokkalfar melted away from him. For a long, taut
moment he and Sorkvir stared at each other. Leifr
stepped out of his hiding place again to torment Raudbjorn and made an offensive gesture at him.

Raudbjorn plunged forward with a berserk yell, plowing a table and two benches ahead of him. Sorkvir broke
off his chilling stare and seized a lance, which he thrust at
Raudbjorn as the thief-taker climbed onto the dais, his

98

small eyes fixed intently upon the doorway into the small hall.

'He's gone mad!' the elder Dokkalfar exclaimed, scuttling away to safety.

'Stop, you animal!' Sorkvir snarled, prodding at Raudbjorn. 'If you've lost your mind, we'll have to keep you in a kennel with the troll-hounds.'

The Dokkalfar laughed appreciatively and elbowed each other, glad to see Raudbjorn disgraced. Raudbjorn glowered at them, halting his advance. Sorkvir sneered and sat down in his chair, darting a wary look in Thurid's direction. 'We are not finished bargaining yet, my friend. As soon as I've disposed of this idiot, we shall resume our discussion about that sword.'

Raudbjorn shook his head violently. 'Raudbjorn not idiot!' he rumbled. 'Fridmarr there in room!'

'Silence! Clear out of here, Raudbjorn, and stay out of my sight until I send for you. You're relieved of all your duties.'

Raudbjorn slowly turned his head to regard Sorkvir with an incredulous stare. 'You throw out Raudbjorn, best thief-taker and warrior in Alfar realm? You shame Raudbjorn?'

Sorkvir smiled coldly, holding the lance carelessly across his lap. 'Yes, I shame Raudbjorn. I'm going to let it be known far and wide you failed in my service. Every chieftain of both Ljosalfar and Dokkalfar will hear you've made an absolute ass of yourself. You're no thief-taker. You're an ox in warrior's armor. I should put you to work at exterminating trolls or catching rats.'

The Dokkalfar guffawed nastily. A mottled rash gradually suffused Raudbjorn's round countenance, beginning with his bottom chin and spreading to the top of his bristling pate. His breathing deepened to quick, menacing huffs, and his small eyes almost disappeared in a deadly squint. Baring his teeth in a ferocious grimace, he took a step forward.

'Raudbjorn angry now,' he rumbled in a voice that

froze the Dokkalfar where they stood. Leifr felt his blood chill, recognizing the symptoms of a berserk fury that knew no reason.

Sorkvir stared impassively, betraying no emotion. 'Take yourself out of my hall, you monstrous freak. It would not even amuse me to torture you.'

Raudbjorn's reason departed. With a terrible bellow, he drew his sword, raised it aloft with both hands, and thrust it through Sorkvir to the very hilt. Planting his foot on his enemy's chest, he yanked the sword out and lashed off Sorkvir's head. Then he began to chop the rest of Sorkvir to pieces.

The Dokkalfar forgot Leifr and Thurid and rushed at Raudbjorn. They fastened themselves to his arms and legs like ants trying to debilitate an angry bear.

'Now you've done it, you great fool!' the eldest of the Owl counselors shouted. 'He's going to change form!'

The Dokkalfar surged backward, away from Raudbjorn, and beat a disorderly retreat. Raudbjorn was too intent upon his mayhem to notice as Leifr and Thurid came out of shadows and slipped toward the doorway.

Suddenly Raudbjorn staggered back in astonishment from his work, coughing and snorting. Instead of fresh blood, Sorkvir's body oozed dust and corruption. As if that weren't astonishment enough, a ghostly image was rising and swelling until it was as large as Raudbjorn. It was a massive, shaggy bear, with silvered fur, humped shoulders, and an enormous, broad head with small eyes that glowed redly. The bear's teeth parted in a low, menacing growl.

Raudbjorn sheathed his sword, gripped his halberd, and backed away as the bear's form solidified. The wooden dais creaked as it padded forward slowly.

At the same moment, Leifr and Thurid plunged for the doorway, with Raudbjorn bringing up the rear. The bear charged after them, clouting aside a heavy table and hurling two benches after them. Raudbjorn took the brunt of the assault, which enabled Leifr and Thurid to get outside first, tumbling almost into the arms of a crowd of yelling Dokkalfar. Seizing Bodmarr's sword from Thurid and brandishing it, Leifr opened a path for their escape. Thurid shoved him around the corner of the horse barn, directing him along the edge of a small creek and over a low green hill. He stopped at a crude ring of rocks. Leifr watched with growing concern as Thurid dashed around the circle as if he were demented, touching all the stones and muttering excitedly.

'Now we're ready,' Thurid said in a voice that shook slightly. 'Hang onto my arm. We're going for a sledge ride – I hope.'

'You must be joking,' Leifr replied indignantly. 'I don't see any sledge.' He started to walk away, disgusted, but Thurid grabbed his arm and pointed back at Gliru-hals.

'We haven't a lot of time,' he said.

The Dokkalfar had freed the troll-hounds. In a dark wave, the beasts poured over the walls and rocks after their quarry, howling and barking with fearsome eagerness.

'Thurid, this isn't going to work, whatever it is,' Leifr tried to protest as Thurid started to run down the hillside, towing Leifr after him, with longer and longer strides until Leifr was certain they would end up at the bottom in a tangle of arms and legs and possibly broken bones.

'Nonsense! It will work!' Thurid panted fiercely, giving an extraordinary leap into the air. Leifr's legs went out from under him, churning frantically in mid-air.

Incredibly, they hurtled over a stretch of rocks and thistles at the bottom of the hill, bounced once on some hummocks in a green, boggy area beyond, and landed on their feet, running. Thurid gave another amazing bound.

'Isn't this wonderful?' he shouted. 'We're almost flying! Pick your feet up, Leifr!'

They sailed over a spring pool, gathering speed, although they were running uphill. When they reached the top, Leifr barely had time to note an excavation of some sort and an upright stone, white nearly to the ground, where it was blackened as if by a fire and glowing in a red-hot ring just above ground level. Its hot breath fanned Leifr's as they plummeted past.

With an exuberant yell, Thurid propelled himself into mid-air off the top of the hill, keeping a tight grip on Leifr's wrist. Leifr closed his eyes. The air whistled in his ears as they descended; then they were climbing again to another rocky hilltop, Leifr glimpsed a complete ring of standing stones, all glowing red-hot at their bases.

Thurid scarcely touched the ground, except to get a running start when their speed slowed at the summit of a hill. 'I think we've gone far enough,' he shouted to Leifr. 'We're in the fells above Dallir. They'll never know what became of their mysterious visitor from Djofullholl.'

He began dragging his feet, braking with his heels, but the force that had them in its grip did not relinquish its riders easily. Thurid muttered at it and swore and cajoled, but it carried them up yet another hill and started down the other side, where he somehow managed to break its hold about halfway down. They rolled the rest of the way, and arrived at the bottom with Thurid coasting along like a toboggan, still clutching his staff in one hand. He stood up immediately and looked at his clothes, which had not been improved by their recent experience.

Leifr felt his bruises. He stood up, feeling shaken and slightly sick and turned to look behind him at the hill, notched long ago by unknown hands to mark the path. 'I don't know what just happened, Thurid,' he croaked hoarsely.

Thurid preened himself like a large, disreputable crow. 'We flew,' he smirked, 'or very nearly so. This is a ley line. The ancient straight way of travel. The only safe way to get through the trolls, Dokkalfar, and giants. Elbegast and his armies will follow these lines one day in the last great battle with the Underground. A great force

102

is conducted through these stones and mounds and notched hills. There are standing stones that men could not have possibly moved without the aid of powerful magic. Whole mountains have been moved away, piled up into mounds and rings and earthworks. It is all terribly ancient, and none of the modern wizards pay much attention to early magic. Too primitive, they say, and difficult to control. But now I can control the powers of the ancient Rhbus.'

Leifr shook his head. 'This didn't happen,' he muttered, looking at Bodmarr's sword in his hands.

Thurid removed a dowsing pendulum from his satchel with a flourish and began dowsing, with his eyes screwed earnestly shut and one hand extended as a pointer. 'Ah,' he breathed. 'The Dokkalfar influence is all to the west of us. West is a favorable direction for me. We shall go north to Dallir.'

'Is Sorkvir dead?' Leifr asked.

Thurid snorted. 'Dead a dozen times over; and each time, he gathers strength from Hel. Raudbjorn merely freed a more evil force temporarily. He'll put his body back together. He can do far more evil with the help of the Dokkalfar than he ever could as a poltergeist.' He tittered.

Leifr saw nothing to laugh at. He held up the pitted, wretched blade of Bodmarr's sword. 'What do we do with this now? I can't believe it was worth all the trouble.'

'The grindstone, my lad, the grindstone.' Thurid's eyes gleamed. 'When we find that, we can sharpen the sword. And with the sword, Sorkvir can be killed beyond his power to return.'

Leifr shivered from the cool night breeze fanning his dew-soaked clothing, and the distant yowls of trolls disturbed by the troll-hounds did nothing to add to his peace of mind. Thinking of Sorkvir changing forms right before his eyes turned his shivering into a shudder. The Alfar realm was more eerie than he had known.

Glancing at Thurid as they strode toward Dallir, he suddenly inquired, 'What happened to your Dokkalfar finery?'

Thurid waved one hand carelessly. 'It went when I dispersed the glamour spell, of course. The horse I left behind will create an amusing uproar. It was that old, bony creature of Latvi's with the walleye.' He chuckled appreciatively, trailing a plume of smoke from his staff.

'It won't take Sorkvir long to realize it was you,' Leifr said. 'He must know sooner or later that there was no new house thrall.'

Thurid stopped his gloating and said. 'I can see you're determined to worry. Well, we may have to hide out in the fells for a few days – depending upon how much time your father has left. I'd venture to guess that the truce won't be worth much after this. We can't leave Fridmundr to die alone, however.'

'What will happen to Dallir when we are gone?'

Thurid knit his brows in a scowl. 'I don't like to think about it. I only hope that Sorkvir will be routed before it falls into a hollow ruin. You won't have much time for farming, now that we've taken that sword.'

It was near dawn when they walked into the yard at Dallir. A lone goose sifted the muddy area near the still house, and all the bars to the folds and paddocks were down. The earth had been churned by many iron-shod hooves into a muddy bog hole in the yard before the house.

'The Dokkalfar were here last night!' Thurid said grimly, striding toward the house. 'You see how Sorkvir keeps truces!'

They cut across the wall into the yard. The barns with their doors standing open struck Leifr as ominous; when he looked more attentively, he saw the spiral marks burned into the wood in fresh, vicious, charred scars.

'We've been marked for doom,' he said.

Thurid stared rigidly, turning slowly toward the house. The doors there, too, had all been marked, but none had been broken down. Yet Dallir was finished. The barns

104

with their doors standing agape lent an atmosphere of desolation that seemed to have been undisturbed for half a century. The only sign of life was a faint wisp of smoke coming out the smoke hole in the roof of the kitchen annex.

They crossed the dooryard boldly and slipped along the wall to the kitchen door. The heaps of grassy debris and crumbled walls, grown so familiar to Leifr, now seemed alien and desolate. Glancing toward the long barn suspiciously, Leifr thought he heard a faint, mocking whimper.

The kitchen door was locked from within, so Thurid tapped urgently with his staff. Pressing his lips to a crack he called, 'Snagi, you old fool, it's Thurid and Fridmarr. Come and let us in!'

Inside, heavy objects grated over the floor, then the door opened a small crack, and Snagi's pale, suspicious eye scrutinized them for a long moment.

'Hurry up and let us in,' Thurid ordered. 'We've got every Dokkalfar in Gliru-hals looking for us.'

The door grumbled open barely enough for them to squeeze through; then Snagi hurled his bony form against it to close it as quickly as he could. Slightly breathless, he shoved a heavy chest against the door and sat down on it weakly. 'Thank goodness, someone is here,' he panted. 'My wits are nearly gone daft. We've had Dokkalfar half the night, besides worrying about you – then there's the master.'

Leifr, not stopping to talk, strode toward Fridmundr's private quarters, with Snagi pattering in his wake, making anxious chirps of distress.

'That wretched Gotiskolker is still here,' he wheezed. 'I tried to send him off, but he's not afraid of me. He said that someone has to sit beside poor old Fridmundr until the last and that he's the one to do it.'

Leifr raised his hand in silence, halting in the doorway. Fridmundr lay on his bed, dressed in his finest clothes, with boots on and his weapons lying beside him.

At his feet lay many of his favorite possessions; his cloak lay ready, and he wore a fine battle helmet, as if he were about to embark upon a journey. Gotiskolker did not look up from his work, piling offerings of new clothing and fine weavings beside Fridmundr so he would not enter the next world impoverished.

Fridmundr's transparent eyelids fluttered slightly. The wondrous light was almost gone from him now, flickering like the last of a dying candle. His expression was peaceful, almost pleasant, as if he found all the funeral preparations satisfactory and anticipated only the prospect of getting on with his journey.

'A pity we've no ship to burn with him,' Gotiskolker said to no one in particular. 'I think the four of us can carry the bier out to the knoll overlooking the hall when the time comes.'

Leifr nodded dumbly, and Thurid patted his shoulder commiseratingly. To Gotiskolker he said, 'You've done a splendid job. Fridmarr could not have done it better himself. You even got those carvings of the deer he was fond of and the antler-handled knife. I think we should leave him with his son for the last moments.'

Gotiskolker bowed his head in silent assent, but Leifr motioned them to stay. 'He should have his friends around him,' he said in a low voice, 'since he has lost almost all his family. Snagi, you too. No one has proved more faithful than you.'

Snagi sank down gratefully on a chair. 'Doesn't he look grand? I can't count the times when I saw him dressed up, going off to the Althing or to visit some high-and-mighty earl or other.'

'He was a generous man,' Gotiskolker added. 'He kept me alive and let me stay in his barrows, although he got nothing in return but tallow. The Rhbus will profit from his kindness.'

Thurid cleared his throat. 'Fridmundr was the only true friend I ever had. When my ship of fame and fortune was sailing high seas, I left him for more glorious

106

ports of call and the exalted realms of the wealthy and powerful. When the wine turned to vinegar in my mouth, and all my rich friends proved themselves cold and uncaring, Fridmundr welcomed me back again and made Dallir my home. Thank goodness for Fridmundr's amazing patience and forbearance, or I would have died a homeless wanderer long ago.' He sighed deeply and clasped his hands over his wrists, shaking his head in direful self-abnegation.

Leifr sensed that it was his turn to speak, and the horror of his false position caused his tongue to stick in his mouth and his throat to lie paralyzed in protest. In shame he stared down at his clenched fists, searching for something he could say honestly and not discredit himself or the dying Alfar. At last the words forced themselves out. 'I never knew him,' he said with a painful effort.

Thurid and Snagi exchanged a sorrowing glance. Snagi rose up to come and pat him comfortingly on the back, which only made him feel like a bigger fraud than ever.

'Don't fret, young master,' the faithful old servant said. 'You're his son. You have his blood. He understood you, for all of your bad ways, and he forgave you. Don't grieve at your badness. All that is past. Soon he'll be past too, and one day we'll be dust ourselves. I really don't see as how our griefs are very important, when you consider how many griefs there must be in this world.'

They sat silently and watched. Each breath that stirred Fridmundr's frail chest seemed more faint, with longer intervals between. Exactly when he ceased to breathe none of them could say. The wan light faded slowly, leaving behind only a gray shadow of the brilliant image Leifr had first seen.

Gotiskolker stirred first, breaking the silence by crossing the room to a small window. For the first time, Leifr wondered how much time had passed. He ought to have been exhausted, but he felt curiously enlivened, as if all his senses were more keenly aware than usual, and sleep was an unnecessary nuisance.

'It's almost sundown,' Gotiskolker announced, in a matter-of-fact tone. Snagi paled visibly. 'The Dokkalfar will be back, looking for the sword. We've got to start the fire now, before they come for the rest of us.'

'The trolls,' Snagi quavered, knotting his hands in his anxiety. 'They'll be back tonight in full force. The word will have spread that Sorkvir has marked us for doom. They'll carry off anything they can get their filthy paws on and smash the rest. I don't think I can bear it. I lived and worked here all my life. I was born in that old hut we use for a granary now. Dallir can't be destroyed this way. It's the end of everything, isn't it?'

Thurid gripped his thin shoulder comfortingly, saying in a gruff tone, 'It's all right, old fellow. One day we'll take this place back from the trolls and the Dokkalfar. Their day is almost finished.'

'Sorkvir's got no right,' Snagi growled. 'He should be destroyed.' He raised his eyes to Leifr in a smoldering gaze, red-rimmed and hate-laden. 'You'll do it, won't you, Fridmarr? When you destroy that beast, give him one mighty whack for Dallir and old Snagi.'

Leifr gripped his wiry hand. 'I'll do that, Snagi.'

Snagi nodded his head in satisfaction, gazing around at the familiar room and all its associated memories.

'This will be the last night that people spend at Dallir,' Snagi said in a wondering voice, looking solemnly at his companions. 'There's one last flagon of Dalliř ale. I think we should drink it, as a farewell – to the master as well as the farm.'

It was a doleful tribute. They sat in the kitchen with the door blockaded, listening to the sounds of the trolls outside. As soon as the sun was sunk from sight, the grunts and screeches began, frequently punctuated by the squalling brawls of quarreling trolls. Overcome by curiosity, Leifr peered through the cracks in the door and shuttered windows and watched knots of trolls scuttling from the long barn, prowling the farm in search of something to eat. One party came back dragging a dead sheep, snarling and defending their catch from packs of ravenous marauders. Other trolls ransacked the thralls' huts. A few trolls thoughtfully donned a pair of trousers, boots, or a long cloak and strutted up and down on two legs as if they were impersonating people.

'I hate to see them do that,' Leifr said. 'They're little more than animals, aren't they?'

'Aye, naught but savage beasts that would as soon tear your throat out for fun as not,' Snagi agreed.

'More than beasts,' Gotiskolker said. 'But less than men.'

Thurid sniffed. 'Trolls are a decadent race. Once they were much more than they are now. They have intelligence, when they care to use it. When they do, they are formidable enemies. The greater gray trolls of the north are far more cunning than these scrawny off-scourings and far more civilized, as far as trolls go.'

'Which isn't far,' Gotiskolker grunted. 'I'd like to see them exterminated as a species.'

'They feel the same way about us,' Snagi said. 'I don't like to think about staying in this house much longer. They're digging a hole in the roof. As soon as the master is well away on his smoke journey, I'm going to my daughter's at Sturmhafn.' Then he looked apologetically at Leifr. 'That is, unless you wish me to stay with you, since you're the master now, although the trolls have taken the farm from us. If there's no land to be farmed, I won't be of much use to you, considering the life you'll be leading.'

Leifr smiled grimly. 'Go to your daughter's, Snagi. You've earned your freedom, and there's no one left to say otherwise. You wouldn't care for the outlaw's life. I can't say that I like it much myself. Fortunately, I'm accustomed to it.' He put Bodmarr's sword on the table and looked at it ruefully. 'And it was all for this. It's going to take a real magic grindstone to make it into a good sword again.'

Gotiskolker helped himself to more of the ale, despite

109

the fact that he had already taken more than his share.

'*Troll's* grindstone!' he muttered thickly. 'That shows what Dvergar know about real powers. It's not a troll that turns it. Any fool knows trolls aren't any good with metal. It was a Rhbu that turned that stone – even if it was in Hjaldrsholl. A plague of boils on Hjaldr!' He swallowed the last of his ale, sagging in his chair as if he might slither to the floor at any moment.

'He's talking nonsense,' Thurid said disgustedly. 'Take the rest of that ale away from him, Snagi, before his temper gets any more sour. We've wasted enough time with our tribute to Fridmundr and Dallir. Let's start the fire before it gets much darker.'

Without speaking, the three of them lifted Fridmundr's bed and carried it out to the knoll where the wood was piled against the red glower of the setting sun. Much of the wood had been torn from the house, the barns, and the fences. The rest was the winter's wood, imported in rafts from wooded islands, or salvaged along the shoreline and thriftily hoarded up, piece by piece.

'There'll be a moon tonight,' Snagi observed. 'This fire will be like a beacon to all Solvorfirth.'

'As well as to the Dokkalfar,' Thurid added. 'Let them come, after we've paid our respects to Fridmundr, and they'll see what their troubles get them.' He raised his staff and sent a spurt of flame into the tinder.

The trolls still lurked in the shadows, hissing and jeering. As the fire climbed higher and glowed more brightly, they slunk farther away, whining and grumbling. The other three watchers backed away also, shading their faces from the heat with their hands.

Leifr scanned the surrounding fields for signs of approaching Dokkalfar. Clearly visible for miles, the black smoke ought to have been a beacon to almost everyone in the settlements. Presently he discerned three horsemen riding up the road from the lowlands. By the time they were close enough to be identified as Einarr and his two sons from Gellirgard, two more riders appeared, coming from the south from Bekanskog. Gradually a ring of old friends formed around the pyre, signifying their regards to Fridmundr's son by curt nods, a few handshakes, and some gruff words of condolence, most of which expressed the thought that at least Fridmundr was free of Sorkvir at last.

The gloom of the twilight did not lessen with the ascent of the moon. The landscape darkened as a mist rose from the sea and slowly filled all the low valleys. The smoke from the pyre drifted seaward, toward a distant opening in the clouds out across the water.

Solemnly, a few old men began to sing the skalds that told the tales of past heroic deeds. The thin chorus swelled with the low grumble of younger voices, and some of those who had arrived on horseback rode slowly around the fire.

At midnight, when the sky was the blackest, the Dokkalfar appeared in a long line across the top of the fell, each bearing a red torch. They stood still, as if awaiting a signal. Old Einarr and Young Einarr turned their backs in contempt.

'Let them come,' Einarr the Elder growled, hitching up his cloak around his shoulders. 'We'll hold them off so you can make your escape. Take my gray horse, and they'll never get close enough to smell your dust.'

His boast at once triggered an argument among the neighbors over whose horses were the best for the travelers to take. After settling on three of the strongest and fastest, Leifr felt obliged to choose one more as a spare, rather than offend the feelings of one of Fridmundr's closest friends. It was an old, black horse, graying around the eyes, but its owner assured Leifr that Jolfr could trot all day and half the night and still outrun many a younger horse, a fact to which the Ljosalfar all attested, some rather ruefully.

Quietly, with no fuss or speeches, the guests all tied contributions to the adventurers' saddles – cloaks, shirts, a small pouch of gold bits salvaged from barrows, lucky

111

amulets, or anything that might be of use on a journey.

'Good luck go with you, young Fridmarr,' Einarr the Younger called out, while the other Ljosalfar watched with less than hopeful head shakings and muffled sighs. Fridmarr had never done anything to win their confidence, but their lack of enthusiasm seemed such a chronic condition that Leifr refused to let it depress his spirits. Tomorrow he hoped to see the first station of the Pentacle, the dwarfs' fortress Hjaldrsholl.

Gotiskolker halted his horse in the lane approaching the decayed barns. 'If we should become separated,' he said, with a nod toward the Dokkalfar, who were descending the fell now, 'we need to agree upon a place to meet. Hroald's last shieling in Stormurbjarg is a good, out-of-the-way place, and there's an upper and a lower path that lead to it.'

'Stormurbjarg it is,' Thurid replied, starting his horse away at a trot.

Leifr had seen the little house from a distance. He also knew that Stormurbjarg was where Ljosa had gone.

As they passed the last barn, Leifr's horse suddenly shied violently away, and a huge, dark shape stepped out into the path.

'Halloa, Fridmarr,' the voice of Raudbjorn rumbled.

Leifr gripped his sword hilt. 'Get out of the way, Raudbjorn,' he said in a menacing tone.

'No, Fridmarr surrender to Raudbjorn.' He hefted his halberd with a creaking of his armor.

'Move aside, or you'll regret it, you swine,' Thurid said, summoning a glow to the end of his staff.

Raudbjorn shook his head. 'Sorkvir wants Fridmarr alive. Mostly alive good enough for Raudbjorn. Try and remember not to kill you all the way.'

'There's not time for this,' Gotiskolker said.

The voices of the troll-hounds rang out from the fell, baying their chilling, direful hunting cry.

Gotiskolker suddenly lashed his horse forward, plunging against Raudbjorn and knocking him off balance.

'Get out of here!' he snapped at Leifr, who immediately clapped his heels to Jolfr's ribs and lunged away at a gallop, brushing past Raudbjorn on the other side and giving him a spin in the opposite direction.

Thurid was chuckling when Leifr heard the deadly hiss of an arrow coming from behind. There was no time to dodge or twist away; the arrow struck Leifr in the shoulder, its shock nearly overbalancing him in his saddle. With his right arm completely numb, he scrambled frantically with his left for a grip around Jolfr's neck. With a toss of his head, Jolfr dumped him back into the saddle and galloped on, his eyes upon Thurid and Gotiskolker ahead.

When they reached the lower pasture, where the ground trembled with quagmires, Thurid motioned Gotiskolker one way while he took the other, glancing over his shoulder and calling something to Leifr in an irritated tone. Leifr gritted his teeth and followed Thurid, too stubborn to let the others know that he was wounded, fearing that all of them would be captured if they slowed down to favor him.

He lost Thurid after Jolfr balked at leaping a wall, necessitating a hasty search for a low spot to climb over. The Dokkalfar came flogging over the crest of a hill at that moment and the troll-hounds spied him, giving chase with a great bellow of triumph.

Jolfr arched his neck and sprang away at a gallop, as if he had been awaiting such an opportunity all evening. Before long, the Dokkalfar were left behind, and the troll-hounds lost the scent when he doubled back to a river crossing and followed it upstream toward Stormurbjarg. His strength was failing, and his wound ached with fiery intensity. Realizing that their course was tending slightly downhill, he turned his horse more often to the upside of the slopes, hoping to approach the shieling from the high trail.

Rounding a shoulder of stone, he heard the startled snort of a horse and a man's muffled exclamation. To his

113

dismay, he recognized the huge hulk of Raudbjorn blocking the narrow path along the rocky face of the scarp.

'Halloa, Fridmarr,' the thief-taker greeted him amiably, hoisting his halberd into battle readiness. 'Narrow path. You back up, then we fight.'

Leifr drew his sword. 'You back up, Raudbjorn. I've got twenty Dokkalfar not far behind me. We could fight here, but one or both of us is likely to go over the edge.'

Raudbjorn chuckled. 'Water long way down, Fridmarr. Better to go to Gliru-hals and live awhile longer. Raudbjorn not let you escape this time. Need to prove talent to Sorkvir.'

Leifr raised his sword, wincing at the pain the movement caused. 'Back up, Raudbjorn, and count yourself lucky I don't have enough time to carve you into bacon.'

Raudbjorn and his outsize horse did not move. He shook his head ponderously, rattling the trophies dangling from his neck. 'Sword arm no good, Fridmarr. Arrow went through it. Time to give up.'

'No one is taking me to Sorkvir alive,' Leifr said.

'Then Raudbjorn glad to kill you. Sorkvir has spells for dead carcass and tortures for live bodies. Better to be dead.' Raudbjorn grinned with infantile glee, taking a firm grip on his murderous weapon.

Leifr shifted his sword to his left hand and tightened his knees to urge Jolfr forward. Behind him he heard the Dokkalfar horses clattering over the stony mountainside with triumphant shouts. Raudbjorn heard them also and made his move to lay claim to the honor of capturing Fridmarr. Swinging the halberd around his head, he sent his horse plunging forward.

Leifr turned Jolfr's head toward the black void below and gave him a smart whack with his whip. Obediently, the horse leaped outward into the blackness of the gorge waiting below.

CHAPTER 7

THE horse somersaulted, and Leifr kicked free of the stirrups barely in time to hit the water upright. His first reaction was gratitude that he hadn't landed on rocks, and his second was the breathtaking agony of plunging into icy water. Floundering and gasping, he thrashed to the surface. Jolfr's head and outstretched neck glided past him, and a shoulder bumped him solidly, followed by a scrape from the saddle. Frantically Leifr groped for a handhold, finding nothing but sleek, wet horsehide churning past him. With a desperate lunge, he caught Jolfr's thick tail floating out behind on the water and he held on grimly while the horse pulled him to solid ground, depositing him on a rocky shoreline and clambering upward with flailing hooves to the turf and scrub above. Covering his head with his arms, Leifr lay half in the water, waiting for the rocks and earth to stop clattering down on him. His shoulder burned with an aching numbness that reached all the way down his arms; from the hot sensation of his skin, he guessed that the wound was bleeding again.

From far above came a thin, echoing shout. 'Fridmarr! Ha-lloo-aah!'

Leifr maintained his silence, gazing upward and trying to see the ledge where Raudbjorn was standing. It was too dark and misty – a thick, cloying mist that seemed to be mostly behind his own eyes. He closed them and rested his forehead against a rock until Raudbjorn gave up shouting for him. Dimly, he heard the Dokkalfar arrive, shouting back and forth with Raudbjorn until everyone seemed to be satisfied that he was dead. Leifr was more than half inclined to agree with them.

Achingly, he crawled out of the water to the turf, where his horse was standing with his ears flattened dejectedly, his back arched under the slipped saddle. Nickering hopefully at Leifr, the horse stretched out his neck and shook himself briskly, showering Leifr with an icy deluge of water.

Leifr wiped his face again and hobbled over to Jolfr's side to pull the saddle into the right position. To his dull surprise, he lacked the strength to pull it up from below the horse's belly; somehow he couldn't find the end of the girth in the mass of sodden leather and swollen straps that, under normal circumstances, was regarded as a saddle. Very weak, he leaned against the horse, appreciating the warmth, until his knees threatened to buckle under him. Knowing he had to keep moving, he fumbled for the reins and staggered away down the rocky gorge, leaning frequently on Jolfr's neck for support. The path, rocky and treacherous enough at best, merged with a small icy stream; presently Leifr found himself floundering along in half a foot of water liberally strewn with rocks of all sizes, and Jolfr seldom had a place to put his feet without sliding and stumbling. Snorting impatiently, Jolfr butted Leifr repeatedly and tried to scramble up the steep bank on either side; finally losing all patience, Jolfr planted his feet firmly and balked. Wearily, Leifr sat down on a mossy hummock and rested his head in his hands, too exhausted to continue until daylight, when he could at least see the rocks he was stumbling over.

Pale dawn found him stretched out on a mossy bed of wet rocks, his feet still in the water, and his head pillowed on a tussock of moss. Jolfr stood faithfully nearby, nibbling at the close-cropped grass and kicking occasionally at the dangling saddle under his belly. His ears swiveled around, catching the familiar sounds of sheep bells, the whine of a dog, and the tap of a shepherd's staff on the stony earth. Since he was hungry, Jolfr whinnied in the direction of the familiar, comforting sounds and watched hopefully as the shepherd came into view.

The shepherd stood still a long moment, then came forward slowly to the prone figure in the streambed.

Leifr awakened at the first soft crunch of wet pebbles. A shadow stood between him and the barely risen sun. Reaching reflexively for his sword, his movement awakened the furies in his shoulder. With a groan, he rolled over and sat up, ready for once to admit defeat.

'Fridmarr, you are an endless idiot.'

He looked up in astonishment at the voice, squinting into the sunlight at the dark, hooded figure before him. In the shadows of the heavy hood he saw Ljosa's face, but he was certain he must be seeing the hopeless visions of a doomed man.

'You tried jumping off that ledge before and broke your leg, don't you remember? It seems to be the curse of your life that you never learn from your experiences.'

Ljosa stood before him, scolding him with a tremor in her voice. She helped him crawl out of the stream onto the soft turf, where he collapsed and shut his eyes, basking in the warmth of the sun after his cold night in the creek.

'What are you doing here? You ought to be Raudbjorn or a Dokkalfar.' He looked waveringly at the shepherd's staff in her hand, thinking it might look like a weapon.

'This is Stormurbjarg, my home,' she told him. 'What are *you* doing here, with your disreputable companions barging into my house? Of all people, you should know you are the most unwelcome here.'

'Stormurbjarg,' he croaked. 'Then we all made it?'

'Yes, although I don't know why you chose my house.'

'I didn't,' Leifr replied, shutting his eyes. 'It was Gotiskolker's idea.'

'Well, you can't stay here. I don't want to get outlawed for helping you escape. I heard about the sword.'

Leifr tried to sit up, but the sky darkened and his head roared sickeningly. 'We won't stay long. No one will

117

know we were here. I don't want you involved, either.'

Ljosa gasped. 'You're hurt! Lie still; it's bleeding.'

'Go get Thurid. He's got powers. He'll help me.'

'Thurid?' Ljosa queried. 'I don't know what powers you're talking about. Thurid is too far away to help now. You've got to move from this spot, because you're perfectly visible from the ledge, if any Dokkalfar come back for another look. I'll get your horse, and you try to sit up without fainting.'

She strode away to catch Jolfr. In a few moments, she had the saddle set to rights and tightened it properly. In the meantime, Leifr had fallen asleep, warmed by the sun.

Exasperated, Ljosa scanned the cliffs above the pool in case someone was watching. She shook Leifr cautiously and failed to awaken him. For a moment she looked toward her house, debating asking her uninvited guests for help. As she hesitated, a dark figure in a tattered cloak watched her from the thickets on the steep slope of the narrow gorge. After seeing her difficulty, he stepped out of the shadows and limped toward her, coming around the horse's heels with one hand touching Jolfr's flank to avoid startling him.

Ljosa started, however, at his sudden appearance and quickly averted her eyes.

'He's completely out,' Gotiskolker said after a brief attempt to awaken Leifr. 'Between the two of us, I think we can get him across the saddle. Three arms are better than two, even if one of them is mine.' He darted her a quick, dark glance. 'I'm pretty disgusting, aren't I?'

'Yes, very,' she said coolly, trying not to inhale too deeply around the smell of his old cloak. 'But I suppose it's kinder to believe that you can't help it.'

'Wrong. I go out of my way to make myself disgusting. It gives me great satisfaction. It's my only form of revenge.'

She hazarded a glance at him then, feeling a stillborn pity for the wretched creature. 'What have I done that you want revenge upon me?' she asked angrily. 'I've never done anything to you. You've always been a stranger to me until now, when you come to my house expecting shelter, food, and protection from your enemies.'

Gotiskolker turned away, scowling and muttering. 'Women always ask too many questions. Now let's get this useless fellow onto his horse.'

Between them, with the aid of Leifr's half-conscious efforts to help, they hoisted him onto the horse and walked slowly back to the mossy house built against the bank.

The door opened a small crack, and Thurid's eye glared out. Then he snatched the door open, reaching Leifr's side in two quick strides.

'Is he all right?' Hurry up, let's get him inside. Someone's bound to be watching, judging by the way our luck seems to be going. He's cold as a fish. Are you sure he's still alive?'

In reply to all his flustering, Ljosa replied, 'Yes.' She helped carry Leifr inside the house. Gotiskolker took the horse to the little stable, scarcely large enough for the three horses already hidden inside. Sighing wearily, he went outside and found himself a place in the sun on the hillside over the stable. Far away to the south, a thin plume of smoke still showed against the sky above Dallir.

Inside the house, Thurid consulted his rune sticks for healing spells, while Ljosa watched him in silent amazement.

'I could go for the healing woman,' she suggested. 'Bergdis will keep her mouth closed.'

'There's no need for Bergdis, with her mumbling, herbs, and weeds,' Thurid replied, trying not to tremble as he read over the spell he had selected. 'We have Rhbu magic to heal Fridmarr. Bergdis has only glimpsed the healing powers of the earth with the corner of one nearsighted eye.'

119

'Then the gossip about you is true,' Ljosa said. 'You used a spell to walk into Gliru-hals and steal the sword from Sorkvir.'

'There's much more, my dear girl,' Thurid replied. 'But now isn't the time to talk about it. Remain perfectly still and use your powers of concentration to heal this wound. If all goes right, we shall leave here tomorrow, with Fridmarr a whole man again.'

Thurid held his staff in one hand and shut his eyes as he intoned the words of the incantation etched upon the rune wand. To be on the safe side, he repeated them nine times and opened his eyes. Ljosa glanced at him doubtfully and returned her attention to Leifr.

Leifr's restless tossings and mutterings soon ceased, and the fever went out of his brow as he descended into a deep and healing sleep. Thurid lost his anxious frown and began to look pleased with himself.

'By tomorrow the wound will have closed,' he said. 'Tomorrow we'll be on our way, and nobody will be the wiser that we were here.'

Ljosa nodded. 'That's good. The eye of suspicion has been on me since Fridmarr returned. Sorkvir believes that I will encourage Fridmarr in his scheme against the Pentacle.'

'It wouldn't hurt if you did encourage him a little,' Thurid said gently. 'I think Bodmarr would want you to forgive Fridmarr. If Fridmarr felt no remorse, he wouldn't be here.'

'Remorse is not enough.' Ljosa turned away and took up a piece of sewing. 'He betrayed the Pentacle to Sorkvir, betrayed Bodmarr, and tried to betray Sorkvir. I can never trust him again.'

'But when he exonerates himself and becomes a hero to Solvorfirth by restoring the powers of the Pentacle and killing Sorkvir, can you forgive him then, Ljosa?'

'When all that happens,' she said quietly, 'the wrongs will be righted, but it does nothing to change the fact that Fridmarr should not have been so weak and foolish as to

120

betray his own people in the way that he did. The Ljosalfar may forgive him, but they will never forget what he did. I won't forget – nor do I wish to forget.'

Thurid shook his head regretfully, drawing a chair into the small alcove where Leifr lay sleeping. 'Yes, I dare say a person can live and thrive on a diet of past bitterness. Fridmarr could have done the same, but he chose to come back to do battle with his dark past. You can escape from your memories, though they may leave scars. What one among us has no scars? Your place is in the present, my dear Ljosa, helping the Rhbus in the forwarding of their plans to rid us of the Dokkalfar and the trolls and all the evil that plagues us. Don't be left behind.'

Ljosa dropped her sewing and stood up, her back and shoulders held stiff, her eyes sparkling with scorn. 'If the Rhbus have a plan, it moves too slowly for me to see it,' she said bitterly. 'If there are any Rhbus.'

As she reached for the door latch, something outside scratched softly on the panels. Thurid hastened to the door and opened it a small crack to peer out.

Gotiskolker stood on the step and gave the door an impatient shove to open it wider. 'Someone's coming,' he whispered. 'You'd better come outside.' His eye traveled across the room from Ljosa to Leifr, lying in the alcove. 'It looks like Raudbjorn. He's not going to rest until he takes Fridmarr back to Sorkvir.'

'Fridmarr must not be disturbed,' Thurid replied. 'If Raudbjorn tries to come into this house, we'll have to kill him. Somehow. He's larger than the trolls I've been blasting.'

'Don't worry about Raudbjorn,' Ljosa said, pushing a small dagger into the waistband of her skirt. 'This is my house and he won't be expecting a mere woman to slit his weasand, which I will do if necessary. Perhaps he won't come in. If he does, I'll pull the curtain across the alcove; as long as Fridmarr makes no sound, we'll all be safe.'

121

Gotiskolker shook his head. 'Too dangerous,' he muttered. 'We'll have to get rid of Raudbjorn before he gets here. Perhaps I could lead him away.'

Ljosa shook her head. 'He'll still be suspicious of Stormurbjarg. It would be better if he saw the inside of the house with his own eyes and convinced himself that Fridmarr was not here. If we have trouble with him, then you can kill him or blast him. You're not afraid that I'll turn Fridmarr over to Sorkvir, are you?'

Thurid looked away from her challenging stare. 'If you are Hroald's daughter, you won't,' he said tightly. 'I know what he would think of such a nithling's deed.'

'Then go hide yourselves,' Ljosa commanded. 'I'll do whatever must be done.'

When they were gone, she made sure there was nothing left in the room to betray the presence of her guests; then she sat down with her sewing.

The loud, solid knock on the door startled her when it came. Most visitors hallooed from the meadow or tapped politely on the window instead of assaulting the door panels so rudely. With her heart knocking fearfully, Ljosa looked first at Leifr, sleeping soundly in the little alcove behind the curtain, then pulled the curtain shut and pushed a chest in front of it, as if concealing an unsightly wall. She went to the door and unfastened it as if she had nothing to conceal. Her courage almost failed her at the sight of the apparition on her doorstep.

Raudbjorn smiled his innocent smile at her and took a clumping step forward, stooping slightly to look through the low doorway, which made his body armor creak menacingly.

'Hallo, Hroaldsdottir,' he greeted her amiably. 'Raudbjorn bring greetings from Gliru-hals. Sorkvir too busy to think about you. Raudbjorn looking for Fridmarr. Maybe catch you later.' He chuckled ponderously.

'What do you want here?' Ljosa held the door open just wide enough not to seem inhospitable. 'Do you want something to eat and a place to rest?'

'Eat, yes. Rest, no. Fridmarr here someplace.' His eyes ranged suspiciously around the small house.

'Is he then? I suppose I can't stop you from searching. Will you eat first?'

Raudbjorn sniffed. 'Blood smell. Fridmarr wounded. Lady find Fridmarr, maybe?'

Ljosa pointed to a pair of freshly killed rabbits on her table. 'That's what you smell.'

Raudbjorn beamed. 'Fix Raudbjorn food. Raudbjorn tired of searching. Fridmarr flew away like genie.'

Ljosa opened her door and beckoned him to come in and sit down. The chair groaned protestingly under his weight, and the table creaked as he rested his hamlike forearms upon it, watching Ljosa's every movement as she skilfully skinned the rabbits and cut up the carcasses for stew.

'Raudbjorn looking for Fridmarr,' he rumbled with an amiable grimace that passed for a smile. 'Much glory for Raudbjorn.'

Ljosa nodded politely and set out a flagon of ale and a horn cup. Raudbjorn beamed at the sight of it and proceeded to empty an amazing quantity of it down his throat before he was forced to stop and take a breath. Wiping his knuckles across his mouth, he nodded approvingly.

'Better than Dokkalfar ale,' he said. 'Ljosa not seen Fridmarr? Up by little lake by cliff, maybe?'

'I heard a great uproar of Dokkalfar and troll-hounds last night on the cliff,' she answered. 'Fridmarr would not dare come back to Stormurbjarg now. He knows that I am no friend of his. Will you stay and eat? I was about to make some bread to go with the stew.'

'Raudbjorn stay.' He hoisted more ale while the bread was baking, his spirits growing more congenial and his countenance rosier until he finally fell asleep, resting on the table, with each snoring breath threatening to shear its legs off.

Ljosa was grateful. She looked at the curtained alcove several times, thankful for the silence behind it.

As for Thurid and Gotiskolker, she trusted them to keep themselves out of harm's way. Raudbjorn had left his huge beast tethered to the wall outside, ample warning to stay out of sight. However, she felt she could not draw a deep breath until this great lout had been fed and sent upon his way.

While Raudbjorn slept, one of Ljosa's sheep dogs ventured out from her hiding place under the bench along the wall to sniff at the unwanted guest, with her hackles bristling and a low growl. The sound awakened Raudbjorn instantly, and he instinctively reached for his weapon. The dog scuttled away with a tremendous uproar of barking, as if she had discovered a houseful of burglars and murderers. Dog and thief-taker glared at each other in mutual dislike a moment; then the dog made a dive for Raudbjorn's leg. Ljosa dived for the dog, who got in a good, satisfying bite just below Raudbjorn's knee, where most good sheep dogs would nip a sheep. Then she wriggled out of Ljosa's grasp, ignoring her scolding, and scuttled under the curtain into the alcove.

'Bad dog!' Ljosa gasped. 'Come here!'

Raudbjorn stopped rubbing his wounded leg and eyed the curtain speculatively, as if he were seeing it for the first time. Then he looked at Ljosa, reaching out one monstrous finger to brush her pale cheek.

'Why so frightened?' he rumbled with a crafty glint in his eye. 'Something behind curtain?'

'Don't kill my dog,' she quavered.

Raudbjorn drew his sword from its sheath. With his other hand, he seized the curtain and yanked it from its hooks, revealing the alcove, with a loom along one wall, bundles of clean wool on another, and a bed cluttered with skeins of wool, where the little dog stood at bay, with every tooth gleaming in defiance and mighty growls shuddering in her small chest.

Ljosa implored, 'She only bit you because you're different – not a Ljosalfar. She hates Dokkalfar.'

124

Raudbjorn's jaw dropped incredulously. 'No Fridmarr! Raudbjorn a great fool. Maybe Fridmarr really dead. Or gone. Raudbjorn thought Fridmarr hiding here.'

Ljosa opened the door, and the dog bolted to safety with a last, fierce bark over one shoulder. Raudbjorn sat down again, and Ljosa served the rabbit stew with steady hands, although she remained pale.

When Raudbjorn had finished off the entire kettle and most of the bread, he went outside to mount his horse. The sun was low in the west, and the gorge was already full of dark shadows when he turned his horse in that direction.

She waited until he was safely out of sight, then she hurried to the alcove and dragged aside the cupboard to reveal a low tunnel. Stooping, she walked quickly toward the dim red light at the far end. Emerging behind a manger, she stood up straight and confronted Thurid and Gotiskolker indignantly. They had dragged Leifr through the tunnel into the horse barn. Apparently undisturbed, he slept on, unaware of his exchange of a straw tick for a pile of hay in a barn.

'How did you know about the tunnel?' she demanded, her angry gaze settling upon Thurid, after a contemptuous flick in Gotiskolker's direction.

Thurid shrugged one shoulder toward Gotiskolker. 'He found it. A clever idea, I must say, for whoever built this house. There's no need for hauling him back. He's used to rougher quarters than this barn. Besides, the sleep spell is showing signs of wearing off already. We may be able to leave sooner than I'd thought.'

'And just as well,' Ljosa replied. 'The Dokkalfar will follow Raudbjorn. He may come back for another look. I know he's still suspicious.'

With his grisly weapon over one shoulder, Raudbjorn rode up the path toward the cliff and the pool. The water chattering over the rocks set up a melancholy reverberation in the gloomy ravine. Thickets clung to the steep rocky walls, leaning out to grasp for the scanty sunlight and clawing at passers-by.

Raudbjorn's horse tossed its hammerhead and snorted uneasily, trying to turn around on the narrow path several times before Raudbjorn reached the small lake set amid jagged black rocks. As the horse danced around nervously, Raudbjorn wrinkled his nose, sniffing. The crackle of twigs betrayed the presence of someone following him up the trail, and a wide, expectant grin split his features as he dismounted from his horse and faced the trail.

In a moment, a dark form swung into view, moving at an unhurried pace. Raudbjorn's eyes rounded in alarm, and his horse took one electrified glance at the creature on the path and vaulted away at a gallop with its tail in the air.

Raudbjorn unshouldered his halberd and backed away a few steps as the huge bear approached, its head lowered, its eyes gleaming with a feral red light.

'Fylgja bear, stop! Listen to Raudbjorn! Sorry for chopping up Sorkvir! Raudbjorn too hasty with weapons!'

'Too hasty by more than half!' the bear growled as it rose on its haunches, displaying a chilling set of sharp, scimitar claws and a mouthful of savage white fangs.

Raudbjorn lowered his halberd placatingly. 'Raudbjorn not do it again,' he offered hopefully.

'No indeed, not ever!' Sorkvir's fylgja replied. 'We've got a score to settle, Raudbjorn. You hacked my body to shreds; now I'm going to do the same for you. It's only fair.'

Raudbjorn shook his head. 'Not fair to Raudbjorn. Life leaks right out of holes and wounds. Sorkvir patches up old body and comes back again. Raudbjorn no wizard of Owl Society. Raudbjorn doomed.'

Sorkvir chuckled. 'Doomed indeed, you great fool.' Lunging forward, he gripped Raudbjorn's thigh and

126

commenced shaking him and dragging him across the ground with savage growling and snarling. Raudbjorn battered at his impervious skull and bristling shoulders, but the bear's thick, loose hide seemed to shrug off his blows. With a quick stroke of one paw, he sent the halberd spinning into the thicket.

'Wait! Sorkvir, listen! Raudbjorn do Sorkvir favor!' Raudbjorn panted, after wrestling desperately and unsuccessfully with the bear, who was going for his throat.

Sorkvir paused, with his forefeet pinning Raudbjorn to the ground, his gleaming teeth only inches from the thief-taker's face.

'What favor, you dolt? I've given you your chances to be of service to me, and you've made too many mistakes every time. What possible reason is there for me to keep you alive, after you let Fridmarr get into my hall and steal my sword?' The claws curved menacingly, sinking into Raudbjorn's battered leather armor.

'Raudbjorn get Fridmarr for you. Sorkvir needs day-farer to get Fridmarr. Raudbjorn loyal to Sorkvir – not like sneaking Dokkalfar. Raudbjorn guard your back.'

Sorkvir grunted. 'The Dokkalfar do not love me dearly, I'm forced to agree, and they take no pains to conceal it from anyone. Their only disagreement is which of their factions will take my place, once they get rid of me.'

Raudbjorn nodded emphatically. 'Raudbjorn not faction. Raudbjorn loyal, like faithful dog. Wants only food and warm place to sleep. Maybe some killing, when Sorkvir wants. Raudbjorn only good follower, not Dokkalfar.'

Sorkvir removed his paws from Raudbjorn's chest and allowed him to rise to his feet. 'I shall let you live this time, Raudbjorn,' he growled. 'A body is a small loss to me, but the Dokkalfar do not have my advantages. You can be useful, Raudbjorn, in keeping them frightened. Perhaps they will behave a bit more discreetly if you are there with that halberd to silence their plotting and complaining.'

Raudbjorn nodded agreeably and grinned until his eyes almost disappeared. 'Raudbjorn glad to frighten Dokkalfar. Dokkalfar and trolls worst part of night-faring.'

Sorkvir growled warningly. 'I could change my mind about you, Raudbjorn, so don't become overconfident too soon. If you want to guarantee yourself a safe position by my fireside, you can deliver Fridmarr into my hands. You were the last to see him. Find where he has gone or who is hiding him.' His gaze turned slowly toward the trail which led down to Ljosa's shieling.

Raudbjorn shook his head. 'Fridmarr not there. Raudbjorn look all around the house. No sign of Fridmarr there, or around lake. Fridmarr at Hjaldrsholl by now.'

'Very likely. I'll send some men to search. And just in case you've overlooked something, I want Ljosa's place searched again – thoroughly. At dusk Hakarl and some others will be coming to question Hroaldsdottir about Fridmarr. If he truly rode his horse off that cliff, it's curious that she knows nothing about it.'

Raudbjorn scowled and edged warily toward the thicket where his halberd had landed. 'That Hakarl. Nasty temper. Raudbjorn like to stir his brains with axe head.'

'You'll do nothing of the kind, unless I tell you to,' Sorkvir snarled. 'Wait for Hakarl and help him with his search of the shieling. Let him know that I'll be watching, whether he sees me or not.'

Sorkvir started to move away through the thickets without making a sound. At the base of a skarp, he turned, his eyes gleaming redly in the failing light. 'That wizard Thurid has been here, and where he is, Fridmarr must be nearby. I want to meet this upstart, with his glamour spells and earth spells and so-called Rhbu magic. He can't be as good as his luck would make him

128

seem. Tell Hakarl to save Thurid, if possible, so I can examine these powers of his and discover where he got them.'

Raudbjorn blinked his eyes. The dark shape of the bear had vanished without a sound, and he could see no trace of it on the steep face of the ravine. His hair bristled and he shivered.

He found his horse on the far side of the ravine and rode it back toward Ljosa's house, not without some reluctance on the horse's part when it discerned the scent of bear on the path. After a hard-won struggle, Raudbjorn brought his horse down to the rocks near the house, where he could hide and wait for Hakarl.

He had not waited long when the wizard Thurid slipped out of the house with a furtive air and started up the path toward the lake. Raudbjorn grinned broadly to himself and crept around a skarp overlooking the path where Thurid must pass below.

Thurid came around the corner of a crumbling granary, oblivious of the threat lurking ahead of him. But to Raudbjorn's vast disappointment, Thurid whirled around and faced the house for a moment, then dived behind a thick stand of blackberry bushes. Always puzzled by the often senseless behaviour of wizards, Raudbjorn craned his neck over the rock to see what had caused Thurid to jump into the bushes.

Ten Dokkalfar rode into the yard of the little house and halted in a half circle around the door. Their leader, a burly renegade named Hakarl, dismounted and thundered upon the door with the hilt of his axe. The others got off their horses and stood behind him in warlike stances, their weapons ready.

CHAPTER 8

When the door opened, the Dokkalfar all crouched defensively, but it was only Ljosa. She pushed the door open far enough to walk outside and stand on her doorstep, gazing at her persecutors with regal hauteur.

'Where is Fridmarr?' Hakarl demanded.

'He isn't here,' she answered. 'Is that your only excuse for battering at my door like a pack of brigands? Have you forgotten the codes of common courtesy? If I were Fridmarr or some other famous outlaw, instead of a lone woman, I suspect you would not forget your manners with such a display of disrespect.'

Hakarl could not resist swaggering before his companions, casting them an amused glance over his shoulder. 'We meant no disrespect,' he said with exaggerated politeness. 'We realize that you used to be the daughter of a chieftain, and you're accustomed to a soft and easy life. But I might remind you that you're in a bad position, if you're harboring Fridmarr inside your house. We know he was here last night, and we don't think he has gone far. You know the penalty for helping an outlaw – banishment or death. You might be forgiven by our gracious lord chieftain Sorkvir, if you allow us to take him peacefully. You could always say he forced his way in without your consent.'

'But that would not be the truth. I kept him here and bandaged his wound and fed him my food. My roof sheltered him willingly from the eyes of his enemies.'

'Then you are guilty, Hroaldsdottir, and there will be no mercy shown you. Where is Fridmarr now?'

'You may search for yourself anywhere you like, but

130

not one of you will set his foot inside this door. No Dokkalfar will ever cross this threshold.'

The Dokkalfar made some covert signs behind their backs, in case she was making a spell against them. Then they withdrew a few paces, coming alarmingly close to the blackberry bushes where Thurid was lying.

'I think he's inside,' Hakarl said in an excited whisper, and the others muttered in agreement.

'He's a cowardly dog to let a woman do his speaking for him,' another said.

'All the more reason he should die, Ljosalfar are all too sly by half. That wizard is probably lying in wait for us, ready to blast us with fire.'

'Then we'll have to be careful not to walk into the trap she's setting for us. If they weren't inside, she wouldn't have made such a challenge to us.'

'But how do we get them to come out? There's only the ten of us, and we don't have days and days. Sorkvir's patience has been thin since that thief-taker cut him up.'

'So is mine. I say we ought to kill Fridmarr and be done with this affair. I don't know what we want with Sorkvir now. He won't come out of that bear shape until it suits him. Give me an ordinary Dokkalfar leader any day; I'm tired to death of wizards.'

'Quiet, he may be around here somewhere, listening. Wouldn't you like for him to hear that speech? We'd all be turned into Gotiskolkers.'

The Dokkalfar snickered uneasily and avoided looking at one another, their narrow faces distrustful and sly.

'It will take all of us to get them out. I think I know the best way. If they come out, they live for awhile. If they don't, they die, and Sorkvir does whatever nasty things he likes to bring them back to some sort of life. Whichever way they choose, they won't be happy.'

The Dokkalfar chuckled grimly, and one said impatiently, 'Get on with the plan, Hakarl.'

'It's quite simple. We'll burn them out.'

With an evil chuckle, they slouched back to Ljosa's

doorstep, where she still stood barring the way, with the light behind her.

'This is our last appeal,' Hakarl said. 'Send out Fridmarr and the wizard, or we'll set fire to your house. Everyone inside will perish.'

Ljosa's composure did not falter. 'House-burning is a cowardly way of getting at your enemies.'

'When one of them is a wizard, we don't like to take chances with our lives. Either they surrender, or we'll start gathering wood.'

'There is no way they will surrender,' Ljosa said. 'Perhaps Dokkalfar surrender, but Ljosalfar would rather die with glory.'

'Is that your final word, Hroaldsdottir? You have no wish to continue living?'

'Not if it means disgracing my family's name even more than it has already suffered.' She turned and went inside, closing the door and barring it from the inside.

The Dokkalfar turned to their task with grim relish, tearing off the gates and bars. Whatever wood they could find was heaped up around the eaves of the low house. A spark was struck, and the first tendrils of flame blackened the green moss growing on the sides of the house.

Thurid leaped to his feet, a roar of outrage and challenge upon his lips, but it died with a faint croak as Sorkvir's fylgja stalked into the dooryard. Swinging his head slowly around, the bear surveyed the Dokkalfar and the wood heaped up around the house. The Dokkalfar stood as rigid as posts, their eyes fixed upon the bear with helpless fascination.

'Whose idea was this?' he rumbled.

Without hesitation, the Dokkalfar indicated Hakarl with shrugs and nods. Hakarl edged away, and Sorkvir followed, raising one evil paw.

Thurid sank slowly into the bushes, reaching for his satchel with trembling hands. His fingers searched among the rune wands until he found one fatter than the others, a spell he had been saving for such a dire emergency as he now faced. He knew the words; to make them more effective, he pierced his thumb with his knife and rubbed the blood into the runes.

'Now we shall see who burns,' he whispered defiantly, drawing deep breaths and beginning to recite the words of the spell.

A rush of power filled him with supreme confidence, opening his eyes and all his senses to the awesome might of the reservoirs of earth magic which he had tapped. As he rose to his feet and crossed the interval to the dooryard, he felt as if his feet scarcely touched the earth. Glancing down, he saw that his hands and wrists already had taken on an eerie glow, and his beard and hair felt as if each hair formed a perfect conduit for the unseen energy that he had summoned into his body.

The Dokkalfar whirled around and stared, properly terrified at the sight of him. Sorkvir froze with one paw in mid-air, then his jaws parted in an ursine grin of welcome.

'So you're not inside with the others,' he said. 'Perhaps you can see now that it would be a good time to change sides. I think I could convince you.'

'I fear I'm not convinced. I won't allow you to burn that house with my friends inside. Command these wretched scums of yours to put out that fire,' Thurid reached out with his staff to point, and all the Dokkalfar dived for the ground, anticipating a raking swath of flames. However, nothing issued from the staff except a small spurt of black smoke that smelled very sooty.

Sorkvir's lips rolled back in a malignant snarl. 'What has become of your magic, Thurid? It seems your fire spell has failed. In my presence, your magic becomes weak and useless. Weak and useless.'

Reeling slightly from astonishment and dismay, Thurid felt the words sink in deeply to the core of his confidence. His amazing strength of moments ago seemed gone. He couldn't find the will to battle Sorkvir's

133

bombardment of negative power. He stood locked in the conflict of powers, unable to stir a finger.

Sorkvir's laugh burbled out of the bear's throat, and he said to the grinning Dokkalfar, 'There's more tinder for your fire. Throw it on, where it's hottest.'

Hoisting Thurid to their shoulders, they charged toward the fire. With a toss, they pitched Thurid headlong into the fire, still as rigid as a gatepost. Overcome with their own wickedness, the Dokkalfar pranced around the dooryard, yelling and howling at the tops of their lungs.

Raudbjorn slunk into the midst of the revelry, and Sorkvir swung his heavy head around to fix him with a commanding stare.

'Raudbjorn,' he rumbled. 'Hakarl has displeased me by setting this fire. I want you to attend to Hakarl in the manner best suited for traitors.'

Hakarl and Raudbjorn exchanged a long, speculative stare; then Hakarl turned and dashed toward his horse. Shaking his head in disgust, Raudbjorn followed at a more leisurely pace, leaving the rest of the Dokkalfar eyeing Sorkvir nervously.

'You see what will happen to anyone who disobeys my orders,' Sorkvir growled. 'The lot of you had better hope that Fridmarr does not die in that house and release his vengeful draug to seek me out. If that happens, I will see to it that each of you suffers exquisitely for it.'

Thurid listened to this exchange, watching through the flames dancing merrily around him. He felt no real discomfort. He felt the crackle and hiss of the flames, and the roar was rather exhilarating. His powers no longer felt weak and useless. The Dokkalfar scuttled back in alarm as he suddenly stretched out his arms and sat up. Although the flames enveloped him, his clothing did not ignite and not so much as a hair on the back of his hand was shriveled. Running his hands over himself assured him that the powerful spell on the fat rune had

134

indeed worked; his body was engulfed by fire without damage to it.

Almost mincingly, he picked his way out of the fire and walked toward the Dokkalfar and Sorkvir as if nothing had happened to him.

'It's just a trick,' Sorkvir growled. 'Anyone can do it if they know how. Seize him, and we'll see if we can't make him a little more uncomfortable this time.'

The Dokkalfar hesitated, their eyes wary. Then a bold one stepped forward and seized Thurid by the arm. Then he suddenly let go with a wild yell, holding up his hands and staring at them in horror. Small flames leaped up his forearms, then the rest of him exploded into a torch. With a shriek, the Dokkalfar vanished, leaving nothing but a collapsed set of clothing on the ground, surrounded by a spreading, wet puddle.

Thurid felt an unamiable grin creasing his face as he surveyed the remaining Dokkalfar. He raised one hand, and they all turned their backs and bolted for the shadows. Galvanized by their desertion, Sorkvir lunged forward with a maddened roar. Thurid blasted his face, setting his fur on fire.

Before Sorkvir could retaliate, the shrill bray of a horn sounded from the hill behind the house, followed by the thunder of hooves. Four horses swept down the slope onto the roof of the house and off the eaves into the confusion of fleeing Dokkalfar trying to mount their frightened horses. The riders plowed to a halt around Thurid, and two of them seized him by the arms and hoisted him onto the back of the horse they led.

'Fridmarr!' a Dokkalfar yelled, and turned his horse to pursue. Looking over his shoulder, he saw no one following. On the contrary, the Dokkalfar remaining were spurring toward Gliru-hals at top speed, heedless of those left afoot or injured.

Leifr had scant recollection of arriving at Ljosa's house and he knew nothing of the healing sleep that

135

Thurid had put him under. When he awakened, he lay still with his eyes closed, taking a tentative inventory of his muscles and bones, gradually realizing not only that he was still alive and not suffering from any disability, but that he felt a peculiar calmness of spirit, a steady glow of renewed resolution to find the grindstone and rid the realm of Sorkvir. As he lay there with his eyes shut, it did not seem like an impossible task.

A voice rudely jarred his peaceful mood, saying in a harsh tone, 'If you're through malingering, it may interest you to know that you'll be expected to ride for your life in just a short while. I hope you'll be awake for it. I'm not going to go back looking for you if you fall off in a ditch somewhere, with twenty Dokkalfar howling at our heels. Or Sorkvir's fylgja may find you.'

'I'm awake, Gotiskolker.' Leifr sat up cautiously and tested his arm, noting some ache and stiffness, which was to be expected in a newly healed injury. Then he took note of his surroundings. He seemed to be in a cave which was doing service as a barn. A narrow shaft of light filtered in from a fissure in the roof, dimly illuminating a row of stalls, a heap of meadow hay, which he was lying upon, and a small spring hollowed out in the stone floor to trap a slow trickle of water. A horse snuffled in its trough, drawing his attention to four saddled horses waiting in their stalls. Beyond them in the darkness, a few streaks of light betrayed the existence of a door.

'Never mind all that,' Gotiskolker said, anticipating a barrage of questions. 'You've had a lovely sleep while the rest of us have been at our wits' end trying to keep you hidden from Sorkvir.'

'I smell smoke,' Leifr said suddenly.

'It's coming from the tunnel. I'd better go back to see if Ljosa is getting out of there.' Gotiskolker bent down and vanished into a dark opening in the earth.

Leifr got to his feet, moving around experimentally to discover how steady he really was and keeping his eyes on the opening. Then he started after Gotiskolker. The tunnel was so low he almost had to go on his hands and knees.

After a short distance, he met Gotiskolker coming back, scuttling along like a rat in the darkness.

'Come on, we've got only a moment to get out of here!' Gotiskolker exploded, shoving Leifr ahead of him back to the cave.

'Where's Ljosa?' Leifr demanded.

'Here,' her muffled voice replied. 'Thurid has got himself into trouble. I don't know if we can save him.'

She brushed past him and began untying the horses. Gotiskolker opened the doors, and the horses surged outward, not liking the smell of the smoke. Leifr swung into his saddle, ducking low so he wouldn't get scraped against the doorposts. Outside, the night air was filled with smoke and the noise of men, weapons, and flames.

'This way!' Ljosa called, leading the way up the slope of the hill where the barn turves were stacked against it. The horses lunged upward with difficulty, scrambling to the top of the hill, then plunging down into the confusion below without hesitation. Leifr clung to his saddle, aghast, as the horses plummeted down onto the roof of Ljosa's house, which was engulfed in leaping flames. A ring of startled faces, dyed scarlet by the fire, gazed upward at the horses leaping straight into their midst.

Gotiskolker reined his horse against Leifr's, shoving him around toward the fire, where a single figure stood waving a staff and blazing like a human torch. Ljosa brought the led horse around. Without bothering to confer, Leifr and Gotiskolker hoisted Thurid off his feet and hauled him over the horse's rump and into the saddle, scarcely breaking stride. A few half-hearted arrows rained down around them, and the shouts of the Dokkalfar turned to frightened yelps as Thurid hurled a parting spell over his shoulder, showering the Dokkalfar with darts of flame. Even the vast form of Sorkvir's fylgja took flight.

The Dokkalfar did not follow them. Thurid stopped several times to dowse for influences and felt quite safe in calling a halt for the remainder of the night at a peat-cutter's hut. Apart from a few new singes and holes, Thurid and his cloak were in far better condition than Leifr had expected.

Leifr's shoulder was also in much better condition than he had expected. He could scarcely believe the amount of healing that had taken place in so short a time.

At dawn when Leifr awoke, he went outside to find Gotiskolker and Thurid quarreling over the fire Thurid had conjured.

'We're not going to roast an ox,' Gotiskolker snapped. 'All we want to do is brew some tea. Do you think you can stoop to such an insignificant task, or are fire wizards too exalted for mundane affairs?'

'I should use you for tinder,' Thurid retorted. 'All that grease on your clothing would make an excellent flame. Halloa, Fridmarr, how are you faring? There's our objective today – Hjaldrsholl, just coming out of the mist. The grindstone is gone, but we must stop and apprise Hjaldr of our intentions, besides touching the site. It has been a fortress since ancient times. A never-ending supply of water flows in an underground river beneath it.'

He pointed to the mountain clearing its spiky crown of mist, but what Leifr saw was Ljosa sitting on a rock with her cloak drawn around her, gazing back toward Stormurbjarg, where the smoke was still visible.

Leifr crossed to Ljosa. 'I'm sorry about Stormurbjarg. It was my fault, and now it's my fault you're outlawed. If there's some way I can help you—'

She arose and glided past him without raising her eyes, saying as she passed, 'I won't burden you for long. I'll travel north to Luster, then up the coast to Fjara-strond. I have relatives there, so you needn't think about my

138

future. You should be accustomed to blighting the lives of everyone around you by now.'

Leifr winced, but knew it was true. He could not blame her for wanting to put as much distance between herself and him as possible. Mentally he upbraided Fridmarr for his unique dislikability. He offered, 'We'll ride with you to Fjara-strond. You won't be safe alone.'

'It's not necessary,' she replied. 'I may be safer alone than with the outlaw all the Dokkalfar in Solvorfirth are looking for. I've made that journey many times with my father and I'm not afraid. Besides, you have more important concerns.'

'More pressing, perhaps,' Leifr said, 'but not more important. Will you come back to Gliru-hals, when Sorkvir is gone?'

'I don't expect to see Gliru-hals again. Your intentions are good, Fridmarr, but I fear you are doomed to failure. You have made too many mistakes in the past.'

'Ljosa, it's not the same – I'm not the same,' he stammered. 'Look at me for what I'm trying to do now – not for all the evil things I've done in the past. I'm not what you think I am.'

She looked at him then with a slight frown. 'It's easy to see what you're not, Fridmarr. You're not as arrogant, not as foolish, not as clever with your powers. In fact, you hardly seem at all what you were. What I don't see is what you really are; only what you aren't. There's a blankness I can't see into, as if you're shutting me out. I can't feel what you are thinking. What are you hiding, Fridmarr? Something worse than your alliance with Sorkvir?'

Leifr looked away from her too-intent scrutiny and saw Gotiskolker watching him. In a low voice he said, 'Ljosa, I want your forgiveness – if that's possible. Bodmarr knew the risks when he took that sword. I know I can't change what happened then, but I can cleanse the Pentacle, and I can kill Sorkvir, once we find the troll's grindstone. If I succeed, I can make a new future for Solvorfirth and for you as well, if you can come to believe in me again.'

'I don't know if I want to believe again,' she replied after a long moment. 'It's too – painful. Not only would I have to accept what you are doing as a good and selfless venture, but I would have to believe that you had your reasons for what you did before, other than your own glorification. Can you tell me now that what you did was not completely for yourself?'

Leifr scowled and shook his head. 'I honestly can't say,' he answered, but he suspected that Fridmarr's intentions centered solely upon grasping as much power for himself as possible. All the signs pointed to his complete selfishness, until Bodmarr died, when he had appeared to come to his senses and tried to make his escape from Sorkvir. The eitur would do its work, though, if it hadn't done it already.

Ljosa was gazing at him, her eyes as clear and golden as amber. 'You're still caught between the two forces, Fridmarr. Elbegast on the one side and the Dokkur Lavardur on the other. One day, perhaps, you'll learn where you belong. Or perhaps you'll lose your life before you find peace.'

'I'd find peace if you'd forgive Fridmarr – the Fridmarr that used to be – and let me hope that I might find you again at Fjara-strond when all this is done with and Sorkvir is dead.'

Ljosa turned away to face Hjaldrsholl and remained silent a long time. Leifr's heart sank further with each moment. Finally, in a guarded voice, she said, 'I suppose you may, should you survive and be successful. But don't hold the Pentacle and your exploits up to me as a trophy, Fridmarr. You must do this for yourself and everyone you've grieved, to make reparation for your crimes. Don't expect me to forget so quickly – or to forgive so easily. Good luck, Fridmarr, and good-bye, perhaps. We'll part at Hjaldrsholl.' She gave him her hand for a moment, then slipped away.

140

Near dusk they came into view of the lower halls of Hjaldrsholl, where a new fortress was being built into the side of the mountain. Tools, carts, and heaps of stone and dirt were scattered around the massive, arched entry. The heavy doors stood slightly ajar, and Leifr could see no sign of a guard. Pausing behind a black skarp of lava, they watched awhile in uneasy silence.

Thurid got down from his horse and walked a few steps forward, his cloak billowing at his heels and his staff spitting a trail of pale smoke. 'I don't like the feeling here,' he said, reaching into the satchel for his bundle of rune sticks. Reading one quickly, he muttered over the words of a spell several times. His stance became rigid, and his eyes glazed over as he gazed toward the fortress.

'The dwarfs are dead,' he whispered. 'Sorkvir's Dokkalfar have been here before us. They believed the dwarfs were hiding us.'

'They might still be lurking inside, waiting,' Gotiskolker said. 'We'd better go higher, toward the old hall. There's bound to be some survivors. We won't be able to touch the troll's grindstone for luck before we start out on the Pentacle journey, but Hjaldrsholl is the place we must start.'

'We'd better not take the road,' Thurid replied. 'It's liable to be watched.'

'We won't get there before dark unless we take the road,' Gotiskolker said.

'Nonsense. I'll dowse the way,' Thurid snorted. 'Just follow me, and I'll have us there in better time than the road would have taken. What are wizards for, after all?'

In a very short time, they were lost and quarreling about the right direction to Hjaldrsholl's upper entrance. The dusk was deepening to the silvery, long-lasting twilight dear to the hearts of night-farers. There was no other solution to their plight except to make camp, which they did on the side of a high fell, looking down onto the rubbly spine of Hjaldrsfell. The horses had very

141

little to graze upon, and the ground sloped enough that sleeping would be difficult. However, the site was relatively safe, with the shoulders of the ravine to screen them from view, along with some stands of scrubby birch to offer further concealment. The place was also fairly defensible against trolls, although most of the troll trails they had seen earlier tended toward the lower settlements.

Gotiskolker broke the gloomy silence with a mirthless chuckle. 'We're making great progress, Fridmarr. We've lost Hjaldrsholl to Sorkvir, the last remaining point of the Pentacle still untouched by evil hands.'

'The Dvergar resisted all these years,' Thurid said regretfully. 'And now they fall.'

Leifr felt all their eyes resting upon him in what he interpreted as accusing silence. Fridmarr's past guilt pressed upon him in an onerous burden, especially with Ljosa's eyes upon him.

He stood up, smothering his resentment. 'I'll go see to the horses. They sound restless.' The horses, at least, were not critical of him, he thought gloomily as he picked his way across the rocky ground in the twilight.

Suspecting that a tether rope was caught on a rock, he climbed over a nest of boulders, feeling for the ropes. The horses stood alertly, snorting and stamping, or pacing in uneasy circles around their picket pegs. As he was trying to soothe them, the sudden clatter of a small stone falling from above alerted his warning instincts. Reaching for his sword, he crept warily around the edge of a skarp, peering around at the bleak fellside and seeing nothing but rocks and the wiry vegetation that grew there. He took another step around the skarp, into black shadow.

He heard a body being launched off the crag above him, and, in an instant, his attacker landed on his back, sending him sprawling. His sword clattered on the stones, almost out of reach. As he groped for it, a heavy boot trod upon his arm, pinning it to the ground, and the sharp point of a sword nudged him behind his ear.

'Don't make a sound, or you'll choke on your own blood,' a voice growled warningly. Then his captor signaled to companions with the fluting whistle of a cricket.

Leifr leaned his forehead against a rock, his arm and shoulder turning numb under his captor's foot, listening to more whistles and covert movements in the crags above. In a moment their camp was taken with no sounds of struggle except a muffled exclamation from Thurid. At Leifr's slightest involuntary movement, the sword poked his neck warningly.

At last his captor received some signal, and he moved his foot from Leifr's arm. 'All right, let's see who we've got here,' a gruff voice said. 'On your feet, my friend.'

Leifr stood up warily, surveying his captors. Two others had joined the original, and the three of them looked very similar – short, barrel-chested, with dense mats of beards covering their chests, except for one whose beard hung in three braids. They wore conical helmets much adorned with devices and embossing, and the metal of their brooches, buckles, and fasteners was worked with fine detail evident even by twilight.

Scrutinizing him with much the same curiosity, the three strangers kept their swords pointing at Leifr purposefully while they discussed their catch among themselves.

'He looks like a rather long specimen for a Ljosalfar,' the one with the braided beard observed.

'And too broad for a Dokkalfar,' the second added.

'And certainly not a Dvergar,' the third chimed in. 'He might be a short jotun.'

'No, I don't think so,' the first said. 'An outsize Ljosalfar, perhaps. It happens more frequently now that they've started trafficking with the Scipling realm.'

'You might ask me, instead of talking as if I couldn't understand you,' Leifr said. 'You might also explain the reason for this unprovoked attack. We're nothing but

143

travelers and we stopped here for the night, hoping we
.were safe. We've done nothing to deserve this sort of
treatment.'

'We'll decide what sort of treatment you deserve,' the
one with the braids said. 'Move along back to your
friends and don't try to escape. There are too many of us
for you.'

When Leifr returned to the camp he was inclined to
agree. Nine more short fellows with axes and clubs stood
around his companions, eyeing him as vigilantly as he
eyed them. Thurid sat on a stone, chafing at the cord
binding his hands behind his back.

'Fridmarr, tell them who I am,' he burst out indignantly. 'Tell them who you are and why we're here.
They don't seem to listen to me and they've taken my
staff and my satchel. You know I'm helpless without
them.'

'I suspect that's why they took them away from you,'
Leifr replied. 'Just be silent, Thurid, and perhaps they'll
explain themselves.'

Looking at the strangers, all bristling and glowering,
he feared that the only explanation he would get would
be from the edge of a sword or axe.

A white-bearded individual stepped forward after a
long, critical survey of the captives from under a hedge
of thick white eyebrows.

'We are the Dvergar of the Grindstone,' he said with a
weighty intonation. 'We have captured four trespassers –
a woman, a wizard, a scavenger, and what looks to be a
warrior of some kind. This is highly suspicious. Especially when we find you trying to creep around our rear
guard. There can be no reasonable excuse for your
presence here.'

'We came here for peaceful purposes,' Leifr said. 'Our
common enemy has made it impossible for us to stay in
Solvorfirth, so we're on our way north to escape him.'

'Sorkvir is after you, then.' The white-bearded leader
did not relax his guard. 'Having a common enemy does

144

not make us friends. The Dvergar are choosy about the strangers they meet blundering around in the fells. In the past, we trusted when we should have attacked.'

As he talked, another dwarf searched through the saddle bags and possessions of the prisoners. With a grave sense of foreboding, Leifr saw him pull out the sword, cautiously unwrapping it and examining it for a long time before bringing it forward. Thurid silenced his indignant huffing and threatening.

'If you'll allow us to explain—' he began.

'No explanation is needed,' the white-bearded dwarf interrupted. 'We know who you are now. This is the Bjartur sword, taken from a barrow in the ancient fortress of the Rhbus and brought to Solvorfirth to cause unimaginable troubles. Fridmarr, you should have left this sword buried, and we would not have been cursed with this alog. The first time I saw it, I knew you'd only succeed in turning Sorkvir against us. Now we've all paid for your foolishness. Bodmarr is dead, Sorkvir has the grindstone, and this sword is ruined.'

'Perhaps,' Thurid said acidly, 'the fault lies in you for not sharpening it the first time he brought it to you, Hjaldr. Your cautiousness led him to the desperate theft of the troll's grindstone.'

Hjaldr snorted, 'He was an ally of Sorkvir. Why should I sharpen a sword for my enemy, especially on a stone with such power as that grindstone had?'

'You knew he wanted to kill Sorkvir,' Thurid replied. 'It shouldn't have mattered, as long as we were rid of Sorkvir. Fridmarr was the lesser enemy, by far.'

'It matters little, now,' Hjaldr said. 'All our hopes are blasted. Half my men were killed yesterday by Sorkvir's Dokkalfar. All that is left to me is the desire for revenge for Bodmarr and all the Ljosalfar and Dvergar who once hoped that Fridmarr would be the bane of Sorkvir. Many is the time I've wished for this very opportunity to slay the man who was responsible for raising such hope and such despair.'

He reached for the short sword hanging at his belt, and the two dwarfs holding Leifr from either side wrestled him to his knees after a sharp struggle.

Hjaldr raised his sword with both hands. 'With your head gracing a pike before our doors, we'll grieve a bit less for our companions who have so recently died.'

CHAPTER 9

'WAIT!' Thurid gasped. 'The least you can do is listen to our side of this issue! How do you know you're not making a fatal mistake, Hjaldr?'

Hjaldr hesitated and cast one eye over his men to observe their opinion. Most of the Dvergar were in favor of taking Leifr's head off then and there, but a few insisted upon hearing out the guilty ones before killing them.

'Very well, Fridmarr, you've won a short reprieve,' Hjaldr rumbled unwillingly, lowering his sword. 'Go ahead and speak your piece, and then we shall decide if you're lying or not. Your head may yet decorate our doors.'

Leifr got to his feet, glowering at his two captors, respecting the amazing strength in their long, burly arms.

'I came back to Solvorfirth to right the wrongs I've committed,' he began grimly, aware that he was bargaining for his life. 'If we can get through the Pentacle, the Rhbus will grant us the object of our desires, which is to sharpen that sword and kill Sorkvir with it.'

The dwarfs shook their heads and hooted in derision.

'The Rhbus are all dead,' Hjaldr said. 'They can't help you, and the Pentacle is all perverted. Sorkvir did his work of destruction well, and you were the one who showed him how to do it.'

'I never suspected what the result would be,' Leifr protested. 'Sorkvir never confided in me about his intention of making an alog that would protect him from that sword. I gave it to Bodmarr, didn't I? Doesn't that show that I was against Sorkvir? If I had given it to him and warned him that it possessed Rhbu magic and would destroy him utterly, then you could say I was Sorkvir's friend. But I gave it to Bodmarr and I came to you to ask you to sharpen it on the troll's grindstone – and you refused.'

'Then you stole the grindstone, and went on with Sorkvir to destroy the rest of the Pentacle,' Hjaldr replied. 'We can never forget that. Either you possess a strange sense of humor or a strong wish to die, if you dare to return here and try to make fools of us a second time.'

Leifr winced away from their sneers and glowers and found himself looking at Ljosa, who stood erect, watching him with dark anguish deepening the shadows of her eyes.

'I have no evil plot this time,' Leifr said, feeling the sweat sliding down his spine. 'I came back to right the wrongs I have committed. I didn't have to return, and a more sensible man might not have done so, but I never was known for good judgment. I want to break Sorkvir's alog over Solvorfirth. I'm going to sharpen this sword and kill him, if it takes me the rest of my life.'

'Which may not be long,' Hjaldr added grimly. 'How do we know all this is true? You were always an accomplished liar before. I doubt if you have learned to be truthful in such a short time.' The dwarfs muttered their agreement.

'It's true.' Ljosa's voice floated above the bass grumble of the dwarfs. 'I am Ljosa Hroaldsdottir, once Bodmarr's betrothed. I will speak for the truthfulness of what Fridmarr says. I believe him when he says he has sworn enmity with Sorkvir. I believe him when he says he has changed and that he will make himself a better man. Already he is not the same Fridmarr we knew.'

Her testimony threw the dwarfs into another debate.

'No matter what he does, he can't bring Bodmarr back,' someone said, 'nor all our friends and kinsmen who died last night.'

'Revenge is the same as cutting off your foot to match the one you've lost,' another Dvergar grunted.

'But he was a traitor once. We can't forgive that.'

'If he gets rid of Sorkvir and the alog, I'll forgive him. Let his brother's death be on his conscience.'

'I don't care about his conscience, as long as the grindstone is brought back.'

'We'll never see it again. He was Sorkvir's once, and no one ever escapes from Sorkvir. He's tainted meat, if ever I smelled it.'

Hjaldr raised one hand to silence the mounting uproar before the dwarfs started going for each other's throats.

'Be still,' he commanded. 'His past misdeeds don't matter much now. The question is, where is the grindstone now? If what you say about it being a Rhbu sword taken from a Rhbu grave in Bjartur is true, until it is sharpened upon a proper Rhbu grindstone, the sword won't work in the hand of Elbegast himself. This is what I told you when you brought it to me before, Fridmarr. How do you know what will happen when that metal touches that stone?'

The dwarfs looked grimly at Leifr, and some shook their heads and spat upon the ground, as if his fate were sealed. Leifr glanced at Thurid, hoping for a cue, but Thurid only stared at him, hanging upon his words with great fascination. The powers of the carbuncle were of no assistance.

Ljosa took a step forward. 'Fridmarr won't speak for himself, but I'm not afraid to speak for him. He knows that the sword and the grindstone are both Rhbu because he has seen the Rhbu who turns your grindstone – not that you Dvergar can truthfully call it yours, since it belonged to your halls long before you named them Hjaldrsholl. Your unbelief does not alter the fact that the magic of the Rhbus lives on. There are still three Rhbus battling the Dokkur Lavardur and they enlist the aid of ordinary Ljosalfar when they find worthy individuals. The Pentacle is one of their tests, as you should know from ample experience, having seen its magic work many times for its travelers.'

Hjaldr scowled. 'I've also seen plenty of travelers who didn't find what they sought when they started the Pentacle. Plenty of them have died, for one reason or another. If any Rhbus were left to tell us how it should work, perhaps it would be a less dangerous journey. As it is today, only a madman would attempt to use its magic. When did you see the troll who turns the stone – or Rhbu, if that's what you care to believe?'

Leifr glanced at Ljosa, wondering desperately what she must know about Bodmarr and Fridmarr's secret plans.

'This is not something I care to discuss,' he growled, glowering around the circle of suspicious Dvergar faces.

'He saw the Rhbu,' Ljosa insisted. 'I know it from his brother Bodmarr. Call it a troll or whatever you will, but we know it was one of the Rhbus.'

'Who's to say the troll or Rhbu was pleased to have the grindstone stolen?' Hjaldr rejoined with a triumphant hoisting of one bristling brow. 'I can't be beaten in that way, my lady. The grindstone is lost now, difficult if not impossible to retrieve. And we have captured Fridmarr Fridmundrsson, the one who is responsible for most of the disasters that have befallen Solvorfirth.'

Gotiskolker spoke for the first time. 'If you were wise, Hjaldr, you'd provision us and send us on our way again with your blessings. The stone will sharpen the sword wherever it lies, but the Pentacle will not shake off the alog until the grindstone is returned to this fortress and placed in its rightful spot in the old forge.'

Hjaldr pursed up his lips in a wry expression. 'Perhaps we can come to a more suitable arrangement than my whacking your head off and placing it on a pike before Hjaldrsholl. Let's see if we can settle upon a satisfactory alternative over some food and drink. Our hospitality isn't what it once was, now that the Dokkalfar have thrown us out of our fine Grindstone Hall, but we'll make the best of what rough circumstances we've got.'

The Dvergar nodded and grumbled in agreement, not without displays of reluctance on the part of the more truculent ones.

'Are we still prisoners, or will our weapons be returned to us and Thurid allowed the use of his hands?' Leifr pointedly ignored their bluff overtures of peace, until Hjaldr issued a sharp command to one of his followers, and Thurid was quickly released.

Hjaldr's rough circumstances were a spacious cave in the cliffs not far above. They rode in the wide opening, and the heavy metal-studded doors were closed behind them with a sound like echoing thunder. The visitors rode down a long corridor, dimly lit by whale oil lamps on long spikes thrust into the earth at infrequent intervals.

To Leifr Hjaldr said, 'These halls used to belong to the trolls. When the Dokkalfar came, we had to clean them out. The trolls are gone, but some of the stink remains. It takes a long time to get rid of such vermin. I hate to think what the Dokkalfar are doing to our beautiful new hall. A thousand years went into the stone carving alone. I can remember when the pillars were nothing but rough columns.'

Leifr said nothing, stealing a covert glance at his companion. Hjaldr was as tough and gnarled as any individual Leifr had seen, as well he should be after a thousand years of battling trolls and Dokkalfar.

'This looks like fine work for trolls,' he observed, nodding to some carvings on the walls where the moonlight filtered in through a distant hole far above. 'The trolls at Dallir were depraved creatures.'

Thurid snorted. 'So they all are. Dvergar made these halls long ago, before the Alfar split into Ljosa and Dokk.'

Hjaldr grunted. 'It was our halls the Dokkalfar took over when they decided to go underground. It's always the Dvergar you Alfar come to when there's trouble above. You come for swords, shields, armor, spells to destroy each other, and curses to curse each other. I wonder what it will be like when you have finally done each other in completely.'

They halted at another pair of heavy doors, and some lesser dwarfs came forward to take the horses away. Inside the doors, Leifr surveyed a vast, gloomy hall, cluttered with benches, sleeping platforms, and tables, all gathering coats of dust from long disuse. In the farthest end, a meagre fire burned in the corner of a monstrous, blackened hearth, with grinning carvings leering out of the soot. A few benches and tables looked as if they were frequently used, and the sleeping platforms on either side were neatly spread with troll- and deerskins and soft down eiders. The furniture was carved for the express purpose of looking grim and uncomfortable, and someone had gone to a lot of trouble to make it so, with scenes of monsters being killed, great battles, and grim moral tales carved into the wood for centuries of Dvergar to look at and feel gloomy. Leifr looked around and felt his hopes being quenched, one by one, until he had no expectation of any support from this meagre outpost of dwarfs.

He discovered that there were only twenty-one of them, and their means of livelihood was rather tenuously supported by a pony train that went over the fells twice a year to fetch provisions from a larger entombment of dwarfs. Before the advent of Sorkvir and his Dokkalfar, the primary function of Hjaldr's settlement was metalwork of some esoteric nature that Leifr did not feel encouraged to inquire into. Dwarfs, he gathered, were rather solitary by nature, distrustful of the above-ground folk, and parsimonious to an extreme degree. The food was of the sternest and plainest manufacture – Leifr had never tasted such unyielding and flavorless meat in his life – and the ale must have been watered down three times to give it such a flat and colorless quality.

When the cheerless meal was finished, all the dwarfs

took out their pipes. In a few moments, the air reeked with bitter smoke of a greenish color. Then Hjaldr began droning the words of a skald, and the others took it up like a swarm of dispirited bees, marking the time with nodding heads and tapping knives, their eyes turned upward to the wall above Leifr's head. Finally he turned around, unable to bear the curiosity of wondering what they were looking at. Twenty-eight helmets hung there, some of them fearfully dented and smashed in, as a silent reminder of their loss.

When the singing was over, the dwarfs took their leave of their guests and went about their business. Leifr heard horses pass the door at the far end of the hall; somewhere someone started hammering, resounding blows that echoed with patient regularity down the echoing corridors of the underground settlement.

Hjaldr folded his hands, resting his elbows upon the table and glowering at his guests. 'I dare say you've noticed the change in our standards of hospitality,' he began rather truculently.

Thurid made a graceful, deprecating gesture with his hands. 'I've partaken of the most famous hospitality known to all Alfar. This, I assure you, will remain one of the most memorable of meals.'

Gotiskolker glared and kicked him under the table. 'As a scavenger, I've eaten much worse,' he said, 'and felt far more grateful. Once I had to eat my own dog.'

Leifr glared at both of them, wondering how to excuse two such extremes. Apprehensively he looked at Hjaldr, who didn't seem offended in the least.

'We Dvergar are accustomed to saying what we think,' he said. 'Perhaps the next time we meet, it will be under happier circumstances.' He glanced up at the rows of helmets. 'We've all foresworn any but the plainest of food and drink and all the creature comforts until our fallen comrades are avenged. Twenty-eight stout-hearted Dvergar died when Sorkvir took the Grindstone Hall from us. We won't celebrate until we return to our

153

rightful place with honor. Then we shall hang these helmets on the wall and drink to them with the blood of our enemies.'

Feeling the hair rise on his neck, Leifr fervently hoped that he wouldn't be numbered among the enemies of the Dvergar.

'Which brings us to the grindstone again,' Hjaldr went on, his voice stiffening in tone. 'I suppose it does you credit that you wish to make restitution. Whether or not you are able is your concern. Whether or not you are sincere is a Dvergar concern. You might decide to abandon the effort to return our grindstone if the opposition is too severe. Perhaps you are lying to us even now, hoping to escape our vengeance.'

'You are courageous to call me a liar to my face, but not very wise,' Leifr replied.

'I said perhaps, and that isn't the same thing as a direct accusation,' Hjaldr returned. 'It makes no difference what your intentions are, as long as you bring back the grindstone. We have ways of insuring your cooperation.'

'I need the grindstone as badly as you do,' Leifr said, not liking the threatening tone of Hjaldr's words. 'I'll do almost anything to get it, without any threats from the Dvergar. You have hinted that I might be a liar, you doubt my sincerity, and you think I might lose heart before I've succeeded. Perhaps you'd like to wait for someone else to try getting back your precious grindstone.'

'We know you as a traitor and a thief. It remains to be seen if you can be trusted. Your word alone is not enough to convince us.' Hjaldr's baleful eyes gleamed from their deepsunk caverns. 'We want you to return with our grindstone; if you don't return, we want you to suffer for it.'

Thurid leaned forward on his elbows. 'What kind of surety do you want? We don't have any valuables to speak of, and the only prospect we have of getting any is when Sorkvir is dead and we take back the treasure he has stolen from the Ljosalfar of Solvorfirth. Then we could give you a share, perhaps.' He winced as Gotiskolker kicked him forcefully under the table again.

'I think not,' Gotiskolker said. 'A surety must be paid in advance. It need not be in gold or valuable property. Perhaps we could leave you as a surety. If we don't come back, the Dvergar can kill you.'

'That seems feasible,' Hjaldr said, plucking at his nether lip thoughtfully. 'A wizard is worth redeeming, if he's any good at all at magic.'

'Out of the question,' Thurid declared. 'Fridmarr will need my assistance in purifying the Pentacle of evil influences. We could better spare a useless scavenger.'

'Or me.' Ljosa's clear voice dropped in the echoing hall like two pebbles into a silent pool.

'No,' Leifr said. 'I refuse to consider it.'

'Come now, Fridmarr, she'd be well cared for,' Thurid said soothingly. 'She'd be safer here than with us or looking for her relatives in Fjara-strond.'

'No,' Leifr repeated. 'I can't risk her life like that. What if I were slain? These dwarfs would kill her.' He flashed a deadly glare at Hjaldr, and it was all he could do to resist drawing his sword then and there in her defense.

'We wouldn't kill her,' Hjaldr said. 'We will simply keep her until you return or someone else comes to exchange her for the grindstone. As the wizard said, she will be well cared for, although she won't see much daylight. She will be safe here until you return.'

Leifr clenched his fists. 'No. I refuse to agree to it. You'll get your grindstone, but not at such a price.'

Hjaldr leaned back in his gloomy black chair and cast a covert glance around the hall, where plenty of dwarfs seemed to be lingering over insignificant tasks. Their presence was not lost upon Leifr, who began to curse himself for stumbling right onto their doorstep and inviting these villainous dwarfs to capture him.

'I fear,' Hjaldr said ponderously, 'that I can't permit you to leave under any other circumstances. The girl must be left for surety that you will return. I think that she matters more to you than the grindstone.'

Leifr looked at her, half-smothered in her old dark cloak, surrounded by warlike elves and dwarfs and the tools of destruction. She belonged in bright surroundings; there her beauty and radiance would dazzle like a jewel, instead of being locked away with the rest of the dwarfs' treasures, where neither light nor admiring eyes ever intruded.

'I can't leave you here,' Leifr said to her, fighting the sensation that he was being slowly strangled from within, beginning with his heart. He had no need for the carbuncle's promptings.

'I said I would stay,' she said. 'No one is forcing me against my will. I want to do this to help you. The Dvergar will help you if I stay.'

'If you stay, then we all stay,' Leifr declared, rising to his feet to pace restlessly back and forth. 'I hadn't thought when we came here that it was as prisoners. You returned us our weapons, but now I suppose we ought to surrender them.' He unbuckled his sword belt and threw it on the table before Hjaldr with a satisfying crash.

Thurid exchanged a terrified glance with a cynical Gotiskolker, who seemed to be looking on with dark amusement at the exacerbations and antics of the others. Seeing no help from that quarter, Thurid slid out of his seat and tried to reason with Leifr.

'Fridmarr, the reputation of Dvergar prisons is deplorable. Ljosa as a hostage and Ljosa as a prisoner are two vastly different things. You wouldn't want to inflict needless hardship upon her, not to mention the rest of us.'

'Speak for yourself,' Gotiskolker interrupted. 'It can't be much worse than what I've become accustomed to. I'd choose the Dvergar over Sorkvir any day as jailers.'

Leifr rounded on him furiously. 'No one's asking you

to choose. You can desert me any time you want to go. You brought me into this mess and haven't done a whole lot to make it any simpler from the beginning. I wish I'd never found you in those barrows. Now I can't make a decent choice. Whichever way I turn, it all seems wrong. I can't put up Ljosa's life as surety and gamble on her future against my ability to find the grindstone. What do you think the odds are of us fighting our way out of here?'

Gotiskolker looked around the hall, counting dwarfs. 'Eleven of them, three of us who can fight – more or less.' He glanced contemptuously at Thurid. 'Those odds stink, Fridmarr, I wouldn't try it.'

'Neither would I,' Hjaldr rumbled, and the other ten dwarfs shook their heads and tweaked the edges of their swords and axes. Leifr noted the powerful girth of their chests and the bulging muscles of their arms, not to mention the fierce and ready gleam in their eyes when a fight was mentioned.

Leifr cast himself into a chair, stifling a groan of despair. Hjaldr gave his sword a push toward him along the table, saying, 'We don't want anyone as prisoners. All we want is our grindstone back. If you had treated us better in the past, we would be treating you better now. Hroaldsdottir will be safe here and as content as we can make her. All you have to concern yourself with is staying alive and returning the grindstone, and we'll release her. Take your weapon and put it on. You have created these circumstances for yourself, so make the best of them.'

Leifr turned toward Ljosa and saw her nod. Feeling a traitor's anguish, he resigned himself to the totally unacceptable plan.

'All right,' he said resentfully, unable to look at her again. 'We'll do it. But if you don't keep your bargain—'

The magnitude of his threat was too great for mere words, but Hjaldr seemed to read his intentions accurately enough without them. His swarthy features were

157

pale and sober as he extended one huge hand to seal the agreement with a slap of palms with Leifr.

'We shall keep our agreement,' he said. 'When you have the word of a Dvergar, you may as well have gold in your pocket.'

'And when you have his anger,' Gotiskolker added, 'you have an enemy forever.'

Hjaldr stood up, signaling to his attendants. 'You must want to rest, so you can start your journey at daybreak. The lady will be taken to her abode.' He nodded to a couple of dwarfs who led Ljosa away through a side door. She looked back once, fleetingly, and then she was gone, leaving a fierce emptiness in Leifr's soul that seemed to crave some sort of violent action to fill the void. Instead of sleeping, when they were shown their spaces on the platform around the walls, Leifr honed his sword, hand axe, and his knives, cut a new set of boot laces, and went over his saddle and bridle, looking for weak leathers to fix. Thurid slept, and Gotiskolker watched Leifr with obvious irritation.

'Save your energy,' he advised dryly. 'You're going to need it for more important things.'

Leifr favored him with a slow, baleful stare and went back to his restless oiling of his boots. 'Couldn't you have helped me get her out of this?' he demanded. 'Was it all you could do to sit there with a smirk on your face? I don't know anything about dealing with dwarfs.'

'Then you've learned a lesson. You can't beat them at their own game. I don't blame them, considering what you did to them.'

'Me! I didn't do anything to them! I'm not Fridmarr. How could he have been such a fool?'

Gotiskolker smiled wickedly. 'You should know how easy it is. You've done it often enough. What a ridiculous display over Ljosa Hroaldsdottir. Do you love her?'

Leifr grabbed a handful of Gotiskolker's cloak, not at all minding that his fingers were digging into one of the thin shoulders. He glowered at Gotiskolker dangerously.

'I'd fight these sour-minded Dvergar for her until I'd killed them all, and the rest of you could rot with Sorkvir forever. I might do it yet. I can't leave her in this place!' He released his grip and flung himself down on the platform to stare at the fire.

'I urge you to do nothing so foolish,' Gotiskolker said. 'You are on a turning wheel which can't be stopped on a whim. You'll have to see this thing through to the end or perish in the attempt. For Ljosa to be yours one day, you have to finish this journey you've begun.'

Leifr shifted his sinister stare to Gotiskolker and considered him for a long moment. 'Keep reminding me,' he said at last, 'that we are old and dear friends, or I fear I'm going to begin hating you. I wasn't doing that badly back in my own realm. I would have got away from those thief-takers. I could have had a relatively pleasant life as a viking. I might never have known that a wizard like Sorkvir existed.'

Gotiskolker shrugged. 'Then you might never have known that a woman like Ljosa existed either.'

Leifr grunted in reply. Stretching out on the platform, he tried to ignore the brooding presence of Gotiskolker, still sitting and gazing at the meagre fire.

Gotiskolker waited until Leifr seemed to be asleep; then he brought a notched stick from his pouch and began counting the notches. Dissatisfied with the result, he counted again and seemed to find no comfort in his computations. With a gloomy sigh, he glanced around the dwarfs' hall as if he had abandoned all hope. Then he quickly counted the notches again before taking his knife and gouging away one of the marks. Surveying it a moment, he shoved it back into his pouch, as if he didn't care for the looks of the stick with one notch less.

In the morning, Leifr was supplied with not only a map of the Pentacle, but a decent supply of traveling provisions, which he realized must have cut into the limited stores of the dwarfs. Hjaldr accompanied them to the outer doors, where he stopped to give Leifr the

159

map without offering a word of explanation, warning, or assistance.

'Each station is a day's journey apart,' was all he said. 'In the old days, a supplicant could make it back here in five days, if all went well. A number of them were killed along the way or otherwise delayed. I don't expect you soon, considering what you will have to deal with. I wish you luck, however, and I wish to offer you a gift before you depart.'

He drew a soft, doeskin pouch from his pocket and removed from it a neck torque of solid silver, made to look like a multitude of twisting strands forming a single rope.

'This is the best craftsmanship of the Dvergar,' Hjaldr said as he fastened it around Leifr's throat. 'I hope it will bring you luck.'

Leifr touched the two interlocking hooks that fastened it at the base of his throat, astonished that the dwarf had wished to honor him with a gift, when they were not parting on the friendliest of terms.

'I'm honored – although the gift I'm leaving behind is far more valuable, I'm afraid.' He let his voice remain stiff and grim, reminding Hjaldr of his resentment.

The Dverg bowed his head in assent, watching Leifr mount his horse before speaking again. 'The torque will bring you luck and is yours to wear with honor for the rest of your life if you are successful in returning the grindstone. It will assist you in your battle with Sorkvir. But if you prove unfaithful to our agreement, it will be your death. It is obedient to my commands, and I have put it on your neck with a spell so you can't remove it. In forty days, it will begin to shrink, unless I stop the spell; so if you try to evade your duty, you will be choked. And don't attempt to remove it by wizardry, or you may hasten your own demise. Farewell, my friends. I hope I see you returning soon with the grindstone.'

Leifr scarcely believed his own ears. Before he could leap off his horse and grab Hjaldr, the dwarf dived between the doors, and they slammed shut with a thundering boom in Leifr's face. Sensing the futility of attacking that much-besieged and assaulted door, he next tried to pry the hooks of the torque over each other so he could get out of it, but to no avail. The metal might as well have been cast as one piece. He strained at it, grimacing and feeling as if he were already choking.

Gotiskolker sat on his horse watching bleakly. Finally, with an impatient sigh, he picked up the reins and led Leifr's horse over to him.

'Outwitted again,' he said. 'You should know better than to accept a gift from a person who has a low opinion of you. It's bound to be something you don't like or can't use. Let's get going. We can get well along the road to Kerling-tjorn before dark.'

CHAPTER 10

LEIFR glared around at him, still trying to pull the torque apart. 'This is a fine time for your advice,' he snarled. 'You might have warned me.'

'You should have known when you saw what a fine piece of work it was. You saw what supper was like last night. Why would such a pinchfisted miser like Hjaldr want to give you a fortune to hang around your neck? Because he's taken a sudden liking to you?'

Leifr answered with a churlish growl. 'I feel as if it's choking me already,' he gritted. 'He isn't going to give me forty days. It's starting right now.'

'Nonsense. Take your hands out of it and you'll have plenty of breathing room,' Gotiskolker said unsympathetically. 'Just leave it alone and try to forget about it. There's no sense in trying to get it off, if a Dvergar spell is holding it on.'

Thurid tried to bend down to get a look at it, but Leifr aimed a kick at him. 'Get away from it, Thurid, or you might get it started. You're not going to touch it.'

'There's no harm in looking, is there?' Thurid demanded.

'If you have to ask, there probably is,' Leifr snapped. 'I guess there's no sense in asking Hjaldr to change his mind and take this thing off, is there?'

'If you have to ask—' Gotiskolker mimicked.

Thurid turned on him, his staff smoking and his eyes blazing. 'This is a tragedy, you fool, and you sit there laughing. What a heathen you are, Gotiskolker. Don't you realize what a predicament Fridmarr is in? Don't you care in the least what happens to him?'

'You'll grieve if he dies?' Gotiskolker demanded sarcastically.

'Yes, I will,' Thurid replied with dignity.

Gotiskolker snorted softly and muttered something about buffoons and humbug.

'I don't like all this talk about dying,' Leifr protested, grabbing his reins from Gotiskolker and swinging aboard his horse. Taking one last vituperative glance at Hjaldr's doors, he said grimly, 'We won't talk about it for the next thirty-nine days.'

'That suits me,' Gotiskolker answered. 'We'll have won by then. After that, you can talk about anything you wish.'

Leifr recovered the map, forgotten in the confusion. The route they were to take formed a five-pointed star, beginning with a trek directly northeast to a place called Kerling-tjorn. Hjaldr's Grindstone Hall was marked with a large number 1, and Kerling-tjorn with a 2. To his surprise, Luster was the third stop, the place Ljosa had mentioned. Glumly Leifr reflected that she might have been on her way there, if not for his interference. It was straight west of Kerling-tjorn, and the fourth stop was to the southeast, Bjartur. The northmost point was Dokholur, and from there they would have to come back to Hjaldrsholl. Thoughts of what he would say to Hjaldr when they next met sustained him for most of the day.

Using a pendulum, Thurid dowsed the straight way they were supposed to follow. In places, rocks and dirt had been brought to build up the roadway slightly, so it showed as a low green ridge across the valleys, and a series of stone markers on the rocky fellsides. From the word *tjorn,* Leifr knew their destination was a lake, and he looked for it from every rocky prominence in their way. When it was nearly evening and they had still spied no lake, Leifr began to wonder if they had somehow strayed off the track, but Thurid steadfastly assured him that the pendulum did not lie and they were very near to Kerling-tjorn.

The green track led them gently downward, under the sharp noses of some overhanging skarps, and gradually faded away into clumps of rank black tules, hummocks, and grass that seemed too tantalizingly green and lush. At intervals, the way was still marked by stones heaped into cairns, but the stones became fewer as the twilight became deeper, and still there was no sign of the lake.

Leifr halted his horse, who did not like to stand still for long on the quaggy earth, which quivered at each step. Frequently a hoof would strike a thin place in the turf and sink over the fetlock in fetid-smelling mud.

'We ought to go back to solid ground for the night,' Leifr said in disgust. 'We can find the lake tomorrow. I don't want to be in this when it gets dark.'

'We must be on the edge of the lake,' Thurid said hopefully. 'It's a marshy lake I suppose.'

'Let's go back,' Gotiskolker cocked his head, listening. 'It's been twilight for hours. I daresay every troll between here and Hjaldrsholl knows where we are. Those cliffs we passed offered some decent cover.'

Leifr tried to peer over the tules and reeds toward their goal, but he saw only black clumps of rank vegetation and bright green grass, with a few rocky islands that offered no comfort for camping. As he gazed, one of Jolfr's hooves sank through the turf. With difficulty, the horse pulled it out again and showed his opinion of the situation by shaking his head adamantly and starting away in the direction they had come, lashing his long tail angrily at the clouds of horse-eating mosquitoes and gnats.

When they were perhaps halfway back to the start of the mires, Jolfr's ears flicked forward attentively, and he raised his head from his weary slogging to listen; but he was unwilling to stand still on the unsteady ground, so Leifr could not hear anything but the squelch of hooves. Urging a little more speed from his tired horse, Leifr managed to pick up the pace for a short while, but the horses had already jogged along most of the day and weren't eager for more.

Gotiskolker suddenly stopped his horse. 'What's that?' he called. 'Stand still and listen!'

'Trolls,' Thurid said, after hearing a gutteral grunt from a distant fell.

164

'No. Something else.' Gotiskolker threw off his hood to hear better.

A yelping howl sounded from the direction of the cliffs, followed by another.

'Troll-hounds!' Gotiskolker cried.

'Hunting trolls, maybe?' Thurid asked, without much hope. He listened to the eager baying scarcely a mile away, shaking his head in answer to his own question. 'No, and where there are troll-hounds, there are usually Dokkalfar. What a miserable place for a battle.'

Leifr turned Jolfr off the marked track, his eyes upon an island that looked steady enough to offer them some slight protection. Jolfr stretched out his neck, picking each step with caution. The others followed silently, while the chorus of the hounds gathered in volume.

Suddenly Jolfr's front quarters sank almost to his shoulders in soft mud. Leifr jumped off so the horse could struggle free, and the other two horses began backing and turning to go back the way they had come.

'This is no good,' Gotiskolker said. 'We'll have to stay with the track. It's more solid than this. We'll have to go deeper into the mires and hope for solid ground.'

They passed the point where they had turned around before. Dimly, Leifr could see the white marking stone ahead. Wondering how many others were completely obscured by moss or tules, he sent Jolfr plunging ahead, hoping he was taking a straight line.

The baying of the hounds grew louder. Twice Jolfr plunged off the safe track up to his neck in slime. Looking back through the twilight, Leifr could see the dark, moving line of the troll-hounds streaking through the reeds, intent upon their prey.

'What a rotten place to die,' Gotiskolker observed.

'Who's dying?' Thurid snapped. 'I'll stay behind and blast the creatures while you two go ahead. They're not much different from trolls.'

'It's time to make a stand,' Leifr said grimly. 'I'm not leaving anyone behind. Is that understood?'

165

'Perhaps there will be something left of us for the Dokkalfar, when the hounds are done with their work,' Gotiskolker added wryly. 'Sorkvir wouldn't want to miss his opportunity either. By all means, let's stop, put up a good show, and hope that none of us live to be captured. I, for one, do not intend to go back to Gliru-hals.'

They dismounted, and Thurid took the foremost position on the path, gripping his staff and mumbling the words of a spell. Leifr drew his sword and stood behind him, while Gotiskolker armed himself with Bodmarr's ruined sword and stood waiting and listening with stoic calm.

To the left, Leifr heard something splashing quietly toward them. 'What's that?' he demanded sharply. 'Are they slipping up on us?'

Thurid responded with a brilliant flare of alf-light, and several large figures lurking in the marsh beside the path crept warily into the shadows of the reeds.

'Who's there?' Leifr demanded. 'If you're going to fight, come out here and make yourselves known. Brave men don't skulk in the dark to do their murdering.'

The skulkers conferred a moment, then crept out of their hiding places, approaching the path and stopping just before they reached it.

'We're not interested in any murdering,' a hoarse voice said. 'We want to help you escape. If you'll follow us, we'll take you to a safer place, where the hounds can't surround you so easily.'

'Who are you?' Leifr demanded, trying to see them better in the flaring glow, but the dark figures turned their faces away from the light. All he could tell for certain was that there were four of them.

'Never mind who we are. Just let us help you. Enough evil has been done in this cursed place. Come off the path and follow us. We'll lead you to a safer place.'

'No, indeed,' Thurid declared. 'I know who you are. You're nisses, and what you delight in most is leading lost travelers astray so they drown.'

'Be silent, Thurid,' Gotiskolker snapped. 'Perhaps they

will help us, if you don't make them angry.'

'It's your decision,' the niss said, sloshing away a few steps in the marshy water. 'We could help you or we could leave you here for the hounds and the foul creatures hunting with them. Our chances for thwarting Sorkvir's plans are not many, but at least we offered to help.'

The baying of the hounds burst upon them with ferocious clamor as the beasts sighted their prey. Leifr grabbed Jolfr's reins and started forward into the water.

'Help us then,' he said. 'We all know there's nothing to lose. Come on, Thurid, this may be our chance.'

'This will be our doom,' Thurid said, following Gotiskolker reluctantly into the water. 'I know nisses. They'll lead us to some deep spot or some particularly sticky mire and they'll drown us.'

'Be quiet or you'll get drowned for sure, and it might not be a niss that does it,' Gotiskolker retorted. 'I'd like to find out what pleasure they get from it.'

'You probably shall, from a very close point of view,' Thurid answered.

Leifr tried to keep his full attention on the four dark shapes that floated just ahead of him, scarcely breaking the surface of the water with a ripple. The ground underfoot seemed firm enough, although he occasionally stepped into a soft spot and floundered around noisily, trying to regain his footing. Each time, he wondered if Thurid's gloomy prognostication was correct.

The baying of the hounds took on a frustrated note, and the beasts seemed to be running up and down the track searching for the scent. Presently the Dokkalfar caught up to the hounds and stood arguing.

'They've gone off the track,' a voice called in disgust. 'We'll never get them before the bog does.'

'Let the nisses have them.'

'Sorkvir won't be pleased if we don't find them. We'll have to go into the bog after them.'

Leifr saw the four nisses gather, whispering, and he glimpsed long hair streaming over their ragged shoul-

167

ders, speckled with duckweed and bits of peat. Filled with sudden misgivings, he stopped sloshing along, wondering where the nearest patch of solid earth might be. The nisses looked back briefly, then floated on. One called back, 'Either follow us, or stay where you are forever.'

He followed, listening to the shouts of the Dokkalfar all around them. The huntsmen shouted at the hounds and exchanged signals with harsh blasts on horns. Over it all, the hounds filled the night with frustrated howling.

Finally, incredibly, Leifr's feet touched solid rock, and he hauled himself out of the marsh onto an island of stones, trees, and solid turf. Jolfr almost knocked him down in his rush to get out of the water, and Thurid lurched face forward when he trod upon his sodden cloak, but he didn't seem to mind. Putting his arm around a smooth rock, he patted it affectionately, then looked more closely at its surface. Hoisting himself to his feet, he went to investigate the dim, rounded shapes of other stones.

Gotiskolker sat down on a rock to wring himself out. Leifr discarded his wet cloak, keeping his eyes upon the nisses. They crept out of the water and sat down on some nearby rocks, pulling bits of refuse out of their long hair and squeezing the water from their ragged skirts. In the Scipling realm, Leifr had heard that nisses were beautiful ladies who lured travelers into lakes and streams, where they invariably tried to drown them. These nisses, however, were shapeless old women, stout and darkened by years of floating around in the peaty water of the marsh. Their arms were long and spidery, their straggling hair matted from years of disinterest.

Spying him almost immediately, one of the nisses said, 'Well now, here's our laddie. Not much to look at are we, my dear?'

'Come and sit down with us,' invited another, whose hair was mostly white. 'Let's get better acquainted. We don't have guests every evening.'

'Especially of the young and handsome variety,' added another niss with a great, sly cackle.

'Finna,' the eldest reproved, shaking her head. 'She's rather playful, I'm afraid, in spite of everything. I am Eydis, and these are my sisters, Goa, Velaug, and –' She sighed impatiently. ' – Finna. In her day, I'm afraid she was something of a minx.'

'Enchantress, you old harridan,' Finna interrupted. 'I was the most beautiful of us all. It was me they all came to see.'

'Hush, witling. You have little to boast about,' Eydis snapped. 'Especially now. It serves you right, considering what you used to do to those young and handsome travelers who were foolish enough to be swayed by your charms.'

'Why is it,' Velaug asked, turning to Leifr, 'that young men always reach for the thing that's going to hurt them?'

Leifr shrugged. 'I don't know – perhaps the forbidden and dangerous has a certain attraction.'

Finna cackled again. 'Forbidden and dangerous – that's exactly what I used to be. The rest of you were good girls, and where did it get you?'

'Finna, be quiet,' Eydis commanded. 'You are the sort to give all nisses a fearfully bad reputation. A necessary evil, and nothing more, do you hear? Your evil days have been supplanted with a greater evil for us all, so stop your preening and cackling about it, you old goose.'

'Something good may come of all this after all,' Goa said gently. 'I haven't given up hope yet.'

'Something good?' Finna snorted. 'Three good nisses and one bad one, and the travelers always chose the bad one. So what is good? Something you hope for and worship – and never get?'

'Finna!' Eydis rose to her feet, rather stiffly. 'I don't know how we've tolerated you all these years. If we hadn't been under a compulsion to endure your presence, we would have gotten Hjaldr to give you away to a husband who would beat you.'

'But she is our sister,' Velaug said. 'We will take care of our own, even if our own is just a bit mad.'

'Mad! Not I!' Finna declared furiously. 'You've always been jealous, all of you!'

'Let's not quarrel in front of guests,' Goa reproved. 'Besides, we all know Finna was only doing what the Rhbus needed done. Just a predator, you realize, to reduce the numbers of the weak ones trying to make it through the Pentacle. Everyone isn't supposed to make it, of course.'

'Of course,' Leifr echoed faintly, casting an apprehensive glance at Finna, who cackled as if she were reminiscing about the most treasured part of her past.

'It's the weak ones who are the most interesting,' she said, turning her long eyes speculatively in Leifr's direction. 'I wonder if our friend here is strong and single-minded or if he could be tempted away from his objective.'

'Finna, hold your tongue,' Eydis commanded. 'Speaking of objectives, however, reminds me that it has been quite some time since anyone has attempted the Pentacle. Since the removal of the Dvergar grindstone, the power of the Pentacle is not what it used to be.'

Leifr tried to ignore Finna. 'Since you mentioned the grindstone,' he said, 'I hope you'll pardon my curiosity, but I'd like to know if you can tell me anything about it.'

Eydis folded her hands in her lap. 'There's not much to tell. It was stolen from the dwarfs' hail inside the mountain by a young acolyte of Sorkvir. Where he took it no one knows, but since its theft, the Pentacle has lost much of its power. Sorkvir desecrated this place.' She pointed with her chin to the surrounding stones and stumps. Leifr looked around him more closely, and felt his gooseflesh rising as he recognized Sorkvir's spiral mark on the stones behind him. Eydis continued, 'He made an insulting pole with a goat's head on it, and he left its hooves and horns with it to drive our powers astray.'

Thurid came around the side of a large, upright stone in time to hear her. 'Insulting pole, and much more,' he said indignantly. 'He's left his mark on every stone. That's what caused the lake to turn into a swamp and the nisses into old hags. What we need to do is change the influence of this place by getting rid of the spirals, to start with. Then we'll see what we can do to drive off the evil land-spirits and attract some beneficial ones.'

Finna scowled at him and tossed her head with an angry clearing of her throat. 'You talk as if you might be a wizard. I warn you, wizard, if you consider me an evil land-vaettir, I won't be driven out of my home.'

The other nisses rose up uneasily and gathered protectively around their sister with a worried murmur.

'You can't drive Finna out,' Eydis said. 'She is necessary here, you must realize.'

Thurid flapped one hand impatiently. 'No, I don't care about her; she can stay and drown all the foolish idiots she possibly can, since we'll never have a shortage of fools, and those of us of superior intelligence will be grateful to her. What I mean to change here is the course of the magic that flows through this place. It's all going widdershins. We'll bring back the lake. We'll get rid of Sorkvir's influences. We'll put pentacles over those spirals, as soon as it's light enough in the morning.'

The nisses gasped and twittered excitedly among themselves.

'One question,' Finna said in a firm, resounding voice. 'Will you make us beautiful again?'

'Yes, I dare say,' Thurid replied, his eyes dwelling with more interest upon a huge, white stone defaced by a black spiral. 'The nisses are a part of the lake; once it is no longer degenerate, the nisses will be their old selves again.'

'If we survive the night uncaptured,' Gotiskolker

interjected over one shoulder as a fresh burst of howling floated over the swamp.

Velaug and Eydis exchanged a significant glance. Velaug said, 'We shall see to it that no one comes this far into the marsh. We have a few of our old ways left.'

'Rest assured,' Eydis said with a stern glare in the direction of the hunters, 'you won't be disturbed here. Come along, sisters, there's work for us to do.'

In a moment they were all four gone, gliding away with scarcely a ripple and vanishing into the shadows of tules and reeds.

After a semblance of a camp was set up, Thurid drew circles around them, hung amulets on the horses, scratched marks in the earth, and mumbled until Gotiskolker could bear it no longer.

'Will you stop it, you charlatan?' he snapped. 'I don't need any help from you. I saw what a big help you were to Fridmarr in the dwarfs' hall. I think I'd rather get into my own trouble, instead of something you've invented.'

'Suit yourself,' Thurid retorted, 'but I'm not a charlatan, and I urge you not to forget it. How do you think we can purify the Pentacle without my carefully cultivated powers?'

'What makes you think we can do it with them?' Gotiskolker demanded. 'We are by no means in a good position.'

'The nisses are going to help us,' Leifr said. 'I think they like the idea of being beautiful again. Especially Finna.' He chuckled ironically. 'It's hard to believe she ever tempted anyone to his death.'

Gotiskolker shook his head and got up to pace back and forth. 'Their victims' bones fill this swamp. Those nisses can't be trusted, once they get what they want.'

'You speak as if you know,' Thurid replied scornfully. 'What would a scurry scavenger like you know about creatures like these? I've read a great deal about nisses, and I assure you I know exactly how to deal with them.'

When he had stationed himself to stand watch for his

share of the night, Leifr invented the pretext of going to check on the horses, who were not very satisfied with their accommodations for the night. The grass was sparse, and the swamp seemed alive with prowling Dokkalfar and their dim lanterns; barking, baying, and yelping hounds; and the shouts of Dokkalfar who seemed to be lost in the dark murk.

He found Gotiskolker propped against a stone, his face contorted with pain, with his breath coming in gasps. He glared furiously at Leifr's approach and waved him away angrily with his hand.

'Are you all right?' Leifr asked, astonished and concerned.

'No, I'm not all right, you fool,' Gotiskolker snapped, raising his head to glare again. 'Now go away and stop bothering me. Can't I die in peace?'

'What is it, the eitur? Sorkvir said it was going to be a rather unpleasant way to die. There must be something—'

'There's not. Don't worry, I'm sure there's enough time to get you back to your realm.' He blotted his forehead with a ragged edge of his cloak. 'Now are you satisfied?'

Leifr went back to his bed among the rocks after his turn as guard and tried to compose himself for sleep. With the sounds that were coming out of the swamp, sleep seemed an impossibility. He heard screams for help, interspersed with the mournful howling of the hounds. Once he heard Finna's eerie laugh not far away, and something about it made his scalp crawl. The carbuncle, he had discovered, was able to treat him to a riveting assortment of Fridmarr's memories – or nightmares – if he permitted it to infiltrate his thoughts. The nisses seemed friendly, but the carbuncle's mysterious influence forbade him from becoming too trusting.

In the morning, Thurid began sorting gleefully through his rune sticks long before sunrise, like a large rat reorganizing its nest. Avoiding him, Leifr went in search of Gotiskolker, whom he discovered looking as ill as before, sitting on a rocky point overlooking the worst of the swamp.

'About that carbuncle,' Leifr began, but Gotiskolker turned toward him with a warning hiss.

'Not so loud,' he whispered. 'You don't know who could be listening.'

Leifr lowered his voice. 'I've figured out that sooner or later the stone will be of no use to me. Fridmarr must have removed it before he took the eitur. What I wonder about is what's going to happen when I reach the same point. The stone will go blank when it reaches the end of its life with Fridmarr, will it not?'

'You won't feel as if you've been there before, but neither will you be completely alone,' Gotiskolker replied a shade impatiently. 'Thousands of years of Ljosalfar knowledge is available to you, if you care to seek for it. You won't be left entirely defenseless.'

'Cold comfort,' Leifr grumbled. 'It never shows me anything pleasant.'

'There might be worse horrors yet, beyond the point where Fridmarr parted company with it,' Gotiskolker said.

Leifr gazed around at the still, dark pools and clumps of secretively whispering reeds and grasses. 'The swamp seems quiet now. I wonder what the nisses did with the Dokkalfar.'

'Misled and mired them,' Gotiskolker said, hobbling toward the horses. 'You heard their voices. Nisses are excellent mimics. They call out in your friend's voice, leading you into the deepest, stickiest mires. I heard your own voice out there, Fridmarr, luring the Dokkalfar to their destruction.'

Thurid looked up a moment from his rune sticks, odd devices, and the random objects that assisted him in his spells. 'I dare say there are still quite a few Dokkalfar lurking about. I wouldn't get careless, if I were you.'

'But since you're not him, you'll be as careless as you

please,' Gotiskolker added. 'What a fine target you make from the edge of the willows over there!'

Glancing toward the willows in question, Leifr saw something moving stealthily through their silvery shadows. Crouching quickly behind a rock, he motioned to Thurid and Gotiskolker warningly. The dark forms slipped into the water without a sound, their presence betrayed only by a slight, rippling swell of the scummy water.

Suddenly, with a splash, a dark head parted the water almost at Leifr's feet, startling him more than he cared to admit, until he recognized Eydis. She combed her lank locks out of her face with her fingers as her sisters surfaced around her.

'Your enemies,' Eydis reported, 'are all put to rout.'

'At least, the ones who were able to get away,' Finna added with her strange laugh. 'It wasn't as exciting as the old days, of course.'

'We are in your debt,' Leifr replied hastily, not liking her looks any better in daylight than he had in the dim moonlight.

Like an oversized lizard, she hauled herself out of the marsh deliberately and sat down on a rock where she could comfortably stare at Leifr with her sinister, slanted eyes. 'It's not a good thing to be indebted to a niss,' she said, casually wringing out a large, tattered portion of her gown.

'As usual, your manners are bad, Finna.' Eydis said disapprovingly as she seated herself nearby. 'For us, it was a small accomplishment. Breaking Sorkvir's influence will be a much more difficult task for them.'

Thurid thrust his rune sticks into his satchel and struck a haughty pose with his staff in hand and his ragged cloak billowing importantly around him. 'No small task, indeed, my good lady, but if anyone should ask you who did it, you may tell them it was Thurid of Dallir.'

Eydis inclined her head. 'Whether you succeed remains to be seen,' she cautioned.

'Who are your companions, wizard?' Finna inquired, darting her slanted eyes sidewise at Leifr and smiling slyly.

Sensing the challenge in her tone, Leifr stepped forward to confront her. 'My name is Fridmarr Fridmundrsson, and you may tell anyone who asks that I have returned.'

'Fridmarr Fridmundrsson!' The nisses all gasped and stared a moment at one another in shock. Then they rose up in an enraged body and fell upon Leifr with their fists, pounding and clawing at him and screeching horrible invectives.

CHAPTER 11

FORTUNATELY for Leifr, they had no weapons and they were rather awkward on dry land, due to the amphibious development of their feet into something more like fins or flippers, rather than feet meant to be walked upon. He rolled out of their grasp, after the initial shock of their unexpected assault, and leaped to his feet.

'Get him! The traitor!' Finna snorted breathlessly.

'Wait! Let me explain!' Leifr protested.

'We should have let the Dokkalfar have him,' Velaug said in disgust.

'I knew it was too good to be true,' Goa sighed. 'The one man who says he will rescue us and our lake is the same rogue who caused our misfortune. Bitter irony!'

'He won't escape from us a second time,' Eydis said.

Leifr raked his hair out of his eyes and composed his rumpled clothing. Curse Fridmarr! Wherever he went, he left a trail of woe and destruction.

'Give me a chance to speak for myself. I'm sorry about what happened back then,' he began, but the nisses hissed and spat at him furiously.

Gripping his staff, Thurid stepped forward. 'Now listen to me, you nisses. Fridmarr has suffered plenty for his crimes. He's doing his best to make retribution to everyone who was injured in any way. He's going to use Bodmarr's sword to kill Sorkvir, if he can find the grindstone to sharpen it on. We're going to purify this Pentacle of Sorkvir's evil influences, whether we have your assistance and gratitude or not. I should think that taking your own revenge upon him now is a shortsighted mistake on your part. You might be wallowing around in this muck forever, if you make him fail now.'

The nisses scowled at Leifr, whispering among themselves. Finally the others pushed Goa forward to speak. Leifr faced her hopefully, remembering that she had gotten in the fewest wallops of any of the sisters.

'You betrayed us to Sorkvir,' she said. 'It's hard for us to forgive your treachery. We showed you this place, our source of youth and all our power, then you gave our secret to Sorkvir. How could you do such a thing to friends?'

Leifr wiped his forehead, glancing at Thurid and Gotiskolker for help. 'It was against my will,' he said, an idea struggling to the light in the dark welter of his racing mind. 'It was a drug Sorkvir gave me that robbed me of my own will. It was beyond my powers to resist.'

Gotiskolker gave him a startled, approving nod.

Eydis eyed him silently, while the other nisses whispered excitedly. 'The eitur,' she said. 'Then you will die from it. I am sorry to hear it. At least we will have something good to remember you by. Go on with your work. We won't hinder you. How may we be of assistance?'

Leifr stifled a huge sigh of relief and beckoned to Thurid. 'This wizard will do all the work. You'll have to ask him how you can help.'

Thurid's eyes sparkled gloatingly. 'You can tell me all about the stones that were here. Are any missing? Did Sorkvir bring any new ones? Where are the rest of the small stones that belong on the altar stone?'

In the ensuing discussion, Leifr found himself blissfully ignored. Finding a level, mossy place that wasn't wet, he stretched out for a nap while Thurid and the nisses went searching for lost stones, markers, and etchings. Gotiskolker squatted nearby, watchful and uncommunicative as usual. Something about his brooding silence prompted Leifr to ask suddenly, 'What did Eydis mean about the eitur? Are you really going to die from it?'

Gotiskolker shot him a narrow glance. 'I'll die from

178

the lack of it, one day, since I don't intend to ask Sorkvir for any more of his poison.'

'Was Fridmarr addicted to the eitur? I think it would explain some of his treacherous behavior.'

Gotiskolker snorted disgustedly. 'Hurry up and go to sleep, if that's what you're going to do. None of us may have much rest later.'

Thurid poked and prodded and dowsed over most of the island. Whenever he came too near the central altar with its attendant standing stones, the pendulum lashed around in a fury, instead of behaving properly. He knew the war between the influences was on when the sky darkened for a storm, all the metal that he chanced to touch spat sparks at him, and the hairs on his head stood out rigid and quivering with unseen energies. Retreating carefully, Thurid found that the only safe place on the island was the spot where they had spent the night. He renewed his circles scratched in the earth, keeping one eye all the while upon the stone circle above, on the crest of the island.

'We're going to have some bad weather,' he said to Leifr and Gotiskolker. 'Stay inside these rings and nothing too dreadful should happen to you.' He glanced up at the boiling, purple clouds above, already veiling the tops of the fells in coils of mist. A chill wind rattled the rank clumps of vegetation in the marsh, and the nisses shivered uneasily and silently slipped into the water, turning their heads warily in all directions.

'That's Sorkvir's influence,' Eydis called nervously. 'He won't like your poking around among those stones.'

'He shouldn't,' Thurid replied. He chuckled, rubbing a rune wand across his palm. 'I've always been a believer in striking the first blow. Stay back, all of you, no matter what happens.' With a last, jaunty salute, he started away up the hill.

Leifr watched him for a moment, noting how the dark cloud had settled among the standing stones, as if it were waiting for Thurid.

179

'I don't like letting him go up there alone,' he said to Gotiskolker, who was checking the picket pins for the horses yet another time.

Gotiskolker replied morosely, 'There's nothing we can do to help him. You're a Scipling with no trained powers, and I'm an Alfar who has lost his. A fine pair we'd be.' He gazed after Thurid for a considerable time, gnawing on his thumbnail worriedly. Finally he said, 'Come on, we're going up there with him. I can't stand waiting down here.'

Following Gotiskolker into the deepening brume, Leifr had the strong impression that he was contributing to his own destruction by being where he was. Nor was Thurid glad to see them. Glowering mightily, he hastily scratched a large pentacle on the ground, saying, 'What a pair of fools! Stand inside this mark and don't stir out of it, if you value your lives. You should have an excellent vantage point for witnessing my triumph.'

Raising his staff with a flourish, Thurid glanced both ways, then spoke the words of his spell in a commanding shout. Red flame burst from the end of his staff, striking one of the stones with a powerful explosion. Hastily Thurid amended his spell, etching a thin red line across the face of the blackened stone; down, then up to form the top point of the star, down again, then across to complete it.

'All right, Sorkvir, what are you going to do about that?' he roared into the wind, with a huge, boastful laugh.

The clouds swirled threateningly, gathering into an immense, indistinct mass towering over the highest of the standing stones. A white blast of wind seared the earth with a deadly cold gale. Leifr instinctively flattened himself on the ground, noting as he did so that everything was frozen white except the star Thurid had sketched. Looking up again, he saw a giant figure standing astride the hilltop, scything the air with a gleaming sword that appeared to be made of ice. Snow

180

and ice crystals swirled in the cold breath of the creature, and its eyes burned with a blue glow in its frost-wreathed countenance. The shifting glance fell upon Thurid, and a glittering bolt of ice shattered against Thurid's upraised forearms, as if it had struck an invisible shield. Thurid staggered back, almost to the edge of the pentacle he stood within, but he quickly recovered and darted a fiery bolt of his own at the frost giant. It smashed against the giant's icy shield into a thousand brilliant sparks with a screaming hiss.

Thurid sent a pencil of fire toward the second stone, etching half the pentacle before the frost giant retaliated with an icy gust of wind that almost carried Thurid off his feet. He dropped to one knee, shielding his face with his flapping cloak until he could summon a fire bolt. With a fiery roar, it struck the ground in front of the giant and splintered into smaller bolts, one of which pierced the giant's lower leg. With a howl, the frost giant strode forward, swinging its monstrous weapon, its eyes darting ice bolts in all directions. Several shattered on the ground outside Leifr's pentacle into showers of deadly splinters, but all that reached Leifr and Gotiskolker was ice water.

Again Thurid blasted the standing stone, hastily finishing the outline of the pentacle before directing another bolt at the frost giant. It struck with a dazzling burst of flames on the giant's shield, and the apparition crouched defensively, darting another bolt that screamed wide over his target and exploded somewhere in the swamp.

Thurid directed his powers again toward one of the standing stones, burning the sign of the pentacle over the black spiral. The frost giant retreated with a grumbling roar from the brilliance of Thurid's fire, which was concentrated into a single, dazzling fireball at the end of his staff, blazing more intensely than any alf-light Leifr had ever seen him conjure before. He averted his eyes and still saw greenish flares superimposed over everything he looked at. Gotiskolker buried his face in his cloak and hugged the ground as the frost giant summoned another mighty gale of icy wind and driving ice crystals.

The alf-light blurred under the assault, but it kept burning brightly until the gale subsided. The giant retreated, still darting ice bolts and leaking ice water in a torrent from the wounded leg. Thurid abandoned his pentacle and dashed after the frost giant, disappearing into the circle of tall stones. In a moment, a thunderous explosion shook the earth, and the frost giant vanished into the clouds with a windy bellow. All traces of the icy wind dissipated, and the dark clouds seemed to evaporate, letting the sunlight straggle through the ragged intervals of cloud.

In the long ensuing silence, Leifr stared questioningly at Gotiskolker, who lay in a huddled heap, listening intently.

'We'd better go look,' Leifr whispered.

Warily they crept out of the pentacle and skirted the standing stones, keeping a healthy distance. Three of the stones still smoked, glowing red and molten in a few spots yet. The ground gleamed with cold, wet spume, and a few fragments of ice glittered among the stones, melting quickly. When Leifr stooped to retrieve a piece, Gotiskolker reprimanded him sharply. 'Don't touch that hateful stuff. It burns forever.'

They found Thurid lying on his face in the mud, his arms around a loaf-sized stone marked with a spiral.

'Thurid!' Leifr gasped, reaching him in two strides.

Thurid's eyes opened and he smiled faintly. 'He almost got me that time, but I got him dead center with a fire bolt. Help me up, won't you?'

'Are you hurt?' Leifr could see no evidence of damage except traces of white frost crystals in the folds of his cloak, which seemed slightly frozen.

Thurid attempted to dust himself off. 'All I need is a little rest.' He prodded the stone he had been embracing. 'Carry this up to the altar stone, Fridmarr. I've been searching all day for this stone. It's the last of the ones we couldn't find.'

'I don't like all these spirals,' Leifr said, after he had placed the stone beside the altar. 'You're not trying to tamper with Sorkvir's own powers, are you, Thurid?'

'No, indeed. These marks were made long before Sorkvir graced this land with his vile presence.' Thurid ran his hands over the rows of stones, fifteen in all, ranging from the size of an egg to the size of a loaf of bread. 'When we get them in the right sequence, we can generate power in this ring.' His moving hand stopped, and he exchanged two stones' positions, his eyes darting keenly over the complete assembly. 'The spiral is a very old symbol, which Sorkvir had no business borrowing for his own evil purposes.' He switched another pair of stones and was rewarded with a burst of sparks. Shaking his fingers, he tried another combination of rocks and holes.

The evening light changed to a sickly, greenish glow, and a cold wind sprang up, thrashing around in the tules and bull-rushes resentfully and thrusting at the standing stones. Shivering, Leifr pulled up his hood and glanced quickly around at the surrounding marshlands, not liking the eerie cast of the light. Gotiskolker nudged him, pointing with a jerk of his chin to the distant edge of the swamp. A long, dark line moved along slowly and purposefully, taking a trajectory that would lead them indirectly to the island.

'Dokkalfar,' Leifr muttered.

Gotiskolker nodded. 'This time they won't be so easily fooled.'

Leifr watched Thurid a moment, standing at the altar with his head thrown back and his eyes closed in an ecstasy of concentration.

'Where are the nisses?' he asked, and Gotiskolker shrugged for an answer. 'They're not showing much faith in Thurid if they've gone into hiding.'

'They're not alone.' Gotiskolker faced the marsh, watching a pair of deer leaping through the hummocks in full flight. In a moment, a fox flashed from its cover in a thicket and vanished among the tall grasses. 'Something is coming which none of them wants to face.'

'Sorkvir,' Leifr said flatly.

After a moment of anxiously watching the marsh creatures slipping away to hide, Leifr turned back to Thurid, who still puzzled over the exact arrangement of the stones in the sockets. With one combination, the standing stones seemed to tremble, and the air was filled with crackling and sputtering. Thurid's face brightened, and he rubbed his hands together in anticipation.

'I think I've hit upon the proper sequence,' he called. 'Stay back from the stones, but don't stray outside the circle. We're safe inside here, I think.'

'Safe from arrows and spears, I hope,' Gotiskolker said. 'We've got a mob of Dokkalfar on the way, and Sorkvir must be with them. You'll have to hold them off somehow.'

Thurid ran his hands over the rows of stones, tracing each spiral with his finger. 'I'm going to turn the stones against Sorkvir,' he said. 'Once the stones are turned, Sorkvir will never be able to return here, and his power will be broken.' He passed his hands over the stones again, and a distinct rumble came from the depths of the earth far beneath the swamp. 'I'm ready to begin. You two can help by staying absolutely quiet and meditating upon the inner reserves of power that conjoin us with the influence of the Rhbus.'

Thurid passed his hands over the stones and began in a loud voice, 'I am turning the stones against Sorkvir of Gliru-hals. May all the land-vaettir rise up against Sorkvir and his house and bring him misfortune. May his powers fail, may his springs turn to poison, and may the earth be blighted to his touch. I am turning the stones against Sorkvir of Gliru-hals. May all the land-vaettir—' He droned the words over and over, while the standing stones grumbled in their sockets and the air crackled with energy.

Leifr eyed the stones uneasily, noting that the bases glowed dull red, and the nearby grass was slowly turning black, forming wide rings around each stone.

'It looks as if it's going to work,' Gotiskolker whispered in amazement.

The sky still gleamed with the harsh, green light, deepening to cobalt at the zenith. The marsh disappeared into shadows and silence, broken only by the infrequent yelp of the troll-hounds and the distant mutter of Dokkalfar voices. Inside the stone ring, the objects at ground level were bathed in red light from the steady glow of the stones, interspersed with sparks that leaped from Thurid's fingers. Low and hoarse, his voice chanted on with deadly intensity, hypnotic in its monotony.

'There they are,' Gotiskolker whispered, pointing with his shoulder toward the edge of the marsh.

The eyes of the hounds gleamed with the light from the circle. For a while, they milled around indecisively, then they spread out along the far edge of the marsh.

'I am turning the stones against Sorkvir of Gliru-hals,' Thurid whispered, his voice almost gone, his sharp features lurid in the red light. Then the sound of his words was lost in the sudden, hissing roar of an ice bolt arcing up from the marsh and shattering overhead with a thunderous explosion.

'It's done,' Thurid croaked, collapsing on the altar among the staring stones. 'This place is no longer Sorkvir's domain.'

More ice bolts exploded overhead, showering them with harmless raindrops. Thurid leaned on his staff, still weakened by his effort, but his expression was one of great satisfaction.

Then Sorkvir in his human form, with Raudbjorn skulking along in his wake, rode his horse from the mists of the swamp to the edge of the water, his staff trailing greenish vapor. He stood and stared across at Thurid, Leifr, and Gotiskolker.

'Thurid, you've crossed me again,' he rumbled in a tone of menace. 'My patience wears thin. Give me Fridmarr, and I shall let you escape from Solvorfirth.'

Thurid's nostrils flared as he stepped forward. 'Never, I say. Your offer is an insult to my honor. You won't dismiss me so easily when we obtain the grindstone.'

'The grindstone! You'll never find it, you fools!' Sorkvir laughed, raising his staff. An ice bolt thundered across the marsh, shattering in mid-air against Thurid's counterspell.

Raudbjorn started forward, swinging his halberd and mouthing threats, but Sorkvir called him back.

'I'd like to see him come across,' Leifr said.

'I'll make a whale blubber lamp out of him, if he does,' Thurid said with a dire chuckle. 'They don't suspect what power I have here at my fingertips.'

Steadying himself by leaning against the altar, he pointed his staff in the direction of Sorkvir and Raudbjorn and uttered a spell. At once the marsh was bathed in blinding white light. The Dokkalfar threw up their hands to protect their faces, but the brilliance melted their hands before their eyes. With despairing shrieks, they crumpled, reduced to nothing but black puddles.

The beam raked over Raudbjorn with no effect except to blind him temporarily, sending him staggering away into the swamp with plaintive bellows for help. The remaining Dokkalfar wasted no time with foolish heroics; they took to their individual heels and left Raudbjorn to his fate. The troll-hounds slunk away, wincing at the painful glare. There was no trace of Sorkvir. In a few moments all that remained of Sorkvir's advancing army were dark spots on the ground and heaps of empty clothing and armor.

Throughout the rest of the night, the marsh rustled with uneasy footsteps and whispering voices, interspersed at irregular intervals by shouting. Unable to

186

sleep, Leifr wrapped his cloak around him and sat down near the altar stone. Gotiskolker rested against a stone just inside the ring of standing stones, while Thurid spent most of the night pacing restlessly from the altar to each of the upright stones. The standing stones still radiated heat from their bases, which felt good to Leifr during the cool, misty night.

'Where is Sorkvir?' Thurid at last exclaimed in exasperation, when the pale glow in the east could no longer be denied. 'I've got the power now to destroy him. Why doesn't he attack?'

Gotiskolker grunted, 'He probably went home and slept peacefully, knowing he has nothing to fear from you. It's Fridmarr who will destroy him with the powers of the Dvergar woven into that sword. If you could kill him with vanity, I dare say he might have something to worry about, since I have seen few engines of destruction half as large as your pride, Thurid.'

'The voice of envy,' Thurid sniffed, averting his gaze after a scathing survey of Gotiskolker's ragged attire. 'One day I'll be a member of the Fire Wizards' Guild, and a lot of people will be glad to know me then. Including you.'

'I doubt it.' Gotiskolker carved another notch out of his calendar stick and shoved it into his pouch without counting the remaining notches.

While they argued, Leifr listened with only half an ear, trying to identify an unfamiliar sound that chattered softly in the chill air, seeming to come from all around him. As the light increased steadily to dim morning, he got up and began to investigate.

It was the sound of running water, Leifr realized, that had tantalized him for so long during the night. Incredulous, he followed the sound around the rocky edge of the island and discovered a spring cascading down the stones into the marsh water below. Farther beyond, he found another spring pouring clear, bright water into a sludgy pool, and the four nisses were there, bathing in the

187

showering water or sitting on the rocks to dry their hair in the sun.

At first Leifr was certain they were four different nisses, much younger nisses with long, shining hair of gold and copper. Their voices were young and mirthful as they bathed in the waterfall and frolicked in the pool. By degrees, it dawned upon him that Thurid's stone-turning had rejuvenated the springs that had once fed the lake, and the nisses also had been rejuvenated, as Thurid had promised. With the springs flowing again, the rank marshlands would soon be covered by clear water. At last, something had worked out the way they had planned.

CHAPTER 12

SEEING him, the nisses swarm across the pool, their bright hair mingling with the moss and duckweed like rays of sunlight. Seldom had Leifr seen women so fair and radiant; their beauty was the untrammeled beauty of wild things, unassisted by studied arts and unembellished by fine jewels or sumptuous clothing. They wore simple gowns fastened at the shoulder, made of a fabric that seemed to repel the water like fish scales or duck feathers.

'Thurid's magic has rescued us,' Eydis greeted him, recognizable only by her solemn air of leadership as the eldest of the sisters. 'The springs are flowing again and soon our beautiful lake will cover this swamp. Our days of misery and bondage are over. We owe our gratitude to you and Thurid. I wish our means of repayment were as great as out debt to you, but we have little to offer, except safe passage out of the swamp – '

'And ourselves,' Finna added with her chilling chuckle, tossing her damp, coppery tresses. Of all the nisses, she possessed the greatest beauty, with dark, flaring brows arching over slanting green eyes, wide cheekbones, and full lips that pouted with a soft, secret smile.

She continued, 'Choose one of us, Fridmarr. Nisses make good wives, once you take them away from their water and keep them from it. The only trouble is their feet, which will persist in looking more like big fins, but that's easy enough to hide.'

'Finna! Be silent!' Eydis commanded, seconded by the other sisters with devastating frowns.

Leifr felt the enchantment of Finna's green eyes and knew how easy it would be to forget all caution and to allow himself to be trapped. With difficulty, he reminded himself of the other adventurers who had forsaken all care and abandoned themselves to Finna's wiles, only to die for it.

'Is it true?' he asked Eydis, tearing his gaze away from Finna's. 'Can a niss be happy away from her lake, once she is taken away by someone?'

'She may be taken away, yes, and made into a wife who will serve you diligently, but happy—' Eydis paused, and the nisses looked wistful a moment, except for Finna, who smiled connivingly.

'I'd be happy,' she said sweetly. 'I'd be glad to leave with you, Fridmarr. You'd never regret it for a moment.'

Velaug gave her a small shove while she was simpering her prettiest. 'She kills them quickly, so it's true they don't experience much regret. Don't take her, Fridmarr; you know what she is. I'm not the prettiest, but at least I'm sensible. I know I'd make a very practical and thrifty housewife.'

Finna's simper turned to an enraged scowl. 'Sensible! Practical! Thrifty! Who cares for all that? A man wants something to look at, not a face like a toad's!'

'Finna! That's enough from you,' Eydis interrupted, giving Finna's hair a good hard yank. 'A man doesn't want a temper, either – even if you were willing to leave the lake and forsake all your evil ways, which I doubt. You are far too lazy, besides.'

Finna retired in defeat, swimming away with murderous scowls over her shoulders at her sisters.

'You'll have to pardon her,' Goa said. 'She can't help being as she is. We are used to forgiving her, since everyone must accept a certain amount of danger in this life. Perhaps Finna is not happy with her fate, either.'

'Well spoken, Goa,' Eydis said. Turning to Leifr she added, 'You couldn't go far wrong to choose Goa. You'd never hear a harsh word from her lips.'

Goa paled under such praise. She murmured, 'I'll accept whatever lot life deals me. One must expect changes.'

190

Leifr took a deep breath, aware that he must tread with utmost care or he might offend the nisses into retaliatory anger. With a regretful sigh, he began, 'I wish that I had the freedom to choose among you, but another's life hangs upon my ability to restore the Pentacle to its former power. I wear this torque as a constant reminder of her in her imprisonment. May I die a miserable death by choking if I allow her to remain without her freedom.'

Eydis and the others nodded their heads in approval, their expressions thoughtful and cautious.

'I'm glad to see you have some honor,' Eydis said. 'Is your heart quite taken up by her, then?'

'Quite,' Leifr replied, with a rather gloomy sigh.

'Ah! You seem sad,' Velaug said. 'Doesn't she return your affection?'

'I fear not,' Leifr answered. 'Not yet, but I haven't given up hope entirely.'

'Well, if she doesn't come to her senses, you must come back to Kerling-tjorn and choose one of us for your wife,' Eydis said. 'We owe you a great debt. What is the name of this haughty creature you are devoted to, perhaps unworthily?'

'Ljosa Hroaldsdottir. You may have heard of her.'

'Yes, I believe she's reputed to be something of a beauty,' Eydis said. 'Although I've never seen her, I'm sure her looks can't compare even to poor, practical Velaug, with that crooked place in her nose. We nisses have claimed almost all of the beauty among women, and there's precious little left over for the rest of them.'

Leifr sighed uncomfortably. 'I never knew about the nisses when I made that oath, or perhaps—' He shrugged eloquently.

'Never knew? Of course you did,' Eydis snapped. 'You were here when Sorkvir corrupted the stone circle and stopped the springs. You saw us then.'

Leifr rubbed his sweaty palms on his knees. 'I meant that I couldn't imagine taking a niss for a wife then, I was

191

so caught up in Sorkvir's evil influence. I had no thought for anything but Sorkvir's eitur.'

'Eitur!' The nisses all recoiled from him in shock. After a long moment, they shook their heads slightly and made sympathetic clucks and murmurs.

'We are saddened to hear of your addiction,' Eydis said. 'He has let you live a long time since you escaped from him. Still, you don't appear to be dying just yet. How long can you go without a dose of his poison?'

Leifr shook his head and got to his feet. 'Not very long,' he said absently, thinking of Gotiskolker and his notched stick suddenly, with a new and alarming insight. Scowling, he glanced over his shoulder toward the camp. 'If you'll forgive me, I think I want to check on Gotiskolker. He wasn't feeling well after the battle last night. I thank you again for your offers. I think you see now that it makes no sense to take away one of the nisses, when I have so little time left to live. Enough to restore the Pentacle and free Ljosa, and little more.'

'We're sorry to hear it,' the nisses murmured. 'We wish you good luck, Fridmarr.'

'I'll need it,' he responded ruefully. 'We'll be on our way today, if all the springs are working now.'

'They are,' Eydis said. 'We'll mark the way out of the swamp for you. Watch for the white scraps of cloth tied to the bushes and trees. Walk in a straight line between them and you won't come to any more grief. Farewell and good luck, Fridmarr.'

He waved, and they slipped into the water and started to swim away, scarcely rippling the weedy surface of the pool.

Eydis called out to him as he was turning to leave, and she came gliding back to the rocks at his feet, leaving her sisters to go ahead without her.

'Just out of curiosity,' she said, 'which of us appealed to you the most? So few escape from Finna. It will help settle any future quarrels among us.'

'If I were free to choose,' Leifr began, thinking fast, 'I

would have chosen you, Eydis. But of course the others could never keep Finna under control as well as you do, so perhaps it is all for the best.'

Eydis smiled. For a moment, Leifr felt regretful, but the regret did not last very long. She waved and slipped under the water. The last he saw of her was a pair of large fins vanishing under the bright green duckweed, and he silently agreed that it would be difficult to conceal the fact that one's wife, however beautiful, had fins for feet.

Thurid was nowhere in sight when Leifr returned to the camp. Gotiskolker glanced up morosely from a cup of steaming tea and silently nodded toward the pot.

'Where's Thurid?' Leifr helped himself to the tea and a piece of bread so dry that soaking in the tea was the only way to render it even remotely edible.

Gotiskolker shrugged one shoulder. 'Looking for the nisses, I suppose. Or maybe another frost giant. He's got a fearfully high opinion of himself, after yesterday.'

'Maybe he deserves a small portion of it,' Leifr said. 'He's done wonders, since I first met him.'

'It won't last.' Gotiskolker spat. 'He's burning himself up too fast. There won't be anything left of him, unless he learns to hoard his powers better.'

Leifr bolted the last of the soggy bread, watching his companion closely. Never too healthy-looking, Gotiskolker looked a little worse than usual – sunken eyes, withered skin much defaced by scars, and very little flesh clinging to his prominent bones.

'You look like the next feast for the ravens,' Leifr observed. 'Isn't there any way to recover from the effects of Sorkvir's eitur?'

Gotiskolker hoisted one eyebrow, much offended. 'It's been a long time since I prided myself upon my personal beauty, and I'm terribly sorry if my appearance doesn't delight you. But if you don't like the way I look, you can go sit somewhere else.' He turned his back pointedly and pulled his hood over his head.

'That's not what I said,' Leifr told the shoulder blades that poked sharply out of Gotiskolker's back. 'I don't like to think about you dying in thirty-seven days.'

'Thirty-six,' Gotiskolker amended, 'and I don't mind it a bit. At least you won't be there to harass me any longer. Why are Sciplings so fond of questioning everything? If I'd known you were such an inquisitive breed, I would have left you for those thief-takers to find.'

'I don't want you to die,' Leifr said bluntly.

Gotiskolker risked a sharp peek at him around the edge of his hood. 'I've tried to make this adventure as unpleasant as I could,' he said in exasperation. 'Why on earth could you possibly feel the least bit of sorrow at my demise? Look at all the grief and struggle I've caused you. I might even cause your death, thanks to that torque Hjaldr put around you neck. I haven't been a friend to your welfare, Leifr.'

'Why does the grindstone and Sorkvir matter so much to you? You aren't going to live long enough to enjoy the gold we recover. The gold never was the reason, was it?'

'Questions, always questions,' Gotiskolker muttered, with another suspicious glance at Leifr. 'Nobody else dared to challenge Sorkvir, so I had to. I have nothing to lose except my worthless life and I have an old score to settle for Fridmarr. There now, is that a good enough answer? I hope so, because that's the only one you're going to get.' After a long pause, Leifr thought he heard him mutter to himself, 'For now.'

Unsure he had heard anything, Leifr gathered up his saddle and his possessions and went to find his horse. The enigma of Fridmarr and Gotiskolker tormented him with the knowledge that he had come this far and spent all this time and he still knew very little about the truth behind the plot that had ensnared him.

After he had saddled his horse, he untethered the other animals and led them all back toward the camp, anxious to get under way out of the swamp. The water level on the edges of the island seemed a little higher to

Leifr's uneasy eye; the longer they delayed the higher the water would get, making their passage much more difficult.

Taking a shortcut past the jumble of mossy tree trunks, he saw Thurid perched on one of the trees, leaning over rather precariously to look into one of the dark, slimy pools beneath. His staff and satchel lay on the ground behind him, the first time Leifr had ever seen them out of Thurid's immediate reach. As Leifr came closer, he heard Thurid talking to himself, which was not unremarkable for a wizard to do; but what chilled Leifr's blood was the sound of Finna's eerie chuckle, self-satisfied and deadly. Leifr abandoned all pretext of minding his own business and leaped from a mossy trunk toward Thurid.

Thurid sat with his bare feet paddling gingerly in the green water. Beside him sat Finna with her arms twined around him and her head resting on his shoulder. Her green eyes glittered venomously at the sight of Leifr, and she smiled her secret, seductive smile.

'Thurid, I've brought the horses,' Leifr said sharply. 'It's time we were leaving, before the water gets too high.'

'We've got hours before the water rises an inch,' Thurid said, flushing an angry red. 'I was right in the middle of an important discussion with Finna when you came barging in so rudely. Now just go away. You had your chance to choose among the nisses and you wasted your opportunity.'

'Thurid, you fool, she doesn't intend to be your wife. All she wants is to entice you into the water so she can kill you. She's done it countless of times to unwary travelers.'

'That's an evil lie,' Finna protested. 'Don't believe him, he's only envious.'

Thoroughly mesmerized, Thurid glared at Leifr as if he were a total stranger. 'It sounds to me as if you want to make a fight of it. I won't let Finna's character be

195

slandered as long as I have an arm to wield a sword with. You'd be wise to apologize and make yourself very scarce.'

Finna chuckled in triumph. 'I think Thurid would rather stay with me.'

Thurid, gazed at her with an idiotic smile and eyes as sensible as a dead mackerel's.

'Thurid, you can't stay here,' Leifr exclaimed. 'We need you desperately. What about the Pentacle? You haven't forgotten about the grindstone, have you? And Ljosa is back there with Hjaldr as a hostage. How can we ever get her away from the dwarfs without you and your magic?'

'Magic?' Thurid's bleary eyes cleared, and he made an attempt to get to his feet.

'Don't leave me so soon,' Finna pleaded, holding his arm firmly. 'Remember what a fine life I promised you.'

Thurid shook his head, wavering. 'Where's my staff and my satchel?' he muttered.

'Tell him to go away, or you'll get angry,' Finna commanded, her tone edged with malice. 'Challenge him to a duel, because he has insulted my character. He has falsely accused me of being a murderess.'

Thurid continued to struggle feebly, mumbling about his satchel and trying to disengage Finna's clinging arms. Encouraged, Leifr drew his sword and moved closer.

'Let him go, Finna,' he commanded. 'You aren't taking Thurid down to a watery grave.'

Finna laughed. 'You shall watch your friend drown, as a reward for your powers of resistance. He was not as strong, therefore he is mine.'

Slipping an arm around Thurid's neck, she slid off the log into the water, dragging him after her. The water revived him completely, and he began to thrash and yell for help as loud as he could bellow, until Finna ducked him under. Leifr dropped his sword and yanked off his boots to leap into the water after Thurid. Grabbing Finna, he tried to wrestle her away from Thurid, but she

196

turned her amazing strength against him instead, twisting her arms around his neck and diving for the bottom of the pool. He broke away from her and shot to the surface, gasping for air, and found Thurid still floundering and bellowing for help.

He took only a few ragged gasps of air before Finna hauled him under again, with a mighty slap of her fins on the surface. Desperately, Leifr wound his hands into her long, floating hair and pulled until she let him go, but she followed at his heels when he bobbed to the surface again. Panting and choking, he shook the water out of his eyes and saw Gotiskolker hauling Thurid out of the water, streaming murky water and green with slime and festoons of moss. Leifr managed to grasp a small limb to pull himself out, but Finna had him by the legs and pulled with tremendous strength until one of his hands lost its grip.

Scrabbling frantically, Gotiskolker clambered over Thurid and seized Leifr's sword. He slashed and thrust around in the water while Leifr tried to writhe out of Finna's grip and avoid one of Gotiskolker's wilder swings. She flinched, as if the metal had touched her, and suddenly sprang away with a bubbling scream, whacking the water with her fins as she dived for the depths of the pool.

Wasting no time in wondering if she were badly wounded, Leifr heaved himself out of the water into a muddy hollow between two rotting trunks and lay there, appreciating the fetid air and the slimy but solid feel of the tree beneath him.

Dropping Leifr's sword next to him, Gotiskolker sank down exhaustedly nearby as if his legs were incapable of holding him up any longer. Thurid dragged himself away in shamed silence to search for his satchel and staff.

'She would have had you both if I hadn't heard Thurid howling,' Gotiskolker said wryly. 'She would have saved Sorkvir the trouble of killing you – a miserable, fishy niss, when so far you've evaded Dokkalfar, a frost giant, and a burning. I wonder how many great heroes have finally died by stubbing their toes or drowning in their own bathtubs.'

'She has a great amount of power,' Leifr said, feeling certain he was going to be covered with bruises after his struggle with Finna. 'She's not as soft and helpless as she likes to appear. She's as strong as the Midgard snake.' He looked back at the pool, which already showed no trace of the deadly struggles that had gone on there. He shivered, wanting nothing more than to leave Kerlingtjorn many miles behind him.

The day promised to be mildly sunny, so he didn't even bother to change out of his wet clothing. Chafing impatiently while the others saddled their horses, he searched the opposite bank until he spied a tatter of white cloth fluttering from a clump of bulrushes.

'There it is!' he called and urged his horse into the water. As the water rose to Jolfr's belly and as high as his chest, Leifr's doubts of Eydis' fidelity also rose, but the going underfoot seemed solid. Presently the water became shallower, and Jolfr scrambled out on dry earth and shook himself from nose to tail, like a dog.

'Say goodbye to your dear nisses,' Gotiskolker said to Thurid as they rode away from the island in a westerly direction. 'You were very nearly a victim of your own magic. Maybe you should have left them as we found them. Finna will captivate a great many more idiots besides you.'

'Don't talk to me of that creature,' Thurid huffed, his eyes glaring with a fanatical gleam. 'Did you ever see such rank ingratitude as that? I wish I could have left her with a monstrous wart on her nose. I brought back their precious lake for them, and all to what purpose? So she can go on murdering innocent travelers? I've half a mind to go back and do something about her.'

'Forget it,' Gotiskolker advised. 'Part of the Rhbus' great plan is opposition. You've just had your little taste of opposition and you've survived it, so you'd better shut your mouth and count yourself lucky. Next time you may not get off so easily.'

Their travel was slow and arduous in spite of the markers. Often they had to dismount and lead the horses, not trusting them with the treacherous footing. Often the next white marker was nowhere in evidence, and they had to explore for it cautiously, which frequently got one of them into trouble with quicksand, mud, or very thin turf.

By late afternoon they were near the edge of the marsh; they could see darker trees and a few gnarled pines on the hillsides ahead, but the worst part of the swamp lay before them. It looked deceptively grassy and safe, but one misstep sucked the unwary traveler into quicksand and black mud with such a powerful grip that Leifr was certain for a while that they would have to leave Thurid's horse behind when it became mired. They also encountered the remains of nearly a dozen Dokkalfar, although nothing was left after a day of sunshine except clothing, armor, and weapons. Several of the troll-hounds also had fallen prey to the swamp, along with four horses who had perished.

The travelers' spirits were at a low ebb when they received the first evidence that they were not the only sojourners in the marsh. A dismal moaning sounded suddenly not far away, as if a cow had been mired. Nevertheless, Leifr unsheathed his sword before he approached any closer. Parting a clump of cattails, he saw a man's head and arms on the surface level of the bog. The man brandished a stick at them, then uttered a despairing, 'Hallooo! Help, help!' like the cry of some vast sea creature in distress.

Leifr could scarcely restrain a laugh, 'It's Raudbjorn,' he whispered delightedly. 'Sorkvir has left him to die. That ought to be a good lesson to him to trust a wizard.'

Thurid coughed indignantly. 'You seemed anxious enough to risk your life rescuing a wizard. I'm astonished that you'd take the trouble, considering how your feel about wizards.'

'You're not Sorkvir,' Leifr reminded him, then stepped out into the clear where Raudbjorn could see him. 'Halloa, Raudbjorn! Are the fish biting?'

Raudbjorn's huge, round face crackled with a welcoming grin. 'Halloa, Fridmarr. Happy to see you. One day we meet on equal ground for final battle. Only one of us walk away.'

'There won't be any battle if you drown in that bog,' Leifr answered. 'Will Sorkvir come back to get you out?'

Raudbjorn managed to shrug. 'Sorkvir knows, but not Raudbjorn. Looks like mud getting deeper. Maybe too long till dark.' He heaved a loud sigh and blinked disconsolately at a swarm of ravens perching not far overhead. 'Raudbjorn never had so many friends.'

Leifr went back to the horses, where Gotiskolker and Thurid waited impatiently. He began assembling all the lengths of tether cords into one long rope.

'Whatever do you think you're doing?' Thurid demanded, his eyes almost popping with indignation. 'You're not going to rescue that assassin, are you? Fridmarr, fair play only extends to the nearer edge of insanity, not all the way across and over the far end!'

Leifr ignored him, deeming his objections unworthy of rebuttal, and proceeded to toss the rope out to Raudbjorn.

'I can't bear the thought of never knowing which one of us is the better,' he called out in reply to Raudbjorn's stunned silence. 'Once you're out, we'll go our separate ways until we meet again under better circumstances. Suffocating in a bog hole is no way for a warrior to die.'

Leifr fastened the rope to his saddle and led Jolfr forward, leaning into a makeshift collar. The ropes stretched tautly, vibrating under the strain as Jolfr lunged against Raudbjorn's weight and the suction of the bog. Finally, with a loud, muddy exhalation, the swamp released its hold, and Leifr hauled Raudbjorn ashore. The thief-taker wiped the slop off his face, revealing a cheerful grin, and he extended one massive paw for Leifr to shake.

'Raudbjorn is grateful,' he rumbled earnestly. 'Fridmarr a noble warrior. Raudbjorn always remember Fridmarr as the best.'

They left him to follow their tracks and the white markers, although Thurid was far from happy about it.

'You've gone soft in the head, Fridmarr,' he growled. 'You never exhibited any symptoms of compassion all the time you were growing up. This is a most unpropitious time for you to start exhibiting such behavior.'

'Raudbjorn isn't evil, like Sorkvir and the Dokkalfar,' Leifr replied. 'Besides, I feel a sort of kinship with him. We're both strangers here.'

Thurid eyed him askance, and Gotiskolker darted him a warning scowl, but Leifr had recognized his mistake the moment it had left his lips. 'Strangers to this miserable swamp, I mean,' he added.

Thurid sighed and shook his head in silent wonderment. 'Fridmarr, Fridmarr, if you were anybody else, I would worry about you, but being Fridmarr, you'll always be a stranger wherever you go.'

They were close to the edge of the swamp when Leifr called another halt. Almost beside the safe path, one of the troll-hounds was mired in black mud almost to its shoulders. The beast yelped at them gladly and tried to wriggle free, using all its ability to appeal for help by wagging its tail frantically and showing all its teeth in an ingratiating canine grin.

Thurid groaned. 'Don't tell me you feel kinship with dogs, too. That's far too preposterous, Fridmarr. This is one of Sorkvir's hounds. Last night it was hunting you and would have torn you to bits if it had found you.'

'Last night he was in bad company,' Gotiskolker said. 'Today he's nothing but a hound. It all depends upon which cause he's following at the time, whether he's only a dog or a demon.' He pulled out his pipe and made himself comfortable, watching Leifr inching on his belly across the mud toward the hound.

All Leifr's doubts about the hound's disposition

vanished when he came within licking distance; the dog ecstatically slathered its red tongue all over his face as he tied the rope around its chest and ordered Thurid to pull. Still muttering curses, the wizard bent his back against the rope.

Once the suction of the mud was broken, the hound bounded freely out of the mire, the gladdest creature under the sun, and placed both paws on Thurid's chest to lick his face. The paws were huge and muddy, but Thurid submitted rigidly to this form of salutation.

'He's harmless,' Leifr assured the wizard. As he crawled wearily out of the mire, he promptly fell victim to the hound's next outburst of gratitude. When he managed to climb into his saddle, the hound stationed himself at Jolfr's heels and trotted along with the watchful pride of a dog who has recently adopted a human being, an object to be defended and prompted to provide shelter and food.

They had not gone far when the hound suddenly pricked up his great, hairy ears and dashed ahead, whining worriedly

'Ah, good, he's leaving,' Thurid said. 'For a while I feared he would follow us.'

Leifr listened to the excited yelps ahead. 'He's found something. Not Sorkvir's bear fylgja, I hope.' He unsheathed his sword and nudged Jolfr ahead cautiously.

The hound was capering up and down the safe track, his eyes fixed upon something in the bog. It was another hound, with nothing of him showing except his head. When he saw the horsemen, he uttered a despairing howl of anguish.

Leifr dismounted, taking his rope with him, and Thurid added a howl of anguish of his own, which Leifr ignored. When the second dog was freed from the mire, he demonstrated his joy with delighted wriggling and fawning around their feet, showing his teeth and lying on his back, paddling the air with his feet, all for the

202

privilege of trotting behind Leifr's horse at the opposite heel from the first hound.

When they found the third hound, Thurid was ominously silent, even when the grateful animal almost knocked him down with its delighted groveling. Each time Thurid took a step, the hound slithered under his feet, gazing up at him rapturously with golden eyes, asking only to be allowed to worship at the shrine of a generous master's boots.

'Fridmarr,' Thurid rumbled menacingly. 'I won't tolerate these puffing, slobbering, stinking brutes. Either you get rid of them, or I'll leave. What monsters they are, and imagine what a lot of fodder they'll eat. Maybe they'll even forget their gratitude and turn on us one day.'

'They're trained to hunt, aren't they?' Leifr asked, wrestling away from one of the beasts so he could mount his horse again. 'They'll provide for themselves and us, too. They would also discourage any trolls from attacking us, if we wander into troll territory.'

'Most likely they'll bring us nothing but troll meat for supper,' Thurid grumbled in a much-softened tone. 'Perhaps they might be induced to bring down a deer, though.'

When they stopped for the night, the hounds stretched out beside the fire, panting amiably, pausing to listen alertly to the night sounds. Once they all sprang to their feet, growling deep in their chests, and tore away without a sound, with all their back fur bristling up like hedges. After a long interval, Leifr heard the distant yammering of trolls and the savage baying of the hounds. When the hounds finally returned, their jaws and chests were soaked with fresh blood.

In the morning, while Thurid was taking bearings with an assortment of devices, the hounds brought down a brace of hares, which Gotiskolker skinned and cooked. The dogs gnawed the bones without any great hunger; their bellies still bulged with troll meat from their night's hunting.

'We're slightly off track,' Thurid at last reported, tapping his long finger on the map with disapprobation. 'We must mend our course slightly northward to find Luster. I expect we could be there by evening, if we have no more delays.' He darted a significant glance toward Leifr, and a resentful one toward the dogs. 'We might have made it last night, if not for certain unnecessary stops.'

Gotiskolker wiped his fingers on his tunic. 'A pity it wasn't you stuck in the mire, Thurid. We wouldn't have wasted our time pulling you out, but we couldn't have allowed three valuable hounds to perish so miserably.'

Thurid elevated his nose and turned his back in a smart about-face and marched away to saddle his horse. For the rest of the morning, he maintained a haughty silence. Once the mud and moss on his clothing had dried, it turned to dust, which he shook out and brushed away carefully, until he could once again present a dignified and imposing appearance. Pointedly, he eyed his companions' miserable attire.

Shortly after midday they sighted Luster ahead, in a green fold in the skirt of the barren fell. The large turf hail boasted four gables and various additions, and the stables and sheep folds rambled outward from it in all directions, enclosing a well-trodden yard before the front door. A dead tree in the center of the yard with a shield hanging on it proclaimed that the house was a house of refuge, a safe haven for all travelers of whatever persuasion, where anyone who left his weapons of war hanging on the tree outside was welcome to come in.

'Luster!' Thurid announced. 'This place is famous far and wide. Alof, the woman who owns it, has kept the peace in this part of the Pentacle for a good many years, as well as keeping a good table for her guests. We should be well-fed tonight.'

CHAPTER 13

As they rode slowly down the lane past the barns and paddocks, Leifr noticed that it all seemed desolate of ordinary use, and all that he could see of any livestock were heaps of bones hither and yon.

'Sorkvir's curse has been hard on this place,' he observed to Gotiskolker.

Gotiskolker nodded abstractedly, peering around him warily. 'This place is dangerous,' he muttered. 'Although there is only one woman here, instead of four. Doubtless Thurid will be glad to hear that.'

Thurid turned slowly to glare over his shoulder, clearing his throat indignantly. 'I don't believe we'll have anything to fear from our hostess, Alof, on any account. She has long been known to this part of Skarpsey as a generous, fearless, and solitary woman.'

'I wonder if she's expecting us.' Leifr noted the freshly hung carcass of a calf in the kitchen annex porch. 'News travels fast in the Pentacle, it seems.'

'You ought to have learned what sort of hospitality to expect by now.' Gotiskolker grunted. 'No one is going to welcome Fridmarr Fridmundrsson with fresh meat.'

'How right you are,' Leifr replied gloomily. 'Not even the dogs will come out to welcome us.' He nodded toward the long barn, where a row of dark snouts showed under the door edge, snarling and growling menacingly. The troll-hounds' fur stood on end, and they would have attacked if Leifr had not called them back sharply.

The riders paused beside a window in the accepted fashion and Thurid tapped at the shutter with the end of his staff. The house seemed silent and watchful.

'What are we supposed to purify while we're here?' Leifr asked Thurid while they waited, speaking in a low voice so he would not be heard by anyone inside.

'A spring,' Thurid answered, 'called Lusterfoss, because there's a small waterfall below it. Hark, someone's coming. They're unbarring the door.'

The door opened a short way and someone peered out cautiously. 'Are you travelers who come in peace?' a woman's voice inquired, somewhat suspiciously, and Leifr could feel himself being scrutinized.

'Yes, we've come with a just and peaceful intent,' Thurid replied pompously. 'We've heard that this is a house of refuge and that we can expect food and shelter here.'

'You are day-farers, and I already have night-farers within. Do you promise to abide one another's presence and refrain from your quarrels while you are under my roof?'

'Yes, we promise,' Thurid said, and Leifr and Gotiskolker nodded their heads in agreement.

'Then you may hang your weapons on my tree and come inside. One of my men will come for your horses.'

As Leifr hung his sword and shield on the dead tree he studied the Dokkalfar weaponry already hanging there – four broad axes, four shields, and four swords with walrus tusks for handles.

'We're outnumbered,' he observed to Thurid.

'They are outwizarded.' Thurid sniffed arrogantly and strode toward the hall with his tattered cloak surging gallantly around the tops of his pretentious old boots. Leifr and Gotiskolker slunk after him, looking like two badly off thralls trailing at their master's heels.

'Pardon the darkness,' their hostess said, after the door had closed behind them. 'My other guests prefer the dark, but they won't mind one small lamp.'

'Are you the famous Alof?' Thurid inquired. For the first time, Leifr got a good look at her. Short and rather stocky, she had little to recommend her except a broad, good-natured face and a massive coil of golden hair. In the Alfar realm, true age was impossible to guess.

Alof laughed, a husky, jovial laugh. 'Have you been hearing stories about me and my house of safety?' she asked. 'I hope you'll find my hospitality deserving of your good opinion, but I must say that times are not what they once were. One rule I must explain first so you will understand. No one is to go outside after the sun has set. I've had guests who slipped away after dark to fight a holmgang and I don't like to have their blood upon the soil of Luster. This house is supposed to be a haven from battle. Also, the trolls are too abundant around here to make any nighttime strolling a pleasant experience.' She smiled broadly and beckoned them to follow her. 'Now come into my hall and make yourselves comfortable.'

The Dokkalfar already in residence looked up suspiciously at the new guests for a moment, then turned their backs to resume their conversation, putting their faces close together and whispering intensely. When the newcomers sat down at the far end of the table, the four Dokkalfar shot them lowering glances and scuttled away to a far corner.

Food and drink were brought. To Leifr's famished eyes, the modest meal looked like a feast. Even Alof's rather coarse features took on a lovely tint by the light of her hospitable fires.

'I feel as if I'm here on false pretences,' Leifr muttered to Gotiskolker, under the cover of a burst of laughter from Alof, whom Thurid was amusing with witty anecdotes.

'You *are* here under false pretences,' Gotiskolker replied in a gruff mutter. 'Now be quiet about it.'

Leifr ate in silence, watching Thurid putting on his best court manners.

'Your two companions are so silent,' Alof said, smiling toward Leifr and Gotiskolker, inviting them to speak.

'They're rather rough fellows,' Thurid said hurriedly. 'Doubtless the splendor of your fine hall and good food has rendered them speechless with admiration. Common creatures such as they are sometimes are very quiet by nature.' His darting glance warned Leifr to acquire a quiet nature or he might pay the penalties for it later. Leifr might have shrugged it off if Thurid had not imprudently added, 'I wouldn't be traveling with such low companions if it weren't so dangerous to travel alone these days. The looks of these two are calculated to frighten off my enemies.'

'Low companions?' Leifr repeated. 'Thurid, you're going a bit too far. Either you tell her who we are and why we've come, or I shall. This is no time for your foolish games. Perhaps if the lady knew our names, she wouldn't be so generous with her hospitality.'

Thurid paled, darting a nervous glance toward the Dokkalfar and then toward Alof. 'Perhaps you have heard,' he began unwillingly, 'that Fridmarr Fridmundrsson has returned and swears to break the alog and kill Sorkvir.'

Alof's eyes widened. 'Fridmarr Fridmundrsson! I thought I knew that face.' She leaned forward to stare at Leifr with what he interpreted as a predatory manner.

'Yes, I'm Fridmarr, the traitor, the despised, the follower of Sorkvir, who caused his own brother's death. You're quite right to hate me for what I've done to Luster, and I've got no business sitting down at you table. If you wish, I'll leave.' He stood up, ready to take evasive action if Alof's opinion of him matched that of the nisses.

'No! No! Please sit down.' Alof held out her hands welcomingly, favoring him with her homely smile. 'For a moment I was surprised, yes, but then I realized that you have indeed come back to right the terrible wrong you did to Luster. I forgive you entirely, and I only desire to help you. Please believe me when I say I bear you no grudge.'

She spoke so earnestly that Leifr sat speechless.

Belatedly he said, 'I am truly sorry for what happened before. I expected you to be angry and to want revenge.'

Alof shook her head, still smiling. 'Revenge has no place at Luster. This is a house of refuge.' Her eyes seemed to bore into Leifr, large and green, with dilated black pupils that glittered like obsidian. Then she went on in a silky tone, 'Do you really believe you can solve the problem of Lusterfoss? It used to be such a pretty little spring, until it started flowing with blood.'

Leifr stiffened, darting Thurid a questioning look, but Thurid merely gazed back at him in blank astonishment. When Leifr glanced at Gotiskolker, he encountered a blaze of silent fury that baffled him further. The scavanger sat glaring at Alof with evident hatred.

'It flows blood,' Leifr repeated carefully, as if refreshing the details in his mind. 'Ah, yes. How often does it happen now?'

Alof shrugged her thick shoulders and gazed into the rafters thoughtfully. 'Sometimes daily. It almost always happens when there are guests in the house, unfortunately. I'm afraid some of them don't carry away a very good opinion of my house when they leave.'

'You're quite sure it's blood?' Leifr asked.

She nodded emphatically and folded her arms. 'Blood and bits of flesh and bones,' she said matter-of-factly. 'There's no doubt about it in my mind. The spring is a polluted, haunted place since Sorkvir made his alog. You were there, you must know what he did to Lusterfoss.' Her eyelids drooped knowingly as she nodded her head at him.

'Sorkvir never confides all there is to know,' Gotiskolker said suddenly in his harsh voice. 'But in Fridmarr's case he made his fatal mistake. He confided too much and he let Fridmarr escape from his influence.'

Alof gazed at Leifr with narrowing eyes. Her pupils shrank to mere slits, almost like a cat's eyes. 'I am very glad to hear it,' she drawled. 'I never thought Sorkvir capable of making mistakes.' She shook herself abruptly, as if banishing unpleasant thoughts. 'Enough serious talk, for now.'

She smiled her empty hostess smile and excused herself, taking a wide course around the three troll-hounds sprawled near the smoldering hearth. They eyed her curiously, growling, with their hackles bristling. Leifr reprimanded them sharply, and they immediately cringed and fawned around his feet in apology.

'I'm sorry for their lack of house manners,' Leifr said in embarrassment. 'Perhaps they saw few ladies in Sorkvir's hall and think you are a new creature.'

Alof laughed, somewhat uneasily. 'I thought I recognized troll-hounds. What do you call the lovely creatures?'

'Kraftig, Frimodig, and Farlig.'

'What very good names. Powerful, Fearless, and Dangerous. If they are like their names, woe betide any trolls they encounter. I'm rather frightened of them myself.' She laughed nervously and edged away into the kitchen, keeping her eyes on the hounds, who kept their eyes upon her. Frimodig growled softly, stubbornly refusing to give up his conviction that Alof was a possible enemy.

'You should leave them out here,' Thurid said angrily when they were outside. 'You don't know what those wretched killers might decide to do.'

'At least, he can watch them, if they're inside,' Gotiskolker said. 'If they're outside, they might kill all of her dogs and a few of her servants for good measure. I've never seen such a scurvy lot in all my days.'

'What can you expect on a farm where the spring flows with blood?' Thurid demanded, fastening an accusing glare upon Leifr. 'If you weren't completely reformed, Fridmarr, I'd think you an evil villain for bringing poverty and affliction on this poor woman. What a nasty thing to do, causing harm to a house of refuge.'

Gotiskolker sighed hollowly. 'I'd heard Thurid had an eye for the ladies when he was in his prosperous days. He never learns his lesson, does he?'

Thurid gripped his staff. 'One day I hope to have the satisfaction of doing something very unpleasant to you, you venomous bit of raven bait. At my present level of powers, however, I don't have anything sufficiently dreadful at my command.'

Gotiskolker snorted. 'Everything has already been done to me that can be done, buffoon. Besides, if you keep going as you are, you won't have any powers.'

'Pooh! What do you know about powers?' Thurid sneered.

'All about losing them,' Gotiskolker answered.

For a moment their eyes locked in a hostile stare. Then Thurid turned away with an indignant shiver. 'What absolute rubbish,' he growled. 'Take me to the spring, Fridmarr, and I'll see what influences are prevalent.'

Leifr had no idea where the spring lay. Recalling a hummocky area behind one of the barns, he started away in that direction, hoping the spring lay somewhere above it. As they passed the barn, Leifr heard something sniffing under the crack of a closed door. Looking down, he saw several ugly snouts pressed into opening between the stone threshold and the bottom of the door. Hurriedly he led the way around the corner of the barn and over a stone wall, whistling impatiently to his hounds, who lingered beside the door, enraging the dogs inside by snapping and barking under the door.

In moody silence, Leifr hiked up the side of the fell, hoping to sight the spring from his high vantage point. Thurid gazed down at the farm below, a speculative gleam in his eyes and his thoughts clearly occupied with something other than finding the spring. Humming softly to himself, he strode along with a sprightly step, letting his cloak billow majestically at his heels. Several times he ran his fingers through his thin hair and tweaked at his wispy beard, as if regretting their mutual sparsity.

Suddenly he stopped in mid-step, completely arrested. Slowly he raised one hand to point, swinging around gradually like a weather vane a few degrees to the west.

'There it is,' he said in a voice choked with awe. 'I can feel it from here. It is a great evil influence.'

He started forward, his hand still extended, his eyes wide and glassy.

Gotiskolker observed to Leifr, 'He reminds me of a bird dog I once had. It was a pointer, too.'

Thurid's nostrils twitched indignantly, but he did not look around. 'Spare us your sarcasm. The influence I feel is no laughing matter.' He took his dowsing pendulum from his pocket and commenced dowsing, although the spring was clearly in sight. 'Stay behind me,' he ordered, as Leifr attempted to move around him during one of his pauses to consult the pendulum. Leifr sighed impatiently, but he remained behind Thurid.

The spring did not boast an inviting appearance. A fence of whale bones had been set up around it to prevent livestock from fouling it, and five tall monoliths stood protectively in a ring, with the dark water pooling around their bases. Long, afternoon shadows reached out like dark, grasping fingers and the air was thick with an unpleasant stench. The turf around the hedge of whale bones was beaten to dust, as if many different paths all converged at that spot. Uneasily Leifr gazed around at the surrounding rocks and thickets, wondering if the prickling sensation in his scalp was caused by watching eyes or by the unseen influence Thurid felt coming from the spring.

As Thurid drew closer to the fence of bones, his pendulum became almost unmanageable. It twirled viciously in tight circles, or swung in wild arcs. Suddenly Thurid's hand dived earthward. Using both hands, he pulled up the pendulum like a stubborn weed with a long root. The sinew string continued to lash around wildly until he forcibly thrust it into his satchel.

'It's no matter,' Thurid said, his ghastly pale face beaded with sweat. 'There's nothing to worry about. We've dealt with Sorkvir's evil curses before. We can

212

deal with this one just as easily. What are wizards for, eh?' Then he added a horrified shout, perceiving Leifr climbing through the bone fence. 'Fridmarr! No! It's not safe!'

Leifr looked around him carefully, seeing nothing to alarm him except Sorkvir's black spirals emblazoned on the standing stones. The earth underfoot seemed smelly and stained, and the smaller rocks ringing the pool were smeared with something that Leifr didn't like the looks of – something suspiciously similar to blood. He moved closer to investigate, ignoring Thurid's cries of protest and dismay.

Thurid finally bent down and crawled through the fence, too curious himself to stay outside while Leifr appeared so interested in his discoveries.

'This place is like a charnel pit,' Leifr whispered, as Gotiskolker slipped silently through the fence, his eyes blazing with a peculiar intensity.

Thurid covered his mouth and nose with a handkerchief, peering into the dark spring water intently. 'It *is* a charnel pit,' he answered in a strangled voice. 'There must be dozens of skulls in that water – and bones and bits of rags. Murders – Alof said that it was dangerous to go out after dark. Someone – or something – preys upon her guests.'

Filled with dark forebodings, Leifr looked into the murky water. A pale shape rose toward the surface slowly, detached from the jumble of bones on the bottom. It was a hand, reaching out toward him as if to shake hands. With a gasp, he drew back from such uncouth familiarity, and the hand floated to the overflow at the low end of the pool and disappeared in the green slime of the slough below the spring.

'There are houses,' he said to no one in particular, 'where the hosts welcome travelers inside and then murder them for their possessions. This could be one of those places.'

'Nonsense,' Thurid said. 'Luster has been a house of

safe haven for many, many years. All my life I've heard of Alof and her golden hair. I've never heard of any murders until lately, since Sorkvir's curse. A great evil has overtaken Luster, and it is because of this polluted spring. We shall purge it of these fell murderers and make Luster a safe refuge once more, instead of a place of horrors.'

'The murderers are trolls, I'd say.' Gotiskolker rose from a close scrutiny of the soft earth. 'Dozens of them, and some are quite large.'

'Trolls! Then it will be as simple as this—' Thurid snapped his fingers confidently and reached out to pat one of the stones. 'Tomorrow I shall have these stones once more—' He had no time to finish; the moment he touched the stone, a heavy jolt ran through his body, spinning him half-around and throwing him to the ground. His open, unblinking eyes stared sightlessly skyward.

Leifr and Gotiskolker rushed to him and knelt down, listening for a heartbeat and trying to feel any breath coming out of his pinched and pale nostrils. They could detect no sign of life after several minutes, and his flesh was beginning to feel cool.

'He's dead!' Leifr gasped. 'What happened? I thought wizards never died!'

'He shouldn't have touched that stone,' Gotiskolker replied gloomily. 'Not until he'd cured it of Sorkvir's influence. He should have known, the buffoon.'

They knelt beside him silently. Leifr touched the silver torque with a flutter of panic in his stomach. It seemed a notch tighter already.

'We can't alter the Pentacle without a wizard,' he began, but Gotiskolker raised one hand warningly, his gaze fixed upon something outside the bone fence.

'He's gone to his fylgja form,' Gotiskolker whispered, as a small owl landed on a rib, staring at them and composing its feathers in a familiar, exasperated manner.

'How will he get back?' Leifr demanded, looking from Thurid to the owl. 'How long will it take?'

Gotiskolker shook his head. 'With the escape spell, no one ever knows for certain if he will get back. We'll have to keep him safe until he returns, if he knows how to reverse the escape spell.' He stood up and looked back toward Luster. 'Let her believe we think he's dead. If she believes it, that's all to the good.'

He refused to explain himself. Under his direction, Leifr hauled Thurid's body out of the circle by the heels, then hoisted him onto his shoulders and carried him down the hill to the house. Gotiskolker trailed behind abjectly with such a weary, despondent manner that Leifr began to be gnawed by fears that he was going to be left to fend for himself in the Alfar realm much sooner than he had ever imagined in his wildest nightmares.

By the time he reached the courtyard, the sun was below the horizon and his strength was almost exhausted. Alof came hurriedly to meet him, and he told her what had happened.

'How very unlucky! How dreadful!' she gasped. 'Bring him into the hall by the fire and we'll see if any life lingers yet.'

'He's dead,' Gotiskolker said gloomily, but Leifr followed Alof's directions and placed Thurid's body on the platform nearest the fire.

Alof brought several lamps nearer to cast their light on Thurid, but she could not detect any signs of life, either.

'We won't give up,' she said with a gloomy sigh. 'We'll sit up with him and watch through the night. We might see the life return to him. Wizards are strange, though. I hope we don't have any trouble.' She shuddered significantly. 'Although he was your friend in life, I doubt if you'd care for him as a draug.'

'Not at all,' Gotiskolker replied darkly.

As soon as it was sufficiently dark, the four Dokkalfar sent for their horses and rode away in a state of muffled excitement. Leifr watched them through a crack in the door as they charged at the tree and reclaimed their weapons. Brandishing their axes and bristling maces, they galloped past the hall, cloaks flying like banners and all their barbarous trophies fluttering from saddles, bridles, helmets, and weapons. From their insignia, he knew them to be from the Order of the Owl and therefore high in status and power with Sorkvir.

Grimly Leifr eyed his sword hanging on the tree, wishing it were at his side where it belonged. Unless he misjudged the intent of the four Dokkalfar, he expected that word of his presence at Luster would soon reach Sorkvir.

Gotiskolker also seemed to be brooding upon that dire possibility as he sat beside Thurid's inert form. 'We can't wait forever,' he said at last. 'Even if this is a house of refuge.' He spoke the last words with bitter emphasis, glancing sidelong at Alof.

'Even Sorkvir won't dare harm you here,' she said earnestly. 'It would be bad luck to break such a long tradition. He won't risk it. You mustn't think of leaving until you know whether Thurid will live or die.'

'The tradition of safety was broken long ago,' Gotiskolker said harshly. 'It would make no difference to Sorkvir anyway. We have no choice, however. We wouldn't leave our friend behind in a place like this.'

'You don't care for my hospitality?' Alof inquired with a brittle smile, eyeing Gotiskolker closely.

'Not much,' Gotiskolker replied coolly. 'I don't know whether I'll be murdered in my bed or up there by the spring.'

Leifr scowled at him, secretly sharing the same fears. 'Thurid's misfortune isn't her fault,' he said. 'She's as opposed to Sorkvir as we are. He's been no friend to her. We can't afford to make any more enemies, Gotiskolker.'

'Enemies are cheaply acquired,' Gotiskolker growled. 'Friends, on the other hand, are very expensive. Ever notice how your friends disappear when your money and luck are gone?'

Leifr decided to ignore him, but Alof gazed at him with particular dislike.

They agreed to take turns watching through the night, but Gotiskolker did more watching than Leifr, who awakened in the morning with a guilty start, realizing he had slept most of the night. Gotiskolker did not appear much the worse for wear and curtly cut off any attempts on Leifr's part to reprimand him. As for Thurid, there was no change.

Late in the afternoon, the sky darkened prematurely and a cold wind moaned in the rugged tops of the fells. The troll-hounds prowled restlessly between the door and the fire, flopping down with fretful groans, listening with pricked ears, and growling softly. The remnants of sky uncovered by scudding black clouds glowed with a sickly yellow light, lending the landscape an unnatural, eerie cast.

Gotiskolker suddenly raised his head, listening.

'Horses are coming,' he whispered.

Leifr sprang to the door and peered through the crack as the riders came thundering up the lane. Looming large among them was the unmistakable hulk of Raud-bjorn, with Dokkalfar banners and trophies fluttering around him. He held his halberd in one hand, dwarfing the Dokkalfar weapons with its size. All the riders were masked, including their leader, but Leifr had no difficulty in recognizing Sorkvir by his spiral insignia. They raced past the hall and came to a plunging halt around the dead tree. Several Dokkalfar examined Leifr's sword and shield with interest, but Sorkvir angrily ordered them away. With a motion of his arm, he banished the nine Dokkalfar to a distant corner of the courtyard, near the cow stable, where the Dokkalfar waited unwillingly. Leifr recognized the four Dokkalfar who had noted his arrival at Luster the day before, knowing them by the spiky devices on their helmets.

Raudbjorn alone remained beside Sorkvir, listening and nodding ponderously as Sorkvir gave him his orders. Then he rode slowly toward the hall, leaning down to peer under the porch.

'Halloa, Fridmarr!' he boomed. 'Come out. Speak with Sorkvir. Time to talk about surrender now.'

Leifr opened the door wider. 'Tell him I may talk, but it's not going to be about surrender.'

Together with Gotiskolker, Leifr warily approached the dead tree, where Sorkvir waited in the lurid glow of the sky.

'This is a house of peace,' Leifr said. 'I've left my weapons hanging on the tree. I suggest you do the same, if you want to talk.'

'Far be it from me to violate the spirit of a house of refuge,' Sorkvir said, hanging his sword on a branch. Glancing at Thurid's satchel and staff dangling there, he hesitated, while Raudbjorn filled several limbs with the assortment of long and short swords and extra axes which he carried.

Raudbjorn scowled, as Sorkvir hesitated over his own staff and satchel. 'House of safe haven is almost sacred place,' he rumbled disapprovingly. 'No need for wizardry. Bad luck to break rules, wizard.'

'Silence, you great fool,' Sorkvir snapped, and hung up his staff and satchel. Then he focused his attention upon Leifr and Gotiskolker, who had approached and halted at a cautious distance.

Leifr called, 'What do you have to say, after Kerling-tjorn, Sorkvir? You were fairly beaten there. One-fifth of the Pentacle belongs to us now.'

Sorkvir removed his mask and headdress and handed them to Raudbjorn to hold.

'And four-fifths of the Pentacle still belong to me,' Sorkvir answered. 'Do you really believe that you can destroy my influence over the Pentacle? Kerling-tjorn was only a fluke, a mistake. Why isn't Thurid here to speak for himself, by the way? Has something happened to him?'

'He's having a nap,' Gotiskolker interposed. 'He's refreshing his powers for his purging of Luster. You'll be able to watch, if you choose to stay.'

Sorkvir laughed harshly. 'Keep squeaking, you wretched rat. It keeps my temper hot. How have you been faring without your eitur, you scum?'

'Better than ever before,' Gotiskolker replied. 'You should know that from Kerling-tjorn and our escapes from you at Stormurbjarg, Dallir, and Gliru-hals. My stars have been rising steadily since Fridmarr's return.'

Sorkvir scowled at Liefr. 'You can go no further, with only this maimed barrow scavenger for a companion. Kerling-tjorn was merely a fluke of luck. You'd never have escaped if those nisses hadn't helped you. You'll never get past Luster, and no man or wizard would dare face what waits at Bjartur. Your knowledge of my spells won't help you any longer, with Thurid dead. You've lost the protection of his pernicious powers, and I can do what I wish with you.'

'Not at a house of refuge, you can't,' Leifr said, and the dogs crouching at his feet growled in agreement.

Raudbjorn nodded emphatically. 'Sacred ground,' he rumbled. 'Can't fight here, or Rhbus get very angry.'

Sorkvir darted him an envenomed glare, silencing him effectively, but Raudbjorn continued to scowl uneasily.

Sorkvir looked at the dogs, and they wrinkled back their lips to show their teeth. 'Ingrates, all of you. You seem to forget that I have seized this house, the spring, and the land around it,' Sorkvir continued. 'If this house is a house of haven, then it is my haven and my influence that protects anyone here – not the power of the Rhbus. I have destroyed their influence in Luster.'

'Not entirely,' Gotiskolker said. 'Your Dokkalfar hung their weapons on the tree in honor of the old tradition, did they not? Perhaps they have more faith in the old Pentacle than in the Pentacle you have created.'

'Impossible,' Sorkvir sneered. 'They are Dokkalfar, and they are my servants. They know who has the most power. They know that Thurid is destroyed. There simply isn't any way for you to continue without your wizard, such as he was.'

'Such as he was, you feared him,' Leifr retorted. 'You wouldn't be here so bold and brassy if you thought Thurid was anywhere near. You fear his knowledge and power.'

'Thurid is destroyed, and I shall give you until tomorrow evening to surrender yourselves peacefully. If you decide to fight, there are nine of us and one of you – unless you want to call this feeble bag of bones a warrior.' He nodded contemptuously toward Gotiskolker.

Raudbjorn scowled blackly. 'You call a battle at house of safe haven? Nine against two? Very unlucky, Sorkvir. Dokkalfar won't like it. Raudbjorn won't like it.'

Sorkvir's sunken eyes blazed. 'And Sorkvir won't like it if you disobey his orders,' he snarled. 'Would you like to learn the meaning of agony, you great lout? A fine thief-taker you are, Raudbjorn. You seem to have far too many scruples for one in your profession.'

Raudbjorn reined his horse around to retreat, muttering over his shoulder resentfully, 'Scruples, hah! Lice maybe, but no scruples, wizard.'

'Remember what I said,' Sorkvir commanded. 'Tomorrow at dusk you'll either surrender or prepare to fight.'

Leifr approached the tree and took down his weapons and shield. 'This is my answer, Sorkvir,' he said coldly. 'When you return, expect to fight for your lives.'

He backed away, holding his sword before him, watching Sorkvir and the Dokkalfar until he had reached the safety of the porch. As soon as he was inside, Sorkvir motioned with an impatient gesture to the Dokkalfar. They rode by slowly, each eyeing the hall with grim speculation. Raudbjorn shook his head dubiously and clasped an amulet hanging from his neck in one huge paw for whatever consolation it had to offer him.

Inside the hall, Alof greeted them stiffly, clasping and

unclasping her hands. 'So there's going to be a battle,' she said. 'The honor of my house is to be violated once again. Is there no end to injustice?'

Leifr sat down beside Thurid and tried again to detect a faint breath from his nostrils. 'There will be an end to injustice when we rid Skarpsey of evil creatures like Sorkvir.' He felt no sign of life in Thurid and stifled a deep sigh.

Indignantly, Alof paced toward the kitchen annex and back again. 'And you think that the two of you can destroy Sorkvir? I admire your courage, but I deplore your lack of wisdom. You have no hope. Sorkvir is the lord of all he covets, and it's pointless to resist.'

'So you haven't resisted,' Gotiskolker answered. 'I didn't expect any help from your quarter.'

'A good thing you didn't, because I won't offer it,' she snapped. 'You are marked for doom, and I don't want your bad luck to rub off on me.'

'So you're telling us to leave?' Leifr asked.

Alof shook her heavy blond tresses. 'I cannot do that, but I will do everything I can to get out of the way of the coming destruction, and you surely can't blame me for that. I'm going to get out while I can and leave you to your fruitless battle.'

'Good riddance,' Gotiskolker said.

With a glower, Alof turned her back and vanished into the passageway. Gotiskolker gazed after her with a considering frown. 'In the old days, the hosts of a house of refuge wouldn't hesitate to defend their guests from their enemies, if they made bold enough to attack. Affairs have come to a sorry state, have they not?'

'I'd say so,' Leifr agreed gloomily. 'You didn't waste any time trying to placate Alof, did you? Usually, if you'd like the help of someone, you don't deliberately insult them.'

'I didn't want her help,' Gotiskolker said. He looked at Thurid with a despondent sigh. 'Just when I was starting to have some faith in him, this had to happen. I think I'm unlucky.'

Although Leifr could not agree more heartily, he said nothing. Throughout the rest of the night, they alternately dozed and listened to the trolls outside. Several times the troll-hounds leaped up in full cry and clawed at the door in a frenzy to be let out at their quarry, and Leifr quieted them with difficulty. He had just managed to fall into a restless doze when another sound awakened him with a start. Something seemed to be scuttling around the smoke hole in the roof, a troll, perhaps, trying to find a way to get inside. Drawing his sword, Leifr crept toward the center of the room, peering upward into the gloom. Suddenly a raucous shriek rang out. He dived behind a pillar for cover, and Gotiskolker flattened himself on the floor, swearing under his breath. With a flapping sound, something plummeted through the smoke hole onto the smoky rafters, winging silently from perch to perch in the gloom.

'It's the owl!' Leifr exclaimed incredulously. 'Thurid! Come back, this way, you fool! You aren't any good to us as an owl. Thurid!'

The owl, however, swooped through the rafters with the utmost wariness, perching to stare down at Leifr, bobbing its head up and down to get a better look at him. After a few more passes through the hall, the owl flew out the smoke hole and disappeared into the night. Devastated, Leifr sank down in a chair and stared at Gotiskolker, who looked more pale and ghastly than usual.

'It must have been just an ordinary owl,' Gotiskolker croaked. He avoided meeting Leifr's gaze, and Leifr likewise looked away, thinking he had made a fool of himself over a wretched owl.

The dogs whined, stretched, and came over to console him by pawing at his chest and gnawing at his ankles in a playful manner. In the silence, the distant grating of an opening door sounded echoingly down a long passageway. The troll-hounds pricked up their ears attentively. A soft whimpering drifted down the corridor, then the clicking of long toenails on the stone flags. The hounds moved as one fluid body in a silent, deadly rush toward the passage, and disappeared into the darkness. In a moment a terrible squalling and growling filled the silence as a tremendous battle got under way in the vicinity of the kitchen.

Leifr grabbed his sword and started to follow, but Gotiskolker raised a warning hand. 'Let the dogs fight the trolls. They're better equipped for it than we are.'

'How did the trolls get into the house?' Leifr peered uneasily into the corridor. 'Someone had to open that door.'

'Someone did,' Gotiskolker answered.

'Alof?' Leifr queried incredulously. 'I thought she never favored one side over the other, according to legend.'

'Nothing is what it seems, especially legends,' Gotiskolker replied.

'Legend or not, I'm going to find out why the lady Alof is still here, letting trolls into the house. If I don't come back by the time you count to five hundred, you'd better get out of the house and leave Thurid to fend for himself.' Leifr took a lamp in one hand and his sword in the other and slowly moved down the long, dark corridor.

The sounds of mauling and snarling suddenly ceased; then the voices of the hounds blared outside in the midst of fresh fighting. The uproar diminished gradually as the hounds pursued their quarry into the fells. When Leifr reached the kitchen, he found the door shut and locked from inside. After staring at it distrustfully for a moment, he went on to explore the dingy, foul-smelling kitchen and the warren of rooms and passages beyond. More than once, he had the feeling that something was flitting ahead of him, just barely beyond the reach of his feeble lamp.

'Who's there?' he demanded, certain he had seen a movement. For a long time he listened, holding his breath, feeling the hairs lifting on his arms under the unseen influence of someone hiding nearby, perhaps in the same room with him. He took a step and heard the soft rustle of cloth in the darkness ahead. Striding forward swiftly, he glimpsed a dark figure darting around behind him and a flash of pale hair.

'Alof, is that you?' he called sharply.

His answer was a low, vulgar chuckle and the thunderous slamming of a door. A bar fell into place on the far side with a crash.

'Alof! I know you're out there! What are you doing?' Leifr threw his shoulder against the door in a mighty effort and was rewarded with only a small creak of protest. 'Alof! Open this door!'

CHAPTER 14

'I'M the mistress of this house,' she answered, 'and I've decided you'll be safer if you're locked up.'

'On whose orders, Alof? Sorkvir's? I thought this house was supposed to be a safe haven for both sides. You're violating the spirit of Luster with such treachery.'

'All that is different now,' she answered. 'Luster belongs to Sorkvir and he has given it over to the trolls. Whoever stops at this house is fair game.'

'I hope this is your idea of a joke,' Leifr said in a threatening tone. 'You've had your fun now trying to frighten me with your tricks. Open this door and let me out, and I'll forgive you for your unfortunate sense of humor.'

She laughed; for a moment, Leifr thought it didn't sound much like Alof. 'You won't think it's a joke much longer,' she said in a grating voice. 'Sorkvir doesn't have a sense of humor. Pain is all that amuses him – as you will soon find out.'

'Then you planned to lure the dogs away,' Leifr said, 'and you led me down here into a trap. This isn't a house of refuge, at all; it's a house of trickery and murder, and you're in the middle of it.' He gave the door a heavy kick to vent his fury, raising a cloud of musty dust.

'I must confess to a certain taste for blood,' Alof replied, with a smack of her lips. 'Unfortunately, we shall have to content ourselves with a cold wizard. Sorkvir forbade us to lay one tooth on you; the other two are fair game, but what poor pickings! Not enough blood in either of them to slake my thirst. I wish it were you we were taking up to the spring tomorrow night.'

Leifr listened with mounting horror. 'Who are you? What are you?' he demanded.

She laughed her coarse laugh. 'Don't worry, you're safe enough from us in there – as long as you're locked up. I don't advise you to come out until dawn, my dear guest. I believe I warned you about that before.'

With a chuckle, she moved away down the corridor, but Leifr could tell she did not go far. Listening through a crack in the door, he heard the patter of several pairs of feet and some hoarse, growling voices. Once an ugly nose poked under his door, sniffing curiously until he trod on it with his foot, occasioning a furious snarling on the far side.

Leifr dismally scouted the narrow room. From its general musty atmosphere, flavored with quantities of mouse droppings, he guessed that it had been a granary at one time. An infrequent breath of fresh air led him to a small, high grate near the roof. Subsequent investigation showed him that the opening was too small to crawl through, and the wall was mortared stone, so he could not hope to dig through it. As long as his lamp lasted, he prowled up and down the room, looking for any weakness in his prison. When the wick at last failed, he searched with his hands. He battered at the door until he was exhausted, but it was a thick, strong door, tightly bound with iron and swollen tight and solid by the dampness of the atmosphere.

Toward dawn, when a bit of light showed in the small grate, the trolls tramping up and down in the corridor ceased their restless prowling and weird chuckling, and the house seemed quiet. Leifr called out to Gotiskolker until he was hoarse, and his head ached from straining to hear an answer. Not a sound came in reply, although he could hear the hounds whining somewhere, unable to get at him. Too exhausted and despondent to think of any more ways to pass the time, Leifr curled up his cloak and went to sleep. Not surprisingly, his dreams were all unpleasant possibilities of what lay in store for him and his companions.

When he awakened, the slant of the sun told him it

was afternoon, and his stomach told him he was hungry. Encouraged by the slender beam of sunlight and a few hours' rest, he investigated his cell another time. When he was finished, he understood his former discouragement. There was no way out, except the way he had come in – through the door. Furiously, he attacked it again, certain that something must give if he kept battering at it; but at last he was forced to concede that his flesh and bones would give out before the door ever suffered much damage.

Gloomily he watched the light fade from his small window, thinking of Alof and her troll companions gathering at the spring to do their evil work, murdering and feasting upon their helpless victims. If Alof opened his door again, he would show her no more mercy than she planned to show Gotiskolker and Thurid. Gripping his sword, he waited for the sound of footsteps.

At last he heard a door open far down the corridor, but the footsteps were heavy and measured and jarred a large amount of metal hanging upon the persons approaching. When the bolt shot back and the door grumbled open, he found himself confronting a pair of burly Dokkalfar, cradling broadaxes on their arms. The expression in their small, glittering eyes assured Leifr that he was looking at a pair of Sorkvir's favorite killers.

One of them grunted. 'Come with us. You may walk, or we'll carry what remains of you after trying to change your mind.'

'I'm sure your methods are very persuasive,' Leifr answered, sheathing his sword. 'I'll walk.'

One of the Dokkalfar led the way, treating Leifr to a view of the long sword he wore in a sheath hanging down his back. The handle was a walrus tusk, much carved with intricate, looping designs, the interstices deeply dyed with blood. The sheath was ornamented with battle trophies, such as long locks of hair or beard, gold-filled teeth, amulets, and quite a few shriveled-up objects that Leifr identified as ears. The rings through the lobes made the job of suspending them from the scabbard much easier.

In the main hall, Sorkvir had taken possession of the best seat on the dais. Raudbjorn stood on one side with his arms folded across his chest, scowling fearsomely, and an armed Dokkalfar stood on the other side. The rest turned and stared at Leifr coldly, their hands uneasy upon their weapons.

'I hope you have passed the time pleasantly,' Sorkvir greeted Leifr. 'My servant tells me you had the best accommodations the house has to offer.'

Leifr glanced around and spied Alof trying to stay out of sight behind a pillar. 'My accommodations gave me no cause for complaint, but I'd like to know what has become of Thurid and Gotiskolker. The quarters she had in mind for them were not nearly so commodious.'

'Well, Alof,' Sorkvir asked, 'have you taken care of Thurid and Gotiskolker as I commanded?'

'Yes, my lord,' she replied nervously and seemed about to add something more, but she shut her mouth instead and smiled rather vacuously.

'Your friends are taken care of,' Sorkvir continued to Leifr. 'Now what is your answer? Do you wish to capitulate or do you wish to resist further?'

'I see no alternative,' Leifr replied. 'I will never surrender. It would be better to die.'

Raudbjorn rumbled disapprovingly and shook his head.

'Death in a house of refuge,' he growled. 'Great, sad evil. Raudbjorn refuse.'

Sorkvir curled his lip in scorn. 'You're a superstitious fool, Raudbjorn. Nothing is going to happen to us. A great number of killings have taken place here, and you can see the earth hasn't swallowed the house yet.'

Leifr kept his hand on his sword. 'So one more murder will make no difference – is that what you're saying, Sorkvir? Why don't you get it started them? Send your best men against me. Let's see how many of them it takes to kill me.'

'Don't be so hasty, Fridmarr. Why are you so willing to die?' Sorkvir bared his teeth in a thin, crafty smile. 'Has Thurid taught you the secrets of death? You think you will be more powerful than I am, once you come back from the dead. He has taught you powers, has he not?'

'I won't answer that,' Leifr replied. 'You have made up your own mind, so why should you question me and expect to hear what you want to hear? I may be defeated, but I refuse to surrender without defending my position as long as I am able to lift a sword. I'm ready; do your worst. You'll never break my spirit.'

Raudbjorn's sullen features suddenly beamed with an admiring grin. 'Good speech, Fridmarr,' he boomed. 'A good warrior's speech.'

'Since you liked it so much,' Sorkvir responded, tapping his long yellow fingers on the arm of his chair, 'you will get to see what reward it earns him. Where is my staff, Raudbjorn?'

Raudbjorn shook his head. 'Hanging on tree, not in house of safety. Raudbjorn no fool.'

Sorkvir transferred his baleful gaze from Leifr to Raudbjorn. 'I didn't order you to leave my weapons on the tree. Now go and fetch them, and we shall allow Fridmarr all the resistance he needs before he surrenders his sword and his desire to fight. The mines of Dokholur will be your next stop, Fridmarr, as long as you have strength enough to wield a pick or spade.'

Raudbjorn heaved a lugubrious sigh and shook his head with genuine regret. 'Someplace else, Sorkvir. Not here. No honor for Sorkvir in killing Fridmarr in house of refuge. Sorkvir's name would stink.'

'Then Raudbjorn's head will roll, if you think you'd prefer it,' Sorkvir replied acidly.

Raudbjorn clasped his huge arms and glowered around him at the Dokkalfar. 'Let them try,' he rumbled. 'Raudbjorn make mouse meat out of them. With bare hands.'

229

The Dokkalfar themselves seemed inclined to agree, evincing no great eagerness to attack Raudbjorn. They stood uneasily with their weapons in hand, viewing Raudbjorn, Leifr, Sorkvir, and even each other with the utmost distrust. Their fear and mutual hatred was Sorkvir's method of controlling them.

Realizing he had reached a stalemate, Sorkvir angrily motioned Raudbjorn aside. 'Go fetch my staff now, if you wish to live. Let me show you how your job is supposed to be done, thief-taker. I had thought I could use a day-faring thief-taker, but I find he is worse than the least talented Dokkalfar.' He stood up and faced Leifr, who immediately drew his sword and held it ready in both hands. 'So you think to confound me with your cold Scipling steel. There are far colder forces, Fridmarr.'

'Then use them,' Leifr said. 'The Rhbus are on my side.' He hoped they were, although he knew almost nothing about them. With Thurid and Gotiskolker gone, he needed desperately to believe that somewhere he had some allies.

Sorkvir raised his hands slowly, his gaze intent, and Leifr felt coldness gathering around him. The sword in his hands began to glow with a faint, frosty gleam. In a moment he heard shrill, humming notes and faint squeaks coming from the metal. The coldness of his hand was a burning, searing pain. He knew he could not endure it an instant longer. He dropped the sword, and the metal shattered like ice, causing the nearest of the Dokkalfar to leap back in alarm.

'That was only a small trick,' Sorkvir said with thinly veiled satisfaction. 'Now you are without your friends, your sword is smashed, and your dogs are in Alof's safekeeping. Surely now you must see you are helpless in my power.'

Leifr allowed his shoulders to sag and he lowered his head, darting sidelong glances at the two Dokkalfar who had brought him from his cell. The one with the sword hanging down his back turned to nudge one of his cohorts. In that moment, Leifr pounced on the Dokkalfar's sword and yanked it from its sheath.

The hall erupted into pandemonium as he dealt two Dokkalfar slashing blows and leaped over them to get his back against a wall. The remaining Dokkalfar armed themselves and charged at him with ferocious yells, yearning for revenge. Leifr parried their blows, greatly assisted by a nearby pillar, which garnered several savage blows from axes and maces that would have ended the battle instantly if they had met their mark. On the outskirts of the mêlée, Sorkvir recovered the staff from Raudbjorn and raised his arms for a powerful incantation.

Suddenly a brilliant explosion rocked the room, and the Dokkalfar recoiled suspiciously, looking around for the source of the spell. In close succession, six more reports and flashes filled the gloomy hall with blinding light and clouds of smoke.

Sorkvir uttered a maddened, choking cry and flung the staff away from him. 'Hawthorn!' he gasped, staggering toward his chair and collapsing after a few steps. 'It's not my staff. I'm poisoned by Rhbu sorcery!'

The Dokkalfar stood as if frozen, staring at their leader as he groped desperately for his satchel. From his position against the wall, Leifr saw that most of Sorkvir's hands had been blown away by the magic in the hawthorn staff, and his clothing also hung in shreds, as if he had been struck by lightning. His body seemed to be disintegrating, piece by piece, sifting dust onto the floor, slumping by degrees out of control, like a sack with the grain pouring out. The Dokkalfar jumped back in alarm when Sorkvir jerked upright in a last spasm, gasping and glaring, trying to speak.

Leifr seized the opportunity to dash nimbly for the door. Raudbjorn rose up from a squat to stop him, but Leifr planted his foot on Raudbjorn's chest and sent him sprawling. In an instant, he unbarred the door and dived into the darkness, bowling over a couple of small trolls who had been lurking on the doorstep. Pausing to take a couple of cursory swings at them with the Dokkalfar sword, he dodged across the porch and leaped into the unknown darkness beyond.

Startled snorts and squeals greeted his precipitate arrival into the midst of a group of horses, who immediately exploded in all directions. Somehow he managed to throw his arms around the neck of one and swing himself onto its back as it raced down the lane in a wild gallop.

As Leifr reached the bottom of the lane, he stopped to look back a moment. The Dokkalfar and Raudbjorn poured out of the house, bathed in an eerie blue light. A windy whistling came from the interior of the hall, which gathered into a mighty roar that sent the Dokkalfar scurrying for cover. While Leifr watched, limbs were torn from the dead tree and driven into the ground fifty feet away like giant hayforks. Sorkvir's wrathful spirit tore the doors off the barns and ripped the gates from their hinges.

Not daring to stay any longer, Leifr clapped his heels to his horse and galloped for the nearest dark ravine, hoping he wouldn't ride right into the teeth of a hundred hungry trolls.

The ravine had a small, swift stream rattling down its dark depths and a narrow sheep path twisting along both sides of the water. Once Leifr saw a group of trolls on the other side and froze, returning their hostile green stares for a long chilly moment. They lifted their lips in dreadful snarls and edged down to the verge of the water, but they wouldn't come across, although it was barely fetlock deep. Leifr moved on cautiously, and the trolls followed for a short distance, growling and making menacing gestures. Then the more businesslike trolls stopped and thrashed several of the aggressive ones and led them away at a shambling trot in another direction.

Leifr encountered several solitary trolls, who refused

to cross the water in spite of lengthy demonstrations of their ferocity and general depravity. One troll gave him a considering stare, then turned his back and hurried away as if he really couldn't be bothered. Wondering what all their important business could be, Leifr rode his horse up to the rim of the ravine for a look across. He saw that he was near the spring, which seemed to be the destination of the trolls he had met. A fire burned at the base of each of the five standing stones, casting a lurid glare on the black spirals burned on the surfaces. Several dark figures moved around inside the circle of the bone fence, and a dark, seething mass of trolls waited on the outside.

Near the edge of the dark water lay an inert form, which Leifr knew must be Thurid. He thought about the small owl that had flown in through the smoke hole last night, wondering if it were a ridiculous coincidence, or if the owl had been Thurid's fylgja. In any case, what was he to do against such a mass of trolls?

As he watched, he noticed that the crowds of trolls outside the bone fence kept a respectful distance between themselves and the fires. When they pressed too close, the figures inside the fence brandished burning sticks at them and they quickly backed away. The common trolls, it appeared, were allowed only to watch while Alof and a few chosen followers conducted their ritual.

Leifr dismounted and groped around in the thickets nearby until he found some dead limbs with leaves and branches intact. With his knife he sawed off the hem of his shirt and twisted it among the branches, hoping the flax and nettle fibers would encourage the rest of the torch to burn. He still had his tinderbox; in a few moments, his makeshift torch had burst into flame. Quickly he got onto his horse and kicked it into a gallop, straight for the spring.

The trolls saw him instantly. A hooded, fire-bearing figure galloping toward them with threatening shouts was an awful spectacle in the superstitious minds, and they scrambled to get out of the way of this emissary of doom. Leifr urged his horse straight toward the fence. The horse hazarded a leap, but it was going too fast, crashing through the fence and plowing into the dark pool beyond.

Leifr jumped off, still carrying his torch, and took up a defensive position over Thurid, sword in hand. Alof and four of her servants picked themselves up from the ground and stared at him with astonishment.

'Fridmarr!' Alof cried incredulously. 'No one escapes from Sorkvir!'

'Sorkvir is dead again,' Leifr answered, 'but he'll come back. You might not be so lucky when you die.'

She tossed her head and chuckled. 'You are in a strange position to threaten me. Hundreds of trolls surround you. At a word from me, they will tear you to pieces.'

She nodded toward the gibbering masses of trolls scuttling restlessly just beyond the whale bones, their green eyes glowing in the firelight.

'How is it that you're one of them?' Leifr asked. 'You wear our clothing and speak our language, and no one would suspect you – until it was too late. What makes you different from those vile beasts out there in the dark?'

Alof smiled coldly and twisted a strand of her hair.

'What makes you think there is any difference?' she asked. Suddenly Leifr saw her concealing spell melt away, revealing the features of a scarred old troll, baring its hideous yellow teeth at him, and the voice became a gutteral snarl. 'Some of us are half-trolls, captured young and taught to be civilized by the Dokkalfar. Sorkvir put me here after the real Alof was killed. In many ways, I am like any Dokkalfar – except for a healthy appetite for fresh, raw meat.' She laughed her coarse laugh. 'Fridmarr, what a fool you've been. We shall relish drinking your blood, still strong and hot from battle.'

Drawing her knife, she motioned to the half-trolls inside the circle, and they all drew their weapons and started edging closer to Leifr, baring their teeth in anticipation.

Leifr waved his Dokkalfar sword. 'I'll make rugs and boots out of all of you,' he growled.

'We shall see what happens,' she said. 'You don't look much like a prophet to me.'

Imperiously, Alof beckoned to her four assistants. They came forward, brandishing their knives and clubs, wearing white gowns embroidered with cryptic symbols and much blackened with dried blood where they had wiped their hands. Leifr stood his ground between them and Thurid.

Just as he raised his sword, a harsh screech rang out. With a noisy flapping of wings, a small owl alighted on the top of one of the stones. With a wary grumbling and spitting, the common trolls drew back, and even Alof stared for a moment.

'Go on,' she said harshly. 'It's nothing but an owl. All they're interested in is mice. Are you mice, or are you warriors?'

The four servants took their eyes off the owl with difficulty and resumed their warlike stances around Leifr.

'Some of you are going to die,' Leifr said. 'Maybe all of you. Are you certain it's worth it?'

The four dull fellows glowered at Leifr a moment, then made a tentative charge, careful to stay out of reach of Leifr's sword.

'Cowards!' Alof spat. 'I could do better!'

They circled warily, seeming more like trolls to Leifr every moment in their slouching stances and scuttling attacks. One of them carried a club made of a root with a heavy rock lashed to its end, with the stubs of roots sharpened and hardened in the fire – a nasty, primitive weapon, but drastically effective, once it connected. Several times it whistled past his head, dangerously near.

Their skirmishes intensified with each attempt, and Leifr managed to pick off one of the half-trolls with a stroke that sent him rolling to Alof's feet. Snatching his weapon from his dying hand, she plunged into the front of the battle with enough ferocity to match the remaining three trolls combined. The common trolls outside the fence applauded their champion with roars and bellows.

In spite of their uproar, Leifr heard the clear voices of baying hounds coming from the direction of the fells. He whistled to them, and they yelped an excited response.

The trolls ceased their cavorting to listen, and Alof backed away to reconnoitre, her pale hair falling down around her thick shoulders.

'That wretched Vitleysa,' she spat. 'He ought to have killed those hounds. Wait until I see him again.'

'My dogs have killed him to spare you the trouble,' Leifr replied grimly. 'They'll make short work of you, Alof.'

Furiously she threw away her club and seized the stone mace from the hands of its owner. 'Get yourself another weapon,' she snarled. 'If you knew how to use it right, he would have been dead long ago. We haven't much time left.'

Driven by Alof's frenzy, the three half-trolls rushed at Leifr like berserkers, unmindful of their own hazard. Two of them went down under Leifr's sword, and the third staggered away with a fatal injury, all without touching Leifr with their weapons. Alof uttered a maddened shriek and plunged forward, whirling the deadly mace, her features contorted by rage. Leifr parried her blows and drove her back with swift feints.

'Why don't you escape while you can?' he demanded, as the baying hounds burst over a nearby hilltop. The common trolls melted away silently into the fells and ravines above.

'Escape to what?' Alof sneered. 'Back to caves and filthy rags and stealing sheep? I'm not one of them any longer. I've learned that there are better ways.'

'Sorkvir's way is not a better way,' Leifr said in disgust. 'Now get away while you can. You're better off as a free troll than a cringing vassal of Sorkvir's.'

From the hillside, some trolls yelped in alarm as three dark shadows streaked toward the stone circle. Alof saw them coming and abruptly abandoned all pretense and reverted to her troll nature. Dropping her weapon, she scuttled through the fence and raced for the shadows of the nearest ravine. The troll-hounds altered their course immediately and raced after her. In a moment, Leifr heard a brief, brutal battle in the ravine, then silence.

CHAPTER 15

LEIFR sank down beside Thurid's inert form. Glancing up, he saw the little owl perched on the standing stone. It fluffed out its feathers and clacked its beak at him.

'Come on, Thurid,' he muttered, scowling at the owl. 'Get yourself back together. I want to get out of here.'

The hounds came bursting into the circle, their jaws red from their night's work, panting and pawing to get Leifr's attention. Leifr commanded them to lie down and watch for any trolls foolhardy enough to return. He heard plenty of them grunting questioningly from the fells, but not one ventured into the meadow surrounding the spring.

Near dawn, he heard the snort of a horse. Arming himself with the stone mace and the Dokkalfar sword, he took a defensive stance and waited to see who it was, with the dogs sniffing attentively and wagging their tails.

To Leifr's enormous gratification, it was Gotiskolker, riding out of a ravine and leading two saddled horses, one of them being Jolfr.

'I wondered where you'd gone,' Leifr greeted him as he tied his horse to a whale rib and came through the gap made by Leifr's precipitate arrival.

Silently Gotiskolker looked at the dead half-trolls, as yet untouched by sunlight.

'You've done quite a job of work for one night,' he observed finally in a gruff tone. 'I slipped out after you disappeared, thinking I'd take the horses and hide them, in case any of us survived and wanted to escape. Where's Alof?'

Leifr nodded toward the troll hounds. 'Ask them.'

'The brutes. But to them she was a troll. I suspected

her from the beginning, when I saw the hall in darkness.'

'Have you seen any Dokkalfar?' Leifr asked.

Gotiskolker nodded. 'Gathering their horses, about an hour ago. I saw Sorkvir in bear form, slinking away to lick his wounds. What did you do to cause such a furor?'

Leifr told him about the staff, and Gotiskolker uttered a ghost of a chuckle. 'I hope it felt like eitur in his veins,' he said with a bitter smile.

The sun rose on a misty day of perfect calm, silently transforming the dead trolls into piles of rocks. As its warming influence touched Thurid's body, he uttered a faint sigh. After a while, he began to twitch, like a sleeper awakening, and finally, with a great snort, he opened his eyes and gazed around with a startled expression until he recognized Leifr and Gotiskolker, who were watching from a rather cautious distance. Stiffly, Thurid sat up, wincing at the movement of long-undisturbed muscles.

'Where's my staff and satchel?' he grunted, by way of greeting.

Gotiskolker nodded toward the horses. 'They're here, safe enough, considering what's happened.'

'Fetch them,' Thurid growled irascibly. 'There's something I'm going to do.'

Leifr went to the horses and brought back the satchel and the staff, noting the blackened places where Sorkvir's hands had touched the wood. Thurid rubbed his hand along his staff with a scowl. 'I couldn't have done better myself,' he said with a fiery gleam in his eye. 'I saw it all from the smoke hole in the roof, cursing myself all the while for being stuck in that fylgja form because of a hastily executed escape spell – one mistake I shan't make again soon.'

He rummaged through his rune sticks, finally selecting an old blackened one and reading it over with a satisfied, grim expression. Then he walked through the gap in the fence and faced Luster in the valley below. 'No unsuspecting traveler will ever be murdered at Luster again,' he said, and began the words of a spell, holding his staff extended before him.

After the third repetition of the spell, the earth responded with a low and menacing grumble far down below. Thurid dashed the sweat off his face with his sleeve and raised his arms, trembling slightly, still repeating the words of a mighty incantation.

The earth trembled under the assault of a series of subterranean explosions. With a ripping, rending sound, a fissure opened up in the greensward, widening and lengthening as it slowly approached Luster. Thurid gritted his teeth, his arms shaking, urging the fissure onward, until it reached the front door of the hall and disappeared beneath the porch. In a moment the porch sagged into the gap; the rest of the house followed by slow degrees as it collapsed gracefully into the black maw of the great crack with a belch of dust.

Thurid staggered back and sat down on a rock, leaning on his staff for support, as he gasped for breath and wiped his face again with his sleeve.

'No one humiliates Thurid,' he muttered.

Leifr gazed at the wreck of the house in awe, but Gotiskolker seemed unimpressed.

'If you're done with your spate of temper,' he suggested to Thurid, 'why don't you get on with your business at the spring? We ought to have been on our way hours ago.'

Thurid stood up. 'I'll be glad to turn my back upon this place,' he said. 'It's enough to sour one's outlook on women entirely, when one of them tries to drown you, and the next one is a troll hag in disguise, who wants to parcel your flesh out like smoked mutton. I suppose Alof believed she could ingest my powers by the most obvious means, true to the trolls' obnoxious obsession with their gullets. Filthy, vile brutes.' He booted the stones that had been trolls out of his path and stalked around the circle of standing stones, keeping a wary distance from the one that had nearly fried him before. He dowsed and muttered over several more rune sticks and stood still for a long time with his eyes rolled up in a trance. Finally he was ready to begin. Raising his arms, he blasted the first stone with fire until the spiral was obliterated, and a brilliant, glowing pentacle took its place.

'That's for the real Alof,' Thurid said balefully.

After blasting the next stone, he stood back away from its glowing heat as if to admire his handiwork.

'That's for Luster, the house of safety which Sorkvir fouled with the blood of innocent travelers,' he said. 'And the next one is for me and my wretched owl fylgja, for all the time we spent in each other's company.'

He blasted two stones in succession and darted a wary glance at Gotiskolker. 'That one was yours, for all you've suffered at Sorkvir's hands.'

Gotiskolker's black brows knit together as he seemed to be pondering some acrid reply, but all he said was, 'Thank you, wizard, I'm grateful.'

Thurid blasted the final stone ferociously, blackening the grass and moss growing around it. When he was done, he turned and looked a long moment at Leifr, then he said simply, 'Ljosa.'

Leifr nodded grimly, silently hoping that one day she would be safe from the actions of evil wizards like Sorkvir and the painful consequences that seemed to swarm around Fridmarr like a cloud of vampire bats.

Gotiskolker watched from a distance, perched on a whale rib like a rusty old vulture. When all the spirals were gone and Leifr and Thurid began packing up for travel, he stood up and walked to the edge of the pool. After a few moments, he beckoned silently to Thurid and pointed at the water.

'Something is happening to the spring,' he called.

The slow bubbling of the spring had halted, and the level of the water on the stones was much lower, leaving a slimy mark. As they watched, a whirlpool began turning slowly in the center of the pool, gathering speed and sucking the vile contents of the pool down into a black maw. In a short while, nothing remained but a basin of stinking mud and a litter of rotting bones.

Thurid gripped his staff, staring at the demise of the spring. Then he heaved a deep sigh and turned away, muttering, 'This is a dismal place. Let's get away from here before we lose our spirits entirely.'

'But what about the spring?' Leifr asked. 'Will the Pentacle work without it?'

'I don't know,' Thurid replied. 'Perhaps the spring will surface someplace else. Perhaps the underground water current is enough. I don't know everything about earth magic yet. All we can do is go on to the next point.'

Before they departed, Leifr collected several of the half-trolls' weapons for his own use. In particular he liked the mace made from the tree root, and he also claimed a hand axe made by lashing a stone into a forked handle.

By the following midday, they came into view of Bjartur, a small settlement gathered around the base of a ruined hill fort.

'I don't know why they call it Bjartur,' Leifr said. 'It doesn't look bright or shining. Bleak and desolate is nearer the truth.'

'It wasn't always a ruin,' Thurid replied. 'Less than a thousand years ago, it was a Ljosalfar outpost. One day, soon perhaps, Elbegast's troops will occupy it again.'

Gotiskolker shook his head. 'You dream, Thurid. Elbegast will never come back to this part of Skarpsey. His embattled kingdom grows smaller every day. His spies and warriors are becoming fewer and fewer.' He cast Leifr a dark scowl. 'You could have become a spy for Elbegast. You boasted about it like a fatuous young fool at one time.'

'Oh yes, I remember,' Thurid chimed in. 'You were insufferable, Fridmarr. A pity Sorkvir was easier to find than Elbegast, or you might have accomplished something to your credit. And I wouldn't be here now, half-starved and half-frozen from sleeping on the damp ground.'

'Nor would you be a practising wizard,' Leifr retorted, slightly nettled. 'If I hadn't pulled you out of your books, you'd be mildewing there now.'

Still feeling irritable and pettish, Thurid replied, 'But if you hadn't shown Sorkvir all the secrets of the Pentacle, Sorkvir's alog would not be so difficult to break.'

Gotiskolker interrupted, 'How else was he to learn Sorkvir's one great weakness?'

Thurid's eyes narrowed and his nostrils flared. 'What a price to pay for that knowledge, Fridmarr? It's Rhbu magic, isn't it? You planned this since you gave me that satchel. You didn't trust me with your secret. I can always tell when you're hiding something. From the moment you returned to Dallir, I sensed something nervous and guilty about you, as if you weren't telling me all the truth. Why have you kept this a secret so long, when I could have helped you immeasurably?'

Leifr glowered at Gotiskolker a moment in helpless perplexity, searching in vain for an appropriate response. 'I don't want to talk about it,' he growled, taking refuge in a display of bad temper and urging his horse forward to remove himself from any more questions, accusations, and alarming revelations.

As they approached the nearest of the handful of scattered houses, Leifr perceived with a sinking heart that it was an unoccupied ruin. The door had been wrenched off its hinges, and the inside was completely plundered and smashed. Not liking to linger in a place with such an atmosphere of untimely death, the travelers rode on in silence.

'No one is left here,' Leifr said, after passing two more battered houses. 'The entire settlement is gone.'

Thurid rubbed his nose with the knob of his staff. 'It must have happened since you passed through here with Sorkvir. I was here shortly before the alog. I shared some of my ideas with a bunch of thralls sharing the same barn I slept in. We passed around a big stone flagon, and the more times it went around, the better I sounded. It was Ofrodur Blue-Nose's barn, I recall, but which place is his, I couldn't say, after all this time. Fridmarr, do you know which one is old Ofrodur's place?'

Leifr shifted uncomfortably in his saddle and stole a glance at Gotiskolker, who was hunched away in his cloak and scowling as if he had no desire to be disturbed.

Annoyed by his unhelpful attitude, Leifr retorted, 'We haven't got to it yet. This place looks all strange to me too, with no people or livestock. I don't like the feeling I get here. Did you notice how those doors were pulled off their hinges by something? I don't think trolls could have done that sort of job. They wouldn't smash the furniture, either, until it was nothing but kindling wood. When we stop for the night, I want to be in someplace safe.' He gazed up at the hill fort crowning the summit of the mountain. Its ramparts had crumbled here and there, pouring fans of scree down the hillside. A pair of round towers peered with blank slits of eyes over the battlements, watching the low ground in silent suspicion.

'Up there?' Gotiskolker questioned, nodding to the fortress.

'Yes, up there,' Leifr repeated, his curiosity suddenly piqued as a flock of ravens surged into the air over the hill fort, cawing raucously in alarm. 'If there's any life left in Bjartur, we'll find it there.'

The roadway up to the hill fort carved a zigzag path across the face of the hill. Years of storms had eroded deep gullies across it, and rockslides blocked it completely at two points, but something had made a path either over the top or around the edge of the rockfall.

At the third rockslide, they halted to decide between a tortuous climb over the rocks or a wretched goat trail overhanging a breathtaking drop to the crags below. Leifr opted for the path over the top, since it was shorter and the afternoon was almost spent. At the top of the

244

rockslide, they passed below the crumbling ramparts of the fortress, where the ravens still cackled among the rocky crenelations.

With an echoing clatter, a rock suddenly bounced across their path and careened into space beyond. Cautiously Leifr started forward again, watching the walls above. Glimpsing a flash of movement, he halted Jolfr quickly and backed him into the protection of a jutting rock as another stone came bouncing down the high wall. This time a considerable amount of rocks and gravel started moving, threatening to bury the trail across the rockslide.

'Someone is up there,' Thurid said excitedly. 'If he throws one more rock, I'm going to blast him.'

'And bring down half the mountain?' Gotiskolker snorted, his hood and beard whitened with dust. 'I didn't come this far to get buried alive.'

'You're not more than half-alive anyway,' Thurid retorted. 'I don't know what your objections would be.'

When the rocks finally stopped falling, Thurid poked his head out cautiously and looked up toward the top of the wall. 'I see him, the miserable rotter,' he growled. 'Halloa! You up there! Who are you? Are you trying to kill us? Stop dropping those rocks, or you'll regret it.'

The answer was another rock, larger than the others, which bounced across the path and vaulted into a thicket far down the slope. A voice called out from above, 'Stay away! You'll be sorry if you come up here. Bjartur is haunted.'

'Haunted! Well, that's hardly surprising,' Thurid mused, his hand straying into his satchel to shuffle through the rune sticks. 'I wonder if this fellow thinks he's a draug.'

'Maybe he *is* a draug,' Leifr suggested. 'Certainly a draug would know if a place were haunted or not.' He was beginning to regret his ill-conceived fascination with the ruined fortress, but he hated to think that they had come a mile over a rough path only to turn back within a stone's throw of the top. He stepped out of his shelter and peered up the face of the hill.

'You there!' he called in a threatening tone. 'If one more pebble falls down on us, this wizard is going to make you suffer for it. You're a day-farer and so are we, you fool, so stop trying to brain us with rocks.'

The scornful reply from above was unmistakable – half a dozen rocks in quick succession clattered down the cliff, generating a rumbling rockslide which fortunately angled behind the travelers, instead of pouring over the top of them like a waterfall.

When the rocks stopped and the dust cleared somewhat, Gotiskolker shook his cloak free of a load of dirt and sand and came forward to Leifr's position.

'I think we'll have to negotiate,' he said, nodding toward the edge of the rockslide.

Four men armed with fearsome stone axes stood blocking the way. Rusty armor of several unusual designs was strapped onto their limbs and torsos by makeshift methods and their helmets were clearly ancient, eagle-winged, and much embellished with superfluous devices and embossing. The axes were made of obsidian, mounted on wooden handles with rawhide and honed to transparent sharpness.

Thurid stepped forward immediately, warning Leifr and Gotiskolker to keep silent with a terse grimace and a scowl.

'What has become of my old friend Ofrodur Blue-Nose?' He struck an indignant pose, rapping his staff on the ground with a shower of sparks. 'I've come all this way, and all the houses are in a shambles. Are you the plundering vagabonds who have ravaged Bjartur?'

'Ofrodur Blue-Nose, did you say?' The strangers lowered their axes cautiously, and their leader stepped forward, a rather thin individual with a brown beard that reached to his waist. 'I'm Borgar Ofrodursson. My father is dead. Did you know him?'

'Know him? I shared his hospitality, his food, his

shelter, his company – and you say he's dead. It grieves me to hear it.' Thurid rubbed his chin meditatively. 'Borgar, you say? I remember you as a small lad.'

'I don't remember any wizards at Ofrodursknoll,' Borgar replied warily. 'What are you doing here now? It's dangerous to wander around Bjartur after dusk.' His three companions nodded grimly and muttered in agreement.

'We were looking for some people,' Thurid said.

'They're gone,' Borgar replied. 'Moved away, sailed away, or carried away, it's all the same. Gone, except for a few of us, who stayed to fight.'

Leifr stepped forward. 'Who are you fighting? Sorkvir?'

Borgar shook his head. 'Sorkvir wastes little time on us, and we keep out of his way. We fight and we wait. Now tell us something about yourself. You look like a warrior and you carry a stone weapon, instead of Alfar steel, and I see you aren't afraid to bare your head to the sun, so you must be a day-farer. Were you also a friend to my father?'

'I fear not,' Leifr answered, and Thurid darted him a warning frown. 'I came here once, before your misfortune. I am a warrior, but thanks to Sorkvir's alog, I have no steel weapons to fight with. I have come here with these companions to offer restitution for an old wrong.'

Borgar and his men exchanged glances, suddenly uneasy.

'We can't stay here to talk,' Borgar said. 'Let's get within doors before the day wanes. We have matters of consequence to discuss, and this is no place for it. Follow me. Let my men bring your horses.' He signaled to the man on the fortress wall, then led the way up the narrow path. 'I hope you'll forgive us for our caution. It's hard to know whom to trust, so we trust no one.'

'You're trusting us, however,' Gotiskolker said. 'Isn't that setting a dangerous precedent?'

Borgar turned to look at Gotiskolker curiously. 'Who

247

said we were trusting you? Until we are satisfied you'll do us no harm, you'll be our prisoners.'

Thurid halted with a deep and regretful sigh. 'I don't wish to be disagreeable, Borgar, since I have such fond memories of your father, but we haven't the time to be prisoners. We're on a journey of utmost importance, and you stand to benefit a great deal from what we do – if we are allowed to do it, that is.'

Borgar inclined his head in an understanding nod. 'In a very short time the sun will be beneath the horizon and we will all be prisoners of these walls until dawn. If you are roaming around out here, sometime before sunrise you'll wish most desperately that you were a prisoner in anyone's dungeon anywhere in the Realm. The thing that walks the outer fortress by night keeps a far harsher prison than we do.'

'But when dawn comes, will we be free to leave, if we wish?' Leifr asked suspiciously.

'Certainly, if you wish,' Borgar replied. 'But for the hours between dusk and dawn, you must be safe behind bars and bolts and thick doors with the rest of us.'

Leifr motioned impatiently to Thurid and strode ahead beside Borgar. 'Wizards are useful when it comes to fighting supernatural forces and powerful enemies. What is it that walks these ruins?'

Borgar darted him a quick glance. 'It's Ognun,' he said quietly. 'I'll tell you about him when we are safe inside. No one likes to talk about Ognun when the sun is about to go down, and there's quite a way to safety yet.'

They reached the main entrance to the hill fort, where the gates lay shattered, with grass and moss growing in velvety tuffets in the cracks. The massive pillars that had held the gate were also skewed and shattered, held together by clumps of grass and trailing vines.

Leifr nodded toward the fallen gates. 'Did your enemy Ognun do this?' he asked.

Borgar shook his head. 'This was long before Ognun,

248

when the fortress fell for the last time to the Dokkalfar and their wizards.'

Inside the wall lay a ditch and another wall, also crumbling and overgrown with the grasses of decades of neglect. An arched gateway led into a courtyard, overshadowed by the walls and the two round towers. By this time, several other strangers had joined the procession. All their weapons were stone, and their clothing was mainly roughly tanned troll skins, with a worsted wool shirt or cloak seen only rarely.

Entry into the towers was gained through a small door barely large enough to accommodate a horse with a pack on its back. Once everyone was inside, a quick tally was taken of the occupants. When everyone seemed to be accounted for, most of the men clumped away to the small courtyard beyond the towers, where dogs barked, horses nickered, and children's voices mingled in a pleasing, home-like babble of sounds. Borgar plucked up a sconce light from where it stood beside the doorway and led his guests across the courtyard to an ancient firehall with a thatched roof, hung with rotting shields. Inside, it was like many a Scipling firehall – much blackened by smoke and age, sparse as to decorations and carvings, with a great hearth at either end and benches and tables in between. Along the sides were platforms for sleeping for guests, or a dozen or so extra fighting men.

Servants were carrying in the supper, threading their way patiently through small children and dogs to serve the meal. Borgar pointed to the places nearest the end of the table for honored guests, then sat down in the chieftain's chair. The hubbub of voices was hushed, and all eyes turned to Borgar and his guests.

'We have visitors tonight, and I bid you all to make them welcome among us,' Borgar said gravely. 'They were here before we took refuge in the old fortress.'

Leifr sensed a sudden heightening of interest throughout the household of thirty-four, from the oldest grandfather to the two solemn babies seated on their mothers' laps. Borgar went on to name all the household, explaining that of the original settlement only three families now remained, and everyone drank in tribute to family members who had perished or disappeared since the advent of Sorkvir's alog. Leifr trembled lest they ask him to introduce himself. Fortunately, Borgar seemed to be politely waiting for him to mention his name without being asked, so Leifr gladly allowed the matter to slip beneath his notice as the evening wore on. Eventually only Borgar, a few of Borgar's people, and his guests were left to themselves beside the fire, where the troll-hounds stretched out with weary sighs.

'Now must be the time to speak of Ognun,' Leifr said to Borgar, who nodded slowly. Without his winged helmet, he seemed about the same age as Leifr, although Leifr knew that, among Alfar, appearances could be deceiving. He was spare and lean, and the firelight played up the bony contours of his angular features.

'Yes, now is the time for Ognun. Sorkvir put him in the Rhbus' well to guard it, in a courtyard on the north side of the fortress. He is a night-farer, so we are able to travel in and out with our livestock or go fishing by day, while he sleeps. At night, he tries to break through our fortifications, unless he knows of any trolls nearby. He often comes home with a brace of them slung over his shoulder, as if they were rabbits.'

'What sort of creature is he, a giant?' Thurid removed his pipe from his mouth and dropped it unnoticed into his satchel as he eagerly dove into his rune wands to find the instructions for a giant-fighting spell.

'No, he is what our elders called a troll,' Borgar replied. 'You seldom see his kind anymore.'

'A troll, eh?' Thurid slapped shut his satchel and felt around for his pipe with mounting irritation. 'Trolls are my speciality. Has anyone seen my pipe around here? It was in my hand a moment ago. Trolls, as I was saying, don't give me the slightest qualm. I'd be glad to destroy this Ognun for you. I wonder that you haven't done it yourselves, if there's only a solitary troll giving you trouble. Drat that pipe, I hope I haven't lost it.'

'Men have tried to destroy Ognun before,' Borgar replied. 'They ended up as Ognun's next meal. He's not an ordinary troll. He has powers. He lives in an old well which is always frozen and fearfully cold.'

'Sorkvir's work,' Gotiskolker spoke up with flat certainty. 'That well used to be a stop for Pentacle travelers.'

Borgar and his three lieutenants exchanged a glance, alert and cautious. 'Not many people speak of the Pentacle any more,' Borgar said. 'Sorkvir has made it a thing of dread. No traveler dares to drink at that well now. In the old days, drinking its water gave a man clearer sight and stronger powers; and for certain ones, there was even more. When a person of extraordinary powers came to the well, five salmon would appear in its water. By catching one and eating it, the chosen one became capable of hearing the voices of the Rhbus – all the Rhbus, not just the ones still in existence now. At one time the Rhbus were a large race of people, like Ljosalfar, only far more gifted in powers. Although they are extinct except for the last three, a person with the gift can hear their voices, thousands of them. This fortress was built by the Rhbus, long before Elbegast, and they put the salmon in the well to insure the preservation of their wisdom.'

Thurid's eyes glittered in the red firelight. 'Then one who eats the sacred salmon has the prospect of one day becoming one of the Rhbus, if he is gifted enough.'

'It is possible – although the selection of a Rhbu is a very rare event indeed. The Rhbus were so far ahead of even the best Ljosalfar wizard that only hundreds of years of training and practice will prepare a candidate.' Borgar prodded another piece of wood into the fire. 'But with the Rhbus' well frozen solid by a spell of Sorkvir's, no one will ever again partake of that knowledge. When the present Rhbus are gone, all their powers and intelligence will be lost.'

Thurid gazed into the fire, absorbed in thoughts so engrossing that he did not notice the smoke oozing from his satchel.

'The knowledge of the Rhbus must not be lost,' he declared, his nostrils quivering with fine emotion. 'We're going to kill that troll and purify the well of Sorkvir's influence. Nothing must threaten the perpetuity of the revered Rhbus.'

At that solemn moment, he noticed the smoke and hastily jerked open his satchel with a fierce oath that rattled the moldering weapons on the walls. Plunging his arm in to the elbow, he fished out his pipe and a feather-covered headdress which was smoldering and smoking. Quickly he extinguished the fire and peered into his satchel, sniffing suspiciously for signs of further trouble. Satisfied, he shut it up again with a brisk snap and continued, 'As I was going to say, we've dealt with trolls before. I daresay you know about Kerling-tjorn and Luster by now.' He leaned back confidently in his chair and relit his pipe by blowing into the bowl gently.

Borgar and his men seemed to have forgotten the ale in their cups, so intense was their scrutiny of Thurid, Leifr, and the enigmatic, shadowy figure of Gotiskolker sitting with his head turned, watching the fire.

'We get very little news,' Borgar said. 'My cousin Lesandi here makes a few journeys each year with a pack train, to fetch needful supplies and to fill his ears with news, but he's between trips now.'

'Then you haven't heard that Kerling-tjorn and Luster have been delivered from Sorkvir's power,' Thurid said with great relish. 'The lake is restored and the safe haven at Luster is no longer a place of terror and death.'

'This is news indeed!' Borgar leaped to his feet. 'Lesandi, go spread the word. This means there's hope for Bjartur. Do you know who is responsible for breaking Sorkvir's power over two points of the Pentacle?'

252

Thurid beamed, and Leifr cringed inwardly, uncertain of Fridmarr's reception in a place that had suffered such harm because of his duplicity. As Thurid opened his mouth to proclaim the news, his satchel suddenly exploded with a murderous report and swatches of soot sailed through the air in all directions. With an agonized howl, Thurid pawed through the blackened remains for any survivors, and came up with a scant handful of intact rune wands.

'I'm ruined,' he said in a voice of despair.

Borgar and his companions withdrew to share the news with the rest of the household, darting a few questioning glances over their shoulders at Thurid and Leifr.

'Can't you remember any of those spells?' Leifr asked.

Thurid heaved a wretched sigh. 'I don't know. If you make one mistake, you get something completely different from what you intended. It even gets dangerous.'

Gotiskolker coughed and fanned at the smoke. 'You've still got your staff magic. Alf-light does an excellent job of killing trolls.'

'But what about Sorkvir's power over that well?' Thurid plucked at his sparse beard with his sooty fingers. 'I don't know what I'm going to do. I wish this had happened before I'd told them we were going to kill their troll.'

'You can do it, can't you?' Leifr asked uneasily, testing the tightness of the neck torque with one finger.

'Yes, yes, of course,' Thurid snapped. 'When the day comes that I can't blast a solitary troll into smithereens, you can put old Thurid out to pasture with the rest of the winter stewing meat. I don't care this much for Ognun, or whatever they call him.' He snapped his fingers contemptuously. 'But those rune wands and all that old magical paraphernalia was priceless and irreplaceable.'

'You'll have to come up with the same powers on your own, then,' Gotiskolker said. 'If you're any kind of wizard at all.'

Thurid glared, but the dogs interrupted him by suddenly scrambling to their feet, with their fur standing on end from ears to tail. With loud, shuddering growls, they slowly stalked toward the far end door, which stood barred and battened. Suddenly Kraftig lunged, shoving his nose under the door and then baying at the top of his lungs in his eagerness to get at whatever lurked on the far side. The other dogs took up the same defiant note and pawed at the door, standing on their hind legs to sniff intently between all the boards.

Thurid hurried to the locked door with his staff in hand. 'It must be the troll,' he whispered. 'Open the peep hole. I want a look at the troll who has devastated an entire settlement singlehandedly and keeps thirty-four survivors living in terror. I don't believe that the troll has been made yet that can do all that by himself.'

For a long moment he gazed out the small window which Leifr had unbarred. Then he hurled himself over backwards as an enormous, hairy hand shot through the window, narrowly missing Thurid with a set of sharp, black claws as the owner of the huge paw groped around for something fo snag, growling fearsomely.

CHAPTER 16

THE only reason that Thurid wasn't hooked like a mackerel on a gaff was the fact that the creature's forearm was too thick to reach through the narrow window any further. The dogs instantly seized the hand with their teeth and shook it furiously, resulting in a deafening, furious bellow from the other side of the door and a series of thunderous blows on the planks. Behind Leifr, Borgar and Lesandi led a rush of men into the hall, all armed with their stone weapons.

Leifr called off the dogs, fearing that the door could not endure much more abuse. Then Ognun put as much of his face against the opening as he could and peered malevolently into the hall with one gleaming green eye. Leifr stared back, hefting the stone mace beligerently, with the dogs snarling around his knees to complete the picture of grim defiance.

Ognun's eye opened wider, perhaps in astonishment, and he peered in with his other eye to make sure the first eye was not deceived. Then he jerked back in alarm as Leifr gave the command and the dogs hurled themselves at the window. Ognun swiped at them with his murderously sharp black claws, rumbling like thunder, until Leifr called the dogs back again, fearing the destruction of the door.

Again Ognun peered into the hall, breathing heavily in hoarse, panting breaths. In a deep, grumbling voice, he called, 'Borgar, I'm going to eat those dogs the way a cat eats rats. Who is this stranger with a cockleburr for a weapon? I don't like the smell of him, nor that smoky one in the long cloak. You're plotting treachery, Borgar. I'll suck the marrow from your bones and pick my teeth with your ribs if you brought them here to kill me.'

'We brought ourselves,' Leifr replied. 'Your quarrel is with us, not Borgar.'

Ognun sniffed through the window, with a huge, wrinkled nose seamed with scars and misshapen from many battles. 'What is your name, stranger?' he rumbled.

Leifr drew a deep breath. 'My name is my own business, and I don't care to reveal it to any troll who demands it.'

Thurid flourished his staff, scattering sparks as he strode forward, almost within Ognun's reach. He had to stoop slightly to peer into the window, where Ognun's eye and part of his warty nose showed through. 'You can't be a troll,' he declared scornfully. 'Trolls don't get that large. Trolls are nasty little vermin with the appetites of sea gulls and the intelligence of weasels. Whatever you are, you aren't a troll.'

'Not a troll? Did you ever see teeth like this in anyone else's mouth but a troll's?' Ognun gnawed at the edge of the peep hole, showing an enormous set of yellowed fangs. 'What about these claws? Don't these look like troll claws to you?' Curving black claws reached inside, biting deep into the wood and pulling off slivers.

'I suppose I'm forced to concede that you are indeed a troll,' Thurid admitted grudgingly. 'Take your claws out of that window, won't you? I find it discomfiting to talk with a seemingly rational being with claws like those. Are you a greater gray troll, or a mountain troll from the inlands?'

'Neither. I am a true troll. All the others are degenerate offshoots. All trolls used to be like me, but now there aren't many of us left.' He peered in with a sly squinting of his eye and went on in his deep, sleepy rumble, 'You look like a wizard and you smell like a wizard. Have you and this warrior come to destroy me? The bones of many would-be heroes lie around the door to my home. I'd be most pleased to show them to you.'

'Indeed,' Thurid snorted. 'We're not interested in the failures. We're going to kill you, Ognun, unless you choose voluntarily to vacate Bjartur and never return.'

'Leave Bjartur and my comfortable home? Surely you are jesting.' Ognun chuckled menacingly. 'And that warrior with the puny stickery weapon is another jest. It will take more than the two of you to kill me. I am thousands of years old and I've learned a thing or two in that time. One bit of advice for you from one much older and wiser is – never attack someone twice your size. Another warning I shall give you – don't go outdoors after sundown in Bjartur or you may find yourself taken down a little red lane whence there is no return.' He uttered a booming laugh at his own joke, then added, 'Better yet, you should leave Bjartur tomorrow while I'm asleep. Do you hear, Borgar? I want these strangers out of Bjartur tomorrow. This is going to cost you when it comes time for the fall tribute.'

With a last noisy sniff through the window, Ognun glowered into the hall for a moment, then moved away with a crunching of rocks beneath his feet.

Borgar shut the peep hole and locked it, and the rest of the men sat down on the benches with a flurry of excited talk, inviting Thurid to tell all he knew about Kerling-tjorn and Luster. Leifr glared at him warningly and made a motion to be silent.

'You're being foolish,' Thurid muttered. 'You've nothing to fear by telling them who you are.'

'Why risk it?' Leifr asked. 'They might decide to make us part of the fall tribute to Ognun. I think I would, in their place.'

'As you wish, then.' Thurid grumbled.

Between them, they parried the questions of the Bjartur men far into the night. Ognun prowled by twice, growling in reply to the dogs. The third time he returned, the hall was dark and everyone asleep, except for the changing guards and Leifr, who heard the heavy tread of the troll and the growling of Kraftig, Frimodig, and Farlig. Slipping off the sleeping platform, Leifr approached the door silently and ventured to peer out the small window, holding it open just a crack.

The troll heard him and turned around suspiciously – a hulking, stooped shape with a massive domed forehead, furrowed into countless wrinkles that sagged past the deep-sunk, gleaming eyes and the scarred and stubby nose. Ognun's hide hung loosely over his great knobby bones, tufted along his spine like an unkempt mane, with clumps of long, matted fur hanging from his armpits and belly. His hind shanks were covered with motley fur, and he trailed a thin, ropy tail with several kinks where it had been broken and mended, leaving unsightly knots. As he turned, Leifr saw his huge, three-toed feet, tipped with claws like scythes.

Then Ognun shrugged impatiently, picked up something, and slung it over his shoulder. To Leifr, it looked like a yearling cow. Ognun staggered slightly under its weight as he bore it off toward the north end of the fortress.

Leifr locked the peephole and thoughtfully stroked the dogs' muzzles. They wagged and stretched, wrinkling up their lips in friendly grins. 'You'd like a chance at him, wouldn't you?' Leifr muttered to Kraftig, removing the great paws from his shoulders and wrestling with the playful beast before he could pass. Then the others followed him, gnawing on his legs so he could hardly take a step. Clearly, they begged to be let out, to go after this larger edition of their natural prey. Irresolute, Leifr turned toward the door leading into the courtyard, where Borgar's guards watched through the night, and the dogs bounded around him delightedly, relieved that their message had at last penetrated his feeble understanding.

Since it was almost dawn, Leifr went outside with the dogs. Several people were stirring around already and lighting smoky fires, their warm breath condensing in the chill air. Leifr pulled his hood over his head and began to explore. The gate leading to the outer compound was still locked, with two guards pacing and swinging their arms to keep warm, glancing up frequently at the paling sky. Nodding to them curtly, Leifr and the dogs took an upward-winding path to one of the round towers, which they found to be uninhabited, except for two more guards and some rumpled, sleepy crows on the broken roof. A gaping window gave access to the top of the wall, which Leifr followed northward until he gained a view of the northern courtyard. He sat down to study it, and the dogs wagged their tails, pleased at his progress in the right direction.

The courtyard was bounded by ruined stables crumbling into green heaps, with only a lintel here and there to show what the structures had once been. An arched gateway led into the court, and there seemed to be no other way in or out. Behind the stables reared the raw mountainside in a sheer cliff; a high wall barred one side, and on the other was a rubble-strewn drop to the valley floor, made more treacherous with blocks of fallen stonework and debris. Inside the court there was no cover or advantage for a fighter, except random blocks of stone and a few thickets.

At first, Leifr was unaware of the well in its natural camouflage, assuming it was a heap of fallen masonry. Then he noticed that the four cornerstones were carved with runes and he discerned the broken curbing of a large well, partially obscured by scrubby bushes that had sprung up between the stones. Part of a stone banister remained, leading down some steps toward the interior of the well.

The hounds suddenly cocked their ears and growled, gazing earnestly toward the well. Presently the disturbance they sensed was silent; they sat down again at Leifr's feet, gazing around them in lofty disdain at the awakening settlement. Their attention sharpened briefly when Borgar, Lesandi, and another man called Skapillur climbed onto the wall from the round tower. They greeted Leifr politely and exchanged a few of the customary amenities before their curiosity got the best of their formal manners.

Lesandi blurted out, 'We were talking, and no one has heard you mention your name. We thought – if you had forgotten, perhaps – or if we didn't understand . . .'

Leifr allowed him to sputter to a confused halt, taking refuge behind a forbidding scowl. Hastily Borgar interrupted. 'Lesandi is saying it very clumsily. Your name is safe with us. If anyone comes after you asking questions, we haven't seen you at all.'

Leifr allowed his scowl to soften. 'You must wonder for a while longer. Perhaps after I'm gone, you'll know.'

Borgar nodded to his companions, who went back to the tower to stand guard; then the chief walked further down the wall, toward the north courtyard. Leifr and the hounds followed, joining him at a black skarp, jutting from the side of the fell and blocking any further progress without ropes and spikes. The place offered a good view of the stables below, and Leifr could see further into the well. A stone stairway spiraled down the wall into the shadowy depths below. Now that the sun was showing over the horizon, Leifr noticed the heaps of whitening bones scattered around the court. He shuddered suddenly at the prospect of going down into that place to do battle with Ognun.

'Ognun is not going to be easily killed,' Borgar said. 'He has the wisdom of ages of evil. Attempts on his life make him angry, and it's difficult for us to live with him after someone tries to kill him. We have to turn out the one who tries, or there's no peace for us. When we leave him alone and humor him with tributes four times a year, he let's us live in relative peace.'

Leifr shook his head incredulously. 'How do you tolerate such a life? After all the murders he has done, you allow him to live and continue to torment you?'

'We don't tolerate it,' Borgar replied with a flash of anger in his eyes. 'We are waiting.'

260

'Waiting for what? Old age to take Ognun away?'

'We are waiting for someone to return, one who promised that he would come back to help us out of our difficulty.' Borgar sighed and gazed moodily toward the north court. 'But he hasn't come back yet, and he's been a long time gone. Some of us think he isn't coming back. So take your crack at Ognun, but if you fail, you can't stay here – if you survive, that is. He'll follow you when you go, and there's not much cover outside these walls.'

Leifr chose to ignore Borgar's warnings. 'Ognun lives inside the well?' he asked.

Borgar nodded. 'You can see a few of the steps that lead downward. You can also see the ice hanging on the edge of the curbing. It never melts, even in summer. It's more of Sorkvir's wizardry, to ensure that no one ever drinks from that well again or eats the sacred salmon.'

'What sort of weapon does Ognun use?' Leifr inquired in a grim tone.

'A big cudgel. His teeth, his claws, his supernatural strength. How do you plan to kill him, when he's twice the size of you?' Borgar fixed Leifr with a piercing gaze when Leifr presented no quick answer to his question. 'Magic, I suppose? I thought your wizard lost a great deal of his magic when his satchel blew up.'

Leifr began to resent Borgar's needling. He whistled to the hounds, who were quartering the hillside above the skarp. 'Is there a way down to the well from here?' he asked, surveying the jagged slope below.

'You can pick your way down, if you're careful. Ognun can't come up this way because his weight causes the rocks to slide. But it would be wiser to wait for your wizard and some of my best men to guard you.' Borgar eyed Leifr challengingly as he spoke.

'We don't need them,' Leifr replied. 'Are you coming with me, or do you have something important to do just now?'

Borgar started cautiously over the edge. 'There's

nothing more important than this,' he answered defiantly. 'No stranger is going to show me up as a coward. Follow me, I'll show you the quickest way down.'

They threaded their way down the rugged jumble of broken stonework with the hounds following eagerly at Leifr's heels, nudging him onward when he hesitated over a difficult traverse. They reached the bottom and crossed a ditch full of bones and nettles, climbed up the wall behind the stables, and rested on the top, looking down into the court.

'You've done this before,' Leifr said. 'Surely there's an easier way into the north court.'

'Certainly, but not when you're a young lad trying to prove his courage to himself and his peers,' Borgar replied with a chuckle. 'It takes a boy to know these walls. We never tired of exploring. Of course we courted danger whenever we could.'

'Naturally. I did the same thing in—' Catching himself quickly, he awkwardly finished with, 'in Solvorfirth. It was quite the thing to spy around Gliru-hals.'

Borgar's attention was caught. 'Solvorfirth? You are from the same region as the wizard Thurid, then. Tell me, did you know Fridmarr Fridmundrsson?'

Leifr composed himself with a deep breath and a steely stare calculated to conceal his nervousness from Borgar. Coldly he replied, 'No one knew Fridmarr. I don't think anybody wanted to, either – except possibly his brother Bodmarr, and one other – Ljosa Hroaldsdottir.'

'How strange,' murmured Borgar, half to himself.

'Strange? I think not, after all the evil Fridmarr was responsible for in Solvorfirth and other places,' Leifr replied somewhat heatedly.

Borgar's frown deepened. 'Fridmarr was regarded as a hero here. He deceived Sorkvir utterly and had gotten into Sorkvir's trust, although it was Elbegast's cause he was always loyal to. He told my father Ofrodur that he was a spy for Elbegast and that one day he would return to undo the evil that Sorkvir put the people of Bjartur into. My father believed absolutely that Fridmarr would return one day, and he raised me to believe it too. Everyone here believes it, more or less, depending upon how discouraged we feel at the time.'

Leifr felt as if all the breath had been squeezed out of him, so great was his shock. Suddenly Leifr felt himself so thoroughly in the grip of Fridmarr's fate that he wanted nothing more than to escape from the situations which Fridmarr had created so many years ago and which reached out now to enmesh him in the unforgiving bonds of cause and effect.

Leaping to his feet, he took a few steps, only to realize the futility of trying to escape. The towering walls of Bjartur were all around him, solid and dark behind their screens of morning mists. There was no escape, and there was no one who could help him. Only Gotiskolker knew that Leifr was not Fridmarr, and Gotiskolker was driven by his own inner demons toward his own inscrutable devisings.

Knowing he was trapped, Leifr turned back to Borgar, who was watching him suspiciously.

'And the people of Bjartur still believe that he is almost a hero, even though he helped ruin the Pentacle?'

'A hero, yes,' Borgar replied.

'But look at the terrible evil that he caused you,' Leifr protested. 'Fridmarr was a traitor to his own kind. He told Sorkvir how to destroy the well. A lot of your people lost their lives.'

'We are at war, and during wars, people die,' Borgar answered. 'If Fridmarr chose to appear as a traitor, it was for reasons that will be explained sometime in the future. Fridmarr gave his word of honor to my father and asked Ofrodur to trust him that one day Sorkvir would be destroyed forever. He promised the people of Bjartur that he would return as their deliverer.'

Leifr gazed around at the ruined fortress, which was coming to life with the rise of the sun. Sheep, cattle, and ponies foraged among the fallen stones, under the watchful eyes of young herdsmen, and three men with bows and lances were starting out for a day's hunting. The smoke and busy noises of a striving settlement rose from the depths of the shadowy old ruin.

For such a diligent and stubborn group of survivors, Leifr reflected, they had certainly been taken in by one of Fridmarr's most blatant ploys. For a moment, Leifr considered the possibility that Fridmarr had intended to come back, but he doubted Fridmarr's word. He had seen very little in Fridmarr's nature to offer him any encouragement.

'How did such a young man as you become chieftain?' Leifr asked suddenly. 'I saw plenty of older, grayer heads than yours around your table last night.'

Borgar's tension relaxed somewhat. 'By the same means that you have earned your status. By fighting – and fighting well. With so few good men and only stone for weapons against the Dokkalfar steel, I must plan our defenses carefully. Less than half of us here are fighting men of full stature and warrior age. Plenty of times, the women, children, and elders have had to put on the appearance of warriors to frighten away marauding Dokkalfar.'

'Why do you stay here? There are plenty of better places, either north or south.'

'Bjartur must not die. This has been our land since the time of the Rhbus. People will come back when the alog is lifted and Ognun is dead.'

'But only if the illustrious Fridmarr returns.'

'He is coming. Someone broke Sorkvir's influence over Kerling-tjorn and Luster. Perhaps it was Fridmarr. Perhaps you have seen him.'

Leifr turned away from Borgar's too-intent scrutiny. 'I think fate is another word for Fridmarr. Haven't we wasted enough time arguing over someone who might not exist?'

'He exists,' Borgar said, rising to his feet and starting

away. 'You shall see. Come along if you truly want to pay Ognun a visit in the daytime.'

The path leading into the north court was littered with bones and skulls of animals and a few bones that looked to be human. Leifr gazed in uneasy wonder at the corner of the gatepost where Ognun obviously liked to rub his back when it itched. What concerned Leifr the most was the fact that the greasy mark was head and shoulders above him, as high as a man's head on horseback. Leifr measured with the stone mace how high he would have to swing to land a blow in a vital area.

'He's bigger than he looked by moonlight,' Leifr observed ruefully. 'I can't reach his skull unless he falls down, or I climb a wall.'

'He'll swat you with that big club he carries as if you were a fly,' Borgar answered.

Warily they approached the curb of the well. Four of the five stones still stood, and the area around them had been paved with flagstones at one time, although by now the stones and the moss had compromised with a checkerboard effect. A well-beaten path disappeared at the edge of the well, and the steps descending into the darkness were blackened with Ognun's grimy footsteps. A skull thrust into a sharpened stake stood as a warning in a crevice of the curbing, and bones and molting skins were scattered within convenient tossing distance around the mouth of the well. A few broken weapons were among the litter. The worst part of it was the nauseating stench hanging over the court.

Leifr approached the well, ignoring Borgar's sharp warnings: 'Don't go near the edge, where he might see you. He hates it when anybody trespasses on his private domain.'

'He'll have to get used to it,' Leifr answered, his voice echoing inside the well. 'His private domain never was his to call his own, so we may trespass here with more right than he has.'

A cold breeze exuded from the well as Leifr peered

down into it from the top steps. It was deeper than he had imagined, spiraling down into the earth until he could see nothing but blackness. The stone walls oozed with clammy sweat, which encrusted them with frost and ice. Far below, he heard something stirring restlessly, moving, then falling silent to listen. Behind Leifr's legs, the troll-hounds licked their lips and rumbled with growls.

Closing his eyes a moment against the dank breath of the well, Leifr allowed the carbuncle to tell him what it could, by way of warning or advice. He felt a strong anticipatory thrill at the prospect of exploring unimagined mysteries. Distinctly he glimpsed a vast galleried chamber veiled in musty dimness – a hollow, echoing place filled with the countless whispers of the long-departed Rhbus.

Startled and uneasy, Leifr stepped back from the well, conscious of Borgar's keen scrutiny.

'Let's see if Ognun's at home,' he said abruptly. 'The dogs would like to meet their opponent without a door between them to spoil all their fun. Ready, Kraftig?'

At the signal from Leifr, they eagerly scampered down the winding stairs and vanished into the gloom.

'You've just wasted the lives of your dogs,' Borgar said grimly. 'They may be death on ordinary trolls, but Ognun is not ordinary. He eats dogs.'

'He won't eat these dogs,' Leifr answered.

In a few minutes, there came a ferocious outburst of barking and snarling from far below.

'Ognun is at home, I'd say,' Leifr observed, and whistled to the dogs. 'Now they've had their look at him.'

Borgar regarded the dogs narrowly when they emerged from the well, panting with satisfaction and wagging their plumy tails. Kraftig pawed Leifr's shoulders, looking straight into his eyes as if he wanted to speak but found Leifr a rather dense subject for communication. Leifr thumped them all affectionately and let them go exploring.

'Let's be going,' Borgar suggested uneasily. 'I expect we've stirred up enough trouble for one day. Ognun will tell us about it tonight. I'd better double the guard.'

'Put everyone up on the walls if you wish,' Leifr said. 'They'll have a good view of Ognun's last battle.'

When they returned to the main gate of the inner keep, they found Thurid holding court with the elders of the settlement. Seeing Leifr, he excused himself and came to meet him. 'There you are,' he said accusingly. 'When I awakened this morning, you and Gotiskolker were nowhere to be found. What have you been doing off on your own, without me to protect you?'

'I went to the well,' Leifr replied. 'The dogs went down for a look at Ognun's living quarters. I heard him moving around down there. The well is deeper than I had thought it would be, and Ognun is bigger than a mounted rider.'

'That's to be expected. What are your plans?'

'I have some ideas, but I thought it was your job to come up with the plans. I don't do anything except the fighting and dying.'

'Don't be facetious. I'm in no mood for levity. This throwback troll is nothing to joke about, Fridmarr. He's far more dangerous and cunning than a hundred regular trolls combined. You'd better have some good ideas for killing him.'

'Have you talked to Gotiskolker yet?' Leifr asked.

'That scumbag?' Thurid snorted profoundly. 'I should say not. I haven't fallen so low as to ask him for advice yet. What makes you think he might know anything about killing giant trolls in wells?'

'Well, it's possible—'

'The trouble with you, Fridmarr, is that you have no respect for your elders and their years of wisdom.'

Leifr glanced around uneasily to see if anyone were near enough to overhear. 'You'd better stop using my name when you talk, Thurid. I don't want them to know who I am. They think that I'm some sort of hero, but I'm not, so I don't want to be treated like one.'

Thurid's eyes bulged wrathfully. 'Perverse, that's what you are. The return of their hero is exactly what these people need to stir them up against this giant. If enough men attacked him, they might kill him.'

'And how many do you suppose Ognun would kill before he died? I don't want to do it that way, and I don't want to pose as a hero. When they find out the truth about my past, they're liable to be furious that I managed to trick them for so long. Gullible people usually get very angry.'

During the day, the word spread that the strangers intended to challenge Ognun. By nightfall, most of the settlement had taken up positions on the walls overlooking the north court. A bonfire burned on the highest rampart in the ruins of a fallen tower, and smaller fires dotted the walls where people watched and hoped. When the sun had vanished, Borgar opened the gate to let Thurid and Leifr out, evincing much reluctance to see them go alone; but Leifr resisted all offers of help. The person he most wanted to see was Gotiskolker, but the scavenger had stayed out of sight the entire day.

The troll-hounds ran ahead, racing straight toward the north court. Ognun had not yet emerged, the watchers on the walls reported, but more mist than usual seemed to be coming from the well, in billowing white clouds.

Leifr glanced frequently at Thurid, wondering at his resolute silence and the grim set of his jaw. It was unlike Thurid to be quiet so long.

'Why do you keep staring at me?' Thurid snapped at last, hesitating at the arched gateway into the north court. 'Are you afraid I'm not competent for the task at hand? I spent most of the day making new rune sticks from memory and finding a new satchel. Are you beginning to doubt my ability?'

'You seem to doubt more,' Leifr replied. 'I don't think you need those rune sticks.'

'Indeed! And what makes you a qualified judge, if I may be so bold as to inquire?'

Leifr paused, knowing he had spoken from Fridmarr's knowledge coming to him from the carbuncle. He rubbed his chest, feeling the slight bump of the little stone against his breastbone. 'You are far too willing to walk with a crutch, when you could be flying without it,' he said.

Thurid sniffed disdainfully. 'Crutch, my eye! I'm only trying to be cautious. With the rune sticks, I'm certain to get the spells right – most of the time. Without them, I have no guarantee and I don't much like relying on my memory alone.'

'You're just looking for excuses not to rely more upon your powers,' Leifr retorted. 'Ready or not, you're going to have to stand up to the test now.'

'I'm ready!' Thurid snapped, with an icy glare as he stepped into the shadow of the arch.

A dark figure waiting in the gloom suddenly lurched forward. Thurid gasped and the knob of his staff flared with a brilliant burst of alf-light. Leifr lowered his raised mace, and Gotiskolker winced in the bright glare of the staff.

'It's only me,' he grumbled. 'I got locked out, so I waited for you here.'

'We've been wondering what had happened to you,' Leifr said chidingly, as the dogs crowded at his heels, urging him to hurry. 'Where have you been all day?' We could have used some help in planning this escapade.'

'I was doing some planning of my own,' Gotiskolker replied, and Thurid responded with a withering snort.

'Our plan,' Thurid said, 'is to attack him whcn hc comes out tonight. Fridmarr and the dogs will keep him occupied, while I blast him with fire magic.'

'That's not the way to hunt bears,' Gotiskolker said. 'You must trap them inside their dens, where they can't maneuver so well, and pierce them with your lance.'

'We're not hunting bears,' Thurid retorted, 'or hadn't you heard?' He damped down the glow of his staff and motioned to Leifr. 'Let's carry on, shall we?'

When they reached the well, Leifr sent the dogs down to draw Ognun out. Thurid paced up and down uneasily, going over his rune sticks. Gotiskolker squatted with his back against a stone and studied the stars. Leifr listened impatiently, growing more uneasy the longer he waited.

'They should have found him by now,' Leifr said at last. 'We should have heard a big uproar.'

'Maybe he found them first,' Gotiskolker suggested. 'He's probably hungry.'

'Shh! There's something!' Thurid warned.

A faint howl, questioning in tone, floated out of the well. Leifr whistled and called, but got no response from the dogs. There was no sound at all, except the drip of the ice melting around the top.

Leifr gripped his mace and stepped over the well curbing onto the steps. Grimly he said, 'Come on, we're going bear hunting.'

CHAPTER 17

As Leifr started down the well, Gotiskolker followed at his heels like a black shadow. Thurid quickly ignited his staff's end with a puff of alf-light and hastened to join them. Inside the well, the alf-light glowed on the icy walls with a fiery blue phosphorescence. When they neared the bottom, the pool of ice below radiated like a frosty eye, growing larger with each descending spiral.

'No troll,' Leifr said, when they had a good view of the bottom of the well. The stone steps ended at a small landing, where the pilgrims had knelt to drink the water. Now there was nothing but ice, polished smooth by Ognun's filthy carcass and littered with bones, hair, and rubbish.

'Maybe he got out earlier than usual,' Thurid said, shining his light around and beginning to sound hopeful.

'Someone would have seen him,' Leifr answered. 'People were watching from the walls before the sun went down.'

Gotiskolker slipped past Leifr and began a circuit around the wall, which was festooned with pillars of ice where the water had dripped down for many years.

'No dogs,' Leifr continued, as Thurid's beam traveled around the well again. Feeling the breath of an air current on his face, he turned toward it and saw Gotiskolker vanish into a fissure behind a thick column of ice. Quickly he followed, trusting Thurid to notice where he had gone.

Thurid was gazing elsewhere and did not notice that he was alone for several moments. He stepped onto the ice warily, stamping on it to sound its thickness. When he looked up, he perceived that he was by himself. In a hoarse whisper he called, 'Fridmarr! Where are you?'

A hand reached out of the fissure behind him and gripped his arm, startling him. He staggered back with a whoop, and his alf-light surged halfway to the top of the well in a bellowing roar of flame that caused several columns of ice to collapse in a thunderous avalanche. Thurid dived into the fissure, narrowly avoiding a falling slab of ice.

'Are you trying to burn the place down?' Leifr cried.

'You startled me,' Thurid protested. 'My magic always overdoes itself when I'm frightened. Fortunately, it happens so seldom that it isn't usually a problem.' As he talked, he peered around him, poking his alf-light into the dark tunnel leading upward from the bottom of the well. 'Very clever of the Rhbus to have a secret tunnel into the well. Those stairs winding around and around are fine for pilgrims, but I'd hate to use them as a daily chore.'

'Hurry up with the light,' Gotiskolker whispered. 'Ognun is somewhere ahead of us.'

The tunnel angled upward, rising with short flights of steps, now nearly obliterated by accumulating soil and rocks from the ceiling above. In places, the fissure had been widened and enlarged and, in other places, it widened naturally into cavernous rooms, where bats hung in clusters from the lofty ceiling, twittering in protest at the unwelcome intrusion of the light into their inky realm. Underfoot, the earth was moist and soft, and Leifr discerned the three sets of hound prints and the large, three-toed track of Ognun, slowly filling with water.

The character of the underground chambers changed suddenly as the three passed through a pair of large doors, torn from their hinges long ago, rudely shattered by some powerful engine of destruction. Beyond the doors were the remains of smooth stone floors, graceful carved pillars, and stone galleries ascending upward, tier by tier.

Thurid gazed around in awe. 'This was the assembly hall of the Rhbus,' he whispered, with a tremor in his voice. 'Imagine so many Rhbus that they filled a place like this! And now there are only three left.'

'And not as many Ljosalfar as there once were,' Gotiskolker added. 'If wizards like Sorkvir have their way, we shall become extinct, too.'

Halfway across the assembly hall, Leifr halted and listened intently for a moment to the distant baying of the hounds, echoing through the underground chambers.

'They've cornered him,' Leifr said, striding forward. 'Hurry up with the light, Thurid. You're crawling along like a snail.'

'A cornered troll is a nasty situation,' Thurid hastened to explain, firing up his alf-light with a quick, muttered spell and scuttling after Leifr and Gotiskolker. 'Perhaps he's leading us on this merry chase deliberately. I don't know what advantage we've got over him down here in the dark where we can't see and he feels perfectly at home. Hasn't it crossed your mind yet that he might have some dreadful surprise in mind?'

Gotiskolker retorted, 'He wouldn't be a troll if he didn't. He's got a number of bolt holes leading out of here to the outside; if we corner him before he gets out, we'll have a better chance of killing him. Wc've got to keep close to him, or he's likely to become the hunter and we'll become the prey.'

Thurid hastened his pace, glancing around nervously.

As they picked their way down a jumbled corridor, the distant reflected light of the staff suddenly illuminated several sets of glowing eyes that came bounding through the shadows toward them. Heavy paws bounded over the rubble, and eager yelps echoed from the damp walls as the troll-hounds burst into view. For a moment, they caracoled around Leifr, leaping up to lick his face and nipping at his heels to encourage him to hurry; then they raced away down the corridor again.

'They've got him treed!' Thurid exclaimed. 'Those worthless mutts are forgiven all their crimes if they help kill Ognun!'

They found the dogs at a rockfall, barking up at the distant roof and dodging the rocks that came hurtling down. Thurid threw himself backward into the safety of the overhanging ceiling of the corridor as a large rock whistled past his head and crashed into the wall with an explosion of particles. The alf-light flaring upward dimly illuminated a hulking dark shape, clawing its way up the rocky dome of the vast vault above.

'He's going to get away from us,' Gotiskolker snapped. 'There are more tunnels up above, and if he gets into them, he'll be stalking us.'

'Is there another way up?' Leifr demanded.

'If there is, I didn't find it,' Gotiskolker replied. 'It would take days to map out this place completely. I was down here only a few hours.'

'Thurid, knock him down with a spell,' Leifr commanded.

Thurid rattled among the runesticks. 'This is the one,' he muttered, taking out one of his new rune sticks. 'I hope so, anyway.' Raising his arms, he recited the words of the spell. At once a hundred small barbs of flame leaped from the ends of his fingers and ricocheted around the vault like a swarm of deadly, bright bees. Thurid dived for cover, and one of the hissing darts pierced the tail of his cloak with a puff of acrid smoke. Leifr and Gotiskolker and the hounds all cowered in a heap as the last of the darts fizzled and died, leaving the cavern in blackness.

'I didn't write that one down properly.' Thurid said in a bemused tone. 'My fire bolt is badly frayed. Perhaps it was only a lack of concentration—'

From above came the rumbling voice of Ognun, and another thunderous crash as a rock came down, shattering on impact. 'You'd better go back while you can, you fools,' he called in a hollow roar. 'These halls are long

274

and dark; when I'm here, they're even more dangerous. Worse things than rocks falling can happen to you.'

The dogs replied with a chorus of savage barking, until Leifr hushed them. He crept out far enough to peer upward, with the aid of Thurid's alf-light. Reaching for the bow slung at his back, he strung it and nocked an arrow.

'More light,' he said to Thurid in a whisper and slipped out of his hiding place.

Thurid spluttered indignantly, 'Fridmarr! Don't be an idiot! Get back under here before he brains you!'

'I said more light, you dolt!'

Thurid responded with a brilliant flare that outlined Ognun clinging to the rocks and the dark mouth of a tunnel just above his clawing fingers. Ognun's shadow loomed huge and threatening as he flung one arm over his eyes when the light swept over him.

'Die, you filthy bag of carrion!' roared Thurid, upping the intensity of his light until the cavern roared with flame and heat, and even he was forced to squint.

Leifr bent his bow until its sinew reinforcing creaked ominously, then sent the arrow flying upward. It lodged in Ognun's humped shoulder, where no amount of twisting and clawing would allow him to reach it. With a bellowing roar, he hurled more rocks down, his eyes blazing with fury.

Leifr dived for refuge until the rocks stopped falling, then signaled to Thurid to fire up the light again. Thurid grimaced and shook his head furiously, but Leifr ignored him and pulled back his bowstring for another shot.

This time the arrow lodged in Ognun's leg, nearly causing him to slip off his precarious perch on the rock face. Seizing the opportunity, Leifr fired off two more arrows, one of which flew wide in his haste, but the other stuck in Ognun's back. Ognun began to slip, clawing frantic score marks on the stone wall and roaring with rage.

Leifr placed two more arrows before Ognun finally

275

arrived at the bottom, still bellowing and lashing around with his deadly claws at the arrows in his flesh. His glaring eyes searched the shadows for his tormentors. When he saw them crouching behind a fallen slab, he rushed at them in a frenzy of hatred. Somewhat impaired by his wounds, he was not able to reach them before they raced away down the corridor toward the assembly hall. Dragging his injured leg, he lumbered after them, snarling vengefully.

'Back to the well!' Thurid panted. 'We've got to get out of here while we can!'

'No!' Gotiskolker cried. 'We've got to destroy him. He's weakened now.'

'Not as much as I'd like,' Leifr said worriedly, listening to the ominous sounds of Ognun's approach. 'What will it take to kill him? Thurid, do you have one good spell that you're sure of?'

'Yes, I have several, but I can't figure out how to apply them to the situation,' Thurid retorted. 'One is for changing the weather; there's one for seeing the future in the way a horse trots, there's one for throwing a whetstone over a house, and the best one of all is curing chickens of the scabs!'

'Well, do something to slow him down!' Leifr snapped.

Thurid quickly perused several rune sticks, then stepped out of his hiding place to confront Ognun. Leifr nocked another arrow and stepped out behind him, ready to cover their retreat if the spell failed.

'Fridmarr,' rumbled Ognun, pointing an accusing claw at Leifr. 'So you have returned after all. I never thought you would keep that empty promise.'

'Then that was a mistake, Ognun,' Leifr replied. 'It will cost you your life, and Sorkvir the Pentacle.'

'Then it was true what they said about you,' Ognun said ponderously. 'You are one of Elbegast's spies.'

'Perhaps,' Leifr answered.

'Fool,' Ognun grunted. 'You can't keep his kingdom

276

alive. Elbegast and all his kind are doomed. Look at Bjartur. Where are the Rhbus now? The Ljosalfar are heading for the same kind of extinction.'

'Perhaps that is true,' Gotiskolker spoke up, 'but you are the one here who is doomed, Ognun.'

Ognun snorted and lashed impatiently at the arrows in his back and shoulders. 'Do you think this is enough to kill me? If you do, then my job will be easy.' He took a step forward, and Leifr drew back his bowstring warningly. The hounds surged forward, diving in for sharp nips at the troll's legs and tail. Slashing at them resentfully, Ognun scarcely noticed his quarry slipping away from him again.

'This way,' Gotiskolker whispered urgently, when Thurid turned toward the corridor that led to the well. He beckoned toward the center of the assembly chamber, where the high roof formed a vast, echoing cavern. Far above, the pale night sky gleamed faintly through an opening. Below the opening stood a dais large enough for a hundred people, with a gallery around it and the remains of benches now crumbled to rubble. Five upright stones stood guarding a pool, where the black water sparkled.

Thurid's breath choked in his throat. 'Rhbu magic,' he whispered. 'This must be the place where they summoned their powers. We can't go there. It's too sacred.'

'It may also save us from Ognun,' Gotiskolker replied. 'I'm not going to die out of mere respect for the Rhbus' abandoned property.'

Ognun came after them with a vengeance, roaring with fury, only slightly impeded by the dogs' skirmishing attacks. His eyes burned like hot coals, and the bloody reek of him excited the hounds to more daring maneuvers in their attempts to get their teeth into his skin. He slashed at them murderously, but they skipped lightly out of harm's way, snarling defiance.

Leifr took a position behind one of the standing stones with Gotiskolker beside him, while Thurid hurried from stone to stone examining the inscriptions and runes.

'It's very similar to my old rune sticks. Rhbu magic!' Thurid leaned against one of the stones with a watery feeling in his knees. 'I'm not worthy.'

'No, you're not,' Gotiskolker agreed. 'But you'll have to do, since we have no other wizard, and you'll have to hurry. Save all your unworthy feelings for later.'

Thurid walked once around the circle of stones, still somewhat dazed, mumbling to himself and making gestures with his hands.

Ognun shook Kraftig off his leg, leaving the hound a mouthful of skin and hair, and climbed up onto the dais. For a long moment his gnarled head swung back and forth, as he considered Thurid and Leifr, deciding which one he wanted to attack first. The hounds leaped at his frayed ears and bit at his back until he lashed out at them with his deadly claws. Then he shambled forward, teeth bared in a snarl, his eyes intent upon Thurid, who had knelt beside the pool on one knee, concentrating upon summoning whatever ancient powers still lurked in that once-sacred site.

Leifr stepped warily between them, his bow drawn.

'Stop, Ognun,' he commanded.

Ognun slowed his pace, turning to regard Leifr while he slunk toward Thurid. 'Without magic, you don't have the power to kill me,' he growled. 'I'll kill this wizard, and then you'll be fair game, Fridmarr.'

Leifr let fly the arrow, a perfect shot. The arrow buried itself in Ognun's ribs, as far as the fletching. Ognun grimaced and clutched at the new injury, but he did not die, as Leifr might have expected from a mortal beast.

'I'm beginning to hate you in a new way,' Ognun said, spitting some bloody spittle on the ground and swinging his fist at the dogs without taking his eyes off Leifr. 'It will be a pleasure to tear you to pieces. I shall be sure to let Borgar and the others know what has become of their hero.'

Leifr nocked another arrow. 'I'll tell them myself, when I throw your head at their feet.'

'Shoot your arrows then. Pain is nothing to me, but you will soon run out of arrows.' Ognun grinned horribly with his bloody teeth and deliberately turned his back on Leifr, moving toward Thurid with slow, dragging steps.

'Thurid!' Leifr called warningly. 'Thurid, watch out! He's coming for you, and I can't stop him!'

Thurid, lost in his trance, did not move. Ognun glanced over his shoulder at Leifr and chuckled, splattering blood from his mouth as he said, 'Nothing you can do will stop me. I am protected by powers that you are helpless against. The powers of the Rhbus are dead. The powers of the Ljosalfar are puny when compared to the force that spawns such as the Dokkalfar, Sorkvir, and the true trolls, such as I. The Dokkur Lavardur will not be defeated.'

'Thurid!' Leifr began to skirt around Ognun, who turned warily to cut him off from Thurid, who still knelt beside the pool, oblivious to his peril as he stared upward at the sky visible through the opening above. Gotiskolker began creeping toward him, but he had the pool between him and Thurid, and Ognun was too alert to be fooled in that way. He moved nearer to Thurid, baring his teeth and raising his claws until Gotiskolker stopped and stood still.

'You hasten his death,' rumbled Ognun, glaring toward Gotiskolker and taking another step, which brought him almost within reach of Thurid.

Preoccupied with Gotiskolker, Ognun missed the moment when Thurid rose to his feet, reaching into his satchel. He held something aloft in his hand which glowed with a faint, fiery light.

'You hasten your own death,' he said.

Ognun froze, and Leifr sensed that he was about to make a last, desperate lunge. Dropping his bow, he leaped onto the troll's back with his knife in his hand, just as Thurid intoned some words and threw the glowing object into the air over Ognun's head. Leifr felt it fly past his ear as Ognun uttered a terrible bellow and began flailing and clawing at him, trying to shake him off. Leifr released his grip on Ognun's neck and jumped as far as he could. Rolling quickly to his feet, he dodged Ognun's slashing claws as the creature turned on him. As he backed away, the hounds swirled around Ognun in Leifr's defense. Ognun staggered forward, still snarling, and Leifr found himself with nowhere to go, unless he chose to jump into the pool. Taking the half-troll's battle mace from his belt, he took his stance and swung the mace overhead.

'Where is your great magic, Ognun?' he taunted. 'I think your wounds are troubling you worse now.'

Ognun seemed to be dying. Sinking to his knees, he struggled for breath, choking on his own blood, his staring eyes incredulous. Leifr called back the hounds, lowering his mace to the ground as Ognun slowly slumped forward. In a few moments his useless, gasping breaths stilled, and the gleaming eyes turned dull and unresponsive. Leifr ventured near enough to prod his carcass with the mace, noticing that Ognun's skin seemed to be hardening and swiftly changing color. It was stone, and the metamorphosis progressed with great speed as Leifr watched, until nothing remained of the troll except a long heap of odd-shaped rocks.

'Are you all right?' Thurid asked.

Leifr nodded and brushed off a little dirt. 'He would have had you in another moment. What was that you threw over his head just then?'

Gotiskolker answered for Thurid, holding up a small stone object. 'A whetstone. A time-honored method of breaking a spell among Alfar – so old that hardly anyone remembers it. The Rhbus would have known it, of course.'

Thurid nodded his head, holding his flaring alf-light aloft to illuminate the ascending rows of galleries above.

'How did you think of it?' Leifr pursued, not liking Thurid's distracted manner.

'This place is full of voices,' Thurid replied, still gazing around at the vast, empty chamber. 'I felt one of them jog my memory about the rune stick for throwing a whetstone over a house, and all of a sudden it made sense to me. I knew if I tossed it over Ognun's head, Sorkvir's spell over him would be broken, and he would surely perish from the wounds Fridmarr had dealt him. There was no doubt in my mind that it would work. It is a Rhbu spell.'

Gotiskolker handed him the whetstone, and he put it back into his satchel. Then he held his staff over the dark surface of the pool, casting a murky light to the stone bottom. Five large fish swam slowly through the light, hesitated a moment with their fins and gills pulsing, then darted away once more into the darkness.

'The salmon!' Gotiskolker gasped, 'Follow them, Thurid. Perhaps we can catch one – although I want nothing to do with Rhbu voices, at this point, and Fridmarr—' He turned and frowned warningly at Leifr.

'Rhbu magic and voices and spells are for wizards, not ordinary people,' Leifr answered quickly.

Thurid damped down his light, shaking his head. 'Almost, but not yet,' he said, as if repeating something he had heard. 'I'm far too inexperienced. Come, let's leave this place at once. You've no idea of the influences swirling around in here.'

'Wait a moment,' Gotiskolker said, turning back to the heap that had been Ognun. 'Get his bone necklace, Fridmarr. You'll want it to prove to Borgar that Ognun is truly dead.'

Leifr pulled the bone necklace from the stones and thrust it into his pocket after a cursory inspection. The bones were knuckle bones spaced by human teeth.

'There's a closer way out,' Gotiskolker said, when Thurid turned toward the tunnel to the well. 'Follow me, it's this way.' He limped toward the far end of the assembly chamber, where another set of heavy wooden doors lay broken from their hinges.

Thurid played his light over the doors, murmuring, 'They put up a brave struggle, even though they knew the torch had already passed.'

'How do you know this?' Leifr questioned, trying in vain to see if there were runes on the doors which Thurid was reading. He glanced over his shoulders uneasily when Thurid looked up and seemed to be gazing past him.

'Knowing is easy, in a place like this.' Thurid motioned to Gotiskolker to lead on, and said no more to explain himself.

Gotiskolker led them down a long, straight passage, which climbed several flights of stairs at intervals. The last flight of stairs ended abruptly at a pair of doors, still standing intact and securely barred from outside.

'It might be a tight squeeze,' Gotiskolker said to Leifr as he opened a small door built into the fortress door, through which no one could pass except by crawling on hands and knees. Ognun might have got his head through it, but certainly there was no room for his shoulders. By turning sideways Leifr managed to squeeze through and found himself standing in the shadow of a massive arched gateway. Beyond was the north court, with its walls jeweled with small fires. It was the place where Gotiskolker had joined them at dusk, seeming to come from nowhere.

A small group of men stood around the mouth of the well with burning torches, which lit up the billowing clouds of mist and spume rising from the well. Muffled creaking and groaning sounds came from the well, punctuated by shattering crashes as the ice released its grip on the walls and fell to the bottom. From the watchers on the walls came no sound, except from an old woman who began a wailing lament, sung to commemorate fallen warriors.

Thurid lit his staff with a burst of white light to announce their arrival without startling anyone into thinking it was Ognun creeping up behind them.

'Halloa, Borgar,' he called. 'Why the lament? Has someone died, or are you grieving for Ognun?'

A gasp rippled around the walls of the court as Thurid led a short triumphant procession to the well, stopping beside one of the standing stones.

Borgar, Lesandi, and the other warriors gathered around them with a torrent of excited questions, unable to grasp the news that Ognun was dead until Leifr held the necklace of bones and teeth over his head so everyone watching could see it. Then the shouts and cheers began, and the entire settlement converged on the hall for the telling and retelling of the tale until the sun rose that morning. The furor died down somewhat by necessity, since there were animals to care for and food to be hunted or fished for and prepared. Leifr found a quiet corner in the old hall and went to sleep, sharing his eider with the three exhausted troll-hounds.

When he awakened, there were more questions and more retelling of the battle with Ognun. Gotiskolker's popularity among the youths and children was magnified tenfold when he passed out a handful of the smaller pebbles from Ognun's petrified carcass. Thurid basked quietly in the glory, smoking his pipe and looking on with a benevolent, superior air.

When Borgar found an opportunity, he approached Leifr alone and said in a low voice, 'You are Fridmarr, aren't you? Isn't it time you confessed it?'

In the midst of the heady wine of acclaim and admiration, Leifr wavered a moment, caught between knowing he was not Fridmarr and the unworthy feeling that he was donating the most heroic deed of his life to a ghost named Fridmarr if he allowed them to honor him under Fridmarr's name.

Regretfully he shook his head. 'One day I'll send you a message,' he said. 'Then you can tell everyone the truth about me. Until then, I will remain nameless.'

Borgar shook his head, mystified. 'I don't understand it,' he said. Then a conspirational gleam came into his

eye. 'Perhaps it has something to do with Elbegast, eh?
A spy for our king must maintain his secrecy, I suppose?'

'I suppose,' Leifr replied with an uneasy smile,
amazed that he had explained himself so well.

After another day at Bjartur, Leifr grew impatient to
set out for the next point of the Pentacle – Dokholur, the
fifth and final station. As they wound down the fell, they
passed several trains of ponies, all loaded with household possessions and farming gear, with smaller children
rocking on the tops of the bundles while the larger ones
ran behind with exultant shouts. Compared to the barren, rocky fortress, the valley was a green and spacious
paradise.

'There are still Dokkalfar around,' Leifr cautioned
Borgar, who was accompanying them as far as the last
house.

'We're not afraid of the Dokkalfar,' Borgar replied.
With a significant sidewise glance at Leifr he added, 'The
Dokkalfar won't be bothering us much longer, when you
finish the task you have begun. When the alog is broken,
they'll take to their heels, or risk their lives on the sharp
new steel of the Ljosalfar.'

Later, when they were well away from Bjartur, Thurid
began to grumble. 'I don't know why you wanted to be
so secretive, Fridmarr, especially when they were almost
certain they knew who you were anyway. You don't
need to be ashamed of what happened so long ago.'

'I don't, eh? Well, you're mistaken,' Leifr retorted,
with a resentful scowl in Gotiskolker's direction. 'As the
Fridmarr who committed such crimes, I don't feel like
being praised now for mending something I shouldn't
have ever broken in the past.'

'Were you spying for Elbegast, Fridmarr?' Thurid
demanded. 'Is that why you're so devious and evasive
now?'

'Maybe,' Leifr replied warily.

Thurid snorted in disgust and rode his horse closer to
Leifr's stirrup. 'I practically raised you, Fridmarr, and

somehow you've always remained a complete stranger, hiding behind your secrets and façades and keeping everyone away with your insults and suspicion. Even now, after I've saved your life and you've saved mine, you still refuse to tell me if you've got connections with Elbegast or not.'

Leifr darted Gotiskolker a haunted look, feeling himself totally beyond his depth. 'Thurid, you wouldn't want to know the truth, and wouldn't accept it if I told you,' he said in exasperation, ignoring Gotiskolker's covert choking motions and frantic grimaces.

'I dare you to try me,' Thurid challenged.

'All right. To begin with, I'm not a spy for Elbegast, and I'd never even heard of Elbegast until this spring.'

'I don't believe you,' Thurid said immediately, sputtering incredulously. 'This is a perfect example of another of your insults, Fridmarr. What kind of fool do you take me for? No, don't answer! Just forget I ever spoke to you, and I'll try to forget I saved you from Ognun by throwing the whetstone over his head. What I won't forget is that you're Fridmarr, through and through, and you'll never change.'

He spurred his horse into a canter and left Leifr and Gotiskolker behind, avoiding each other's eyes.

'I've had just about all of Fridmarr I can stand,' Leifr muttered. 'I'm getting more like him every day. When and how are we going to end this masquerade, Gotiskolker?'

Gotiskolker rode along in silence for a few moments, his hood drooping over his face. 'We'd better do it before my time is up, or you'll be stuck here forever as Fridmarr, like it or not.'

'I can tell you right now that I won't like it,' Leifr snapped. 'You'd better not die before you get me back to my own realm. How much time is left?'

Gotiskolker pulled out his notched stick and counted.

'Thirty-two,' he said. 'Plenty of time. How's the torque, by the way? Does it seem any tighter yet?'

Leifr slipped his finger under the ring. 'I feel as if it's strangling me every moment.'

'Perhaps you'll die before I do.'

'Then you'd better watch out for a vicious and vengeful draug, because I'll not rest until I've wrung your neck with my own hands,' Leifr snarled. 'I'll make you regret you ever brought me here.'

Leifr dropped behind, sunk in an angry silence made more painful by thoughts of Ljosa waiting to be released from Hjaldr. Bleakly, he stared at Gotiskolker's bony carcass, sagging wearily in his saddle, and wondered if he would be able by himself to convince Ljosa that he was not Fridmarr. But as Fridmarr, at least he would be entitled to inherit Dallir, in case he managed to survive the next thirty-two days and the coming battles.

Thurid waited impatiently near the summit of the next ridge, motioning for them to hurry. He tied his horse to a dead thicket and crept up to the skyline to peer warily around a stone pylon someone had erected there long before.

Leifr tied his horse and started up the hill. Gotiskolker dismounted and sat down to rest on a mossy rock, waving Leifr away when he turned and started to come back down to see what was wrong with him.

'Go on,' he rasped. 'I'll wait for you here.'

Leifr climbed up the rocky ridge to Thurid's position and gazed down into the next valley, disbelieving his eyes until he began to comprehend the method behind the destruction below.

The valley lay desolate and barren, heaped with mounds of rock and dirt like the massive skeletons of extinct monsters. One large fell seemed to have been blasted with some poisonous blight, clawed from top to bottom with gouges and craters and fans of sliding scree. Roads traversed the once-green face of the mountain, leading from one gaping cavern to the next. Around the portals, the rocks were blackened with soot, and wisps of smoke still issued from the openings in lazy black puffs.

In the silence of the fells, the muffled clangor of the working of the mines sounded an ominous note.

Leifr knew by instinct that the feeling of dread and gloom hovering over the place signaled a location associated with evil – and Sorkvir. He knew without asking that they had arrived at Dokholur.

CHAPTER 18

'THIS used to be a holy hill,' Thurid said finally, his voice choking slightly. 'In the winter, no snow would stay on its summit. No blood was ever shed here, and no night-farer dared to attack anyone sheltering here. This mountain, according to old legend, is actually a giant who lay down and went to sleep so long that the dirt covered him up and trees started to grow on him. Perhaps that was just a way of explaining the frequent earthquakes near Dokholur. I do know that the mountain is a site of special powers, and Sorkvir knows it too. This must be his most ambitious destruction project yet – the complete leveling of Dokholur, and the gutting of its valuable minerals. There used to be a river that surfaced here, but you see that Sorkvir has done something to change its course. Underground water seems to be the secret for much of the Pentacle's powers.'

He dangled a dowsing pendulum as he talked, shaking his head and scowling over its behavior before stowing it in his satchel once more, adding as an afterthought, 'Enough disturbance of this kind can destroy an important site forever. We'll have to find the aquifer first and consider the damage to the mountain second.'

Leifr stared at him in horror. 'No one could fix this wreckage,' he said. 'The Dokkalfar have spent years digging up the mountain and hauling it down to the valley. The mountain is destroyed, and the valley is full of rocks. Dokholur does not exist anymore.'

'So it would appear,' Thurid replied wearily. 'But the least we can do is stop any further destruction. Perhaps all the magic and power is not diverted.'

'How many Dokkalfar do you suppose it takes to dig

away that much of a mountain?' Leifr asked suspiciously.

'Quite a lot, I imagine,' Thurid answered with an evasive shrug. 'Let's get a bit closer, to see what we're up against.' He pointed with his staff to the ruins of a house at the foot of the slope. 'We'll get down to there, where there's some cover. Where's Gotiskolker?'

'He's staying with the horses,' Leifr replied, with an uneasy glance over his shoulder down the hillside. 'He wasn't looking too good.'

'I daresay he'd like another swallow of eitur,' Thurid said. 'We ought to keep an eye on him, in case he decides to go in search of Sorkvir and his poison.'

'Don't be any more of a fool than you can help,' Leifr retorted. 'He'd rather die than go on with that poison.'

Thurid smiled darkly. 'You might be surprised how a man's mind changes when he comes eye to eye with dying. I hope you're not wrong about your unsavory friend.'

By the time they had crept down the hillside to the ruined house, slithering from one scanty cover to the next, the sun was touching the horizon. Nothing occupied the house except a family of owls, who seemed undiscomfited by the growing heap of scree that had come down the mountain to build up against the side of the house.

As the sky darkened, the excavation came to life. Pony trains, loaded with sacks of earth and rock, wound their way down the mountain to dump their cargo in the valley, with rivalrous shouts from the Dokkalfar of each procession. Above, on the ravaged mountainside, more Dokkalfar hacked away at a new road, with a busy clashing of picks and hammers and shovels. The mine portals glowed with fiery light, outlining the many scuttling forms of Dokkalfar, carts, and horses and lending the entire valley a lurid, foreboding cast of light. Clouds of acrid smoke belched from the tunnels and showered the slopes below with sparks and cinders.

Thurid watched, muttering to himself and clutching

his staff. The knob of his staff glowed, shining through his fingers when he passed his hand over it.

'How does he dare do this?' he growled restlessly. 'I've never seen such a desecration. He's even mining the rocks for their minerals to make the destruction of the mountain's power more complete. He must be stopped.' He turned his blazing eyes upon Leifr. 'Fridmarr, this will be your greatest triumph.'

'If we can do it,' Leifr interrupted gloomily.

'We can do it. There are powers within this mountain yet. I can feel them, like a voice calling out for help.'

'Help? We're the ones who need help,' Leifr protested. 'We can't do it without some powers that will help us, instead of us helping them. This isn't going to work, Thurid. I have a nasty feeling in my bones that this is going to turn out very badly.' He stood up, stretching his cramped muscles. 'Let's go back. I want to talk to Gotiskolker.'

Stealthily they left the house and climbed up the hillside, gaining a better perspective on the hellish scene below them. As they started down toward the horses, Thurid suddenly reached out and gripped Leifr's arm in warning. 'Something is wrong,' he whispered. 'Back over the top, quickly!'

They dived into the shelter of some rocks and looked down. Leifr murmured, 'I don't see any horses. Nor the dogs either.' He had commanded them to stay behind, which they had done with the utmost reluctance. He whistled once and got no response.

'Gotiskolker must be gone too, or dead,' Thurid said. 'I hope he's dead, because if he isn't, it means he has left us to look for Sorkvir and his eitur.'

'Maybe not,' Leifr answered. 'Maybe some Dokkalfar were getting too close, so he moved. We'll have to look for him. He might have left a signal to show which way he went.'

Thurid grunted and shook his head with a fatalistic sigh. 'I've seen how eitur works before. There's no loyalty to anything but the drug when the victim begins to feel the need for it.'

Leifr quelled the panic rising within him, swallowing hard against the silver torque. 'We've got to find him,' he said grimly. 'Our horses were carrying all our provisions and equipment. We can't get along without them.'

'I fear you won't see them again, once the Dokkalfar get their hands on them. At least I still have this.' Thurid pulled Bodmarr's sword out of his satchel, then thrust it back in, although it was considerably longer than the satchel was deep or wide. Astonished, Leifr felt the satchel to see if a sword were sticking through the bottom of it. There wasn't, and Thurid snatched it away, snapping, 'Don't touch that satchel, you fool; it's got spells on it to protect it from thieves. How would you like your hand to wither up and drop off? Don't be curious about wizards' satchels. They're unpredictable things.'

Leifr wondered whether he meant the wizards or the satchels and looked forward to the day when he would have no dealings with either.

'Come on,' he whispered sternly. 'We're going down for a look to see what happened to Gotiskolker.'

'We'll look, but we'll do it my way,' Thurid said, raising his staff aloft and lighting it with a spluttering roar, bathing the little ravine below in instant light.

'Look at that!' he gasped, as eight or ten dark figures scurried away. 'It was a trap! Gotiskolker must have helped set it!' Ignoring Leifr's bleak glare of protest, he stifled his light. 'Back to the house,' Thurid whispered. 'They won't think of looking for us that close.'

The Dokkalfar rallied quickly from their fright at the alf-light and scattered over the mountainside on horseback. Gradually they worked their way closer to the ruined house. From their insignia and headpieces, Leifr recognized them as Sorkvir's Dokkalfar guardsmen.

'So they won't think of looking this close, eh?'

Leifr growled as they watched the Dokkalfar quartering the hillside above. 'We're trapped, Thurid.'

Thurid fidgeted with his rune sticks, listening to the Dokkalfar outside. 'I wonder what the whetstone spell would do to them?' he mused.

'I'm not going to sit here and wait for them to find me,' Leifr said. 'Especially if you're going to experiment with your spells on them.'

'We'd both better go while we can,' Thurid replied, putting all of the rune sticks into his satchel except one, which he concealed inside his sleeve.

Outside, Leifr silently beckoned toward the west, away from Dokholur, and dodged from the cover of the house to a fallen stable and pigsty and from there into the rocks and thickets beyond. The Dokkalfar had discarded their broken equipment by shoving it down the mountainside, so Leifr discovered huge fractured cauldrons, slabs of broken furnaces, worn-out sledges and carts, and the bones of many unfortunate horses. As he crouched half-inside some huge old mining machine, waiting for Thurid to catch up, the Dokkalfar surrounded the house in a concerted move that Leifr might have admired under different circumstances. As it was, two Dokkalfar rode by so close that he could have touched the horses' legs as they passed. Silently he cursed Thurid, wondering what was delaying him.

Thurid waited until all the Dokkalfar were gathered around the house, their attention focused on the search of the interior. Then he crossed his fingers and recited a spell on the rune wand, hoping he had remembered it correctly. Closing his eyes, he stretched out his staff for the final words of the incantation. The force of the explosion staggered him backward a few steps, and a brilliant fireball lit up the sky as the ruin exploded with a deafening report. Rocks, timbers, Dokkalfar, and horses were tossed in all directions. Those of the Dokkalfar who were able staggered out of the ruins in tatters, while most of the horses picked themselves up and dashed away in desperate panic.

After watching a moment to be sure the Dokkalfar

were no longer interested in stalking their quarry, Thurid turned and followed Leifr. He passed the machine where he had seen his companion hiding, after peering into it to make sure he wasn't there.

'Fridmarr!' he whispered in mounting irritation.

There was no answer, nor did any of his subsequent whispers receive answers. By the time he had searched all around the ruins and halfway up the western slope, his mood had gone from angry to worried. His explosion had summoned forth more Dokkalfar, who picked through the ruins for the dead and injured. A growing number of them were casting speculative glances around the nearby hillsides.

Thurid crept from clump to clump of gorse until he reached some rocks on the top, where he sank down dejectedly to consider his situation. He had scarcely made himself comfortable when the tail of his eye caught a movement. A dark shadow reared up from the shelter of a rock. Thurid grabbed his staff and scrambled backward, spluttering over a spell that had suddenly escaped from his memory.

'Thurid, it's me – Gotiskolker!' a voice called softly.

Thurid recovered his aplomb quickly. 'Where have you been? We didn't know if you'd been captured or if you'd gone back to the eitur.'

'Neither. I had to hide, and they took the horses. But the worst of it is that they've got Fridmarr now. I saw them take him while you were watching your fire. If you'd only turned around, you might have saved him.'

Thurid gaped at Gotiskolker in dismay and shock. His thin shoulders slumped. 'Alive, I hope?' he asked.

'I don't know. There were six of them. They hauled him away, slung across a horse, into the mine. One thing I do know is that once a man goes into Dokholur, he never comes out alive.'

Thurid's nostrils quivered, and his eyes gleamed with a fanatic light. 'Well, this is one time it's going to be different. We're going into that mine and we're not going to give up searching until we find Fridmarr – and we're going to bring him out. Is that understood?'

Gotiskolker sat down and rested his forehead wearily in his hands. 'We have no equipment, no supplies—'

'We'll steal them. Whatever it takes, we're going to find Fridmarr.'

When Leifr realized that he was not dead, his first reaction was surprise. The six Dokkalfar had been waiting for him with cudgels and clubs. For a short while, he had fought brilliantly with his mace, stirred on to a masterful performance by sheer desperation. The last thing he remembered was a great wallop on the back of the head and finding himself lying on his back somehow, with the twisted faces of the Dokkalfar and their weapons spinning around him in a garble of unintelligible voices. It all went black, and then he awakened to firelight and a stale, earthy smell in the damp air.

His entire body ached from bruises, and one of his eyes defied all attempts to open it. A swollen mass gripped half his skull; when he raised one shaky hand to feel what on earth it might be, a voice murmured something in the same strange garble the Dokkalfar had used, and a cold rag was placed over his battered eye. Through one narrow slit, he discerned a woman bending over him and he felt that it must be his sister, the gentle Thora, who always bandaged up his scrapes and bruises. He was lying on the ground on an old cloak. For this small bit of comfort, he felt inordinately grateful.

'Thora?' he muttered. 'Where are we?'

A huge, untidy heap separated itself from the shadows and descended to stare into his face with small, bright eyes in a vast, tranquil countenance.

'Still talking out of head,' a voice rumbled.

Leifr's senses were beginning to clear, and he recognized Raudbjorn. 'I'm not out of my head,' he growled. 'Where's my sister? She was here, wasn't she?'

'No,' the woman replied. 'I've been watching you. Do you know who I am?'

Her voice haunted him. He risked shaking his head slightly and was rewarded with shooting pains. 'No. Not here. It can't be Ljosa.' He tried to focus his good eye, but all he could get was a blurry image of a woman in a gray cloak, her face almost hidden by her hood.

'Yes, I fear it is true. Sorkvir came to Hjaldrsholl and brought me here as a hostage. He'll trade me for the sword, Fridmarr, but you mustn't do it. Don't worry about setting me free. It's more important to finish the Pentacle and find the grindstone so you can sharpen Bodmarr's sword.'

Raudbjorn shook his head. 'No chance now. Thralls can't escape from Dokholur. Fridmarr never see sun again. Life here bad for poor thralls.'

Leifr felt himself slipping away helplessly, and their voices once more burbled in meaningless confusion. When he next awakened, he was still aware of the discomfort of each bone and muscle that had cause for complaint. Forcing open one eye a crack, he peered around himself, seeing the walls of a cave, a small fire, and heaps of rags that seemed to be breathing, moaning or snoring. On the other side of the fire sat Raudbjorn, smiling upon him with great good fellowship.

'Halloa, Fridmarr. Better today? Ready to go to work, old thrall?'

'Don't call me thrall, you lard-bucket,' Leifr grunted. 'What are you doing here, anyway? Where's Ljosa?'

'Sorkvir took her away. You all right now.' Raudbjorn pursed his lips and clucked with sympathy. 'Sorry fix you in, Fridmarr. You don't remember. Sorkvir sold worthless carcass to Skrof, thrall-driver. Too bad, too bad. Should have let Raudbjorn kill you, eh?' He chuckled ponderously.

'I'm not a thrall,' Leifr snapped. 'I'm the son of a well-off landholder in Landslag. No one is going to hold me thrall.' He struggled to rise to one elbow by slow and calculated degrees, inventorying his injuries and deciding with relief that no bones were broken and nothing seemed too badly beaten to mend eventually.

Raudbjorn slowly shook his head. 'Sorkvir sells enemies to Dokholur as thralls. Dying too good for some people.'

Leifr sank back with a stifled groan. Sorkvir was perfectly within his rights to sell a vanquished enemy into slavery. Death had a certain nobility for the defeated, but nobody cared to remember the degradation of being sold into thralldom. Such a fate made a man more dead than a funeral pyre or a barrow mound, and escape did little to improve the lot of the reluctant thrall.

'I'm not staying here.' Leifr felt the torque around his throat. 'How long have I been out of my head?'

'Three days.' Raudbjorn looked at Leifr critically. 'Escape, hah! No thralls escape from Dokholur.'

'I'm not a thrall. I'm a warrior, with the freedom of the earth and my fate in my own two hands, and I'm going to escape. You can tell that to your master Sorkvir.'

Raudbjorn grunted dubiously and scowled. 'Raudbjorn no thrall either.'

'You are, as long as you grovel around Sorkvir's feet and lick his boots,' Leifr retorted, ignoring Raudbjorn's dangerous expression. 'What about Thurid and Gotiskolker? Were they captured too?'

'No. Just Fridmarr. How you kill that great, ugly Ognun? Raudbjorn tried to fight him and had to run like big chicken. What weapon you kill him with?' He made the inquiry in a strictly professional tone not untinged by admiration.

Leifr replied shortly, 'Arrows and a whetstone.'

Raudbjorn's brow puckered. 'Whetstone. Rhbu magic. Bad sign for Sorkvir.'

'Sorkvir is going to be killed, Raudbjorn. If I were you, I'd get out now, before you get caught in the middle. All these Dokkalfar are going to be driven underground. You're a day-farer. You don't belong with them.'

'Raudbjorn likes fire and food and Sorkvir's gold. Night-faring not so bad. Better than thief-taking.'

Leifr snorted in disgust. 'You're willing to lose your good name and your pride for nothing more than gold and a full belly?'

Raudbjorn winced. 'Used to be proud, but poor. Now Raudbjorn not so proud.'

'Well, give it up, then.'

'Too hard to give up good life, Fridmarr. Sorkvir a hard master, but hungry belly worst master of all.' Resuming his expression of benign vacuity, he posted himself against the wall to watch Leifr, with his halberd held across his chest.

On the next day Leifr was awakened by the shuffling of the wretched thralls on their way to their labors. They did not raise their dull eyes to Raudbjorn, but they glanced at Leifr knowingly, offering him no encouragement with their rueful expressions. When they were gone, a group of Dokkalfar came striding down the tunnel into the thralls' quarters, stopping in a menacing circle around Leifr, who rose to his feet, tottering like an old dog rising to his last battle, beaten but not defeated.

Sorkvir shoved his way through the ring to confront Leifr, suppressing his gloating into a pleased smirk.

'Still alive, I see,' Sorkvir said, thrusting a torch almost into Leifr's face, but failing to make him flinch. 'Perhaps old Skrof didn't make such a bad bargain after all. A thrall such as you should be good for years in the tunnels of Dokholur.'

A gaunt and unwashed face crept out of the shadows behind Sorkvir, nodding nervously. 'Yes, I dare say he'll last a long time, my lord, although it is rather close to winter and nobody really wants another thrall to feed this time of year. I'll be lucky if half of them don't freeze or starve before next spring.' He looked at Leifr with great gloom. 'He still doesn't look too good. Do you really think he's ready to go to work?'

Leifr answered grimly. 'You needn't worry yourself about my welfare. You should look out for yourselves, considering what has happened at the other places where I have stopped for a while.'

Skrof blanched and slunk back into the shadows.

Raudbjorn nodded approvingly. 'Right, right. Ognun not feeling too good now.'

Sorkvir whirled spitefully on Raudbjorn, giving him a shove with the end of his staff. 'Silence, you bullock. It's not your privilege to speak anything that comes into that bird-sized brain of yours, so hold your speech. You might inadvertently convince me I don't need your presence, if you're not more cautious.'

Raudbjorn retreated, scowling and muttering, and the Dokkalfar seemed to enjoy his discomfiture and humiliation, winking at one another and stifling nasty chuckles.

'And you,' he continued, turning back to Leifr, 'are in no condition to boast. You have interfered in matters more important than you are. That's what earned your friend Gotiskolker his reward. I don't know what gave you the audacity to interfere with the Pentacle. You could not have done it without the knowledge I entrusted you with. No ordinary fire wizard could have broken my influence.'

'But Rhbu magic might,' Leifr answered. 'As long as Thurid remains free, you're in danger, Sorkvir.'

'In danger!' Sorkvir's cloak surged as he raised his staff in a threatening gesture. 'You are the one in danger, my insolent friend.' He nodded to the Dokkalfar, and they all drew their swords, gleaming in the firelight and etched with blood-blackened runes.

Skrof edged forward and ventured to tug at Sorkvir's sleeve, protesting, 'You can't kill him unless you give me my two marks back. You've lost your rights to murder him. Begging your pardon for speaking up, of course,' he added hastily, retreating into the shadows when Sorkvir bent an angry eye upon him.

Leifr said, 'Perhaps it would be well worth two marks for you to kill me now, Sorkvir. This may be your best opportunity.'

Sorkvir's hard eyes glittered as he stared at Leifr. 'I dare not, just yet,' he said with hatred in his tone. 'You know far too much of my own knowledge. You would return as a vengeful fylgjadraug, made more powerful by your journey into Hel and back. I shall keep you here, working like a mindless animal, until there's little left of your mind or body, like Gotiskolker.'

'It didn't work with Gotiskolker,' Leifr replied. 'He's the one who brought me back. I see little evidence that he's under your power.'

Sorkvir's eyes flickered with rage. 'It was Gotiskolker, was it? I'll have to settle with him later. His time is near at hand, when he'll want to seek me out for the eitur.'

'Not any longer, Sorkvir. He's going to die free.'

'You should know that none of my enemies die free, Fridmarr. Perhaps you have forgotten Kaldi and Barmur, or you might never have ventured to dare my wrath. Or have you forgotten that I have Ljosa Hroaldsdottir here as a prisoner? I have brought her to Dokholur to convince you to return Bodmarr's sword to me. She was much more comfortable at Hjaldrsholl, I am ashamed to confess. Here she is forced to work for her keep, the same as any other prisoner.'

Leifr restrained his fury, speaking with cold deliberation. 'For that alone, I shall be glad to kill you. She is a chieftain's daughter and not accustomed to such treatment. If she had any brothers left to protect her, you wouldn't dare to treat her this way.'

'She has no one left to defend her – except you. Unless you return that sword, Hroaldsdottir is likely to die this winter when the trolls get hungry and start stalking the tunnels, preying upon the weak and unwary. She shall go free as soon as you summon that madman Thurid and put Bodmarr's sword into my hands. I'll see to it that she is taken to her relations in Fjara-strond.'

'How can I believe anything you say?' Leifr retorted. 'You wouldn't let her go. Maybe she's not even here now. For all I know, she might be dead.' The thought was like iron stuck to his soul.

'She is here and alive.' Sorkvir nodded towards one of the Dokkalfar. 'Go and fetch her from the cauldron area. Be quick about it.'

The Dokkalfar favored Leifr with a malevolent grin, and Leifr recognized him by the dried ear trophies hanging from his sword sheath as the same Dokkalfar who had brought Leifr out of Alof's musty storeroom as Sorkvir's prisoner. He had also garnered a chin-to-temple slash from Leifr's sword, now partially healed into a fulsome puckered scar. Seeing Leifr's present battered condition seemed to afford him a great amount of satisfaction.

'That's Greifli,' Sorkvir observed. 'He holds a particular grudge against you. It was all we could do to restrain him from leaving a similar beauty mark upon your face. He thinks you've quite spoiled his looks.'

Leifr was about to retort, when the mountain suddenly began to tremble slightly around them. Hollow, groaning, grinding sounds echoed through the network of tunnels.

Sorkvir cocked his head to listen intently, and the Dokkalfar guards exchanged uneasy glances while the tremors continued.

'Skrymir the mountain giant crushes us all one day, digging in his body like worms,' Raudbjorn said.

'Not before we find his heart or whatever keeps him alive,' Sorkvir replied, speaking to Leifr. 'I've heard that his heart is a single large ruby, big enough that one man can't reach all the way around it. One day we'll find it, and Skrymir will be dead, as mountains are intended to be. He has weakened a great deal since you saw Dokho-lur last, Fridmarr. I suspect you never thought that you would one day be one of the wretches carving out Skrymir's vitals.'

Leifr scarcely noticed the jibe. His thoughts were too busy with the idea of a mountain that lived. Another rumbling groan ran through the mountain, as if some huge creature were in pain.

Greifli came back, pushing Ljosa along before him, a slight, very ragged figure with a regal composure about her that filled Leifr's heart with fierce pride. Greifli shoved her into the circle of torchlight, and Sorkvir reached out one withered hand to draw back the hood that hid her face. She flinched away, tossing back her hood to gaze around the ring of her captors. Her glance settled on Leifr with rock-steady calm. Leifr could not speak, only gaze with furious resolve to rescue her from the loathful condition he had brought her to in his clumsy and unwilling parody of Fridmarr.

'You see, she is here,' Sorkvir said. 'Enjoy looking at her; she won't keep her looks long in this place. Unless, of course, you do the noble thing and set her free by giving me Bodmarr's sword. What is your answer, Fridmarr?'

'Let her go, Sorkvir,' Leifr said in a deadly tone.

'Then will you give me the sword? At least then you could spend the last of your days thinking of her freedom, which you bought for her.'

Ljosa turned her angry stare upon Leifr. 'Don't do it for my sake, Fridmarr. I refuse to be used as a pawn in Sorkvir's vile games. I can suffer and endure as well as you can. If you help Sorkvir get Bodmarr's sword, even if I do go free, your name will be an anathema to me forever, Fridmarr.'

'Quiet, spitfire!' Sorkvir rasped. 'Greifli, take her out of here. I might have known she'd have a streak of self-immolation in her.'

Greifli seized her arm roughly and started to lead her

away. She called back, 'Remember, Fridmarr! Anathema!'

Raudbjorn grinned and nodded approvingly. 'Brave girl. Spirit like tiger. Anathema something poisonous?'

'Silence, fool!' Sorkvir spat, shifting his brittle stare to Leifr. 'Well? What is your answer?'

Leifr shook his head slowly. 'As long as I live, you'll never get the sword by any means of mine.'

'Are you mad? That girl can't survive here. She'll have a lingering and wasting death before her – supposing that a troll doesn't kill her and carry her off.' Sorkvir smiled his thin and sinister smile. 'I had thought that you cared for her, somewhat.'

Leifr's response was a cold and menacing stare. 'Have you any other business to conduct?' he asked sarcastically. 'I thought I was supposed to work in the mine, not stand around listening to a lot of useless chatter.'

Sorkvir folded his arms across his chest and moved a few paces to the side. 'Many's the time, Fridmarr, in the old, pleasant days when you were my acolyte, that I wondered if you would be worth all the trouble of teaching and retraining you in the ways of the Dokkalfar. You were in so many ways a bright and eager pupil, but somehow I always suspected you lacked the true, single-minded devotion that a student of mine would require. Indeed, when I killed your brother, Bodmarr, I learned where your true loyalties dwelt – with the Ljosalfar and their dying cause. I wonder how many years you will have to reflect upon your wisdom in choosing that cause instead of mine. Five years? Ten? Thirty?'

Leifr shook his head doggedly, weary but determined to sustain his passion for survival. 'I think of it as five or ten or thirty years to escape,' he replied.

'I thought you would say that.' Sorkvir beckoned again to Greifli, who again unsheathed his sword with a ringing hiss and a broad, evil smirk. 'Are you certain you've reconciled yourself and Hroaldsdottir to such a despairing fate? Think of those five or ten or thirty years filled with the agony of the eitur slowly devouring your vitals from the inside out. Not a pleasant prospect, is it, Fridmarr? A dose of the eitur would do you good now, after the beating you've taken. Come now, I'm offering you a painless way out of your situation.'

He produced the small blue vial from the tail of his sleeve and uncorked it. The tantalizing fumes drifted lazily through the musty smell of the room.

Leifr shook his head doggedly. 'Take yourself and your poison out of here.' In vain he groped for a stray thread of memory from the carbuncle, but its voices were all distant and faint now. Searching, he caught a faint clue. 'I took the eitur once to prove my loyalty to you – or so you would think. It was a small price, if I had succeeded in destroying you then. I deceived you, Sorkvir. Do with me what you will, but carry that thought with you.'

Sorkvir's face darkened with fury. 'I'm not likely to forget your treachery. However, the sting of it will be greatly soothed by picturing you here, slowly dying from the eitur.' He nodded toward Greifli and stepped back. 'But first there's a small matter of unfinished business I want attended to before you depart for your labors.'

Greifli stared at Leifr with a tight little smile, his eyes large and black like a cat's, about to pounce on its quarry. His sword gleamed sharp and deadly in the torchlight.

Skrof whimpered in protest. 'Have you decided to kill him after all, Sorkvir? You'll owe me two marks!'

With a quick thrust of his blade, Greifli slashed the tendons behind Leifr's knee. Leifr doubled over, clutching the wound with both hands to stop the bleeding, and pitched to the ground, his meagre strength suddenly exhausted by this new insult to his weakened condition.

Pandemonium erupted as Raudbjorn's furious bellow echoed through the underground vault. Swinging his halberd, Raudbjorn came after Greifli with a roar of red-eyed fury and challenge.

Sorkvir raised one hand, and an ice bolt shattered with a loud explosion on the wall behind Raudbjorn. Halting his weapon's downward swoop, Raudbjorn froze a moment, with his eyes widening as he contemplated the black mark on the wall, realizing how near it had come to him.

'This is your last warning, you ignorant ox,' Sorkvir said. 'The next time, the bolt may not miss its target. This is what comes of trying to make use of a day-faring killer. I fear you will come up lacking. Raudbjorn.'

Raudbjorn's face furrowed in thought and the halberd wavered uncertainly. He let its butt drop to the floor with a clank and leaned upon its handle to calm his furious breathing.

'Not a fair way to fight,' he grumbled in an abashed tone, retreating toward the shadows, watching the Dokkalfar warily. Greifli made a feint at him, and all the Dokkalfar chuckled unpleasantly when Raudbjorn whirled around to defend himself.

Sorkvir beckoned silently and started to leave, his cloak swirling around his heels. Skrof risked seizing the moment to dart a quick scowl over the rock that sheltered him. 'That was a treacherous thing to do, Sorkvir,' he quavered indignantly. 'I could make a grievance of it at the next Althing, if I was of a mind to. You lamed my thrall, and after I paid you good money, too, when nobody could tell if he would live or die.'

Sorkvir turned and tossed a small pouch to Skrof, who opened it up feverishly and gasped at the contents.

'Now I have bought him from you,' Sorkvir said, 'and at a far better price. I want you to take care of him for me and keep him alive and as healthy as you can in a place like this, but not so healthy he'll think of trying to escape. If such an accident should occur and Fridmarr comes up missing, your head will be the first to fall. You do understand me, don't you, Skrof?'

As he talked, Sorkvir caught a shred of Skrof's raiment. The thrall-driver sidled back and forth, nodding and shaking his head in an ecstasy of self-abnegation. Sorkvir wound up the shred of cloth, drawing Skrof unwillingly nearer, like a gasping, glassy-eyed, unwholesome species of fish.

With a last, intimidating glower, Sorkvir thrust Skrof from him and stalked away, calling to his warriors to follow. He bestowed a last triumphant sneer upon Leifr; then he and his men were swallowed up by the cavern amid the tramping of boots and the rattling of weapons.

Skrof smote his brow and stooped to look at Leifr's wound with an exasperated, proprietary air. Leifr at once knocked him sprawling.

'Mind your own business, you maggot,' he snarled. 'Now get me a bandage for my leg.'

Skrof picked himself up, shaking his head in disbelief. Backing away from Leifr cautiously, he went out into the corridor and underwent an astonishing transformation from abject worm to towering tyrant, all in the space of a few moments, shouting in a mighty voice for a cart and a horse and someone to bandage a wound. When the objects of his desires were slow in presenting themselves, he flew into a terrible fury, taking care to stay out of Leifr's sight. When he came back, his shoulders sagged and his belligerence left him.

'I'm glad I sold you to Sorkvir,' he muttered. 'I'm not looking for trouble, but trouble always seems to find me. I knew poor old Skrof would catch it in the neck when Sorkvir arrived.'

When his leg was bandaged, Leifr climbed into a cart behind a bony wreck of a horse and Skrof glumly drove him down the tunnel on the most miserable journey of his life. He tried to remember the turns, but he lost track when the torches became too few to see much. They passed groups of wretched thralls, chipping at the rock and tossing the pieces into carts and sledges. The journey ended in a large, dank room where another troop of prisoners was sleeping the sleep of exhaustion and deprivation. One of the guards pointed to an empty pallet by the wall, where Leifr lay down gratefully, without wondering much what had become of the former occupant. He did not suppose it would lift his spirits any if he knew.

They put him to work with a heavy pickaxe, since he was taller and stouter than most Ljosalfar or Dokkalfar. The only light he had to work by was a small whale-oil lamp wedged in a crack, and the food portion was inadequate, as he soon discovered. Perhaps worst of all was the constant threat of rockfalls and cave-ins, when the mountain shook under their feet and all they could do was crouch helplessly and wait for the tremor to cease, hoping their tunnel would not collapse.

'Skrymir feels the pain,' they would say when the mountain trembled. But there was no choice except to work or starve, as Leifr soon discovered.

After six days of watching for his opportunity, he managed to slip out of the prisoners' quarters after a long day's work and threaded his way almost to the main portal. Each dragging step of his injured leg was an agony. If he had possessed two good legs, he might have eluded his captors and escaped, but they recognized him and hauled him back to Skrof. To discourage any further departures from duty, and to save his own throat, Skrof fastened a shackle around Leifr's leg and chained him to a large stake pounded into the ground.

For several days Leifr enlivened his existence by refusing to work and menacing Skrof whenever he came near, so Skrof left him alone in the dark in the prisoners' quarters to do nothing until his pride subsided. The involuntary abstinence from eating did as much as the boredom to convince him that working was better than doing nothing, so he promised that he would behave himself and received his pickaxe and resumed his mindless battering at the rock walls. At present he could do nothing but wait for another opportunity, all the while giving the appearance that he had reconciled himself to his fate.

As near as he could guess, there were twelve days left before Hjaldr's alog took effect. Every clank and rattle of the chain reminded him of his captivity, and he berated himself for not trying harder to escape before. In a fury, he attacked the chain with his pick, hoping to break free, but the metal defied all his efforts. Skrof caught him at it and he lost the privilege of eating his share of stale black bread and rancid dried fish that night. The other prisoners offered their silent sympathy by slipping him bits of their own meagre fare, which fired his resolve to deliver them all safely from Dokholur.

Although talking was strictly forbidden, everyone seized any opportunity for a few moments of whispering; by this means, Leifr learned that Dokholur was the final stop in the lives of hundreds of thralls and wanderers who had fallen upon bad times. Even a cripple such as Leifr could swing a pick or shovel ore into the carts. Every year, dozens of thralls died from cave-ins, falling down deep shafts, or getting lost in the maze of tunnels. Lungs gave out in the cold, damp air, and occasionally the miners encountered deadly vapors. If nothing else menaced the lives of the prisoners, trolls could always be relied upon to seize victims in the dark tunnels, particularly in winter.

A prisoner might last a day at Dokholur or many years, but eventually Dokholur and its hazards won. When a thrall died at his work, his companions silently loaded the body onto a full ore cart and it was burned with the next batch of molten ore at the nearest furnace, so the thrall's final contribution to the mines of Dokholur was the remains of his own poor husk. From the least, scruffy orphan child that dragged food and water to the prisoners, to the sickest old beggar, everyone was expected to give his all to the mine. Leifr encountered old thralls, outlaws, wanderers, and many others who had fallen into disfavor with either fate or Sorkvir.

With ten days left, Leifr saw Ljosa for the first time since his arrival. Rising water had made further work

307

impossible in their tunnel, so Leifr's troop was being taken to another place until the water was dammed up. As the captives shuffled wretchedly past the furnace area, he saw her in the red light, throwing fuel onto the fire. Sensing his eyes upon her, she straightened and look around, spying him towering over his bent, skinny companions. A brilliant light of recognition suddenly illuminated her weary features, and Leifr could see that she was calling something to him, but it was lost in the roaring of the furnaces.

Leifr started toward her, ignoring Skrof's frantic attempts to drive him back by prancing around him menacingly and brandishing a staff. Keeping his eyes upon Ljosa, Leifr seized the staff and broke it over one knee, tossing it away in contempt. Skrof scuttled away in alarm. In another five strides, Leifr would have reached Ljosa, but two armed Dokkalfar interposed with bared steel. Reluctantly he backed away, still straining to understand what Ljosa was trying to convey to him. When she gave it up in defeat and turned back to her work, he permitted himself to be prodded along once more with the rest of the prisoners, but he kept his eyes upon her until his view was blocked. Feeling more chafed than ever by his dragging chain and the endless, mindless hacking at the stone, he worked furiously all that day, waiting only for another chance to see Ljosa, even if he couldn't talk to her.

However, at the end of the day, his troop was taken back to their quarters by a different tunnel, and he didn't get to see her. In a frenzy of gloom, Leifr gave away his supper and sat with his back to the stone, racking his brains for a way to escape.

When he finally fell asleep, long after the other prisoners, his fine-tuned senses suddenly discerned a soft sound that did not belong to the usual repertoire. A lumbering sledge, twelve snorting, scrambling ponies, and half a dozen shouting Dokkalfar could go grinding past without disturbing him, but the soft whisper of stealthy, padding feet awakened him instantly. Thinking it was a troll, he reached for a rock and waited. To his surprise, the soft glow of a candle shone on the rough, oozing walls, and a slight, dark shadow crept warily toward him. As the largest and most able of the thralls, to deal with the trolls, so he had a good view of anyone approaching.

The intruder paused, listening. After a long, taut silence, a voice whispered, 'Leifr! Is that you?'

CHAPTER 19

LEIFR dropped the rock, astonished at hearing his own name. A few thralls stirred uneasily in their exhausted slumber, but Skrof continued snoring away beside his small fire in the driest area of the cave.

'Who's there?' Leifr whispered, still incredulous. 'Gotiskolker, is that you?'

'Yes, who else? Finally, I've found you.' Heaving a long, weary sigh, Gotiskolker sat down near Leifr, shading his candle with a hand that seemed almost translucent, like a dry leaf trembling on a twig. 'I've been searching for you since the day you disappeared. I found Ljosa, and now she found you for the first time today.'

'You're not a prisoner? How do you manage to live?'

'I steal a little food now and then. Mostly I hide. If someone comes along, I just bend down and scrabble along picking up rocks and everyone thinks I belong here.'

'Where's Thurid?' And the sword?'

'Safe. Thurid is prowling the lower levels, looking at the dams and planning some powerful magic.'

'The dams? It's frightfully dangerous down there.'

'Indeed. It's the weakest point of the entire mountain. If the dams were all to break at once, nothing on earth could save the mines.'

'What about Skrymir? Is this mountain really alive?'

'Alive is not exactly the right word for something so motionless and silent that trees grow on it and animals live there, but yes, the mountain is more than rocks and dirt. It's part of the Pentacle, and it has been here longer than anyone knows.'

'If Sorkvir finds the heart of the mountain, what will happen?'

Gotiskolker shrugged. 'He'll take the ruby away and Dokholur will become as any regular mountain. No difference that you would notice – but it would be quite a difference for Skrymir and the Pentacle. Our first concern is getting you out of here. Ljosa said they unstrung your knee. How bad is it?'

'I can walk. They didn't do a thorough enough job to leave me completely useless. What slows me down the most is this.' He rattled the chain resentfully.

Gotiskolker looked at the shackle and the stake by the light of his candle, scowling. 'That's going to be a problem, but I'm sure Thurid will think of something. There may be another way yet that I'm working on. I'd better get going now, before the outside guard comes back.'

'Wait. What about the rest of the prisoners? We've got to get them out safely. Some of them have been kind to me, and none of them deserve this kind of fate.'

Gotiskolker heaved another sigh. 'We'll get them out, Leifr. The Dokkalfar are another matter, though. I'd like to destroy as many of them as possible.'

'Gotiskolker! Wait!' Such a brief touch of the outside and the freedom beyond Dokholur was almost too tantalizing to bear. 'How long will it take you to get me out of here?'

'Less than nine days, I assure you. I'll be back, don't worry.'

Daily Leifr expected him, but he did not return. For the next five days Leifr worried in excruciating detail, wondering if Gotiskolker had fallen down a crevice somewhere, if Thurid had drowned, or if he had dreamed the whole episode.

At the end of the sixth day, while the dispirited thralls were eating their meagre supper, the mountain shook beneath their feet; far below, deep grumbling sounds rumbled up through the tunnels. Everyone froze, listening.

'Sounds like tremors on the lower levels,' one of the thralls near Leifr muttered. 'Skrymir will bring it all down on our heads one day.'

'Or drown us all, if he breaks the dams in the water tunnels,' someone added grimly.

The tremors continued, and Skrof paced up and down nervously, peering frequently out into the main corridor and listening for news.

'One of the dams is leaking badly,' he reported, mopping the sweat from his unsavory yellow brow. 'But something seems to be happening to anyone who goes down into the lower level to patch the dam.'

The thralls grunted and nodded uneasily. A sense of foreboding and gloom descended over the prisoners as the tremors continued, punctuated by sudden sharp cracking and booming sounds, like an ice breakup in spring. The sledge and cart drivers began to have trouble with their horses. The dead, stale air was moving, bringing with it the smell of water and wet earth.

At last, the uneasy waiting ended decisively when boots came tramping into the chamber and a torch flared in the dark, revealing the monstrous bulk of Raudbjorn. Skrof leaped up immediately and scampered toward him, babbling anxiously about his orders. Raudbjorn shook his head, like a bear annoyed by a buzzing bee, and declared, 'Water coming up main shaft! Time to get out! Mine is flooding! Get outside, thralls!'

The thralls leaped up immediately and made a rush for the doorway, ignoring Skrof's shouts and threats.

'I take orders from no one but Sorkvir!' he shrilled, almost losing his footing as several thralls shoved him out of the way. 'I can't go outside. It's daylight! All these thralls are going to escape!'

Raudbjorn thrust Skrof out of the way and approached Leifr. 'Take off chain, scumbag. Let Frid-marr go.'

Skrof shook his head frantically. 'I daren't, without special orders from Sorkvir himself. He said to keep the

312

chain on him, and that's where it's going to stay, no matter —'.

Raudbjorn seized Skrof and held him aloft by his skinny legs as he shook him to dislodge the contents of his pockets, which rained around Raudbjorn's boots.

'No key,' grunted Raudbjorn in dissatisfaction. 'Where is key, scumbag Skrof? Tell Raudbjorn, if neck doesn't want breaking.'

Skrof shivered and shook his head, croaking in wordless terror as Raudbjorn shook him again. 'No key,' he finally gasped. 'Sorkvir had me throw it down a shaft.'

Raudbjorn lost interest in Skrof immediately and deposited him in a heap, with a kick in the direction of the door. 'Raudbjorn doesn't need key anyway, Halloa, Fridmarr. You ready to escape? Friends waiting.'

Leifr glowered at him suspiciously. 'You're going to help me escape? I'll believe that when the moon turns to milk and witches don't sit out at crossroads.'

Raudbjorn shook his head emphatically and drew his sword to kiss its hilt. 'Raudbjorn swears fealty to Fridmarr forever. Sick of Sorkvir. Sick of shame. Raudbjorn wants to be free and proud again. Sorkvir and evil must die.' His cherubic expression turned into a murderous grimace as he bared his teeth in a berserk grin.

Skrof stopped his astonished gaping and began to scramble toward the tunnel outside, mostly on his hands and knees, as if he didn't trust his legs to hold him up.

'This is treason,' he panted, pausing a moment when he felt safe. 'Sorkvir will hear about this, Raudbjorn!'

Raudbjorn flourished his sword, and Skrof scurried away, still shaking with fear and outrage.

'It's a bargain, then,' Leifr said, and whacked palms with Raudbjorn to seal their agreement. 'I don't know why you want to swear fealty to me, when I suspect I'm going to drown before much longer.'

Raudbjorn shook his head. 'Not drown. Raudbjorn pull out stake.' He ambled forward to take the chain in his hands. 'Heavy chains. Hard metal. Stake driven in almost to top. Maybe a little pull get it out.'

Wrapping the chain around both big fists, he braced his feet against the wall and pulled until the veins stood out on his massive arms, neck, and forehead. With a final mighty heave, he gave it up and sat down, wiping the sweat from his face and trying to catch his breath.

'It won't come out,' Leifr said. 'You'd better leave while you still can.'

'It will come out. Plenty of time for Raudbjorn.' Again he wrapped the chain around his bleeding knuckles and planted his feet. Fixing his eyes upon the stake he began to pull, with the muscles in his arms knotting like straining ropes.

Fearing Raudbjorn would pull until his heart burst, Leifr seized the thrumming chain below Raudbjorn's hands and pulled with all his strength. With a jolt, the stake came out halfway. Raudbjorn collapsed with a wheeze, beaming in triumph and rubbing his skinned hands.

'You see?' he rumbled. 'It comes out for two brother warriors.'

'Once more,' Leifr said, his deliverance suddenly shining bright before his eyes. 'Three is a lucky number.'

They gripped the chain again, and this time, after a mighty heave, the chain snapped off at the stake.

'Where are the others? Is Ljosa safe?' Leifr asked.

'All safe. Gotiskolker help her while Raudbjorn help you. Crazy wizard Thurid climbing big shaft, hunting Dokkalfar. We go up to highest level to get out.' He beckoned Leifr toward a vertical shaft, with the sound of water churning away far below.

Leifr risked a quick look down into the blackness of the shaft, then swung onto the ladder, climbing straight up into the blackness above. Raudbjorn followed, with the rungs creaking in protest at each step. Holding up his torch, he illuminated the way above, where timbers jutted at crazy angles from slipped supports and pieces of

314

broken ladders showed what had happened to other climbers before. Portals opened onto nothing in the shaft or to the remnants of broken walkways, waiting to take someone to his death.

Leifr's weak leg tired soon, and he was forced to halt several times for a few minutes to stop its aggravating tremble. During one of these rests, Leifr noticed that the ladder was quivering, as if someone were up above. His suspicions were confirmed by bits of mud and pebbles that pelted down occasionally.

'Drop the torch, Raudbjorn,' he whispered. 'Someone's above us.'

The torch plummeted downward and vanished.

The voices from above neared the spot where Leifr had stopped. A few timbers offered a slightly larger foothold and an additional support for grabbing. Raudbjorn watched intently as the dim red light from above descended swiftly. Drawing his sword, he gripped it between his teeth and started climbing up to meet them.

'Who's that down below?' someone called warily, and several other voices muttered together. 'You can't get out this way. That wizard has blocked all the portals from outside. He's on the top level, blasting anyone who comes up the shaft. You'll have to back down.'

As he spoke, a bright splinter of flame cleft the darkness like a lightning bolt far above, exploding with a report that jarred some small rocks loose.

'Hurry up, back down!' growled a chorus of irate voices, perhaps six in all.

'You go back up,' Leifr answered. 'There's nothing below but water. Start moving.'

'Who's down there?' demanded one of the Dokkalfar.

'Raudbjorn,' came the rumbling response. 'Back up.'

'Raudbjorn!' muttered the Dokkalfar. Then one called, 'We're not backing up for you. If you don't like it, you can jump. I hope that fire wizard burns you like bacon.'

315

The Dokkalfar laughed nastily, and the ladder creaked as they descended another step. Their faces caught the red glow of their torch – lowering, sinister faces. With an unpleasant shock, Leifr recognized Greifli, who had cut his leg. At the same moment, Greifli recognized Leifr.

'It's Fridmarr,' he said in disbelief.

'Kill him, then,' someone growled. 'We've had too much trouble from him already. Day-farers should all be killed.'

'Do it and hurry up,' another voice said. 'I think that fire wizard might be coming down after us.'

Raudbjorn fastened the chin strap of his helmet and pulled his shield up over his shoulders to the top of his head. Gripping one of the hand-holds in his teeth, he started climbing upward, expressing his feelings with an inarticulate roar of wrathful challenge. He held onto the ladder with one hand and took swipes with his sword with the other, driving back the Dokkalfar above. They hailed him with blows and rocks to no avail; he advanced inexorably, hacking at their feet when he got near enough. The Dokkalfar soon abandoned the ladder for the jumble of timbers crosshatching the shaft and fired arrows at Raudbjorn when they got the opportunity. Most of their arrows went wide of their mark in the darkness, but a few whizzed by dangerously near, and one hit Raudbjorn's shield. Motioning Leifr to stay under cover behind a timber, Raudbjorn sheathed his sword and unslung his deadly halberd. Still protected behind his shield, he stepped off the ladder onto a beam, inching his way across with his halberd to balance him. The Dokkalfar climbed farther downward on the scaffolding to escape from him. One, who stood his ground a little too long, was swept from his perch by the halberd and sent plummeting down with an echoing shriek.

Suddenly the entire structure shifted with an ominous groan as Raudbjorn reached the middle, and everyone froze, not breathing, until the creaking and shuddering stopped.

'Raudbjorn,' Leifr called. 'Come back from there before it collapses and takes you with it.'

'Need to get rid of five Dokkalfar first,' Raudbjorn replied. 'Lighten the load. Dokkalfar trapped now, no place else to go.'

Raudbjorn stalked the remaining Dokkalfar and picked them off the timbers one by one until only Greifli remained, holding the torch and waiting at the lowest part of the scaffolding. As Raudbjorn reached the lowest timber and stepped onto it cautiously, the scaffolding creaked again. Raudbjorn waited until the structure had steadied and crept after Greifli with catlike grace along a beam, with nothing on either side to hold onto.

A look of cunning overspread Greifli's face. He jumped on the timber under his feet, causing the scaffold to sway alarmingly.

Leifr was almost straight above Greifli; if he leaned out a bit he could drop a rock right on him. Groping around for a loose one, he heard the cracking of wood.

The scaffold folded in on itself, tearing away from the walls of the shaft, a section at a time. Raudbjorn clung to a timber, looking up with astonishment.

Still holding his torch, Greifli sprang desperately from timber to timber even as they sagged, making a last flying leap toward the ladder. Then the whole structure of timbers gave way at last, sinking into the black void and taking Greifli and Raudbjorn with it. The red light of the torch winked out, leaving Leifr alone and trembling with shock on the ladder.

'Raudbjorn!' he shouted, when the uproar of falling timbers had ceased. There was no answer. 'Raudbjorn! Answer me!' he roared in despair.

'I hear you,' a voice said, not far above, and a burst of blinding alf-light filled the shaft with twisting black shadows and harsh glares. 'Come on, Fridmarr, there's nothing you can do to help him now.'

Leifr gazed down the tangled maze of the shaft, which

had been considerably cleared out by the collapse of the scaffolding.

'I've got to be sure,' Leifr answered, staring down. 'He saved me once. It's the least I can do for him.'

'Fridmarr! Stop! What a mutton-headed – Fridmarr! You're not going down there again!' Thurid clambered down after him, his eyes glaring with rage.

Leifr stopped to rest a moment, allowing Thurid to overtake him. 'Shine your light down there, Thurid. We may be able to see him.'

Thurid obliged with a blaze of light, but the bottom of the shaft was a dark tangle of groaning, shifting timbers and black water. 'I hope you're pleased,' Thurid growled. 'Thanks to you, the Dokkalfar are all going to escape. If you'd climbed up as you were supposed to, I would be up there now, blasting Dokkalfar. I don't see him, Fridmarr. Let's go back up. Look how fast that water is rising.'

Leifr resumed his descent. The water was rising at a visible rate, gurgling around the timbers. 'How did you get so much water to come up, Thurid?' he asked. 'I thought it would take days to fill all these tunnels.'

'Ordinarily it would, but I was afraid it wouldn't fill up fast enough to suit me, so I used a water spell from one of my rune sticks.' Thurid sighed and followed Leifr downward. 'Do be careful, Fridmarr!' he warned sharply as the whole jumble creaked dangerously, grinding against the walls and splintering some of the timbers. Part of the ladder pulled away from the wall as the treacherous mass shifted upward with the rising water.

Leifr climbed onto the tangle of wood, occasioning even more violent groaning and shifting.

'I see him!' he called, identifying a dark, sodden lump trapped not far below among the timbers.

Raudbjorn raised one hand in a feeble wave and exerted another mighty shove against the timber that was trapping him. Already the water was past his waist.

Raudbjorn looked up at Leifr and smiled his gentle smile.

'Knew you'd come, Fridmarr. This time Raudbjorn won't get out.'

'Don't be a fool,' Leifr said, motioning Thurid to hurry. 'I've got Thurid with me. He'll get you out with one of his spells. Isn't that so, Thurid?' The look he turned upon Thurid left no doubt about his determination.

Thurid stepped onto the tangle with great trepidation, yelping when it creaked threateningly. 'All right, Fridmarr, we'll try it, but we've got to hurry. Before long there won't be any sense in pulling him out.'

He positioned himself over the timber that held Raudbjorn and hastily read over a few rune wands. Then he polished his staff nervously and held it aloft and began to chant strange words. The timber groaned and trembled, and Raudbjorn's eyes widened as it rose inch by reluctant inch off his chest. The water was nearly to his chin by the time Raudbjorn wriggled out from under the beam and clambered upward, still clutching his prized halberd.

Thurid stopped chanting, and the timber fell back with a crash. Heaving a huge sigh of relief, Thurid helped Leifr hoist Raudbjorn out of the tangle of wood, shoving him toward the dangling ladder. Thurid brought up the rear, with his alf-light glowing very pale. Brusquely he brushed off Raudbjorn's thanks, urging him to climb faster and stop talking so much. A large part of his irritation was due to the water streaming off Raudbjorn's clothing and dripping into his face.

When the last ladder was behind them, they stumbled gratefully into a short tunnel that was barely more than an airshaft. Raudbjorn had to bend nearly double as they crept toward the small patch of light at the end.

Suddenly a deep and ominous rumble shook the rough ground beneath their feet with the most powerful tremor yet. Leifr lost his footing, and Raudbjorn fell to his hands and knees, blocking the tunnel effectively. Thurid battered him in a frenzy, gasping, 'Get up, you great ox! Skrymir's going to do it this time! The whole mountain might fall in! We've got to get out!'

A thundering crash behind them filled the tunnel with dust as tons of rock plummeted down the shaft. When the dust had settled somewhat, Leifr raised his head from the protecting cradle of his arms and looked around at a peculiar red light which suffused everything. A dome of stone had fallen down the shaft, leaving a high, vaulted ceiling above. The light seemed to come from the top of the vault. Leifr glanced at Thurid, who gaped at it just as incomprehendingly and made only a faint croak of protest when Leifr stood up and picked his way back toward the domed chamber.

Looking up, he gasped and shaded his eyes from the dazzlement streaming down into the dusty pit. An enormous red stone hung like a brilliant plug in a natural shaft that looked straight up at the sun. A thousand facets caused the light to sparkle and dance on the walls. Up near the ruby, runes had been carved into the stones.

'Skrymir's heart,' Thurid whispered in awe, with his face turned rapturously upward. 'There was a chamber beneath it. This is what the Rhbu candidates sought for. They came to Skrymir's heart to learn.'

'That's why Sorkvir wanted it? It's full of power?' Leifr questioned, unable to remove his gaze from the wondrous vision twinkling above him.

Thurid nodded. 'He was terribly close. The floor of the chamber must have been only a few feet thick. There are voices here, too. This disturbance has awakened them.'

'Old dead Rhbus talk to Thurid?' Raudbjorn queried 'Maybe Thurid a Rhbu someday.'

Thurid shook his head quickly. 'It's not for anyone else to say. When the Pentacle is cleared, others will come who have a greater gift than I do.'

'The Pentacle won't be complete until the grindstone

320

is returned,' Leifr said. 'We have three days left. After that, if we're not successful – you'll have to find another swordsman, Thurid.'

Thurid turned away from his rapt contemplation of the stone. 'Three days is three days. Plenty of time,' he snapped fiercely. 'Let's go. Gotiskolker and Ljosa will think we're all dead.'

When they crept from the small, rough opening at the end of the tunnel, they found the remains of several petrified Dokkalfar. Thurid nodded to the west where the sun had not been long below the horizon. 'They were a bit too hasty. Sorkvir was patient enough to wait for the sun to set. If he'd waited for Skrymir's last tremor, he would have seen what he has been digging for all these years. Perhaps if he had, he wouldn't be so willing to forsake Dokholur.' His keen eyes discerned a group of horsemen riding southward, far below. 'I believe his next and final stand will be wherever the grindstone is hidden.'

'Grittur-grof,' Raudbjorn said.

Thurid turned on him incredulously. 'Grittur-grof? The center of the Pentacle? What makes you think it's there?'

'Raudbjorn carried it there, after Sorkvir heard Fridmarr came back. Sorkvir hid it from Fridmarr. Lot of fuss over one old grindstone.' Raudbjorn shook his head in wonderment at the vagaries of wizards.

'It's a Rhbu grindstone, you dolt,' Thurid told him testily. 'The only one that will sharpen a Rhbu sword, which is the only weapon that can destroy Sorkvir forever. That's Sorkvir's great weakness – Rhbu magic is his bane.'

The mountain shuddered again, dislodging several black skarps and boulders that crashed thunderously into the valley below, scattering the thralls, Dokkalfar, and horses that lingered there. All the portals were blocked by rockfalls, and water oozed out from beneath, cascading down the steep, scarred slopes. Fissures opened as the earth slipped downward in landslides. Where the tunnels collapsed underground, deep craters pockmarked the mountainside. The glaciers at the summit of the mountain cracked and heaved, sending blocks of ice the size of hay barns rumbling down the ravines, casting up sheets of misty spray and ice particles.

Thurid led the descent from the mountain, muttering magic to himself the entire time, until they arrived safely on the far side of the fell to the south. By then, Leifr's strength was exhausted and his damaged leg dragged almost lifelessly as he hauled himself grimly along with the aid of a rough crutch torn from a thicket. At the bottom of the fell was a ruined farmhouse, where watch fires burned in a ring around it. Leifr halted suspiciously, but Thurid assured him. 'It's nothing to worry about – just some of your old friends from the mines watching for us. We've got an army ready-made, armed with pickaxes, mauls, and shovels, and a strong desire to remain free of Sorkvir. There are about four times as many thralls as there were Dokkalfar. Even Sorkvir would think twice about attacking them.'

The first watchman spied them and sounded the alarm, which went from post to post down the mountain. In short order, a horse and sledge came rumbling up the fell with a welcoming jingle of bells and harness. None of it seemed real to Leifr until the sledge had delivered him to the ruins of the house, where Ljosa and Gotiskolker had taken possession of the last remaining piece of standing roof, which had been part of a barn.

Gotiskolker was too weak to rise from his pallet and could only welcome Leifr with his dark, pain-laden eyes and a slight quirk of a smile. To Leifr, he looked already cadaverous, with his skin drawn thinly over his battered facial bones, showing every scar.

Seeing Leifr's stunned expression, Ljosa came forward quickly and led Leifr aside to explain tersely, 'He's dying, Fridmarr. It took the last of his strength to rescue me. He said that he has something important to tell me, but I fear he won't live to tell it.'

CHAPTER 20

Leifr drew a deep breath and sank down on a sheep fleece to stare across the fire at Gotiskolker. 'I believe I know what he wants to tell you.' He was certain it was the secret of Leifr's identity; or perhaps Gotiskolker wanted Ljosa to help Leifr return to the Scipling realm.

'He can't die and leave me here,' Leifr said wearily. 'We've come so far together.'

Thurid held his hands over Gotiskolker a moment, as if testing the heat of dying coals; then he sat down with an exhausted grunt next to Ljosa's fire.

'Don't look so bleak, Fridmarr,' he said, meaning to be kind. 'The eitur has been killing him for years. He's been living on borrowed time. His life could not have been very pleasant for him.'

'He's not finished yet,' Leifr said doggedly. 'There are things he has to do first.'

'Is there anything to eat around here?' Thurid asked, and Raudbjorn grunted a second to that motion, his eyes brightening at the prospect.

'Nothing but black bread and dried fish,' Ljosa replied.

Leifr shuddered. 'I'll never eat black bread and dried fish again for the rest of my life.' He lay down, bone-tired and gloomy, unable to think of anything but being marooned in the Alfar realm and unable to convince anyone that he was not Fridmarr Fridmundrsson. He felt the torque around his neck as the idea occurred to him that he might have only three days to worry about it. But if he were successful in finding the grindstone at Grittur-grof, he would have to spend the rest of his life as Fridmarr, an uneasy occupation with frequent

323

unpleasant surprises as more of Fridmarr's past came to light.

Eventually he went to sleep. In the morning when he awakened, he looked first to see if Gotiskolker was still breathing. By daylight, Gotiskolker looked far worse than by firelight, but he was still holding on to the thread of life. He opened his eyes a moment to look at Leifr, then closed them slowly, drifting away again.

Leifr prodded the frosty heap that was Raudbjorn, who awakened with a snort and blinked around at the ruins, as if he had no idea how he had gotten there.

'Raudbjorn, go find us a sledge and three horses. See if you can find us some riding horses.'

Raudbjorn's face puckered with doubt. 'Old mine ponies no good to ride,' he grumbled. 'Dokkalfar took best horses. Maybe have to walk.'

'While you're doing that, Raudbjorn, spread the word that we're all going to Grittur-grof.'

Glad for the opportunity to strike a few blows at their former slavemasters, the outcasts of Dokholur rallied themselves into an efficient traveling company, ready to follow Leifr south to Grittur-grof. Gently Leifr placed Gotiskolker in the sledge, noting that there was almost no substance left to his body.

'He might have lived longer if he'd never come on this expedition,' he observed bitterly to Ljosa, who was to ride in the sledge with Gotiskolker.

She smiled at Leifr sadly. 'Yes, but look at all the strength it took for him to go so far, when he knew he was dying. He must feel proud; and so should we, to have known such a brave and tormented soul.'

To cushion the rough ride, she held him in her arms, swaying as the horses started forward. The spectacle of the chieftain's daughter comforting a dying beggar sent a thrill through the motley army of perhaps a hundred tattered, homeless men, instilling their resilient souls with the strength to shoulder their packs of salvaged provisions and march grimly toward Grittur-grof

324

and the expected confrontation with their bitterest enemy.

Leifr found himself miraculously reunited with his old black horse Jolfr, who had been deemed unworthy of Dokkalfar possession and set to work in the mine, much as Leifr had. Raudbjorn brought Jolfr to him in the company of several former prisoners Leifr recognized, ones who had shared their food with him when they had not enough for themselves. Leifr made them captains. Under their leadership, the army moved southward.

Near sundown they came into view of Grittur-grof. Ancient barrow mounds covered with stones rose from the barren earth, long barrows where kings might have been buried, and round barrows for the lesser dead. No bushes or thickets grew among the graves, and the grass and moss clung to sheltered pockets between the stones, where the piercing wind could not penetrate. Leifr viewed the vast, desolate area with grim dismay, wondering how a grindstone could be found among so many thousands of ordinary stones.

Raudbjorn deployed his watchmen, and a dozen small fires soon sprang up in a circle around the main encampment. Leifr found a sheltered area for Gotiskolker and Ljosa within the doorway of a large barrow. As the sky darkened, the Dokkalfar appeared on the tops of the barrows, their helmets and weapons glimmering redly by the light of their torches and their battle-standards flapping in the cold wind with a rattling of bones and metal symbols. Presently Sorkvir appeared, riding the length of a long barrow, with several of his captains following at a respectful distance. Greifli would no longer be among Sorkvir's evil train, Leifr thought with grim satisfaction, and neither would Raudbjorn, who had taken a prominent position atop a small barrow to yell derision at the Dokkalfar.

Sorkvir halted and conferred with his captains for a few moments, then rode his horse down the side of the barrow toward the former prisoners' encampment. The former thralls took up their weapons and presented a bristling defense. Stopping at a safe distance, Sorkvir sent in word that he wished to speak to their leader, and the message was carried quickly to Leifr. He rode his horse out to meet Sorkvir, in spite of Thurid's advice not to, and persuaded Raudbjorn to stay at the edge of the watch fires only after a lengthy argument.

Leifr stopped at a cautious distance, not trusting the glowering wizard to maintain the truce.

'Fridmarr, we ought to be able to reach some agreement,' Sorkvir began, his eyes burning with the fever of a hunted animal. 'I believe we can both continue to exist, once we come to a truce.'

'There will be no truce,' Leifr replied.

'I could give you Gliru-hals,' Sorkvir said after a long, taut pause.

'Gliru-hals is not yours to give,' Leifr said. 'It belongs to Ljosa Hroaldsdottir, now that Hroald is dead by your hand. Driving out the trespassers is only one of our goals. Not one Dokkalfar will remain in Solvorfirth.'

Sorkvir snorted. 'You wouldn't be so arrogant if not for that Rhbu wizard.'

'Perhaps not, but Rhbu magic will be your doom.'

'Be sensible, Fridmarr. I could make you rich and powerful. I see now that I was foolish to think I could subdue your spirit by imprisonment and deprivation, when it was your intelligence I should have appealed to. We are not so different, you and I.'

'Only as different as night and day, Sorkvir,' Leifr said. 'Only one can exist at a time. It does you no good to try to sway me. I won't change my mind. I will sharpen that Rhbu sword and destroy you with it.'

'You are only doing this to assuage your own conscience about your brother Bodmarr. You think it will remove your guilt for his death, but treachery to your own brother is a crime the Ljosalfar will never forgive. They may tolerate you, but their backs will always be turned to you. You will always feel a secret self-loathing because you were unable to come to Bodmarr's aid when you could have saved him. What a weak fool you were in those days! You were out of your mind with eitur while I was killing Bodmarr. You killed him almost as much as I did. One day the eitur you took then will kill you, Fridmarr. Sometimes it takes many years, but one day you'll begin to feel it burning away in your vitals, in your very brain. All that can prevent it is more eitur. Aren't you afraid, Fridmarr? It's an unpleasant way to die. I have the means to save you from such a miserable and protracted death.'

Sorkvir held out a small flask to Leifr. 'Go ahead and take it, Fridmarr. As long as you have a supply of eitur you'll never have to worry about the pain of being without it.'

Leifr's thoughts were upon Gotiskolker. With a sudden flare of hope he realized that saving Gotiskolker's life now could ensure him a way back to his own realm later. But his hope died a sickly death when he pictured himself forcing the poison on his friend in order to desert him to the evil consequences of such a deed. He gazed at Sorkvir, feeling the powerful influence of the wizard's skills trying to draw him under the spell of Sorkvir's words.

'It's useless to try to save yourself,' Leifr said after a long, silent struggle. 'You know that fate is on my side; otherwise, the Pentacle would not be almost cleared.'

'The damage is quite easy to remedy,' Sorkvir said, making a visible effort to control his temper. 'Fridmarr, I have tried in vain to appeal to your common sense and I have tried to frighten you about the eitur. I had thought that you might listen to reason, instead of being so obdurate. You have not changed from the stubborn fool you were before.'

'As you said, we are not so different.'

'Is that your final word, Fridmarr?'

'Yes, unless you wish to tell me where the grindstone is hidden.'

327

Sorkvir chuckled drily. 'And tempt fate?' Your challenge is tempting, Fridmarr, but I'm no longer young and foolish, as you are. What if Bodmarr's magic Rhbu sword doesn't work in your hand? What if he was the chosen hero, and you are nothing but a presumptuous usurper? If that should be the case, and you are unable to kill me, have you contemplated what your immediate future might be?'

Leifr turned his horse sharply, backing away from Sorkvir. The wizard broke into a wild laugh that echoed off the rocky barrows. 'Give it up now, Fridmarr, while neither of us knows what the truth actually is. This question will keep the peace between us.'

'I think I stand to lose more by not knowing,' Leifr replied, feeling the torque's cool metal around his neck. 'I know from Raudbjorn that the grindstone is here. Maybe he will remember exactly where it lies.'

Keeping a watchful eye upon his enemy, Leifr turned and rode back to the encampment. Obviously working himself into a rage, Sorkvir lashed his horse into a gallop and raced away into the barrows, with his captain following warily.

Thurid strode after Leifr, once Sorkvir was safely out of sight. When he caught up with Leifr, his face was drawn and gray with anxiety.

'Fridmarr,' he whispered, darting a resentful glower at Raudbjorn, standing rigidly nearby, guarding them. 'What about the eitur? How could you have swallowed that stuff? Even a fool such as you were should have known—'.

'Thurid,' Leifr interrupted, 'do I look like I'm dying of poison? I've never tasted eitur in my life.' He started to go around Thurid, but Thurid again blocked his path, using his staff as a bar.

'Fridmarr, if you've used eitur—' Thurid seemed to have trouble slowing down his rush of words into coherent words and sentences. 'If eitur has been in your bloodstream only once, then the magic of the Rhbus isn't

328

going to work for you. The corruption begins immediately, although it may progress very slowly for many
years. Even if we sharpen the sword with the proper
grindstone and you thrust it through Sorkvir a hundred
times, it isn't going to destroy him and prevent him from
taking Hel's journey back to life again. What I mean to
say is, if we're doomed to fail, it would be better not to
try until we find someone who is free of Sorkvir's fatal
taint.'

'Thurid, I told you—'.

'Yes, but I think you're lying in an attempt to keep me
from worrying.'

'It's not working then, if that's what I'm doing,' Leifr
retorted. 'If I'd taken eitur, I'd tell you. I don't want to
face Sorkvir in battle and fail. If you're through
bothering me, will you let me by now?'

'I'm not through,' Thurid protested as Leifr pushed
him aside. 'You've already got your bad leg to slow you
down. Sorkvir might kill you before you kill him, even if
the sword magic will work for you.'

Gnawed by his own grave doubts, Leifr retorted
furiously, 'I didn't come here willingly; if I'd known what
it would be like, I would have done anything to prevent
it. I am not Fridmarr, and this shouldn't be my quarrel. I
was virtually kidnapped and forced to interfere with that
Pentacle. Gotiskolker is the one who brought me here,
and he's not going to be able to get me back. Gotiskolker
is—'. Leifr had a grip on Thurid's collar piece, shaking
him for emphasis at each point.

Then a pure revelation pierced his anger to the core,
dissolving it into amazement and awe. Releasing Thurid
from his grip, he turned slowly to the barrow, where
Raudbjorn stood watching interestedly.

'Gotiskolker is Fridmarr,' Leifr whispered.

Thurid's glazed eyes did not blink as he stared at Leifr
for a long moment. Then he said, 'Brain fever. It must
have been from that beating in Dokholur.' He clasped
his hands around his staff and rested his forehead against

them as if this new affliction were too much for one wizard to bear.

The knowledge of Fridmarr's final secret and the dark torment of Gotiskolker, finally resolved, left Leifr almost weak with relief. Leaving Thurid to his distraught muttering and groaning, Leifr went inside and knelt beside the still figure on the pallet. Ljosa already knelt on the other side, holding one wasted hand between hers. Tears spilled on the withered hand as she smoothed it and kissed it.

'You know,' Leifr whispered, and she nodded, raising eyes to him that regarded him as if he had suddenly become a stranger to her.

'Who are you?' she asked.

'Leifr Thorljotsson – a Scipling. He brought me here to do the things that he couldn't.'

Ljosa bowed her head. 'All these years among us, and no one suspected. What wretched little comfort anyone gave him – except Fridmundr, from the generosity of his own kind heart. If he had known—'. Blinded by scalding tears, she gently kissed the thin, scarred hand.

The long-lost Fridmarr opened his fragile eyelids a crack and whispered, 'Hush, it doesn't matter now. My father did know who I was. He also knew I was too proud to accept more than almost worthless offerings. All I took from him was the reverse glamour spell that got me into Gliru-hals. Then he carried me to the hut in the barrows and treated my wounds, instead of leaving me on the dung heap to die, as he ought. I almost didn't forgive him for that. Not until he was nearly gone did I speak to him again. You see what a fool I've been. Don't grieve for this miserable carcass. I'm glad to let go of all this old pain.'

Leifr glanced up as a shadow passed before the fire and met the astounded gaze of Thurid, gaping at him with a complete lack of comprehension. Slowly the wizard sank to his knees beside Fridmarr to listen to the long-kept secret.

Leifr burned with mounting shame, struck by a sudden awful realization. 'Then Fridmundr knew from the first moment that I was not his son. What a fool he must have thought me. And I was a bigger fool for thinking that even this would deceive Fridmarr's own father.' Leifr removed the carbuncle from his neck and placed it in Fridmarr's wasted hand.

Fridmarr shook his head weakly and smiled. 'No. He knew the carbuncle, of course. He knew that I was finally making the effort to restore the honor to our family name, after wasting so much time. He saw you as Fridmarr reborn in all his former strength and power and courage – reborn from the ruin of eitur, abuse, and wretched suffering caused by his son's terrible pride.' Fridmarr's eyes glowed faintly for a moment. 'I saw you that way myself and felt horribly jealous, so I wasn't kind to you, Leifr. But I tried to swallow some of my pride in order to destroy Sorkvir.'

'Even to the extent of destroying and denying your entire identity as an Alfar?' Thurid demanded brokenly, his hand closing gently over the carbuncle and Fridmarr's feeble hand clutching it. 'We could have helped you without all this misery. To think of you, outcast among your own family, sacrificing your jewel for the sake of revenge, and poisoning yourself with Sorkvir's eitur—'. He shook his head, unable to continue.

'Thurid. My old teacher and friend.' Fridmarr tried to raise his head to see, but the effort was too much for him. 'You should know how it is with me. I never took the easy way around, did I? Some of us need to suffer and make our own mistakes. Now it's time to pay the price. I'm sorry for the misery and pain I've caused all of you – but it was a good deception while it lasted, was it not?'

Thurid lifted his pinched and pale features to look at Leifr, bafflement and suspicion in his eyes.

'Yes, it was an excellent deception,' he said musingly. 'Even I was fooled, and I prided myself at one time upon

331

my perspicacity. And you were there in the barrows all this time, scavenging useless bits from the settlements. Fridmarr, you might have told your secret to me, and I would have helped you.'

Fridmarr shook his head, his unfocused gaze traveling blindly in Thurid's direction. 'My truest and oldest of friends, I could not abide anyone's pity. Sorkvir might have guessed who I really was, had you come flocking around. I knew Sorkvir would punish anyone who was too kind to me, whether or not he knew who I was, so I kept you all away.'

Ljosa raised her tear-stained face. 'I would not have been afraid of Sorkvir, Fridmarr. I wouldn't have pitied or scorned you when you needed my help. It would have taken away this bitter feeling in my heart that I've cherished all these years, if you had allowed me to forgive you.'

'I'm too stubborn,' Fridmarr answered with a tortured scowl. 'I'm not the fine spirit that you are, precious one. I was too ashamed of my weakness and my mistakes. So when I found Leifr, I used him to hide behind. Leifr, will you ever forgive me for all this I've put you through?'

'Of course I will,' Leifr said gruffly. 'I never meant half those wicked things I said about Fridmarr, before I knew he was you. It must have been hard watching me make such a fool of myself and not giving yourself away by saying too much.'

'You did well, my friend. Far better than I had expected. My only regret is that I won't be here to see your final victory. I know you must succeed, Leifr.' He sighed and closed his eyes. 'Thurid, you'll see to it that Leifr gets back to his own realm, won't you?'

Thurid looked disturbed and twisted a strand of his thin beard. 'I've never done anything like that before. I'll be glad to experiment, though. Perhaps the rune sticks contain such a spell.'

'Forget the rune sticks. You don't need them, Thurid. You're going to be one of the finest wizards in the realm

one day.' Fridmarr's voice was faint and tired. 'It's time
to make an end to all this talk. Leifr, take the carbuncle.
Where I'm going, there will be no use for it. I think the
day will come when you might want it. You could stay in
this realm. The Ljosalfar need good fighters.'

Leifr took the carbuncle reluctantly; it was a dying
friend's last wish, and he knew he must honour it. 'I'm
grateful, Fridmarr – but I'll have to go it as a Scipling
from now on. One day maybe I'll change my mind,
though.'

'The choice is yours, my friend.' Fridmarr's voice
faded to a mere whisper. 'The time has come to say
good-bye, my dear ones. May the Rhbus guide you, until
we meet again.'

As they gazed, his withered skin began to glow softly,
blurring and shifting in changing patterns, until it was
Fridmarr as he had been long ago, before his afflictions
laid him low. His likeliness to Leifr was distinct, but the
light shining from within illuminated his countenance
until ordinary flesh seemed dull dross by comparison.

'The last gift of the Rhbus,' he whispered. 'Remember
me as I once was – not as Gotiskolker.'

The glorious light began to fade, although the youthful
likeness remained. Ljosa clutched his hand, whispering,
'So little time! Why couldn't we have just one day? I had
him back, and now he's gone again!'

Thurid leaned forward. 'Fridmarr, if ever I do achieve
honors and fame and power in this realm, it will be partly
yours. Farewell, my dear boy!' His voice choked, and he
hid his face in his hands.

'Good-bye, dear friend. Good-bye, Leifr, battle companion and true friend. Good-bye, Ljosa – my love.' He
sighed and relaxed his tremulous grip on the thread of
life, smiling peacefully as his spirit slipped away.

'Fridmarr! I always loved you!' Ljosa cried out in
anguish.

'I know you did, my love,' Fridmarr's voice whispered, as if from a great distance. His last breath rattled

in his throat, and his eyes opened with a brief flicker of glad astonishment before fading into a lightless, vacant stare.

For a long moment no one stirred. Then from outside came Kraftig's mournful howl, echoed by Frimodig and Farlig, rising in an unearthly chorus that tightened the band of grief around Leifr's heart until he feared it would burst. Rising quickly, he left the barrow and limped away into the darkness blindly, guided by the voices of the hounds. They stood atop a barrow, pointing their long noses skyward, shivering in a crouched pose, with their fringed tails drooping.

When the dogs were done with their howling, they slunk down from the barrow to Leifr, pressing close to his legs and growling fearfully at every small sound, still shivering. Raudbjorn loomed suddenly around a large black cairn, setting off a ferocious salvo of barking and snarling, which Leifr quelled sharply to conceal his own startlement.

'Raudbjorn, I meant to find you earlier,' Leifr began, glad for some distraction from his grief and despair at Fridmarr's death.

'Fridmarr?' Raudbjorn's voice quavered questioningly.

'No. My name is Leifr. The real Fridmarr is dead.'

Raudbjorn shook his head slowly. 'Real Fridmarr always be you. This Leifr somebody I don't know.'

'Maybe we'll become friends, when you get to know me as Leifr, instead of Fridmarr.'

'Maybe. Leifr fights like Fridmarr, brave as Fridmarr, looks like Fridmarr. But Raudbjorn always miss Fridmarr, somehow.'

'Me, too,' Leifr replied with a sigh. 'I wanted to ask you about the grindstone, Raudbjorn. I have two days to find it and return it to Hjaldr, or my life will be cut short as if I were a common horse thief. Do you remember where Sorkvir hid the grindstone?'

Raudbjorn heaved a regretful sigh. 'In rocks. Rocks all Raudbjorn remember. Raudbjorn search tomorrow and maybe find grindstone for Leifr. Maybe find Sorkvir and Dokkalfar too.' His teeth gleamed in the moonlight, and he strummed the edge of his halberd with his thumb to test its sharpness.

During the night, Ljosa prepared Fridmarr's body for burial, as well as she was able with such limited resources. The news of his true identity and his death swept through the encampment almost immediately. At dawn, the ragged assembly gathered before the open barrow to pay their last respects and hear Thurid give his funeral recitation. Then Leifr and three of the stoutest of the former prisoners carried the remains on a pallet to an open barrow for burial, with the others streaming behind, singing skalds. Ljosa stood beside Leifr as the barrow opening was filled with stones. When it was done, she turned away with a sigh.

'I saw you limping as you carried him,' she said. 'Your knee must be very painful.'

'No, not at all,' Leifr lied manfully.

She walked beside him in silence, darting him a covert glance now and then. At last she said, 'Fridmarr is dead. You don't have to maintain the pretense of being infatuated with me.'

'It never was a pretense. If I really were Fridmarr – if Fridmarr had come back as himself – would you have forgiven him then, instead of waiting until he was dying?'

Ljosa let her blowing hair screen her face as she bent her head. In a broken voice she replied, 'I don't think I have ever been humble in my life, until now. Nothing Sorkvir could do to me broke my pride. I vowed I would never forgive Fridmarr because of Bodmarr's death. I didn't know if my hard heart could forgive him. But to think of him living just a few miles away, all those years, and never saying anything!' She wiped her eyes on a tatter of her cloak and walked a bit faster. Then she turned abruptly and asked, 'Did he do this all for me? You knew him better than anyone else, so you should know what his reasons were.'

Leifr considered carefully and slowly shook his head.

'No, he did it because he knew that something had to be done and he was the only one with the knowledge to get it done. Gotis – Fridmarr was tormented by his past and he knew that nothing could take the pain away altogether.'

Ljosa bowed her head, nodding in assent. 'I'm glad he was doing it for the sake of rightness and not just to prove himself to me. He must have suffered greatly under the burden of his guilt. I don't think I will ever forget this pain – no more than you can forget your knee.'

'Many people walk with a limp,' Leifr said. 'It's better than not walking at all.'

Ljosa darted him a small smile through the curtain of her hair. 'That must be Scipling wisdom. Yours must be an enduring and determined race of people.'

Leifr shrugged, never having thought about it before. 'We have to be, as harsh as Skarpsey is.'

The thralls gathered near the open barrow where Fridmarr had died, and Thurid divided them into groups for searching Grittur-grof, reserving the western section for himself, Raudbjorn, and Leifr, since that was where he expected to encounter the Dokkalfar. As they saddled their horses, Ljosa also saddled a horse and rode forward to join them with such a set, composed expression that even Thurid dared not contradict her. He stuffed a handful of rune wands back into his satchel and disentangled a dowsing pendulum.

'Silence, please,' he commanded, extending the pendulum at arm's length. 'Think of nothing but the grindstone, so your mental powers will assist me.'

Raudbjorn obediently squeezed shut his eyes, but after a few moments he gave it up with a groan. 'Nothing but food in Raudbjorn's mind,' he grumbled.

Thurid glared at him as a fresh source of aggravation and thrust the pendulum in his pocket. 'I shall try later when there is less interference. Raudbjorn, doesn't anything at all look familiar to you?'

Raudbjorn slowly shook his head. 'Grittur-grof all the same everywhere. Nothing but rocks and barrows.'

'Rocks and barrows,' Thurid muttered witheringly, darting a covert glance at Leifr, perhaps the thousandth one since he had learned that Leifr was not Fridmarr. With a huffy snort, he urged his horse along faster.

Leifr nodded Jolfr into a trot, overtaking Thurid so he could ride beside him and look at him as he asked, 'Why do you keep on staring at me like that?' Don't you think I can be trusted?'

Thurid's eyes slid over him uneasily. 'It's just that I've never seen a Scipling before and I feel as if I've been betrayed somehow by having one deceive me for so long. I don't know how I could have mistaken you for Fridmarr. You're nothing alike. I had a strange nagging feeling all along that something was wrong, but I was too stupid to see what was right before my nose. I suppose it was a clever hoax. You must feel awfully proud.'

'I can't say that I do,' Leifr replied. 'I'm sorry if my being a Scipling upsets you, but I'd like to remind you that we've spent a long time together, and I, at least, have grown to trust you. Am I not the same person I was when I first came to Dallir?'

'No, you're not,' Thurid answered decisively. 'You were Fridmarr then, and now you're a strange Scipling. It will take me a while to get used to the idea. I'd always thought there was something rather evil about Sciplings; I'm trying to decide what it is.' He rode a few moments in moody silence, then burst out with, 'You might have confided in me! Didn't you think I was worth trusting?'

'Not at first, no,' Leifr replied.

Thurid sniffed indignantly, 'You weren't fair to me at all.' He paused and dismounted to make another attempt to dowse with the pendulum, daring a murderous glare at Raudbjorn. 'Ride to the other side of that barrow, Raudbjorn. I don't want any more of your mutton and duck than I'm already forced to endure.'

Thurid struck his pose, concentrating magnificently,

but he had scarcely got into it when Raudbjorn rode back from the other side of the barrow.

'Something strange, something strange!' he babbled.

Thurid put the pendulum back in his pocket with jerky, irritated movements, muttering, 'What's the use of trying to think with this brute in our midst? Sorkvir was wise in palming him off with us, I'm beginning to think.'

Raudbjorn pointed upward. 'Look! Clouds!'

'Clouds!' Thurid seethed, but he glanced upwards nevertheless.

Black masses of clouds with a greenish tinge boiled up at the horizon, spreading over the rocky face of Gritturgrof like advancing night. Thurid leaped off his horse and dug frantically into his bundle of rune sticks, selecting one with shaking hands and reading it over several times in great haste. Extending his staff, he spoke the words of the spell in a loud voice. A jet of white cloud hissed from his staff into the sky, but the black clouds rolled over it with a crackling of thunder and lightning. Several more times, in quick succession, Thurid tried to halt the advance of the storm, until the black clouds were almost overhead, blotting out the sun and half the sky.

'Blast!' Thurid muttered, rummaging through the rune wands in a frenzy of impatience. 'That's one I must have copied wrong! I can't get enough power into it! I hope there's another way to stop those clouds, or we'll have a battle such as no Scipling has ever seen and lived to tell about.'

CHAPTER 21

A DEADLY cold wind lashed at the horscs' manes and tore at everyone's cloaks. Thurid tried another spell, which happened to be the sputtering firebolt that had failed so drastically inside the tunnels of Bjartur.

'Look!' Raudbjorn gripped Thurid's arm in the middle of another spell, turning him around to look to the west. 'Sorkvir!'

Sorkvir and a long line of Dokkalfar rode slowly toward them, spanning much of Grittur-grof. The thralls sprang from their hiding places like flushed rabbits, retreating from the grim apparition of the masked Dokkalfar and the menacing clouds.

Determined not to retreat so ignominiously, Leifr rode to the top of a barrow and waited, armed with a heavy pickaxe from Dokholur, a weapon he had learned to respect and use with good effect against prowling trolls.

Sorkvir and his men halted within shouting distance, and Sorkvir rode ahead alone until Leifr advised him, 'Come no closer. What you have to say can be heard from there.'

Sorkvir unmasked himself, after a glance upward to note the progress of the clouds. When he revealed his face to Leifr, he was grinning with maniacal glee.

'Fridmarr is dead,' he hissed malevolently. 'I heard it from one of my spies. You are nothing but a lowly Scipling.'

He laughed a harsh and bitter laugh that the wind carried away across the barrows. 'Now you'll know the meaning of my wrath, Scipling. With Fridmarr gone, I have nothing to fear by destroying you. The Pentacle is still mine. Fridmarr might have saved himself the trouble

339

of coming back and suffering as he did. I am indestructible and your Rhbu wizard is a contemptible, inept amateur.' He shook his head in disgust as another of Thurid's failed spells fizzled overhead, showering the barrows with a spray of harmless sparks.

Leifr glanced at Thurid, who did not bother to conceal his desperation; rune sticks lay scattered around his feet. His hair streamed in the icy wind, and his eyes had a mad, furious glaze. Leifr signaled silently to Raudbjorn to take Ljosa and depart. Raudbjorn nodded, and Leifr turned back to Sorkvir, who was still preening himself with monstrous self-satisfaction.

'Our dispute rests in the hands of fate,' Leifr said. 'You don't know that a Scipling won't be your bane. I was not brought here to fail.'

'Nor have I raised this empire of mine to fail,' Sorkvir retaliated. 'Half of my assurance lies in a good defense. You won't have the chance to kill me, Scipling. Your bones will rot here in Grittur-grof with the remains of the Rhbus and the Ljosalfar.' He raised one arm aloft and the clouds responded with an earth-shaking explosion of thunder. Needles of greenish lightning struck the tops of the barrows nearby, blasting fragments of rock in all directions, which lent great impetus to the fleeing thralls.

Sorkvir masked himself and drew his sword. With a defiant roar of challenge, he spurred his horse down the side of the barrow, with the Dokkalfar thundering close behind,clashing weapons and shields.

Leifr fought to control his frightened horse, winding his pickaxe around his head and letting it fly just as Sorkvir's horse came plunging up the barrow. The pick struck Sorkvir in the chest, knocking him backward off his horse and sending his sword flying end over end into the rocks.

Thurid suddenly struck upon a workable spell with a wild yell of exultation. A wall of flame sprang up, towering before the charging Dokkalfar. Their horses veered and stumbled, shooting several riders off over their necks.

Sorkvir was rising to his feet slowly, shaking both fists in the air and saying the words of some spell directed toward the roiling black clouds.

The clouds glowed with an eerie, lurid light, churning into the shapes of horses and riders galloping through the flying turmoil of clouds with a mighty thundering roar.

'Storm giants! Take cover!' Thurid shouted, scuttling into the lee of the barrow. The wall of flame faded the moment his concentration was broken, and the Dokkalfar regrouped for another rush.

Leifr abandoned his horse and plunged after Thurid, who was making for the doorway of an open barrow. Midway, a barrage of ice bolts from above sent them diving into the meagre cover of some large rocks. The storm giants swirled overhead, darting ice bolts and furious gusts of snow and hail.

Looking back for Sorkvir, Leifr saw him climb to the top of the barrow, calling the storm giants and brandishing his staff aloft, with the wind whipping his red cloak out straight behind him. Heeding his commands, the storm giants wheeled around and started another barrage as they traveled the barrow field. The unfortunate thralls scattered before them in confusion, many falling prey to ice bolts and flying fragments of shattered rocks.

During the brief interval between attacks, Leifr noticed a nearby hole and dived into it. Fervently he hoped that Raudbjorn had managed to take Ljosa back to the barrow at the encampment where they would be safe. No living thing stood a chance against the shrieking green bolts that were shattering against the stones, exploding into thousands of smaller missiles. Not far from Leifr's retreat, three dead thralls lay stiff and blue, mute testimony to the deadly effects of the shattered ice bolts. He saw nothing of Thurid in the murky brume that settled over the barrows.

Eventually the roaring winds and thunder ceased, and the silence was almost harder to endure than the uproar of the storm giants. Twice Leifr heard horses tramping past outside, but whether they were loose horses or Dokkalfar horses he had no way of guessing, so he kept still in his barrow, waiting until the dark mist had lifted and the sun winked between the clouds before he dared to come out.

The hail, snow, and green ice were melting into the earth. Leifr saw no sign of the Dokkalfar or Sorkvir, except more dead thralls. He heard no sound except the crunch of his own boots. At the encampment, he found the earth churned into mud by many hooves. Raudbjorn and Ljosa were gone. Despairing, he traced his footsteps back to the last place he had seen Thurid, when the storm giants made their first attack. Thurid's satchel lay not far beyond, almost hidden by snow and ice. He picked it up and scraped it off. Cautiously he opened the satchel and looked inside for the sword, seeing nothing but Thurid's all-important chaos of seemingly unrelated objects. Gingerly he poked through the mess until he located the hilt of the sword. When he pulled it out, he discovered that Thurid had acquired a sheath for it at some point in his travels, a lovely sheath embossed with silver designs. With a sigh, Leifr buckled it around his waist, somewhat comforted by its presence, even if it was dull and useless. Without Thurid, it was his only defense.

The silence of Grittur-grof made his solitude even more appalling. He searched around for signs of his friends, fearing the worst each time he had to turn over another body, but he did not find Ljosa, Raudbjorn, or Thurid. A goodly number of the thralls must have escaped, a thought which cheered his spirits, and possibly his friends were among them. If that were the case, they would come back for him – or at least for Thurid's satchel with the sword, even if they no longer considered a Scipling worth saving.

Entertaining as such thoughts were, Leifr knew it was

342

senseless to sit and wait for something that might not happen, particularly in view of the fact that tomorrow was the last day of Hjaldr's alog. As far as Leifr was able to see, the only recourse for him was to get to Hjaldrsholl and humbly ask for more time, since he now had an idea where to find the grindstone. Surely Hjaldr would be sensible and allow him to continue his search.

Grimly resolved, he set off straight southward, hoping to arrive at Hjaldrsholl by sundown, in spite of his recalcitrant knee. Walking ten miles or so would have been nothing to him before his injury; but to his disgust, he found himself stopping to rest repeatedly and he was not even out of Grittur-grof yet. The low angle of the sun warned him that he was more likely to spend the night in an open barrow, fighting off the trolls, than he was likely to spend it at Hjaldrsholl.

His rest stops were getting longer, with less distance in between. Dejectedly he sat down on a rock. The sun was almost touching the horizon when he heard the familiar sound of paws pattering over the stones behind him. Three hairy faces peered at him over a rock momentarily, then three hairy bodies hurled themselves at him with yelps of wild delight. Laughing, he exulted in the feel of their rough coats and the wriggling, panting, bright-eyed life within them. For too long, he had thought he was the only living thing left in Grittur-grof. Now, at least, he wouldn't have to worry about trolls. Maybe the dogs would even hunt him something to eat.

With his thoughts on food and finding someplace to hide for the night, Leifr followed the dogs into a dark avenue between two long barrows. His leg was hurting, so he sat down and pulled his cloak up around his ears and his hood down to his eyes against the piercing wind, which the barrows seemed to channel especially for his benefit. After a few moments he could no longer stand it and stood up impatiently to hobble on to a less windy spot to do his resting. Whistling to the dogs, he started around the edge of one of the long barrows. Suddenly, for the first time he was aware of a soft, steady sound which had come to him intermittently since he had sat down, but which he had been too weary to give much heed.

Stopping in his tracks, he stood still, listening until he discerned which direction the sound was coming from. It was a singing, grating sound that seemed as familiar to him as the memory of his father's old grindstone, standing in the moss beside the kitchen door, where it had stood for seven generations. Leifr had grown from cradle-size, hearing the song of that grindstone as it sharpened knives, farm tools, and once his father's sword when a neighboring earl revolted.

It was the sound of a grindstone he was hearing. Slowly he turned around. It stood on the top of the long mound, a larger grindstone than the old one at home, and a small, bent figure pumped the treadle with one foot, all his attention upon the blade he was sharpening. A shower of sparks flew away into the wind with the shrill singing of metal and stone. Leifr could see little more than the silhouette of the ragged little man against the soft pink glow of the setting sun.

Scarcely breathing, Leifr climbed up the side of the barrow, stopping at a respectful distance, with the dogs clinging around his knees, silent and alert.

The little, bent man held up the knife he was working on and felt its sharpness with one thumb, seeming to take no notice of Leifr. Satisfied with his work, the stranger put down the knife on a sheep fleece nearby, along with several other knives he had evidently sharpened previously. He moved with the stiff deliberation of the aged, every movement judged to perfection, with none of the extravagance of youthful energy. Straightening, he looked up at Leifr, gave him a single, thrifty nod of welcome, and extended his hands for Leifr's sword without speaking a word. For a long moment, Leifr was too stricken with awe to move. Then he reached for Bodmarr's sword and drew it slowly, placing

it gently in the hands of the little man, who bent over it
with a scowl, turning it over several times. Leifr knew
with a certainty that he was going to give it back and say
he could not sharpen a sword cursed by Sorkvir. He
expelled his pent-up breath with a long sigh of bone-
weary despair.

The stranger darted one quick glance at him, his
wizened features still hidden in the shadows. Pumping
the treadle vigorously, the stranger put the sword to the
grindstone with a ringing shriek of metal. The dogs
shook their heads and pawed at their ears. Leifr listened,
totally rapt, certain that he would never again hear a
more thrilling sound.

When the sword was finally sharpened, the wizened
smith held it up for a last, critical examination before
surrendering it to Leifr, almost with reluctance, perhaps
regretting that his fine handiwork would soon be undone
after the inevitable clashing with other swords, hacking
shields in twain, cleaving helmets, and other acts of war.

Leifr accepted the sword. From tip to hilt, it gleamed
golden with a radiant light somehow trapped within the
metal. Leifr swung it cautiously, unable to take his eyes
off it.

'It's perfect,' he said with reverent awe, letting the
last, red ray of sun touch the gleaming metal. 'I've never
seen anything like it. I'm not the one it was intended for,
although I'll make the attempt as if I were. Tell me – do
you believe it will work its magic for a lowly Scipling?'

He turned around to look at the smith when there was
no immediate answer. To his amazement, the smith had
quietly vanished, taking his knives and sheep fleece with
him without making a sound or saying a word. Leifr stared
at the grindstone, still turning slowly, and hastily peered
all around for the small, bent figure in the rusty black
cloak. He could not have traveled far and must still be
visible in such a barren landscape.

'I meant to thank you,' Leifr called, although he saw
no sign of the little smith. He waited a moment and

345

heard no reply except the hiss of the wind through the dry, wiry grasses. The dogs crept forward humbly and crouched at his feet, trembling with suppressed excitement and gazing up into his face expectantly.

'It's a hunt you want, isn't it?' he said softly, rubbing Kraftig's silky ears. 'Then a hunt you shall have, only it's Sorkvir we're stalking, not trolls.'

With a yell of challenge, he swung the sword around over his head, facing the western edge of Grittur-grof where a few red fires twinkled. Presently two horsemen appeared atop a barrow about half a mile away, staring in Leifr's direction. He yelled again in obvious defiance, and the two Dokkalfar returned his challenge in a similar fashion before turning back toward the fires.

Leifr positioned himself in an advantageous spot and waited, dividing his attention between watching for the Dokkalfar and admiration of the sword. Its first trial was not long in forthcoming; the Dokkalfar rode out at a brisk gallop to find him, their banners snapping and grisly trophies rattling jauntily on bridles, shields, and armor. The sky, always slow to lose its light, bathed the Dokkalfar warriors in an ominous green afterglow as they plowed to a halt about a bowshot from Leifr and surveyed him suspiciously.

'What, only six of you?' Leifr called. 'Either Sorkvir is running out of loyal Dokkalfar, or he doesn't count me for much as an enemy. Which of you is the spokesman?'

One Dokkalfar rode forward slowly, a thickset, dark-bearded fellow wearing the insignia of the Fox Society.

'I am Grunur,' he said. 'Do you wish to surrender?' Is that the reason for calling this attention to yourself?'

'Not at all,' Leifr replied, keeping the sword out of sight; but it was harder by far to keep the triumphant edge out of his voice. 'I see you are from the Fox Society. That's getting rather low in the hierarchy for you to be a leader, isn't it? What has become of the Owls and the Wolves and Eagles? Surely they can't all be dead.'

346

The Dokkalfar eyed him coldly. They were all younger members, as evidenced by their insignia of Bats and Skulls. Grunur urged his horse a few steps forward.

'It makes no difference which class we're in,' he growled. 'You'll find that we can kill you just as dead as the older Dokkalfar – who may be more renowned for their discretion than for their valor.'

'Thirsty for a little fame, are you?' Leifr taunted. 'Do you think Sorkvir will give it to you – or will it be an early grave?'

Grunur shifted in his saddle with an impatient creak, but Leifr had read correctly the gleam in his eyes.

'We didn't come out here merely for the pleasure of your conversation,' he replied, loosening the loop over his sword hilt. 'If you don't wish to surrender, then you must want to fight.'

'Or to talk to Sorkvir,' Leifr added. 'Send one of your men back to deliver my message that I wish to speak to him.'

'Sorkvir is occupied with important affairs,' Grunur said, after a moment's hesitation. 'You'll have to come with us, and we'll take you to him.'

'In how many pieces? Somehow I distrust your offer.'

Grunur darted a glance over his shoulder at his five companions, waiting with their hands on their weapons. At his signal, they rode forward cautiously to join their leader, all studying Leifr warily.

'Forget the offer, then,' Grunur said. 'We'll take you to him in the way that suits us best.' He drew his sword and held it aloft. 'I'm sure Sorkvir would rather see you dead than alive, now that he has nothing to fear from your draug, Scipling.'

Clapping his spurs to his horse, he charged straight at Leifr, with his cohorts howling and cheering at his heels. Leifr kept the sword hidden at his side until the last possible moment, when Grunur's horse slithered to a halt almost within arm's length of him. Grunur's sword came whistling down at him, striking Bodmarr's sword

347

with a resounding clang and a brilliant flash of light. Half of Grunur's sword swung away among the stones, smoking. For a split second Grunur reeled back in astonishment, his eyes following the flight of the broken piece of metal, but he recovered almost instantly, taking a backhanded slice at Leifr with his broken weapon – a choice that cost him his life. Had he waited or retreated to unsheath his axe, he might have survived, but he was eager for any chance to enhance his reputation and unwilling to let his subordinates take all the glory.

Leifr parried the blow with another flash of fire, and a large shard of Grunur's sword ricocheted away with a shrill whine. The other five Dokkalfar were blocked by Grunur's horse from joining the attack, and the large rocks in back of Leifr's position prevented them from riding around behind him. For a few moments they wavered, watching their leader fighting with increasing desperation as his sword disintegrated, bit by bit. Then two of the Dokkalfar dismounted and started to climb up to Leifr.

It was then that the battle ended for Grunur. Leifr drove the sword through his body in one deadly thrust, just as the two Dokkalfar came into striking distance.

Grunur sagged slowly backward, turning his face upward to the ghastly sky and gasping, 'The soul-destroyer! I'm done – Sorkvir is finished!'

He dissolved like mist, his cloak and armor collapsing and toppling to the earth, steaming slightly. The three Dokkalfar still on horseback took to their heels, and not in the direction of Sorkvir's encampment. The other two started a desperate scramble down the rocks toward their horses. At a nod from Leifr, the dogs tore after them eagerly, worrying and menacing their prey to a standstill. Leifr followed more slowly and mounted one of the horses, keeping his attention upon his prisoners. He pointed his sword, and they made haste to drop all their weapons, which amounted to a surprising number.

Leifr pointed the sword at one of them. 'You get on

the horse. And you,' he said to the other one, 'go after the others who ran away. None of you had better come back. Be grateful I'm sparing your life. You may not be so lucky the next time you cast your covetous eyes on land that doesn't belong to you Dokkalfar.'

With a last, apprehensive backward glance at the gleaming sword in Leifr's hand, the Dokkalfar turned and ran, leaving his companion as Leifr's prisoner apparently without a qualm. The prisoner stared at the sword in helpless fascination, crouching miserably on the back of his horse as if he expected to meet Grunur's fate at Leifr's casual whim.

'Now take me to Sorkvir,' Leifr commanded, motioning the Dokkalfar ahead of him.

The prisoner jogged along with many a fearful glance over his shoulder. He gasped out, 'That's a wretched way for a Dokkalfar to die. Much worse than being made into a draug or fylgjadraug. I'm just a new recruit, you know, scarcely worth your time to kill. If you'll let me go, I swear I'll stay underground for the rest of my life.'

'First you'll show me where Sorkvir is,' Leifr said, 'and then you can go. I've no objection to Dokkalfar as long as they stay out of sight.'

Uneasily the Dokkalfar replied, 'Sorkvir was getting ready to leave for Hjaldrsholl when I saw him last. He's taking the woman and your two friends as hostages.'

'Then ride on,' Leifr advised grimly. 'I'll be right behind you.'

Whipping his horse into a gallop, the Dokkalfar leaned forward along its neck to urge it along with greater speed, and Leifr rode close at his heels. Presently the Dokkalfar drew rein atop a long barrow, pointing wordlessly to a dark, moving object outlined against the lowering sky. It was a sledge and three horses; not far behind, a long line of horsemen followed.

'That's Sorkvir's sledge,' the Dokkalfar gasped over the panting of the horses. 'He heard the sound of that soul-eating sword being sharpened, and he's frightened. The oldest Dokkalfar have left him already. Now that I've taken you this far, can I go?'

'There's only one more thing I want from you,' Leifr said. 'Your helmet.'

'Take the cloak too,' the Dokkalfar said, gladly handing over his helmet. Lifting a hand in salute, he backed his horse away cautiously, not trusting Leifr for a moment; then he turned and rode away at a gallop toward the east.

Leifr started toward Sorkvir's train at a canter, measuring his speed against that of the sledge so that they would meet at a level space between two barrows, where the sickly sky had cast a long shadow. In the darkness, no one would look twice at another Dokkalfar joining the procession.

Lest the dogs reveal his identity by their presence, he stopped and commanded them to stay behind on a small barrow. Their ears flattened in disappointment and they crouched on their bellies, ashamed of their unknown disgrace, gazing at Leifr with appealing golden eyes as he rode away.

As Sorkvir's sledge drove into the shadow, Leifr rode forward to meet it.

'Who's that?' Sorkvir's voice demanded. He halted the sledge abruptly, hauling on the horses' jaws without mercy. In vain, Leifr tried to recognize the silent cargo of the sledge as his three companions.

'Halt the column,' Leifr commanded in a low voice, unsheathing the sword. 'Your Grunur was unsuccessful, except at getting himself killed.'

Sorkvir drew in a hissing breath. 'The Scipling!' He stood up and motioned with his staff toward the Dokkalfar following, its glowing knob making blue arcs in the darkness.

'Now what do you want?' Sorkvir inquired coldly. 'Do you wish to see your friends die before your eyes? Is that the reason for this senseless attack?'

'Let them go,' Leifr said, 'and I will meet you at the Grindstone Hall to settle all our differences.'

'Give me that sword and you shall have your friends,' Sorkvir countered.

'And you would then proceed to kill us all,' Leifr retorted. 'This is inevitable, Sorkvir. Let them go. They have nothing to do with this.'

'Will it prolong my chances for survival, as long as you possess that sword? I think not,' Sorkvir said. 'Time is my best ally. Perhaps we might talk about my captives in a fortnight's time.'

Leifr brandished the sword. 'I don't want to wait that long. Now is the time to talk.'

'Why now, and not tomorrow?' Sorkvir inquired silkily. 'Is there some reason for your impatience?'

'I can see you enjoy flirting with death,' Leifr said. 'Once you come to know it intimately this time, there will be no coming back for you again.'

'Kill me now and you'll never know what I've done with your friends,' Sorkvir replied. 'What corner of my mind is their prison, Scipling? Which of my powers are required to bring them back? Destroy me and you destroy them also. Perhaps it's a cheap price to a barbaric Scipling.'

'But one you'd be glad to make me pay,' Leifr replied. 'Think again which one of us is barbaric, Sorkvir. I've never been known for any remarkable qualities of patience. I want to see that my friends are alive, here and now, or I'll assume there's nothing to be lost by killing you on the instant.'

Leifr started his horse forward, but Sorkvir raised his staff warningly. 'Come no closer, Scipling. They are with me and quite safe enough – at least until tomorrow. With any luck, after tomorrow you will cease to be a thorn in my flesh, and that Rhbu sword will be safe in my possession.'

Leifr thought of the torque with a burst of silent fury and desperation. Unless he got to Hjaldrsholl before sundown, the torque, the sword, Sorkvir, and his associates would all cease to be thorns in Leifr's flesh. Leifr's flesh would be irretrievably dead.

'I'll meet you at the new Hjaldrsholl at dawn,' Leifr stated, gathering up his horse's reins. 'If you don't meet me there to fight for your life and your honor, you'll be known as a coward forever among the Dokkalfar.'

'I'll set the terms of our holmgang,' Sorkvir said. 'And I say it won't be tomorrow at dawn.'

'I say it will,' Leifr retorted.

Sorkvir stood up in the sledge and beckoned furiously to the Dokkalfar watching silently from a distance. 'We'll see what your arrogance costs you!'

'We'll more likely see what it costs your Dokkalfar followers,' Leifr replied, swinging the sword in a glowing arc. 'You're rather generous with their lives. No wonder so many have deserted you. Or do they know your cause is lost?'

Leifr backed away toward better cover as the Dokkalfar approached the sledge. Sorkvir pointed toward Leifr. 'It's the Scipling. He's killed Grunur's patrol. I want you to capture him and bring him to the hall in Hjaldrsfell. Kill him if you must, but that sword belongs to me. Digur, I shall hold you personally responsible for bringing it to me.'

Digur rode forward a few paces, halting as Leifr flourished the sword menacingly.

'*Endalaus Daudi*,' Digur muttered. 'The Endless Death is nothing I want to touch.' His followers rumbled in agreement, gathering around Digur in a truculent mass of bristling swords, lances, and horned helmets.

Sorkvir pointed threateningly with his staff. 'Do you dare disregard my commands, Digur? There are worse things than your dreaded *Endalaus Daudi*, and I know how to make you realize the worst of them if you dare disobey. No one dies as hard as a traitor dies.'

Digur hesitated, scowling bleakly in Leifr's direction, then he slowly raised one hand and beckoned his men to follow.

352

'Remember what I said about that sword,' Sorkvir called after the Dokkalfar. 'Bring it to my hand, Digur, or you and all your kin for generations are going to be cursed with unimaginable curses. Whatever you do, the Scipling must not reach Hjaldrsholl except as your prisoner – or dead.'

Cracking his whip over the horses' heads, he sent the sledge lurching away over the stony ground, leaving the Dokkalfar and Leifr facing each other in grim determination. Holding the sword aloft, Leifr nudged his horse forward a few paces. The Dokkalfar halted, fanning out in a long line to face Leifr. Digur rode forward a few steps and stopped.

'Sorkvir is afraid to meet me in battle,' Leifr said. 'I have challenged him to a holmgang tomorrow at dawn. I say he is a coward, beside an evil and treacherous wizard. I also accuse him of being a liar, a thief, and a murderer. He is a wrongful usurper of Gliru-hals and the killer of many innocent Ljosalfar. I have challenged him, and he has set his allies against me and has run away in the craven manner of a coward.'

'These are strong accusations,' Digur replied. 'You can't make accusations like this without expecting to make an accounting for them. Your speech has offended Sorkvir's honor. He must defend himself against your charges, and you must either fight him or withdraw your accusations and suffer the loss of your own reputation for it.'

'Fighting him is what I want to do,' Leifr replied. 'Are you going to try to stop me? Are you afraid for Sorkvir to meet me with this sword?'

He raised the sword so they could all see it glowing in the pale darkness. Endless death – the name suited it perfectly, and Leifr smiled with grim pleasure.

Digur unsheathed his axe. 'I have my orders not to let you go to Hjaldrsholl,' he said.

The Dokkalfar beside him rode forward and leaned over to speak to Digur, but Leifr could hear plainly what was said. 'Orders to die, you mean. I say let him challenge Sorkvir to the holmgang. What do we want with a leader who is afraid to defend his name against accusations of this kind? All the Dokkalfar in Skarpsey will know that Sorkvir was afraid to fight and that we helped him in his cowardice.'

'You're speaking treason,' Digur snarled. 'I should bury this axe in your brain rather than listen!'

'Listen you will, because you know in your heart it's the truth.'

'We can kill one Scipling, no matter what weapon he has in his hand. There are twenty of us against one of him.'

'Do you want to be the first to taste the Endless Death? I don't. Whom of your friends will you send to die?'

'It will be an honorable death,' Digur answered after a short pause.

'We've had enough honorable deaths for Sorkvir's cause. I say let the Scipling go. Sorkvir is doomed. Let's not go to our own senseless doom by backing a loser with our lives.'

'How many of the others think as you think?' Digur turned in his saddle to look up and down the lines beside him. The Dokkalfar returned his look uneasily, gripping their weapons.

'All,' the other Dokkalfar said firmly.

'So the lot of you are treasonous cowards,' Digur said. 'You seem to have set yourself up as their leader, haven't you, Ragur? What will you do if I order them to attack the Scipling?'

Ragur replied calmly, 'We won't do it. We'll kill you if you force us to it, but we'd rather you joined us.'

'Then I'll give you my answer.' Digur dove for his sword, making a wicked thrust at Ragur, but Ragur defended himself skilfully.

Leifr watched them fight a few moments, then turned and rode away slowly in the direction of Hjaldrsholl.

When he heard no more clashing of steel on steel, he paused and looked back. Nineteen mounted Dokkalfar rode away in the opposite direction, with Digur's riderless horse following in the rear. Sorkvir had lost the major part of his allies, except for whatever number he had left to hold Hjaldrsholl.

Leifr whistled for the dogs and started after Sorkvir at a brisk pace. In a few minutes, the dogs caught up and fell to smelling out Sorkvir's trail with the utmost dedication to their task.

After passing the last of the barrows of Grittur-grof, Leifr came into view of Sorkvir and the sledge. Halting, Sorkvir stood up to look back for a long, silent moment as Leifr rode slowly out of the shadow of the barrow.

'Your Dokkalfar have killed their leader and abandoned you,' Leifr called. 'They're carrying word of our holmgang to the rest of the Dokkalfar.'

With a curse, Sorkvir raised his arms and sent a bolt of green flame hurtling toward Leifr like a lance. Stepping aside, Leifr slashed at the bolt with the sword and was rewarded with a jolt that nearly tore him off his horse. The bolt arced upward, returning toward Sorkvir in a cartwheel of ice shards. The sledge horse plunged away in alarm, nearly jerking Sorkvir off his feet and thus preventing him from returning another bolt at Leifr.

'You'll never make it to Hjaldrsholl in time,' Sorkvir shouted over the rumble of the sledge, finally bringing it to a halt on the slope of the fell. He shoved something from the rear of the sledge, then cracked his whip over the horses with a defiant yell.

'Here's one of your dear friends, Scipling! Take care of him well and keep him warm, or he will die! You can't leave him until the sun comes up to break my spell!'

Leifr followed the dogs, who raced toward the inert mass Sorkvir had pushed from the sledge. Shoving them aside, Leifr knelt beside the huge hulk of Raudbjorn, who was snoring heavily and as cold and stiff as a slab of dead mutton. No amount of shaking would awaken him.

Hastily Leifr scratched together enough wood for a small fire. The dogs licked Raudbjorn's face and prodded him with their sharp noses, finally eliciting a rumbling grunt as the warmth of the fire gradually penetrated Sorkvir's spell. Anxiously Leifr scanned the eastern sky, already discerning the first traces of early dawn. Raudbjorn had a long way to go yet before he was unthawed enough to travel, and Leifr had no idea how long the sun would take to unravel Sorkvir's spell.

Dismayed, he sat down and stared glumly at the dogs clustered contentedly around Raudbjorn. Kraftig came to sit beside Leifr, perhaps sensing his master's low spirits, and sought to cheer him up by trying to sit on his lap like a puppy. Battling against the hairy, friendly beast, Leifr was struck by a sudden idea.

'Kraftig! Come here!' He managed to escape from the huge paws braced against his shoulders and led the dog over to Raudbjorn, commanding, 'Lie down, Kraftig. Stay here. Watch Raudbjorn.'

Kraftig understood the idea immediately, curling up next to Raudbjorn and stretching out over his chest like a furry, living blanket. When Leifr rode away, Kraftig was licking Raudbjorn's ear, perhaps relishing the unwashed taste and glorious smell that always accompanied Raudbjorn and his sordid trophies.

By the time Leifr caught up with Sorkvir again, it was nearly dawn, light enough for him to plot his course to get in front of the sledge. Sorkvir drew up immediately the moment Leifr's dim form took shape in the mist, riding slowly toward him.

'So you abandoned Raudbjorn to die, faithless Scipling?' Sorkvir chuckled. 'It will haunt you, if you live that long.'

'Raudbjorn is provided for,' Leifr answered. 'I have no doubt you'll see him at the holmgang.'

'He may be there, but he'll see no holmgang,' Sorkvir replied. 'This time when I lighten my load, you'll have no chance of catching me again. Here's your friend

Thurid, stiff as hardfish. I had plans for him; but if you revive him, I can always find him later, after I've taken care of my business at Hjaldrsholl.'

'Leave Ljosa also and you can make your journey all the faster,' Leifr said.

Sorkvir rolled Thurid out of the sledge with one foot. 'No, she weighs hardly more than a feather. I'll keep her as additional insurance. Then I shall return her to Gliru-hals where she belongs. I need more winter shepherds, since I lost so many to the trolls last year.'

Cracking his whip and laughing harshly, Sorkvir sent the sledge bounding down the slope.

Thurid was stiffer and bluer even than Raudbjorn, to the extent that Leifr wondered how he could be alive at all. Frozen with his staff in his hands, Thurid glared at him, frosty and unblinking, as Farlig and Frimodig nosed around him, whimpering and tasting the frost ridged along his beaky nose and eyebrows.

Again Leifr built a fire and commanded Frimodig to lie on Thurid and keep him warm. He tucked the satchel under one of Thurid's stiff arms and said a silent farewell, hoping Thurid would not be too annoyed when he awakened to find one of the hated hounds slobbering in his face and smearing its huge, muddy paws on his clothing.

Leifr cantered his weary horse into Hjaldrsholl just before sunrise, finding the great outer gates standing open. The horse's hooves rang on the cobblestones of the tunnel leading to the hall. When he reached the hall, he found the doors there standing open also, blocked by the bodies of two dead dwarfs, blasted and whitened by Sorkvir's ice magic. Leaping from his horse, almost falling when his weak knee buckled under him, Leifr staggered past the bodies and into the hall, dreading what he would find.

CHAPTER 22

SORKVIR could not have been an hour before him. Ice bolts lay melting in the dark pools among the scattered corpses of more dwarfs. At last he discovered Hjaldr, still sitting in his chair, pinioned by the sword thrust through his chest. Knowing after the first glance that Hjaldr was dead, Leifr turned away and sank down in one of the few upright chairs, fingering the torque around his throat. In a matter of hours it would strangle him, although he had found the grindstone and sharpened the sword, thus ending the alog over Solvorfirth. Somehow Sorkvir had learned of Hjaldr's alog; hence his haste to reach Hjaldrsholl before Leifr did.

Leifr did not waste much time brooding over the unfairness of the trick fate had played upon him. His temper began to boil, infusing him with the needful wrath to finish his quarrel with Sorkvir. Standing up and facing the wall where the helmets of the fallen Dvergar hung, he drew his sword and raised it to his forehead in salute. Filled with grim resolve, he strode out to the hall to retrieve his horse.

When he rode out of the outer gates, the first rays of the sun pierced the misty horizon, touching the high peaks and leaving the valleys in shadow. Without hesitation, Leifr guided his horse down the rugged path to the hall in the mountainside. Once a Dokkalfar guard barred his path with a long, deadly lance.

'Who's there?' the Dokkalfar demanded, seeing nothing of Leifr but a dark Dokkalfar cloak and a Dokkalfar helmet.

Drawing the gleaming sword, Leifr answered, '*Endalaus Daudi*. Either die or let me pass. I have no particular preference.'

'Pass!' the Dokkalfar gasped, falling back into the shadows.

Leifr urged his horse a few steps nearer. 'Did Sorkvir pass this way in a sledge not long ago?'

'He did, not a half hour before.'

'And he's in the new hall Hjaldr built?'

'Aye, with the doors barred.'

'A piece of advice I'll give you before I go on. Take yourself back underground where you'll be safe. The alog is broken now, and the Ljosalfar will be looking for any Dokkalfar to take revenge upon; their swords will be sharp.'

'I'll do it, even though it means abandoning my post. They've been gathering all night around the new hall, ugly as can be. I wouldn't be caught here for anything.' He vanished into the shadows.

As Leifr approached the gates to the new Hjaldrsholl, he passed covert knobs of Ljosalfar, all armed with newly sharpened swords, axes, and lances. They stared with blatant curiosity at Leifr, busily nudging their neighbors with their elbows. 'Look, it's the Scipling.'

They all regarded him with a mixture of suspicion and awe, even the Ljosalfars who were neighbors to Dallir, as if they had never seen Leifr before in all their lives. The first to make a move of recognition was Young Einarr, who cautiously raised one hand in salute as Leifr rode past.

'Be you needing any help?' Old Einarr rasped, leaning on a villainous old halberd with a gleaming half moon of sharp edge showing through the rust. 'If it was Fridmarr, we might not offer – unlucky fellow, you must surely know. I wouldn't mind following a Scipling into a fight. I'm not the sort to be overproud.'

Leifr looked into his earnest, weathered features and nodded slowly.

'I could use some good Ljosalfar at my back. I wish Fridmarr were here to see it, though.'

Both Einarrs shouldered their weapons, shaking their

359

gray heads ruefully. Young Einarr passed the back of his hand over his mouth. 'Fridmarr was always high and mighty with pride, even when he was rendering tallow. I always felt something peculiar about that old Gotiskolker. And him Fridmarr all along.'

The Elder Einarr beckoned imperiously to another group of neighbors watching from a cluster of rocks.

'Some of us wasn't fooled,' he growled darkly. 'I knew Fridmarr wouldn't give up easy. I always wondered what plot he'd hatch out.'

'Odd he'd pick a Scipling to help him,' Young Einarr added thoughtfully. 'There were plenty of willing Ljosalfar just waiting for an excuse to rise against Sorkvir.'

Leifr turned his horse and rode on, saying over his shoulder, 'Waiting? How long were they willing to wait? Forever wasn't long enough for most of you, in my opinion.'

The Ljosalfar uneasily avoided looking at each other. They rode at Leifr's heels in silence, until Einarr the Elder cleared his throat and spoke. 'It wasn't for us to go into heroics. That's the stuff for young Ljosalfar and Sciplings and other fools. Like that Thurid. Now there's a man who was born to be a wizard or a hero – or a fool. He never was one to plod along like the rest of us, working our hearts out on this ungrateful, hardhearted land. Thurid and Fridmarr both fretted and chafed at the idea of being broken to harness. The ordinary life wasn't for them. You're the same way, young Scipling. But don't get hot and impatient with us common folk. You need us; and maybe the rest of us need the cross-grained ones like you and Thurid and Fridmarr.'

Leifr stopped and gazed around at the work-worn faces of his small band of allies, feeling himself properly chastened by Old Einarr's wise words. In their demeanour, he saw respect and admiration, but he sensed that their complete acceptance was reserved for others like themselves, whose largest worries in life concerned their land and their prosperity, instead of the killing of dangerous wizards and breaking of alogs. It was for the protection of these ordinary souls that the Rhbus in their inscrutable wisdom had plotted the course that had brought Leifr to the Alfar realm.

'We're not out of danger yet,' he said gruffly. 'There's one more job of work to be done.' He nodded toward Hjaldr's hall. 'Sorkvir must be fought and destroyed. It looks as if we'll have to batter down the doors first to do it.'

Einarr the Elder took charge of the improvisation of a battering ram, setting the younger men to work on it immediately. They commandeered a sledge from the settlement of Laukur, extracted its long, heavy keel, and appropriated men to help batter the doors of the hall.

Exceptionally strong and thick, the doors withstood the battering longer than three teams of batterers. The fourth team consisted of six of the Dvergar who had escaped the carnage of Hjaldrsholl at far-flung outposts. Relentlessy they smashed the doors they had lovingly carved and hung, shattering the fine wood brought from afar and sending the doors reeling off their finely crafted hinges. Dropping the battering ram with a crash, they unsheathed their axes and stood waiting for Leifr's commands. Leifr rode his horse into the tunnel, with Farlig casting ahead eagerly for Sorkvir's scent.

The tunnel entered a high-domed underground court-yard, dimly lit by fissures far overhead. With a trium-phant howl, Farlig discovered Sorkvir's sledge and sniffed all over it with a chorus of growls and excited yelps. Then he hurled himself off the sledge and fol-lowed the scent to a dark corridor, where he stood with stiff legs and bristling fur, sniffing into the darkness beyond with obvious unease. The tunnel was too low for a man on a horse, so Leifr dismounted, motioning to the Dvergar to wait where they were.

'What's down there?' he asked their leader, a young dwarf with a bushy red beard and a premature scowl etched into his broad brow. He had changed his name to

361

Hegna as part of his vow to punish Sorkvir for his crimes.

Hegna stepped forward, shouldering his axe. 'It's the rearward way to the great hall. A door opens onto the dais at the back. Other doors and tunnels lead to the horse quarters, the smithy, springs, mine shafts, and empty places. If Sorkvir has gone down there, he has chosen a good place to hide himself.'

'Not so well that I won't find him.' Leifr took a torch down from the wall and fanned it into brighter flame. He hesitated for a moment, wishing he had Thurid and his powers with him; but he dared not wait any longer. 'Bar the front doors to the hall from this side, in case Sorkvir tries to escape that way. Wait for me here, and don't allow anyone to come into this tunnel, no matter what you think may have happened.'

By their scowling and muttering, Leifr knew the dwarfs were not fond of the idea, but they stayed where he had ordered them to, watching as the red light of his torch diminished in the long dark tunnel.

Farlig's faithful nose led him past several side tunnels with hardly a glance in their direction. Suddenly Farlig halted, blocking the tunnel rigidly as he sniffed at something on the ground. Leifr held the torch down to investigate and discovered a splatter of fresh blood, still wet and glistening. His throat constricted as he thought of Ljosa, wondering if Sorkvir had decided he had nothing further to lose by killing her. Farlig glided forward a few steps and froze again, sniffing loudly and intently over more splatters of blood, enough to show that a major injury had been suffered. It appeared as if Sorkvir had dragged his victim along after him.

Leifr smoothed Farlig's soft ears in an effort to control the commotion of his rising fear and anger.

'Come on, Farlig, enough of this laziness,' he whispered. 'Now, we've got to hurry.'

He forced his weak leg to endure the fast pace. The pain became a fierce numbness, but the leg still held him, so he kept going until the tunnel bent abruptly to the left. Halting, he grabbed Farlig and peered around the corner, sensing a faint illumination on the sweating stones. A massive double door stood open at the end of the corridor, with pale sky light filtering through, very gray and distant. Farlig thrust his long, pointed muzzle around the corner and sniffed eagerly, shivering with excitement and panting, his lips drawn back in wolfish anticipation.

Quietly Leifr drew the sword and stepped around the corner, walking step by cautious step along the wall toward the doors, which opened on a vast, silent chamber, lit by random streaks of sunlight from fissures high above. The dwarfs had not finished their work before Sorkvir and his Dokkalfar had driven them out, but Leifr could see that the vast hall would have been a glorious monument to the craft of the Dvergar. Portions of rough pillars had begun to take graceful shapes. At either end of the massive hall reared a gigantic hearth, large enough for roasting an entire ox with room to spare; and some skillful craftsman had begun the work of carving a history into the stones surrounding the hearths. A black trail of blood led across the dais before Leifr and onto the marble floor. A heap of excavated stone blocked Leifr's view of the end of the blood trail.

Commanding Farlig to follow, Leifr started across the dais with the dog at his heels. Warily he surveyed the rough interior of the great hall. The jumble of stones and masonry afforded Sorkvir hundreds of places to hide.

Guided by soft but audible cracking sounds, Leifr advanced to the marble pavement and followed the blood spots with his eyes to a dark mass lying near the far hearth. He stared at the heap without comprehension, until it suddenly shifted, and two red eyes fixed an evil stare upon him. A low rumbling growl echoed through the hall, and strong white teeth glinted in the pale light.

Farlig answered the greeting with a shuddering growl of his own as the massive form of a bear lurched to its feet to confront its attackers.

363

'Is this the way you prefer to fight for your life, Sorkvir?' Leifr called, his voice echoing hollowly. 'I had thought it was a cowardly deed to retreat to fylgja form in the face of battle.'

Sorkvir's voice rumbled from the bear's throat in a guttural growl. 'What finer fighting form is there than this? A bear is harder to kill than a cat. Only a direct thrust to the heart will keep him from tearing his assailant to shreds with his teeth and claws, even as he dies from a hundred lesser wounds. Your *Endalaus Daudi* will not save your life if you don't strike it true.'

Leifr stood rigid, not failing to notice that the bear's muzzle and claws were stained with fresh blood; beneath one set of scimitar claws, the bear held a bloody leg bone, almost gnawed free of flesh.

'Where is Ljosa?' he asked, his voice thick with menace.

'There,' Sorkvir replied, pointing briefly with his muzzle over his silvered shoulder toward the hearth. 'She's safe enough, for now. I have saved her all along for this moment, when you must choose between her and that sword.'

A shadowy figure stirred within the dark grotto of the huge hearth, and Leifr saw a pale face lifted in his direction. In a low and clear voice she said, 'The choice is on your side, Sorkvir. You can escape and live until the sword finds you, or you will die now.'

'Then you shall die first,' Sorkvir replied, lying down once more, but keeping his eyes alertly upon Leifr.

'I can die gladly with that assurance,' Ljosa answered with cold disdain. 'I have the blood of warriors and fighting queens. Death is nothing that I should fear.'

Leifr approached slowly until he stood near the center of the hall. 'This is the place where we will fight,' he said, drawing a line on the floor. 'Will you come to meet me, Sorkvir, or do I have to come for you?'

The bear rose to his feet with a grunt and shambled slowly along the marble pavement toward Leifr, swinging his massive head from side to side. Farlig crouched before Leifr's feet, growling and bristling with all the menace he could muster.

The bear moved with astonishing speed. One moment he was lumbering along at a ponderously slow gait; in the next instant he lunged, swiping Farlig away with one swing of his huge, deadly paw and slashing at Leifr with the other. Reeling backward a few steps, Leifr raised the sword defensively to prevent another assault. He was certain that he had felt the bear's claws lay bare the bones of his right shoulder and rip through the muscles of his chest. A quick inspection indeed revealed that his cloak, tunic, and shirt were a mass of fluttering ribbons and threads. At any moment, he could expect a gush of blood that would quickly drain away his strength.

Slicing at the bear in a determined effort to make his last moments count, he scored a smoking slash in the heavy fur of Sorkvir's neck. Black fluid welled up in the injury but did not spill over. Sorkvir backed away a few steps, shaking his head with a roar of pain. Leifr pressed his brief advantage, making a daring thrust at the bear's ribs. With lightning speed Sorkvir whirled around and struck at him with his deadly claws, shredding the sleeve on his right arm in one stroke. It was a glancing blow, miscalculated and poorly aimed, or Leifr might have been sent spinning.

Farlig, who had lain in a twitching heap for a few moments after Sorkvir's breath-taking wallop, regained his consciousness and leaped back into the battle, fastening his teeth in one of the bear's ears and swinging around to avoid being clawed away.

Leifr glanced ruefully at his arm, feeling no pain, although he was certain the claws had scored his flesh. Yet he saw no ragged wound, only perfectly healthy and intact skin. A quick inspection revealed the same results for his shoulder and chest. Elated, he silently thanked the Rhbus for the protection that must be part of their sword's magic.

Watching him with maddened red eyes, Sorkvir knocked Farlig away with another heavy clout, scarcely sparing the dog a glance. Farlig shook his head and wobbled to his feet, still game for another assault on his master's foe.

Sorkvir reared to his hind legs, towering over Leifr with a thunderous growl, taking two ponderous steps forward.

'The Rhbus have betrayed me again,' he rumbled. 'They mock me even from their graves. Look to yourself, Scipling, and don't let that sword out of your hand if you wish to live much longer. My claws and teeth may not harm you because of the Rhbu spell, but you must come closer than that, if you want to kill me. I won't die without taking at least one of you with me on Hel's journey.'

Leifr swung his sword invitingly. 'Then come on and fight Sorkvir. We'll see who celebrates tonight and who lies in a cold bed.'

From behind, Leifr heard the flurry of running paws and throaty snarls as something burst into the hall from the door behind the dais. Out of the corner of his eye he saw two white, furry forms streaking across the rough floor. Farlig threw back his head in a joyous howl, which was echoed by Kraftig and Frimodig. Circling Sorkvir with annoying barks and yaps, they took turns diving in to worry at him, dodging his furious blows almost tauntingly.

Leifr risked glancing behind him and saw Raudbjorn striding into the hall with Thurid slung around his neck like a muffler. Raudbjorn put Thurid down hastily. With a wide grin, he unslung his vicious halberd and strummed its edge with his thumb with an approving nod.

'Now Sorkvir ready to die,' he said with a rumbling chuckle of pleasurable anticipation.

Sorkvir strode forward to meet his adversaries, his jaws gaping open in a savage roar of challenge. The dogs leaped all around him, snapping at his ears and face.

Reaching over their clicking teeth, Sorkvir raked at Raudbjorn's shield, almost tearing it out of his grasp. Leifr retaliated, but the bear whirled on him instantly, slashing at the sword with both murderously armed paws and losing two long claws as a consequence.

Between them, Leifr and Raudbjorn baited the bear back and forth, dealing him small injuries that served only to enrage him further. None of his wounds bled, and none seemed to weaken him in the least. In his rage, the bear seemed to increase in size and his eyes blazed with a fanatic light. The dogs kept a wider distance, exercising more caution in their attacks as they garnered more powerful wallops from Sorkvir's paws.

Leifr's leg felt like an inert mass of red-hot lead. Clenching his teeth, he stood his ground as Sorkvir made a furious rush, which Raudbjorn deflected at the last moment so Leifr could make another attempt to shove the sword between Sorkvir's ribs into his heart. Each time, however, Sorkvir was faster than Leifr and managed to block the attack and save himself. With each failure, Sorkvir's confidence seemed to increase. He initiated more of the attacks than Leifr and Raudbjorn, until they were on the defensive, backing away gradually toward the dais.

Leifr's eyes sought out Ljosa, standing beside the great hearth watching as if entranced.

'Ljosa! Run!' Leifr called out to her. 'Get out of here while you can!'

She certainly could have made a dash for the door, with Leifr and Raudbjorn to hold Sorkvir back from giving chase. She looked toward the doorway, then shook her head.

'I belong here,' she replied. 'No one can run away from his fate.'

The bear gathered itself for another rush, charging through the shoal of snapping dogs straight for Raudbjorn, dealing him a tremendous swat with one paw and following it up with another blow that destroyed his shield and sent him reeling. The dogs instantly leaped on the bear's back in an attempt to delay the murderous rush, and Leifr lunged forward with a mighty two-handed blow to Sorkvir's head.

It was no use. Sorkvir had determined to eliminate Raudbjorn from the fight. He clamped his teeth onto Raudbjorn's leg, shook him like a dog killing a rat, and threw him aside into a pile of rocks. Then he turned toward Leifr once more, ignoring the frantic sallies of the dogs.

'This is the end,' Sorkvir growled. 'You have failed, Scipling. You can't kill me. You're too weak. A pity your Rhbu magic won't help you now.' He tossed his head contemptuously toward Thurid, who lay stiff and stark, staring toward the ceiling above. A faint beam of sunlight had crept over one shoulder, thawing the ice spell into a dark puddle.

Leifr fought away his doubts, knowing that to fear was to go down in defeat.

'We're not finished yet, Sorkvir. Not as long as the two of us are still alive.'

A slender shadow crept around the pile of rock where Raudbjorn lay groaning and grunting like a fallen war-horse. Straightening, Ljosa lifted Raudbjorn's axe with both hands.

'There are still three of us,' she said. 'Two of us may die, but one of the two will be Sorkvir, and that is all that matters now.'

Leifr had not time to protest, only time for an indignant, despairing smile at Ljosa, who returned him a sweet and peaceful smile. For the first time Leifr saw that the dark and troubled expression in her eyes was calmed, as if an inward storm had gone out of her. She thrust at the bear with the pike on the head of the axe to good effect, turning back Sorkvir's first charge.

Shaking his head, Sorkvir backed away a few steps and fixed his murderous gaze upon Leifr. Then he lunged forward, ignoring the attacking dogs, and struck a diving blow at Leifr's faulty leg. The leg collapsed instantly, as if it had been waiting for such an excuse to give up the pretense of strength beyond natural endurance, and Leifr fell backward on the marble pavement. The dark hulk of the bear blotted out the dim light from above. A heavy paw came down like a hammer on his sword arm, and another stroke sent the sword clattering across the floor into the rocks, far beyond Leifr's reach. For an instant all Leifr saw was the huge, dark maw of the bear gaping in his face, reeking of troll meat. Then the teeth closed on his helmet with a rending screech. Sorkvir crushed him to the ground and began to gnaw through the helmet at his leisure. Ljosa screamed and battered at the bear's skull with her axe. Then she dropped the axe and turned to look for the sword. At the same instant, Sorkvir lashed out with a wicked blow to stop her, shredding her cloak from top to bottom and jerking her back within reach of his deadly claws. Ignoring Leifr's struggles to escape, Sorkvir hooked at Ljosa as she scrambled away, pinning one of her feet to the ground with his paw.

Nearly deafened by the growling so close to his ears and half-smothered by the stench of the bear's fur, Leifr struggled desperately to escape from the bear's clutch, but he was hopelessly pinned. The dogs made no headway against Sorkvir's thick fur and tough hide.

Ljosa twisted and kicked at the claws holding her foot, her face white with pain. Sorkvir growled, grinding his teeth on Leifr's helmet until its seams began to pop.

'You were wrong,' he said to Ljosa in a guttural snarl. 'You are the two who will die. Three counting that idiot Raudbjorn, and four, after I'm finished with Thurid. Killing this Scipling will be pure pleasure. I'll rid myself of an intolerable nuisance.'

He bit Leifr's helmet again, and this time one of his sharp teeth punctured the metal.

Ljosa seized the axe she had dropped and attempted to wedge the handle between Sorkvir's grinding teeth.

With a splintering sound, Sorkvir's teeth sank into the wood, snapping it easily, and Leifr heard another great fang puncture his helmet. The thick fur and loose skin of the bear's neck defied his attempts to discover its windpipe.

Sorkvir suddenly released his death grip with a suspicious grunt, and lifted his paw to let Ljosa escape. Thurid, mostly unthawed but still stiff in the joints, stood with his staff propping him up, extending one shaky hand in a sorcerous gesture, although his blue lips were still too stiff to form the words he wanted.

'Fool,' Sorkvir snorted, closing his teeth around Leifr's helmet once more, scoring long, bright gouges in the metal. 'Your powers will be depleted for days. There's nothing you can do to stop me.'

'Let him go,' Thurid grated stiffly. 'He's not Fridmarr. This isn't his fight.'

'I wish he were Fridmarr,' Sorkvir snarled, biting the helmet vindictively. 'It's his fault Fridmarr escaped from me, so he'll taste my wrath, as an example to those craven Ljosalfar waiting outside.'

Ljosa glided from behind a block of stone. 'The Ljosalfar are not craven!' she said, her eyes flaring and brilliant with resolve. 'And since you did not put me under your ice spell, thinking I could not escape or harm you in any way if I did, my Alfar powers are not depleted.'

She took Thurid's staff from him and advanced towards Sorkvir, leaving Thurid to steady himself against a rock. She held the staff upright in both hands and touched her forehead to it. Sorkvir kept his eyes on her, shifting his teeth to the other side of Leifr's helmet.

'There's nothing you can do,' he growled. 'Hawthorn won't damage me unless I grasp it in my hands.'

'Get the sword, Ljosa!' rasped Thurid. 'You can use it! There's no bear crushing you!'

Ljosa shook her head. 'It's not for me to use the sword. I'll use the powers that all Ljosalfar possess to save them from deadly peril.'

'You can't,' Thurid spluttered. 'You haven't been instructed. You'll destroy yourself – and Leifr with you!'

Ljosa raised her arm and tilted her face upward to the sun filtering in through the distant roof. Sorkvir paused a moment in his casual gnawing to listen to the faint murmur of words she was speaking, then he redoubled his efforts to crush the helmet and Leifr's skull inside it. Thurid uttered a despairing howl, staggering forward and gripping the bear's jaws in a vain attempt to pry them apart. Contemptuously, Sorkvir shook him off, taking a murderous swipe at Thurid with one paw.

While he was thus distracted, he did not observe the sudden radiance that suffused the staff in Ljosa's hands and traveled from her fingers into her arms. She trembled, as if lifting a great weight, then suddenly the bear's jaws snapped shut on empty air with a jarring clash, and Leifr had vanished. Sorkvir glared beneath his paws, disbelieving that Leifr was not securely crushed beneath him, awaiting his destruction. Whirling around warily, he saw where the girl's spell had dropped his quarry. Then he moved swiftly in retaliation against her interference.

With the screeching of Sorkvir's teeth on his helmet still in his ears, Leifr found himself sprawling in the rocks safely out of the bear's reach. Every bone and muscle reverberated with the fiery tingle of magic, made familiar to him by the influences of the carbuncle. Scrambling to his feet, he saw Ljosa still holding the staff, reeling from the power of her spell, while the bear strode toward her, his eyes smoldering vengefully.

'Ljosa! Run!' he bellowed, hurling himself forward with all his might, yet feeling that he moved with dreamlike slowness. The bear reached her in two lumbering strides, towering over her, mouth agape in a triumphant roar. In an instant the cruel fangs would close upon her unprotected, fragile body.

Ljosa's eyes turned upward, calculating the bear's rush. When the dripping jaws seemed inches away from her face, she thrust the knob of Thurid's staff into

371

Sorkvir's roaring maw. Instantly a white light exploded inside the dim cavern, setting off the echoes into a series of thundering reports. Leifr plowed to a halt as the flames washed over him like a monstrous hot breath. He tumbled backward, smelling his own singed hair and clothing, his dazzled eyes retaining the image of Sorkvir standing upright, clawing at the staff even as it spun away like a straw in a tempest, with shreds of bearskin flying apart in flaming tatters. The figure of Sorkvir stood inside the fireball, slapping at the remains of his disguise in a frantic and futile attempt to extinguish it. Leifr barely noticed the form of a small gray cat shooting away from the conflagration, like an arrow into the darkness.

As Leifr groped for shelter among the heaps of rock, still dazzled by the brilliance of the explosion, his fingers brushed cool metal with a thrill of recognition. Snatching up the sword, he turned. Sorkvir was no longer flaming, but the tattered mass confronting Leifr was scarcely recognizable as either wizard or bear. Elements of both were melted together; the bear's face dangled in blackened shreds with Sorkvir's face underneath, seared and sooty and twisted with rage as he struggled to tear the remains of the bear's paws away form his hands. The bear's rippling hide now flapped in tatters from Sorkvir's shoulders, like a disreputable hairy cloak saved by mistake from a fire.

Thurid tottered forward with a triumphant crow. 'It's not his fylgja! It's only a bearskin spell! Except when he's coming back after he's killed, he doesn't have the power for a bear fylgja! Destroy him, Leifr!'

Sorkvir whirled around to face Leifr, crouching like a cornered beast, teeth bared in hatred.

'No Scipling will kill Sorkvir!' he snarled, lifting his hands for a spell.

Leifr raised his sword and spoke its name, guided by an impulse born from the reactions of the other Dokkalfar. '*Endalaus Daudi*', he said. 'The Endless Death awaits you, Sorkvir.'

372

Sorkvir held his blustering pose for another moment, then his hand dived for the sword hanging at his belt. As it cleared its sheath, the main doors of the hall slowly grumbled open, revealing Hegna and the dwarfs standing ready with their weapons, and the Ljosalfar crowding close behind.

With a curse, Sorkvir struck the first blow at Leifr, muttering the words of spells that would not work. He fought with skill and the courage born of desperation, striking glittering sparks from his sword each time it clashed with Leifr's, until the edge was pocked with jagged notches. The point of his sword snapped off and spun away onto the marble floor, scoring the stone with a black, steaming mark.

Leifr fought grimly, knowing that a touch of Sorkvir's sword would inflict the same deadly ice magic as the bolts of the storm giants. His cuts and thrusts slashed away more of the charred bear skin. To his surprise, the wounds he dealt to the bear's hide bled profusely.

'You're weakening, Sorkvir,' he panted. 'Your pelt is bleeding now. Is your ice magic failing?'

Calmly Sorkvir replied, 'Failing, yes, but the fight is not yet finished. Remember that a bear is hard to kill.'

Leifr dealt the first telling blow of the battle by slashing Sorkvir's leg. Sorkvir fell back, grimacing.

'We're even now on that score,' Leifr said grimly.

Sorkvir parried his next thrust and retorted with a twisted leer, 'But there's a torque, or did you forget?'

'You won't be here to watch,' Leifr answered.

Sorkvir made a desperate rush at Leifr, swinging his long sword with both hands.

Leifr ducked and thrust his sword through Sorkvir's body with a sense of disbelief. Sorkvir staggered, crumpling to his knees on the marble pavement, shaking his head slowly as he, too, were unable to believe.

'Dokkur Lavardur,' he gasped, 'you've betrayed me. Djofull, my lord!'

He collapsed slowly to the pavement, sinking into a

misty form that flattened and dissipated until nothing remained but a dark discoloration in the shape of a prone body and a heap of charred bearskin and singed clothing.

Hegna and the others approached cautiously, surrounding Leifr and the evidence of his vanquished foe. Leifr, scarcely aware of anything but his own overwhelming exhaustion, sank down on a rock with the sword still in his hand, glancing up only briefly when Thurid gripped his shoulder with tremulous fingers.

'Wheres Ljosa?' Leifr asked.

Thurid sank down beside him, his face gray and ravaged as he gazed intently at Leifr.

'She's gone,' he said in a stricken whisper.

Leifr lifted his head a moment, then let it sink down again. 'I see. She didn't want to stay. It was Fridmarr she loved from the beginning, wasn't it?'

'Not like that! It's – worse than you think, Leifr.' Thurid revealed a bundle hidden under his cloak which Leifr recognized as Ljosa's tattered blue cloak. Inside that was her long gown and the rest of her habiliment. Leifr gazed at Thrurid in blank incomprehension.

'She used the escape spell to rescue you from Sorkvir,' Thurid said. 'It's a power all Alfar possess. With proper training, an Alfar can escape and return unscathed. But she was untrained, and without proper training, there may be no coming back from that void where all power comes from.'

Leifr stood up unsteadily, still staring at Thurid.

'Then she's gone – into that void? She disappeared?'

Thurid heaved a heavy sigh, his breath burbling inside his chest. His eyes slid away from Leifr, haunted and weary.

'She isn't lost. She has returned to the starting place for all Alfar. Perhaps the Rhbus are there. All I know for certain is that she used the last of her power to blast Sorkvir. With some help from this.' He held out his hawthorn staff, badly charred in the two places where Ljosa had gripped it with her hands. Leifr gazed at the

374

mark of each finger, choking back a hideous sense of his own unworthiness.

'She shouldn't have done it,' he muttered. 'This was wrong. She did it because she couldn't bear to live any longer without Fridmarr.'

Thurid looked at the ground. 'She wanted to help you – was willing to die to save you.'

Leifr winced. 'Then she is dead.'

'What does dead mean? She used up her powers pulling you out of Sorkvir's grasp. Then he tried to kill her and she used the last of it to blast him. After that, she went into the void. With magical powers, you can't take without giving something in return.'

Leifr shook his head. 'I don't understand it. I thought that good deeds were rewarded. She gave her life to save me. Where's the reward in that for either of us?'

'You're alive, aren't you? That's the only reward she wanted. You should feel grateful, instead of cheated. You're a hero, and you're still alive. That's quite an accomplishment.'

'Aren't you forgetting this?' Leifr showed him the torque, and Thurid turned white with shock.

'Why haven't you removed it yet?' he gasped. 'It's only a matter of hours before it starts—'

'Hjaldr is dead,' Leifr said. 'Sorkvir's last evil trick.'

Thurid clasped his temples with his hands. 'This is hideous!' he whispered. 'There must be a way to get rid of it!'

'You're not messing with it,' Leifr snapped. 'If I've got only a few hours left, I want every moment of them. You'll rob me of even those if you try tampering with it.'

Thurid shriveled, defeated. 'My powers are depleted. I doubt if I could do you much good, even if I knew how.'

CHAPTER 23

WHEN the news of Sorkvir's death spread, more Ljo-salfar poured into the hall to examine the murky outline on the marble floor and the charred remains of Sorkvir's garb, assuring themselves that he was truly destroyed. Next their attention turned to Leifr with much the same mixture of awe and disbelief. To spare them the embarrassing necessity of gratitude, Leifr seized the first opportunity to disappear, hobbling out a low rear entrance in the company of Thurid and some of the Dvergar who bore Raudbjorn on a litter, in spite of his protests that he would rather hobble along like a hero than be carried out like a loser. Leaving the new hall to the celebrants, Leifr and his companions sought out the sombre refuge of Hjaldrsholl.

His leg was still aching, and he stopped twice on the way to sit down and rest it. The second of these times, he thought he detected movement out of the corner of his eye. Turning quickly, he caught a glimpse of a small gray cat. Remembering the image of the cat he had thought he saw shooting away when Sorkvir bit Thurid's staff, Leifr struggled to his feet. But when he looked again, there was nothing there.

In Hjaldrsholl, the dead had been cleared away and buried, along with the helmets that had hung on the wall. Now that Sorkvir was dead, the dwarfs had no need to cherish their desire for vengeance. Their morose and silent natures were not particularly uplifted by Sorkvir's destruction; their losses had been too grievous to be easily forgotten in revelry and song, a compunction not shared by the Ljosalfar.

Leifr eased himself into Hjaldr's chair with a weary

groan and rested his head on his hands. Thurid sat across the table and spread out all his rune wands for an exhaustive scrutiny. Then he scowled over them and finally pushed them aside impatiently. Standing up, he upended his satchel on the table and shook out all the contents, which amounted to an astonishing pile of random objects.

'I'll return to my original, privitive methods of divination,' he explained. He gathered the rune wands and put them back in the satchel, then began pawing through the other objects, looking for anything else he wanted to keep.

Suddenly Thurid paused, examining a small, wax-covered packet which he had discovered in the jumble of odd objects. He stood still, staring fixedly at it.

Leifr's curiosity was piqued. 'What's that, Thurid?' he asked. 'Your face looks as if you'd just seen a ghost.'

Thurid nodded slowly and tossed the little packet on the table. 'I feel as if I have. Fridmarr gave me this just before the last time he left. He said, if ever I was in trouble, I should burn it, and it would summon help. But only if I were in the direst of need. Somehow I never used it, although I ought to have when that Irskur jarl wanted to cut my throat, or that time when I was thrown in prison for bad debts. Ah, Fridmarr.' He shook his head with a rueful little smile. 'It was the only time he ever tried to show that he was looking out for me. He did sort of like me, in his own, peculiar way.'

'He thought of you as his only friend,' Leifr replied.

Thurid sighed and picked up the package again. 'I only wish this would work for us now. It was probably only a joke at the time. I remember how he threw it at me and laughed when it landed in my ale horn.' His eyes were opaque with memories and old regrets. Then he slowly turned toward the hearth, where a small fire was burning, and dropped the little packet into the coals. 'Well, Fridmarr, this is the end of your joke.'

In a few moments a plume of black smoke filled the

hearth, swarming up to the smoke hole in a choking, inky cloud. Hegna and the other dwarfs stifled their coughs, swabbed their stinging eyes, and went to open some doors to let the pungent smell out. Thurid sat glowering, and Leifr had the urge to laugh.

'He fooled you again, Thurid,' he said with a wry smile. 'Come now, there's no sense being angry at him.'

'It's myself I'm angry at,' Thurid snapped. 'I should not have forgotten so soon, in my silly sentimentality, that Fridmarr loved nothing better than to embarrass me. I'm frightfully sorry for all this.' He nodded brusquely toward Hegna.

'It's a minor inconvenience and nothing more,' Hegna replied graciously. 'We've had worse guests, I'm sure.'

As he spoke, he darted a glance toward Raudbjorn, propped upright on his sleeping platform and combating the pain of his wounds with large quantities of Dvergar ale, clutching his fearsome halberd in one first.

Rather than persistently inquire how much longer before sundown, Leifr limped to the outer gates several times to mark the descent of the sun in the sky. Between Raudbjorn's ravings and Thurid's smoke, the dwarfs' hall was well-nigh uninhabitable anyway. The dogs followed Leifr, with their tails drooping and their golden eyes overflowing with tender concern for their troubled lord. Leifr sat on a rock with his cloak drawn around him, almost tasting the expectancy he felt closing in on him as the time grew shorter.

When little more than an hour remained, Thurid joined him outside in silent disgruntlement.

'I'm sorry for all this,' he finally burst out in helpless rage. 'How like Fridmarr to create such a mess. He never thought much about consequences – especially the consequences of his own stupidity.'

Leifr shrugged. 'It's all right, Thurid. Nothing lasts long in this life anyway. The only part that I really regret is Ljosa. But I suppose I was a fool for ever thinking she might care about anyone else, after Fridmarr.'

Thurid stood up to stalk around impatiently. 'Sciplings must be dense creatures to protect themselves from the truth when it is smacking them in their faces,' he exclaimed. 'Among Alfar, there is no greater gesture than to expend one's last powers for another. You didn't see her doing that for Fridmarr. She lived for him, because he made her miserable. You, Scipling, freed her by becoming her cause, her purpose for existence. You took away all her pain and regret and the poison of long-embittered pride. If she didn't love you with a far better love than she loved Fridmarr, then I have no idea what love must be.' He dabbed at his smoke-reddened eyes with the tattered tail of his sleeve. 'I loved her too, you know – as well as Bodmarr and Fridmarr. They were my pupils. I helped raise them from children. Now they are all gone, and I have nothing left of my past.'

In gloomy silence, they sat watching the sun descend closer to the horizon, seemingly moving faster the closer it got. The dogs, lying around their feet, suddenly lifted their heads, breaking the reverie with a chorus of growls and suspicious woofs as a lone traveler appeared on the rugged path to Hjaldrsholl. Leifr and Thurid eyed him a trifle resentfully as he plodded toward them.

'Is this Hjaldrsholl?' he called out when he was near enough. Little of him was to be seen beneath a long black cloak and closely drawn hood.

'Hjaldrsholl it is, although Hjaldr is dead,' Thurid replied. 'I suppose it will be called Hegnasholl now. The hospitality is somewhat rough, but you're welcome, as long as you're a day-farer.'

'That I am, one of the things I know for certain.' The traveler stopped beside them and leaned on his long staff. 'No doubt you know all about Sorkvir's death,' he said, in the manner of one who doesn't and would like to hear more. 'I've just heard the news myself and I came as fast as I could to see if it was really true.'

'It's true enough,' Leifr replied guardedly. 'You'll hear all about it down below, if you want to walk down the mountain. I'd walk with you, but I'm waiting here and can't leave just yet.'

'Waiting, eh? Then I don't mind waiting with you. I've taken a liking to your company.' The stranger sat down on a rock and removed a pipe and pouch from an inner pocket. He stuffed the pipe and blew gently into the bowl to ignite the leaves, and Thurid's eyes widened in recognition of a fellow wizard. The stranger nodded and silently puffed at his pipe for a few minutes.

'I've traveled far to get here,' he said in a satisfied tone, casting one long, appraising stare at Leifr, blowing the fragrant smoke in his direction. 'It's a momentous day when lost land is regained by the Ljosalfar. I hope there's room here for me and a few traveling companions.'

Thurid nodded a trifle curtly. 'Plenty of room down below in the new hall. Hjaldrsholl is not a festive place, I fear. There are too many unhappy memories up here. Down in the new hall, they've got plenty to celebrate about.'

The stranger peered toward the outer gates of Hjaldrsholl. 'I think this suits us better up here. New halls are not as homelike as fine old ones, even with their age and sorrows. It's not fine hospitality we're looking for.'

He stood up and signaled with his hand, and some riders and a sledge came out of a thicket on the side of the fell. A trio of white horses pulled the sledge, tossing their heads with a jingling of small bells. The last rays of the sun glinted on gold-inlaid harness, and the helmets of the riders also gleamed with golden light and the occasional flash of red jewels. As the horses approached, Leifr could see the fine, fur-trimmed cloaks of the riders, stitched with gold and silver thread. The horses ranged in color from black to pale silver dapple and white, and all were arrayed as splendidly as their riders.

Thurid hoisted one eyebrow and straightened his bent shoulders into a more dignified posture.

380

'I see you are traveling with someone of considerable importance,' he observed with grudging respect.

'Yes, indeed I am,' the stranger agreed, raising one hand in salute as the sledge rumbled past, bearing its glittering driver and a lone passenger.

Leifr stood up to see better as the sledge passed, and what he saw convinced him that he was having a hallucination. The lone rider in the sledge looked like the ragged little smith who had sharpened his sword, and he sat cradling the grindstone in his arms to steady it. He spared Leifr one sharp glance from beneath his peaked hood and a glimpse of a crusty smile before the sledge bounded through the outer gates and vanished into the tunnel.

Leifr leaped to his feet, startling Thurid, who turned pale and cried out furiously, 'It's not sundown yet! The alog can't have started already!'

'No! Hush, you dolt! It's him! The troll – or Rhbu. He sharpened my sword!' Leifr started after the sledge. 'He's brought the grindstone back to Hjaldrsholl!'

He shoved his way through the horses and riders gathered in the courtyard until he got to the sledge, where he found a pair of Alfar hoisting the grindstone to their shoulders and bearing it into the hall, amid the cheers and battle cries of the jubilant Dvergar. Of the ragged little smith there was no sign.

The torque remained as tight as ever around his throat. Disgusted at himself for his foolish hope that the smith could break Hjaldr's alog, he hurried back to Thurid, meeting him halfway as he strode along arm in arm with the stranger.

'Gone,' Leifr said tersely. 'He must have slipped away in the confusion.'

'I saw nobody in that sledge except the driver,' Thurid said testily.

'And the troll's grindstone,' the stranger added. 'Or so it is called by the Dvergar. It may not be a troll at all who turns it.'

381

'I saw no one.' Thurid made a slight effort to extract himself from the stranger's companionship, politely saying, 'Through there you'll find Hegna. He'll make all of you quite comfortable. Right now I fear I must go and attend to something. Leifr, come along. There's not much time left.'

'No, no, you must both come with me,' the stranger said warmly. 'I know who you are. I wish to hear the story from your own lips, since poor Fridmarr is not here to tell me himself. I wish he had lived to see this day. He devoted his life to the destruction of Sorkvir. Now, after many wrong turns, he has finally accomplished his objective.'

The stranger strode into the hall, with Thurid and Leifr following in his wake. At once, a hush fell over the Ljosalfar and Dvergar, and they looked up expectantly while the stranger seated himself in Hjaldr's chair.

'Who is this arrogant trespasser?' Thurid muttered between his teeth to Hegna.

'He knew Fridmarr,' Leif said. 'We can expect the worst – or, at best, the totally unexpected.' He shook his head in silent wonder and covertly tested the tightness of the torque for any signs of its imminent shrinkage.

The stranger must have heard; he turned to Leifr with an amused gleam in his eye as he removed his hood and unfastened the brooches of his cloak.

'Yes, expect the unexpected,' he said. 'I have things to say that no one will expect to hear. To begin with, I wish to thank Thurid for sending for me. It was a message which I have waited long to receive.'

Thurid's jaw gaped as all eyes turned toward him. He spluttered, 'I don't recall sending for anyone, if you'll forgive me for saying so. I think I'd know if I had.'

'You did send, Thurid, and I have come, just as I promised young Fridmarr.' The stranger's beard was wiry and golden, and his long fair hair was bound at his forehead with a plain band, allowing the rest to fall to his shoulders. His eyes were the color of amber, sparkling with amusement and vitality. Leifr knew a natural leader when he saw one. If not for the torque, he would gladly have followed this man wherever he commanded, in perfect faith.

'Who are you?' Leifr asked, forgetting the etiquette that forbade such impertinent questions. 'You know us, but we've never seen you, and you knew our comrade Fridmarr. A friend of his who sought for the destruction of Sorkvir is a friend of ours, so tell us what your name is.'

The dwarfs nudged each other and leaned forward to listen. The stranger placed his staff across his knees and did not appear annoyed by Leifr's blunt manners.

'The night-farers have a variety of names for me, which I don't care to claim, since they are invariably derogatory. I have been known as Schmelpfinning, and the Lord of Snowfell, but most will agree in calling me Elbegast or the Ganger or the Wandering King.'

Thurid gasped and clutched Leifr's arm, shoving him forward.

'The torque!' he cried. 'Remove Hjaldr's torque! There's very little time left! He cleared the Pentacle of Sorkvir's evil, and the grindstone has been returned, but Hjaldr's alog will not be stopped. Elbegast, Lord of Ljosalfar, use your powers to save Leifr, and I'll be your servant for the rest of my life. Or you can take my powers and do with them what you will – such as they are.'

Elbegast rose to his feet and regarded Leifr gravely for a moment. 'Where is the grindstone? Is it restored to its usual place?'

'Aye, it's in the forge,' Hegna replied uneasily. 'King of the Ljosalfar you may be, but it's a dangerous thing for anyone to go alog-breaking. I wish you wouldn't be doing it here.'

'Here and now is the best place and the only time,' Elbegast said, raising his hands with a shimmering glow, as if seen through a curtain of flame. 'The grindstone is

383

in its place. The Pentacle is purified of evil. What more remains to prevent the earth powers from flowing again? What influence interferes? What is missing to complete the circle of power?'

White light glowed around his form, and the Dvergar squinted and shaded their eyes from the unwonted glare. In the brittle silence, as Elbegast stood entranced, with his arms outstretched, a faint but familiar sound threaded its way into the shadowy hall. Leifr recognized it instantly as the grating whine of a grindstone being turned somewhere down the echoing tunnel of Hjaldr-sholl. He pushed past Thurid, who was staring at Elbegast, half-entranced with reverence. Jolted from his reverie by Leifr's abrupt departure from the hall, Thurid seized his staff and rushed after him, seething with outrage.

'Fridmarr! Dradgast it, *Leifr*!' he spluttered. 'Your Sciplings' manners are abysmal, do you realize that?'

Leifr found the forge, following the red glow of the fires as well as the whine of the grindstone. As he passed under the wide arch of the doorway, with the three hounds at his heels, he saw the ragged old smith bent over the grindstone in a circle of light, sharpening a tool with loving concentration. The sparks danced on the bright blade of the knife, showering over the smith's wrinkled hands and bouncing playfully over his sleeves and the patched knees of his trousers.

'Are you glad to be home again?' Leifr inquired softly, during a pause in the grinding, and the smith answered with a slight nod.

'I know who you are now,' Leifr went on. 'You're one of the Rhbus, the last of the living ones. My fate has been in your hands from the beginning. Now I am ready for your final decision. Are you finished with me, or is there yet more that I will be able to do for your cause?'

The Rhbu put down the knife and took up a large pair of pincers, motioning for Leifr to come closer. Leifr approached the stone, and the Rhbu reached up with the pincers and cut through the torque in one easy motion. It fell to the ground at Leifr's feet in two pieces, and the cut ends glowed with molten heat.

Leifr rubbed his neck, wondering how he had missed being burned. When he raised his eyes again, with a fervent word of gratitude on his lips, the Rhbu had vanished, leaving the grindstone still turning. Leifr searched the shadowy forge with his eyes, and Thurid found him standing beside the whirling grindstone, still staring around in amazement.

'The torque!' whispered Thurid. 'Hjaldr released you after all! To think how I reviled him! I should not have been so blind and distrustful. The powers I serve are just.'

Leifr turned around quickly. 'Did you see him? The small, bent smith? He was here. The same one who sharpened the sword. The one Elbegast brought in the sledge.'

'The sledge was empty,' Thurid insisted. 'If one of the Rhbus was there, a Scipling wouldn't have seen him.'

'A Scipling did see him. Three times,' Leifr replied.

'Impossible,' Thurid snorted enviously, peering around the forge, which suddenly filled with the burly Dvergar, all regarding Thurid and Leifr with utmost suspicion.

'Who started that stone turning?' Hegna demanded, shouldering his way to the front of the glowering crowd. 'No one uses that stone. No one is allowed to touch it. The Pentacle may be upset forever by the treatment it's gone through today.'

'I didn't touch it,' Leifr said. 'It was turning when I came into the forge.'

Elbegast came into the forge as he spoke, and the dwarfs hastily parted before him. 'You should know, Hegna, that it always turns when it is needed, and no one sees who is turning it – not unless they are particularly favored by the Rhbus.' His eyes traveled to the broken torque at Leifr's feet; then he smiled into Leifr's eyes as he repeated, 'Particularly favored by the Rhbus. I believe the powers of the Pentacle will flow again, as of old, at least until you see this stone turning by itself again.'

'A Scipling, favored by the Rhbus!' murmured the dwarfs and Ljosalfar, gazing at Leifr speculatively as their minds entertained such a novel idea.

Hegna was the first to step forward to extend his hand to Leifr in friendship and trust. 'If the Rhbus accept a Scipling, then a Scipling is good enough for the Dvergar.'

They all offered Leifr their fealty and their lives, if he required them, while Thurid stood nearby, preening himself unashamedly.

'I knew there was something unique about Leifr, even before I knew he wasn't Fridmarr,' he confided to Elbegast pridefully. 'I daresay he's eager to get back to his own realm. I promised Fridmarr I'd send him back, although I have no idea how to go about it.' He chuckled uneasily, glancing sidewise at Leifr. 'It seems a shame to lose such an ally, just when he might be a help to us against others like Sorkvir.'

'Others like the Dokkur Lavardur and Djofull.' Elbegast gazed straight at Leifr with his amber eyes. 'We need the arm that can wield that sword.'

'A limping swordsman is no asset,' Leifr replied with a grim smile.

'Our healers can mend the leg,' Elbegast said. 'There is a place for you in Solvofirth. Hroald is dead. Take Gliru-hals, if you want to stay. A warrior needs a home, a place of peace between battles. Other captured settlements will follow the example of Solvorfirth and overthrow their Dokkalfar warlords, particularly with you to lead them.'

The forge rumbled with approval, with a louder rumble from the archway as Raudbjorn hobbled in, using his faithful halberd for a crutch.

'Raudbjorn stay with Leifr,' he growled with an earnest scowl furrowing his brow. 'Sorkvir's bane. Scourge of Dokkalfar. Hammer and sword of Elbegast. Plenty heads will roll, eh, Leifr?'

'Adventure and fame,' Thurid added approvingly.

386

There was an ambitious gleam in the wizard's eyes at the prospect of such opportunities. 'Not to mention the glory.'

Leifr considered his choices for a short moment. If he returned to the Scipling realm, he would live the life of a hunted man for the rest of his life. And here, it seemed, he was expected to spend all his days in wild combat against the most powerful leaders of the Dokkalfar – wizards mightier than Sorkvir.

Slowly he shook his head.

Thurid's nostrils twitched incredulously. His eyes blazed with outrage. 'What! You reject all that? Fridmarr wouldn't have turned down such a chance!'

'You'll get your glory and wealth some other time, wizard,' Leifr told him. 'You're not going to rest until you've found Ljosa and brought her back from the void.'

'Me!' Thurid gasped. 'Such a feat requires a master wizard, not a mere beginner such as I am. It's incredibly dangerous to reach into the void after someone. It takes enormous amounts of power. It takes—'.

'But it can be done?' Leifr interrupted.

Thurid shrugged doubtfully. 'Yes, it can be done, but whether by me or not is a great question. It might require a Hel journey, which I have never done. Death rather frightens me as yet, even as a means of acquiring wisdom and immortality. I think some other wizard might suit you better.'

'I think not,' Leifr said. 'You'll do it, Thurid.'

Elbegast shook his head. 'All you need to know is in those Rhbu rune sticks Fridmarr gave you, Thurid.'

'But some of them were destroyed,' Thurid protested. 'I've tried to make copies from memory, but—'.

Elbegast smiled. 'I think you'll find that those copies are now quite accurate, with no errors. I wish you the best of luck in finding Ljosa and bringing her back. When you are done, however, summon me with this.' He put a small, wax-covered parcel in Leifr's hand. 'Or you may save it for some hour of direst need, and I shall

387

come for you as I would have come for Fridmarr. Use it wisely.'

He gripped Leifr's hand in his strong grasp, and Leifr felt a wave of power break over him, drawing him under the spell of Elbegast's influence.

'One day it will be the Dokkur Lavardur that your followers destroy,' Leifr said. 'Sorkvir and all his kind will have perished.'

Elbegast smiled, and his eyes darkened for a moment. 'I hope you're speaking a prophecy, Leifr. But I fear it will be a longer time than either of us are given by the Norns before Skarpsey is rid of the Dokkur Lavardur and Djofull. The Dark One has outlived the Rhbus, who once possessed the powers to destroy him. We must find the strength again, and the Ljosalfar need the help of warriors like you, Leifr.'

'And Raudbjorn, too,' Raudbjorn rumbled. 'Now Raudbjorn needs drink and food. Even Dvergar food.'

Hegna raised his arms to quiet a mutter of agreement and the wry chuckles of the dwarfs. 'My fellow Dvergar, we have received a challenge. We'll show our guests that our hospitality isn't always meagre and thin. Bring out our best ale and meat; and from now on, there will be no more watering it down. This will be a celebration such as these ancient halls have not seen in many a long day.'

Amid shouts and cheers, they trooped back into the main hall, where the hearths were heaped with fuel and more lamps were filled with whale oil and lit. Harps, lutes, and horns that had not seen much use in many years were brought out and tuned up.

When the feast was about to start, Elbegast rose to his feet and addressed the company.

'The time has come to reveal the truth about Fridmarr,' he announced, casting an amused glance at Leifr, who saw nothing humorous in his memories of impersonating Fridmarr and was not certain he wanted to know anything more about him.

'Fridmarr was unjustly accused by many people,'

Elbegast continued. 'Everything he did was under my orders, except his taking the eitur to prove his loyalty to Sorkvir. He thought it the quickest way to learn Sorkvir's secrets. Too late, he realized that he had taken one step too far down the road to doom.

'It was I who guided him to the ancient fortress of the Rhbus in Bjartur, where *Endalaus Daudi* was hidden. I told him how to find the Rhbu and grindstone in Hjaldrsholl to have the sword sharpened, but it was too late.

'Sorkvir discovered the scheme and made the alog against all metal among the Ljosalfar. To do so, he corrupted the powers of the Pentacle. He played cat and mouse so well that Fridmarr never knew until too late that his duplicity was discovered.

'Bodmarr was allowed to think that he stole the sword, believing Fridmarr wanted it for Sorkvir. But Sorkvir was too clever to fool. When Bodmarr was killed, Fridmarr wanted revenge, but I took him away before Sorkvir could kill him.

'True to his loyalty to me, Fridmarr never revealed that he was my spy, although a few guessed the truth at Bjartur when he took away the sword and a very old satchel of Rhbu magic. He took the satchel against my orders, but he said there was someone who could use it.'

Thurid pretended to cough so he could hide part of his face in his sleeve. 'I doubted him sometimes myself,' he muttered. 'If only he had told me. But I guess he couldn't, if he wanted to deceive Sorkvir.'

'No, he couldn't trust anyone, not even Bodmarr – or me, in the end.' Elbegast sighed. 'I thought him safe, but he was not finished with Sorkvir. He came back as Gotiskolker to make one more attempt to regain the sword and try to salvage something from all the harm that had been done. He wanted to purify the Pentacle, but he had eitur in his veins, and it was destroying his Ljosalfar powers. The rest you know.'

Elbegast resumed his seat, and the feast began.

While the celebration went on, there was no one in the

lower hall to see the dark-hooded figure that crept from a crevice and stole onto the marble pavement, to crouch beside the dark, charred mass of Sorkvir's ruin. Long, skilful fingers poked and pried among the remains of the bearskin, discovering a few fragments of bones, sweeping together small heaps of ash, and funneling them into a small leather pouch. After a thorough search for any remaining physical particles of Sorkvir, the intruder glided away and disappeared into the dark tunnels behind the vast hall.

Word of Elbegast's arrival spread quickly, and before dawn came, nearly every Ljosalfar within a day's travel had convened at Hjaldrsholl, hoping for a look at the Wandering King. Most brought food and drink, pooling it all together for a feast of epic proportions which threatened to last for days.

At dawn of the second day, Elbegast and his honor guard rode from the gates of Hjaldrsholl, accompanied by Leifr, Thurid, Raudbjorn and a few of the leaders of the Ljosalfar settlement of Solvorfirth. Elbegast halted to say a last farewell to the assembled farmers, fishermen, and laborers.

'Enough speeches have been made already,' he called to them, and they applauded his statement vigorously. 'As my final words, all I have to say is this: Guard your freedom.' Waving, amid cheers and shouts of acclaim, he turned his horse to ride away with those who followed him.

'Now I want to see where Fridmarr is buried,' he said quietly to Thurid. 'I wish to pay him my respects.'

Taken aback, Thurid gaped a moment in astonishment. But recovering quickly, he moved triumphantly forward to lead the way.

Leifr dropped to the rear, glad to be out of the center of attention for a time. He let the horse follow the others with little guidance. His thoughts were filled with the choices he must soon make.

A hint of motion caught his eye as he chanced to

glance backward. The little gray cat was following. But almost at once, as his eyes fell on it, the small form seemed to fade into the shadow of a rock and was gone.

With his suspicions renewed, Leifr urged the horse to faster progress. But when he finally caught up with Thurid and tentatively voiced his speculations, the wizard snorted explosively.

'You're suffering from hallucinations, Leifr. You've let yourself be carried away by feeling guilty over Ljosa. I never saw a cat dart away from Sorkvir; it was far too brilliant a flare for anything to be seen in it. And it couldn't have been Ljosa's fylgja. She couldn't have had enough power for shape-shifting after dragging you away from Sorkvir. Stop brooding about things your Scipling mind cannot possibly understand. Leave magic to the wizards.'

Thurid elevated his nose and rode ahead.

By midday they reached the long barrow of Gritturgrof where Fridmarr was buried. Elbegast went forward alone, with his head uncovered to the harsh wind, and stood a long time before the barrow. The chieftains and elders stood quietly until he returned.

'We judged him wrong,' Old Einarr admitted grudgingly, and Young Einarr sighed glumly. 'I don't doubt his loyalty now, but he was a wrongheaded youth and fiery proud sometimes.'

Elbegast nodded. 'He was flawed in many ways, which led him to his difficulties. He should never have come back as Gotiskolker, but he couldn't bear the shame of knowing how he was remembered as a traitor. I grieved to see what Sorkvir had done to him, but his spirit was never humbled. To the last, he was looking for a way to clear his father's name of shame. Now, with Leifr's help, he has finally succeeded. Fridmarr spent his life trying to free Solvorfirth of Sorkvir. He must have loved this land with all of his noble heart.'

The two Einarrs nodded their heads, drawing themselves up with fierce pride. 'Nobody will ever forget

Fridmarr – the hero of Solvorfirth. The first of many, I should hope.'

Elbegast bade them farewell and rode away, disappearing with the same abruptness with which he had arrived. A mist was rising out of the low ground of Grittur-grof, shrouding the barrows almost to their tops, leaving only their rocky spines visible. Elbegast and his riders galloped along the crest of a long barrow, waving a last salute with their weapons, and disappeared into the rolling gray fog. In a few moments when the fog cleared, there was not a trace of man or beast.

The chieftains and elders heaved a collective sigh and began pulling up their hoods against the cold wind, resuming their habitual expressions and manners.

Einarr the Elder beckoned to Leifr. 'Well, come on. You'll be staying at my place until Gliru-hals is mucked out. No one else has a house worthy of such an honor.' He shoved his horse into the foremost position and led the cavalcade away from Grittur-grof.

As they filed past the barrow where Leifr had found the Rhbu and the grindstone, he looked toward the spot, but it was empty now.

Thurid eyed him narrowly. 'You're not seeing little cats or Rhbus again, are you? If you are and continue to do so while I see nothing, I might avail myself of this gift from Elbegast.' He held up a rune wand. 'The spell on this will send you packing back to the Scipling realm and put an end to your superior attitude about Rhbus. Why don't they show themselves to me? I'm the one trying to follow in their footsteps.'

Leifr reached out and plucked the rune stick from Thurid's fingers. He tossed it to Raudbjorn.

'Put that in your trophy pouch, Raudbjorn, and don't let Thurid have it. Not until he rescues Ljosa Hroaldsdottir and I've grown tired of the Alfar realm.'

Raudbjorn smiled his gentle assassin's smile and shoved the stick into his pouch. 'Safe now, Leifr. Raudbjorn keep stick forever. Wizard lose arm if he tries to take it.'

392

Thurid favored him with a haughty twitch of his shoulders. 'I've nothing to fear from you, lard-bucket. I'm not afraid of what lies ahead. I'll find Ljosa one day, with the aid and protection of the Rhbus. Your nasty weapons and bloodthirsty tactics will only help you to an early grave.'

Raudbjorn snorted and shook his head, patting the haft of his halberd. 'Strong arm and good steel better than powers. Always ready. Always sharp.'

Leifr rode on, letting their arguments fade from his attention. For the moment, he was content.

THE END

THE SWORD AND THE SATCHEL
by Elizabeth Boyer

The Impossible Quest

Kilgore had long dreamed of great adventures and magic. But when he alone proved able to draw the magic sword Kildurin, he found himself embroiled in more than he had wanted. With the aid of a crotchety old wizard, he set out for the far north across lands beset with trolls, frost giants, dark elves, and all the minions of dark sorcery. It was his duty to find and destroy the evil wizard Surt, who was threatening to bring never-ending darkness and eternal winter to the land or Skarpsey.

If he could survive the perils of the journey, he would then have to face Surt alone – one man and his sword against the might of the greatest wizard and all his cohorts. And there was a further problem.

There had been twenty previous attempts to end the life of Surt, and all had failed. Surt, it seemed, could not be killed!

0522 127582

THE ELVES AND THE OTTERSKIN
by Elizabeth Boyer

The Reluctant Hero

Ivarr had been sold to the witch Birna. But now Birna was dead, slain by the evil sorcerer Lorimer. Ivarr was stranded in the land of the elves. His only chance to return to his own realm was to become a hero for a group of outcast, incompetent elves and a wizard of doubtful qualifications.

As he discovered, being a hero was a little difficult. First he had to seek out a magic sword concealed somewhere in the land of the fire giants. Then, to seize a horde of gold, he must somehow find and destroy a terrible dragon. And, finally, he would have to overcome the power of Lorimer and an army of dark elves.

Ivarr knew nothing about being a hero, and the more he heard, the less he liked the idea. But a hero he'd be – or else!

0552 12759 0

THE THRALL AND THE DRAGON'S HEART
by Elizabeth Boyer

War of the Dark Elves

Brak just wanted to help Ingvold, the elfin girl who was cursed by the witch-queen Hjordis to act as a hag. He never expected his efforts to lead him through a strange gate to the world of the Alfar, where the dark elves were fighting to destroy all the light elves. As a humble thrall, he had no business there.

But he was trapped. Ingvold had given him the dragon's heart, the only hope the light elves had to summon aid from the Rhbus. He could not let that fall into the hands of Hjordis or Myrkjartan, the dreadful necromancer who was mustering armies of the dead against all that was good in the world.

Betrayed by the wiles of the wizard Skalgr, Brak struggled to master the magic of the dragon's heart and recover the weapons of power that would, perhaps, bring victory to Ingvold and her people.

It was too much, even for a hero. And Brak was no hero!

0552 12760 4

SHAPECHANGERS
Chronicles of the Cheysuli: Book I
by Jennifer Roberson

They were the *Cheysuli*, a race of magical warriors, gifted with an ability to assume animal shape at will. For centuries they had been allies to the King of Homana, treasured champions of the Realm. Until a king's daughter ran away with a Cheysuli liege man and caused a war of annihilation against the Cheysuli race.

Twenty-five years later the Cheysuli were hunted exiles in their own land. All of Homana was raised to fear them, acknowledged the sorcery in their blood, call them *shapechanger*, *demon*.

This is the story of Alix, the daughter of that ill-fated union between Homanan princess and Cheysuli warrior, and her struggles to comprehend the traditions of an alien race she had been taught to mistrust, to answer the call of magic in her blood, and accept her place in an ancient prophecy she cannot deny.

First of an eight-part dynastic epic of a magical race and the compelling prophecy which ruled them!

0552 131180

THE WORDSMITHS AND THE WARGUILD
Chronicles of an Age of Darkness Volume 2
by Hugh Cook

'Thanks to the wizard of Drum,' said the Brother, 'we know where to find these boxes. The nearest is in the bottom of a green bottle in Prince Comedo's Castle Vaunting in Estar. A monster protects the bottle from those who would acquire it.'

'Charming,' murmured Togura. Togura would not have chosen the profession of questing hero but in the end he had no choice. He was caught between The Wordsmiths and The Warguild, the two organisations which vied for power within the dismal kingdom of Sung, a land famous for being so often and so richly insulted.

Besides, if he did not find the *index*, the key to the magical treasure chest known as the *odex*, he would never be able to claim his love from its mysterious depths.

The second volume in a spectacular fantasy epic.

Volume 1: The Wizards and The Warriors
Volume 2: The Wordsmiths and The Warguild
Volume 3: The Women and the Warlords

0552 13130X

THE CENTRE OF THE CIRCLE
by Jonathan Wylie

Silver spiral, black as night,
Turning ever, ever still.
Circle's centre at its edge . . .

Luke was an extraordinary young man. King's son, child of magic, heir to a destiny prepared for him centuries ago, he had always been thought unusual – even by his mentor, the wizard Ferragamo.

Sheltered and protected by his family, Luke had been free to follow his own nature. But when the ancient evil, that had almost overcome his father many years ago, threatened Ark once more, reaching out in a massive network of foul and vicious magic, Luke must put himself to work.

Aided only by a stranger – a bizarre young girl whose nature he already seemed to know – Luke was forced to challenge the armies of darkness, and confront the awesome heritage that had long awaited him.

The Centre of the Circle continues the enthralling fantasy trilogy, SERVANTS OF ARK, begun in The First Named (also available from Corgi Books).

0552 131342

A SELECTED LIST OF FINE FANTASY TITLES
AVAILABLE FROM CORGI BOOKS

☐ 12760 4	THE THRALL AND THE DRAGON'S HEART	ELIZABETH H. BOYER	£2.50
☐ 12759 0	THE ELVES AND THE OTTERSKIN	ELIZABETH H. BOYER	£2.95
☐ 12758 2	THE SWORD AND THE SATCHEL	ELIZABETH H. BOYER	£2.50
☐ 12761 2	THE WIZARD AND THE WARLORD	ELIZABETH H. BOYER	£2.50
☐ 12566 0	THE WIZARDS AND THE WARRIORS	HUGH COOK	£3.50
☐ 13130 X	THE WORDSMITHS AND THE WARGUILD	HUGH COOK	£2.95
☐ 12284 X	BOOK ONE OF THE BELGARIAD: PAWN OF PROPHECY	DAVID EDDINGS	£2.50
☐ 12348 X	BOOK TWO OF THE BELGARIAD: QUEEN OF SORCERY	DAVID EDDINGS	£2.95
☐ 12382 X	BOOK THREE OF THE BELGARIAD: MAGICIAN'S GAMBIT	DAVID EDDINGS	£2.95
☐ 12435 4	BOOK FOUR OF THE BELGARIAD: CASTLE OF WIZARDRY	DAVID EDDINGS	£2.95
☐ 12447 8	BOOK FIVE OF THE BELGARIAD: ENCHANTERS' END GAME	DAVID EDDINGS	£2.95
☐ 12638 7	EXILES OF THE RYNTH	CAROLE NELSON DOUGLAS	£2.95
☐ 12682 9	SIX OF SWORDS	CAROLE NELSON DOUGLAS	£2.95
☐ 12848 1	THE LIGHT FANTASTIC	TERRY PRATCHETT	£2.50
☐ 12475 3	THE COLOUR OF MAGIC	TERRY PRATCHETT	£2.50
☐ 13118 0	THE CHRONICLES OF THE CHEYSULI: SHAPECHANGERS	JENNIFER ROBERSON	£2.50
☐ 17282 4	SONG OF SORCERY	ELIZABETH SCARBOROUGH	£1.95
☐ 12852 X	ISLE OF GLASS	JUDITH TARR	£2.50
☐ 12834 1	THE CHRONICLES OF MAVIN MANYSHAPED	SHERI S. TEPPER	£4.95
☐ 12849 X	THE REVENANTS	SHERI S. TEPPER	£2.95
☐ 12620 9	THE TRUE GAME	SHERI S. TEPPER	£4.95
☐ 13101 6	SERVANTS OF ARK 1: THE FIRST NAMED	JONATHAN WYLIE	£2.50
☐ 13134 2	SERVANTS OF ARK 2: THE CENTRE OF THE CIRCLE	JONATHAN WYLIE	£2.95